PASSIONATE PRAISE FOR THE NOVELS OF PATRICIA CABOT

An Improper Proposal

"If your tastes run to strong-willed heroines, alpha-male heroes, lots of action, pirates, treasure maps, and sensuous romance, look no further: AN IMPROPER PROPOSAL fills the bill. Written with dash and verve, Patricia Cabot's latest novel offers enough humor, adventure, and love to satisfy connoisseurs of the genre."

—*Under the Covers*

Portrait of My Heart

"A wildly sexy black comedy, set in Victorian England . . . Witty dialogue abounds from the first page, but what sets this romance apart are the hero's charm and keen sense of humor, which immediately endear him to readers . . . A jewel of a romance."

—*Publishers Weekly*

"Sexy, romantic . . . delightful."

—Jill Jones, author of *Bloodline*

"Patricia Cabot warms the heart with this charming, often funny and poignant spin-off from WHERE ROSES GROW WILD. Readers will fall in love with the characters and their exploits."

—*Romantic Times*

Turn the page for more critical acclaim . . .

"Charming, witty, and complex . . . filled with fun and authenticity. However, it is the motives and actions of the fully developed characters that make Patricia Cabot's novel an entertaining tale that will bring much-deserved acclaim to the author."

—Harriet Klausner, *Painted Rock Reviews*

"Wickedly funny, wickedly sexy, and just downright wicked . . . If you have found yourself in a romance reading rut and can live with a hero who is an unrepentant rake, I recommend PORTRAIT OF MY HEART. At every turn, there will be laughter, love, and joy."

—*All About Romance*

Where Roses Grow Wild

"Passion, wit, warmth—thoroughly charming."
—Stella Cameron, author of *Wait for Me*

"Ms. Cabot is a delightful read with her humor and verbal sparring between the two main characters. Splendid!"
—*Bell, Book and Candle*

"Snappy dialogue . . . a good read."
—*Old Book Barn Gazette*

"A charming and delightful read from beginning to end. The story flows freely and the characters will capture and entertain you."

—*Rendezvous*

A LITTLE SCANDAL

PATRICIA CABOT

St. Martin's Paperbacks

A LITTLE SCANDAL

Copyright © 2000 by Patricia Cabot.

ISBN: 0-312-97413-2

Printed in the United States of America

St. Martin's Paperbacks edition / June 2000

St. Martin's Paperbacks are published by St. Martin's Press, 175 Fifth Avenue, New York, N.Y. 10010.

10 9 8 7 6 5 4 3 2 1

For Benjamin

Part One

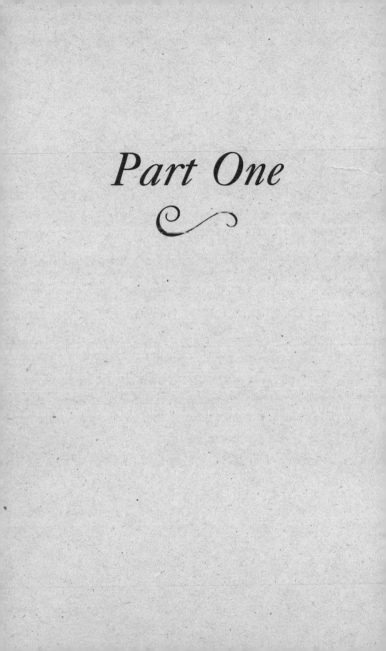

Chapter One

London
April 1870

"I'm not going." She twisted in his grasp. "I told you before. Let go of me!"

He was tired of reasoning with her. Sometimes it seemed to him that all he'd been doing these past seventeen years was reason with her.

"You're going," he said, his deep voice nothing more than a menacing growl. So menacing, in fact, that the footman straightened up beside the chaise-and-four, and looked everywhere but in his master's direction.

"I won't," she cried. Again, she gave the wrist he held a jerk. She'd grown slippery as a cat lately, and it was all he could do to keep his hold on her slender, silk-clad arm. "I said *let go of me.*"

He heaved a sigh. So this was how it was to go. Oh, well. He ought to have known. Everything had pointed to it. An hour earlier, when he'd been retying his cravat in the looking glass—Duncan was an exemplary valet, it was true, but he was getting on in years, and had become quite intractable in his ways, so that subtle changes in men's fashion now only served to irritate him. He continued to tie the knot in his employer's cravat in the exact same manner that he had for over twenty years, thus forcing Burke to resort secretly to undoing his valet's work and retying it himself—Miss Pitt had burst into his sitting room, quite unannounced, and in a state of considerable agitation.

"My lord," the old woman had cried. Quite literally cried. There were tears streaming down her corpulent cheeks. "She is impossible! Impossible, do you hear? No one—*no one*—could be expected to put up with that kind of abuse. . . ."

Here the woman had pressed a shaking hand to her mouth and fled the room. Burke hadn't been completely certain, but it had seemed that Miss Pitt had just given her notice. With a sigh, he'd begun undoing his cravat. There was no sense in looking his best now. He would not, as he'd originally planned, be enjoying the company of the inimitable Sara Woodhart that evening. No, now he would be escorting Isabel, in the unfortunate Miss Pitt's stead, to Lady Peagrove's cotillion.

Damn it all to hell.

Now the minx was writhing in his grasp, actually attempting to bite him—yes, *bite* him—in order to loosen his hold. He sincerely hoped none of the neighbors were watching. It was getting to be damned embarrassing, these public displays of temper. It had been different only a few years ago, when she'd been younger—and smaller—but now . . .

Well, now he found himself longing, more often than not, for a pipe and the comfort of the fire in his library.

Yes, even more than he longed for the company of the estimable Mrs. Woodhart.

Good Lord! How repulsive! Could it possibly be true? *Was* he getting old? Duncan had told him so, on more than one occasion. Not in so many words, of course. A good valet never implied that his master was in anything but his prime. But just the other morning, the fellow had had the nerve to lay out a *flannel* waistcoat, of all things. Flannel! As if Burke were approaching fifty-seven, and not a still relatively youthful thirty-seven. As if he were infirmed, and not the prime physical specimen he knew himself to be—that many of the most attractive women in London, including the discriminating Mrs. Woodhart, had assured him he was. Duncan had learned a sharp lesson that day, that was certain.

Just as Isabel would learn one now. He was not going to

be trifled with. Particularly not since it was for her own good, in the end.

"And I"—he bent down, and with the ease of long practice, threw her bodily over his shoulder, as if she were a sack of wheat—"said that you're going."

Isabel let out a shriek so shrill it seemed to pierce the thick yellow fog that had fallen like a curtain across Park Lane—across all of London, most likely, knowing his luck. It would be hours before they managed to wind their way through the traffic, backed up because of the fog, to the Peagroves' door. It was all he needed, really, this thick, smothering fog, on top of Isabel's hysterics. The only thing he needed more, perhaps, was a bullet in the brain. Or maybe a blade to the heart.

And a moment later, it appeared his second wish was about to be granted. Only instead of a blade, the interloper, who'd appeared from the fog as if from nowhere, was pointing the tip of an umbrella in the general direction of his heart.

Or where his heart would have been if, as Isabel was insisting at the top of her lungs, he happened to own one, which, according to her, he did not.

"I beg your pardon, madam," Burke said to the umbrella's owner—quite calmly, too, he flattered himself, for a man with a reputation of being so very hot-blooded. "But would you mind lowering that thing? It is impeding my progress toward that carriage waiting there."

"One more step," the umbrella's owner said, in a surprisingly hard voice, for a creature so . . . well, puny, "and I shall seriously endanger your hopes of siring an heir."

Burke glanced at his footman. Was it his imagination, or was he being accosted on his very own doorstep—and on Park Lane, of all places, the most exclusive street in all of London—by a perfect stranger? Worse, a perfect stranger who happened to be a young woman . . . exactly the sort of young woman whom Burke so assiduously avoided at social gatherings.

Well, and who could blame him? It always rather alarmed him when, in the middle of a conversation with one of these creatures—who were not, truth be told, generally very scintillating conversationalists in the first place—the girl's heavily jeweled mamma swooped down suddenly from out of nowhere, and politely but firmly steered her little darling away from him.

Yet here there was no jeweled mamma. This young woman was quite alone. Quite absurdly alone, and on a night as gloomy as any he'd come across in a good long time. Where was her chaperone? Surely such a very young woman ought to have a chaperone, if only to keep her from threatening gentlemen with the business end of her umbrella, as appeared to be her habit.

What was he to do? If she'd been a man, Burke would merely have struck him down, stepped over the limp body, and been on his way. If necessary, he'd even have called the fellow out, and taken great pleasure, in his current mood, in putting a bullet through his head.

But she wasn't a man. She was even a bit on the smallish side for being a woman. He supposed he could have lifted her out of the way, and easily, too, but laying hands upon any woman, particularly one of the youthful variety, had a tendency to cause all sorts of trouble. What was he supposed to do?

Perry, whom Burke made the mistake of looking to for aid, wasn't the slightest help. He too was staring at the young woman, his already slightly protuberant eyes bulging to their very limits—not, of course, at the sight of the umbrella tip waving in his master's direction, but at the sight of the young woman's very slim ankles, quite plainly observable beneath the hem of her skirt, which had hiked up a little in the front when she'd assumed her fencer's stance.

Stupid boy. Burke would see that he was sacked upon the morrow.

"Put her down," the young woman said. "At once."

"Now, see here," Burke found himself saying, in a tone that was far more reasonable than he felt. "Don't go jabbing that thing at me. I'll have you know that I happen to be—"

"I don't give a whit who you happen to be," the young woman interrupted, and very smartly, indeed. "You will put that girl down, and count yourself lucky I don't call for the constable. Though I'm not at all certain I shan't. I've never seen anything so disgraceful in all my life, a man of your advanced years taking advantage of a girl who can't be half your age."

"Taking advantage!" Burke nearly dropped his burden at that point, he was so surprised. "Of all the impertinent suggestions! Do you honestly think—"

To his horror, Isabel, who had grown suspiciously silent since the approach of this umbrella-wielding termagant, lifted her cloaked head and said, in a plaintive voice quite unlike her usual self-assured tones, "Oh, please help me, miss. He's hurting me dreadfully!"

The umbrella tip pressed upon his lapel, the metal point pricking the flesh just above his heart. Now the young woman did not bother addressing Burke at all, but turned her head and said to his footman, "Don't just stand there, you ignorant boob. Run and fetch the magistrate."

Perry's jaw dropped. Burke watched irritably as his footman's face contorted as he struggled with himself, torn between his loyalty to his employer and his desire to obey the girl with the very commanding voice.

"B-but," the idiot boy stammered. "He'll sack me, miss, if I do—"

"Sack you?" The girl's already ridiculously large grey eyes widened with outrage. "And you'd prefer a sacking, would you, as opposed to being jailed as an accomplice to abduction and intimidation?"

Perry wailed, "No, miss, but—"

Here Isabel could restrain herself no longer. Burke could feel her quivering against his shoulder. Even the whalebone stays of her corset couldn't suppress the violent spasms of her belly as she burst out laughing.

Only, of course, to the girl with the sharp-ended umbrella, the laughter sounded like sobs. He saw the pale face, framed by a bonnet that had at one time probably been quite expensive, but was now several seasons out of fashion, tighten with anger, and then she drew back her arm, intent, he didn't doubt, on skewering him bodily with her umbrella.

That, he decided, was the last straw.

"Now, see here," he said, swinging Isabel from his shoulder and setting her, not very gently, upon her own two feet beside him. He kept a firm hold on her wrist, however—he was no fool—to keep her from slipping off into the night, a recent trick of hers. "Although I haven't the slightest idea how it is that I come to be slandered so rudely—and at my own doorstep, no less—I ask that you allow me to assure you that this situation is, in every way, respectable. This young woman happens to be my daughter."

The umbrella did not waver. Not even an inch.

"A likely story," its owner said woodenly.

Burke looked around for something to throw. He truly felt as if he might suffer an apoplexy. Really, what had he ever done to deserve *this*? All he'd wanted—all he'd *ever* wanted—was to get Isabel married off to a decent fellow who wouldn't beat her or squander the money Burke had settled on her, leaving him free—at last—to spend a pleasant evening alone with an agreeable woman like Sara Woodhart. Or a book. Yes, even a book by a nice, roaring fire. Was that so much to ask?

Apparently so, as long as there were umbrella-wielding madwomen roaming the streets of London.

Perry, perhaps for the first time in his stupid life, opened his mouth and actually said something helpful. And that was: "Um, miss? She—the young lady—*is* his daughter."

Isabel, who'd been struggling to suppress a fit of the giggles since Burke had set her down, could do so no longer, and now let loose a peal of laughter that likely was heard all up and down the street.

"Oh," she cried gaily. "I *am* sorry! But it was so rich, your threatening Papa with your umbrella. I couldn't help myself."

The umbrella wavered. Just slightly, but noticeably.

"If he is your father"—beneath a fringe of dark blond hair, slim eyebrows knit in bewilderment—"then why, in heaven's name, were you shrieking so?"

"Oh, la!" Isabel rolled her eyes as if the answer were obvious. "Because he insists upon me attending the Peagroves' cotillion."

To Burke's utter astonishment, the young woman—this perfect stranger, this lunatic—accepted that statement as if it were completely understandable. Burke watched, thunderstruck, as the umbrella lowered from his heart, until the tip struck the ground.

"Good Lord," the woman said. "You can't possibly go *there*."

Isabel reached out and tugged upon Burke's coat sleeve, rather more forcefully than playfully. "You see, Papa?" she said. "I told you so."

Burke was absolutely certain now that he was going to succumb to an apoplexy. He did not understand what was happening at all. Just seconds ago, the young woman in front of him had been threatening to go for the police. Now she was calmly discussing social engagements with his daughter, as if the two of them were sharing a gossip in a milliner's shop, and not standing in the middle of Park Lane at nine o'clock in the evening on the foggiest spring night he could remember.

"It's a crush," the young woman was assuring his daughter. "Lady Peagrove invites twice as many people as can possibly fit into her house. It's a nightmare just getting anywhere near the place. And no one who actually *matters* attends it. Hangers-on and country cousins, is all."

"I *knew* it." Isabel stamped a daintily slippered foot. It made no noise whatsoever on the soft pile of the carpet Perry had rolled out to keep her train from collecting mud as she climbed into the carriage. "I told him that. But he won't listen to me."

Burke, aware that he was being spoken about as if he were not even standing there, began to feel more annoyed than ever.

"He'll only listen to Miss Pitt," Isabel went on. "And Miss Pitt had some absurd notion that Peagroves' was the place to go."

"Who is Miss Pitt?" the stranger had the audacity to inquire.

And before Burke could say a word, Isabel was replying,

"Oh, she was my chaperone. Until she gave notice an hour ago, anyway."

"Chaperone? Why in heaven's name must you be saddled with a chaperone?"

"If you must know," Burke replied acidly, "it's because her mother is dead. Now, if you'll excuse us, madam—"

"La!" Isabel said. "That isn't it at all, Papa." To the stranger, she confided, "Mama *is* dead, but the truth is, he hires chaperones for me because *he* can't be bothered to take me anywhere. *He* wants to spend all his time with Mrs. Woodhart—"

Burke's grip on Isabel's arm tightened. "Perry," he said. "The door, please."

The footman, who'd been listening to the conversation with more wide-eyed attention than he'd ever paid to any of Burke's instructions, jumped at being so suddenly addressed, and stammered, "M-my lord?"

Burke wondered if it would be considered brutish of him to deliver a swift kick to the back of Perry's trousers. He decided it would.

"The door," he growled. "To the carriage. Open it. *Now*."

The hapless footman hastened to obey his master's orders. Meanwhile, to Burke's utter fury, Isabel was still chattering away.

"Oh," she was saying, "I kept telling them Dame Ashforth's was the place, but would they listen to me? Not a bit. It wasn't any wonder I had to be rude to Miss Pitt. I mean, if no one will listen to you—"

"Oh, is Dame Ashforth's ball tonight?" The young woman was leaning nonchalantly against her umbrella handle now, as if it were a croquet mallet, and they were all standing on a summer lawn, enjoying a friendly game. "Well, that's it, then. You simply can't miss Dame Ashforth's."

"Yes, but it's all a plot, you see, to keep me away from the man I love—"

"Into the carriage," Burke interrupted stonily. He was proud of himself. He hadn't yet booted her into the vehicle, which had been his first impulse. He was learning to control his temper. Lord knew it had been sorely tempted, these past few weeks. But he was keeping it in check. If they could just escape this talkative young woman and her umbrella without any blood being shed, he would be well pleased.

"But Papa." Isabel looked up at him, round-eyed. "I thought you heard the lady. The Peagroves' cotillion is simply not—"

"Get in the carriage!" Burke roared.

Isabel staggered back a step, but he was too quick for her. He caught her up and tossed her—but gently; even the shrew with the umbrella would have to admit he did it very gently, indeed—into the chaise-and-four. As soon as the last bit of her train had disappeared into the confines of the vehicle, he turned and said, to the very astonished young lady standing on the street, "Good evening."

And then he too disappeared into the carriage, barking at the driver to get a move on, which he did, right smartly.

Isabel, recovering herself, said, from the opposite seat, "Really, Papa. There was no call to be so rude!"

"Rude!" He let out a humorless laugh. "I like that! And I suppose it was out of sheer politeness that a total stranger pointed her umbrella at me and threatened to fetch the police, as if I were some sort of escaped convict."

"She wasn't a total stranger," Isabel said, as she arranged the yards of white satin that made up her skirt. "She's Miss Mayhew. I've seen her before, out and about."

"Good God." Burke stared at his daughter in astonishment. "That creature lives on Park Lane? I don't know any Mayhews. To whom does she belong?"

"To the Sledges. She's governess to all of those wretched little boys."

"Oh," Burke said, somewhat mollified. No wonder he hadn't recognized her. Well, that was one thing to be grateful for: the woman was only a servant, and wouldn't go prattling around the neighborhood about the fact that Burke Traherne, third Marquis of Wingate, had no control whatsoever over his headstrong daughter.

Or at least, if she did, no one who mattered was likely to listen.

Then he asked, with some indignation, "If you've seen her before, why the devil didn't she know you're my daughter? Why did she think I was about to despoil you?"

"She's only just started working there," Isabel said, tugging on her gloves. "Besides, when would she ever have seen you before? Certainly not at church, considering how often *you* make it to bed before dawn of a Saturday night."

Burke glared at her in the light from the carriage oil lamp. It didn't seem to him that a man's daughter ought to speak to him in such a familiar manner. This is what came, he supposed, of having married so young. His father had warned him. And his father hadn't been wrong. Other men—older men, who, unlike him, had waited until they were past twenty before marrying—had daughters who didn't speak to them so flippantly. Or at least, Burke supposed they didn't. He didn't happen to have that many acquaintances, thanks to his somewhat checkered past, and the reputation that came along with it.

But he supposed that if he *had* had male friends, and they'd happened to have daughters, their daughters would be docile and dainty things, like the daughter he'd always imagined he'd have, instead of this unmanageable creature who'd emerged from the expensive ladies' seminary she'd attended up until a month and a half ago, and had been speaking to him so uncivilly across the dinner table ever since.

"Isabel," he said, as evenly as he could. "What did you do to Miss Pitt?"

Isabel studied the ceiling of the carriage very deliberately. "If the carriage pulls up in front of the Peagroves, I shall run away. I'm warning you right now."

"Isabel," he said again, with what he considered admirable patience. "Miss Pitt is the fifth chaperone I've hired for you in as many weeks. Would you like to tell me what you found so objectionable about her? She came very highly recommended. Lady Chittenhouse says—"

"Lady Chittenhouse," Isabel said, her disgust evident.

"What does *she* know? None of her daughters ever *needed* chaperones. No man in his right mind would ever go near any of 'em. I've never seen such dreadful complexions in my life. You would think they'd never heard of soap. It's a wonder any of them married at all."

"Lady Chittenhouse," Burke said, ignoring her, "wrote a very glowing letter of recommendation for Miss Pitt—"

"Did she? And did she happen to mention in her letter that Miss Pitt, besides being fantastically boring, with her endless prattle about her precious nieces and nephews, has a tendency to *spit* when she speaks, particularly when she is attempting to correct what she calls my wild ways? Did she happen to mention that?"

"If you found Miss Pitt so offensive," Burke said, as gently as he could, considering the fact that he longed to throttle her, "why didn't you come to me and ask me to hire someone else?"

"Because I knew you'd only find someone worse." Isabel peered out the window at the mist-shrouded street. "You know, if you'd only let *me* interview the candidates—"

Burke couldn't help smiling at her elaborately casual tone. "And who would you consider a suitable chaperone, Isabel? Someone like that Miss Mayhew back there, I wouldn't doubt."

"What's wrong with Miss Mayhew?" Isabel demanded. "She's a spot less disagreeable to look at than that horrid old Miss Pitt."

"You don't need someone agreeable to look at," Burke growled. "You need someone stern, to keep you from running after that wretched Saunders fellow—"

The minute the words were out of his mouth, he knew he'd said the wrong thing. Suddenly, a storm erupted on the seat opposite his.

"Geoffrey isn't wretched!" Isabel cried. "Which you would know, Papa, if you'd only take a moment to get to know him—"

Burke rolled his eyes, and turned his own gaze toward the window. Unfortunately, they had already become stuck in traffic, and the carriage was now being besieged by flower and ribbon sellers, beggars and prostitutes . . . the usual riffraff one encountered on the streets of London of an evening. The glass was up in the windows, so no one reached in, but Burke could see their hands plainly enough, empty palms lifted toward them, dirty, chafed from work and hardship. He could not restrain a sigh. This was not, by any means, how he'd envisioned spending his evening. He'd planned, by this time, to be in his box at the theater. Now he'd be lucky if he made it to the stage door before Sara slipped through it, into the usual throng that gathered there nightly, to pay homage to her unequaled talent. . . .

Or so she liked to think. Burke knew good and well what they were there paying homage to, and Sara Woodhart's talent had very little to do with it.

"I don't need to get to know Mr. Saunders, Isabel," Burke said, with more equanimity than he was feeling at that moment. "You see, I'm fully acquainted with all the particulars concerning that gentleman, and I can only say that the day that jackanapes darkens our doorway is the day he tastes lead."

"Papa!" Isabel sucked in her breath on a sob. "If only you'd *listen*—"

"I've been listening to you drivel on about Geoffrey Saunders for as long as I care to," Burke said. "You're not to mention his name in my presence again." There. That sounded very forthright and forbidding, the way fathers were supposed to sound. "And now we'll be going to the Peagroves', since I happen to know that Mr. Saunders has not been invited there."

Isabel let out another sob, this one much louder than the last, and said, in the tones of the tragically wounded, "You mean *you'll* be going to the Peagroves'! I'm going to Dame Ashforth's!"

And before Burke knew what she was about, Isabel had thrown herself upon the carriage door, flinging it open and hurling herself through it with a dramatic flair even the unparalleled Sara Woodhart might have envied.

Burke, finding himself suddenly alone in the chaise-and-four, sighed. God preserve him from young women in love. This was really *not* how he'd planned on spending his evening.

He tugged on his top hat and heaved himself out the still-open door, and into the teeming street after his child.

Chapter Two

❧

A blast of heat from the fire in the great kitchen hearth
was not the only thing that greeted Kate Mayhew as she
slipped through the door: Posie, the day maid, blasted into her
as well, a veritable hurricane of rosy cheeks and lace petticoats.

"Oh, miss," Posie cried, racing to the older girl's side before Kate had even had a chance to shut the door behind her.
"What do you think? You'll never guess!"

"Henry's put another snake in the pocket of his father's
dressing gown," Kate said, as she stripped off her gloves.

"No. . . ."

Kate worked the buttons to her pelisse. "Jonathan's said
that word again in his mother's presence."

"What word, miss?"

"*You* know what word. The one that begins with the letter *f*."

"Oh, no, miss, nothing like that. It's who's in the front
drawin' room, waitin' for ye."

"If it's his lordship, I should sincerely hope so." Kate untied
her bonnet strings and hung the hat on a wooden peg by the
door. "He was supposed to have met me at the recital, and I
spent an hour searching high and low for him."

"He says he must've gone to the wrong church." Posie
trailed after Kate as she wound her way through the kitchen.

"Ol' Fusspot is right put out, an' the master's beside himself! He's pacin' a hole through the floor outside the drawin' room door, tryin' to think up things to go in there an' say."

Kate stopped in front of a mirror at the bottom of the stairs, hung there especially so that the maids could adjust their caps before heading through the baize door out into the rest of the house, and tried, ineffectually, to fluff out the fringe of hair that covered her forehead. Her cheeks, already pink from the chill spring air outside, didn't need pinching, but her nose looked a little shiny. A fingertip of flour, taken from the sack in the pantry and rubbed in well, did the trick admirably.

"Poor Freddy," Kate said. "How long has he been here?"

"Since right after you left, nearly." Posie stood at Kate's right shoulder, and spoke to her reflection.

"Oh, dear," Kate said with a sigh. "Is Mrs. Sledge cross?"

" 'Course not! She'll be preenin' like the Queen of the May tomorrow when the ladies in her missionary sewin' circle ask about the carriage what was pulled up out front of the house, an' she's able to tell 'em it was the Earl of Palmer."

"Come to pay a call on her children's governess?" Kate adjusted the cameo that held the lace collar of her blouse closed. "I rather think not."

"She won't tell *them* that. She'll make it sound as if he was here to talk to *her*—"

The baize door burst open, and Phillips, the butler, appeared at the top of the stairs. Both girls started, and Posie threw herself at the large plank table where an assortment of copper pots had been set out, which she industriously began to polish.

Kate, however, was not so lucky. She had no duties belowstairs, and, in the butler's way of thinking, hadn't any business being down there in the first place. Descending the narrow staircase with great effrontery, Phillips said, "Miss Mayhew, I believe I have mentioned a number of times that it is not one of the master's expectations that you utilize the servants' entrance. As the children's governess, it is perfectly acceptable for you to use the front door."

Kate opened her mouth to inform the butler cheerfully that

she preferred the trade door to the front door—primarily because by using it, she was able, most days, to avoid running into *him*, though she'd never be fool enough to admit *that* out loud—but he kept right on speaking.

"And if you had utilized the appropriate door in this instance," Phillips went on, with what she began to realize was barely suppressed rage, "you would have realized that his lordship, the Earl of Palmer, has been waiting for you for nearly two hours in the front drawing room."

"Oh, Mr. Phillips," Kate said. "I *am* sorry. Lord Palmer was supposed to meet me at a recital this evening, and I suspect we missed each other somehow. I can't tell you how—"

"In the future, Miss Mayhew," Phillips said, as emotionlessly as an automaton, "if you are going to invite titled personages to this house, would you be so good as to inform me beforehand, so that I might decant the good brandy well enough in advance for it to make a difference."

Phillips, Kate realized, was furious. He wasn't screaming, and he wasn't throwing things—a man of Phillips's training would never stoop to such a display of emotion. But his very lack of inflection made it clear to Kate that he was angry, furiously so . . . and all because he'd been demoralized by having to serve inferior brandy to an earl. A butler of Phillips's status might never recover from such an ignominy.

And he would certainly never forgive Kate. No, it was all quite finished between the two of them. The fact that she had brought a cat with her into the house—an unforgivable offense, in Phillips's eyes, cats being, in his opinion, filthy creatures, fit only for rat-catching duties belowstairs—had been bad enough. But now she had humiliated him, too.

She might as well start looking for another position.

"Honestly, Mr. Phillips," Kate began, knowing it was futile, but determined to try at least to make amends. "If I'd had any idea, I—"

"Don't apologize to me, Miss Mayhew," the butler said stiffly. "It's the master who's been at his wit's end, trying to entertain the earl these past few hours you've been away."

Kate frowned. It wasn't *her* fault Freddy was so scatterbrained he couldn't remember a simple address. And it wasn't her fault he'd chosen to park himself in the Sledges' drawing room to wait for her. And how dare Phillips imply, with his "these past few hours you've been away" that she was off lollygagging about, when it was, after all, her night out. Surely, on her one night out, she should be allowed...

But there was no use arguing. Not with a man like Mr. Phillips.

Lifting her skirts, Kate started up the stairs toward the baize door. She had to brush past Phillips as she climbed the narrow staircase, but he stonily ignored her, which, she decided, was just as well, because if he'd said another word, she was just in the sort of mood to do something rash, like point out to the odious man that she knew perfectly well he'd replaced the good claret with an inferior brand, yet had presented their employer with a bill for the former.

Or worse, poke a finger into the gut he sucked in so carefully, as she'd witnessed her young charges do upon occasion.

Outside the door to the front drawing room, Mr. Sledge was, as Posie had said, wearing a hole through the thick pile of the Oriental runner. He looked up when he heard Kate's step, and then rushed to her side.

"Oh, Miss Mayhew, I'm so very glad you've returned," he gushed. "The earl—the Earl of Palmer, don't you know. He's right inside there, waiting for you. I brought him today's newspaper. I hadn't thrown it out, you see. I thought he might enjoy it."

Kate smiled up at her employer. Cyrus Sledge, despite his unfortunate name, was not a bad man. He was only a rather dull man, who had married an ugly cousin without the slightest idea that she might one day inherit a fortune—the fortune that was currently supplying Kate a salary, as well as keeping several missionaries, and hundreds of natives in Papua New Guinea, in shoes and Bibles.

"I thought," Mr. Sledge whispered, "about giving his lordship one of the Reverend Billings's tracts, you know, about the mission. Do you think he would be interested, Miss Mayhew? Many of our country's finest young men, I've found, are not particularly interested in the less fortunate. Their heads are full of hunting and the theatre. But I often wonder if that is only because they don't *know*. They often haven't been made *aware*, you see, of just how badly off the Papua New Guineans *are*, having neither hunting nor theater, let alone any sort of decent appreciation for the Lord—"

Kate nodded. "I quite agree with you, Mr. Sledge. Next time his lordship comes to call, be sure to speak to him about it. I believe he'll be *quite* fascinated."

Mr. Sledge's ordinarily pale face flushed with pleasure. "Really, Miss Mayhew? Do you really think so?"

"I really do." Kate took him by the arm and steered him away from the drawing room door. "In fact, I think you and Mrs. Sledge should put together a bundle of Reverend Billings's tracts for Freddy—I mean, his lordship—to read tonight, and then the next time he calls, you should both quiz him on their contents."

Mr. Sledge gasped. "Splendid idea! I shall tell Mrs. Sledge at once. We have some lovely new ones, don't you know, Miss Mayhew, all about the wretched conditions under which the average Papua New Guinean woman gives birth, and how the Reverend Billings has been working feverishly to improve those conditions—"

"Oh," Kate said. "That will be *perfect* for his lordship."

Mr. Sledge hurried away, eagerly rubbing his hands together. Kate, smothering a laugh, threw open the doors to the drawing room and said, "Well, Freddy, you're in for it now. Mr. Sledge is getting his tracts out. The childbirth ones, no less."

The tall, fair-haired man standing before the fire spun around guiltily. A second later, Kate saw why. He had made good use of her employer's newspaper, twisting pieces of it into small balls, then flinging the balls into the fire, where they burst into flame before being carried up the chimney by the draft from the flue. He had worked his way through the social pages, and had just started on the financial section when Kate happened to walk in.

"Really, Freddy," she said, looking down at the wreckage

of the newspaper which had, only that morning, been neatly pressed—with a hot iron, no less—by Phillips, in order to dry the still-tacky ink. "You're far worse than Jonathan Sledge, you know, and he's five years old."

Frederick Bishop, ninth Earl of Palmer, stuck out his formidable chin and said, "Well, you were forever coming, Katie. I had to occupy myself somehow."

"And it wouldn't occur to you actually to *read* a paper," she said, bending down and attempting to straighten the pile of crinkled newsprint. "Tear it to pieces, certainly, but never actually look at it."

"What's to look at?" Freddy wanted to know. "Just boring bits about the trouble in India, and whatnot. I say, Kate, what kept you? I've been here for hours and hours. I went to that church, and there wasn't any concert going on. There was just the vicar's wife—a horrid, nasty thing, fastening dead sticks to the wall for some festival or other. She was downright rude when I asked when the Mahler was starting. Looked like a dead stick herself, now that I think of it."

"You went to the wrong church again. And it wasn't Mahler, it was Bach." Kate sank down onto one of the Sledges' hard, formal chairs. "The polonaise was lovely."

"Bugger the polonaise," the Earl of Palmer said, quite violently.

"Really, Freddy," Kate said with a laugh.

"I don't care." Freddy flung himself onto the chair opposite hers. "I missed the concert, and now it's too late to take you to supper. The Sledges will be retiring soon, the stupid sods, and you'll have to go. And you don't have another night off until next week. So bugger the polonaise!"

Kate laughed again. "It's your own fault, you know. When *are* you going to start writing addresses down so that you'll remember them?"

The earl said, with sudden slyness, "If you'd only quit being so bullheaded, and marry me, I wouldn't need to write addresses down, because you'd always be around to remind me."

"Well," Kate said cheerfully, "you're certainly going about

it the right way. I don't imagine there's a girl in London who could resist a man who calls her bullheaded."

Freddy pulled at one end of his thick golden mustache. "You know what I mean. Why d'you have to be so stubborn?"

"I'm not being stubborn, Freddy," Kate said. "You know I love you. Just not as a wife should love a husband. I mean— I'm not *in* love with you."

"How do you know?" Freddy demanded. "You've never been in love before."

"No," Kate admitted candidly enough. "But I've certainly read about it in books, and—"

Freddy made a rude noise. "You and your books!"

"You ought to try reading one once, Freddy," Kate said mildly. "You might actually like it."

"I doubt it. Anyway, what does it matter whether or not you're in love with me? I'm in love with you, and that's all that matters. You could always *learn* to be in love with me," Freddy said, warming to his subject. "Wives do it all the time. And you ought to be better at it than most of my friends' wives. You're a quick study, after all. Everyone said you'd never last a minute at this governessing business, but look how well you've done for yourself."

"*Who* said I'd never last a minute at governessing?" Kate demanded, but the earl waved her indignation aside.

"I can be quite lovable, you know," Freddy informed her. "Virginia Chittenhouse was mad for me last spring. I assure you she cried dreadfully when I was forced to admit that my heart would always belong to you, even though you haven't a penny to your name anymore, and that in your old age, you'd developed an acid tongue in that head of yours."

"You ought not to have put Virginia Chittenhouse off," Kate said, with some effrontery. "She's hardly acid-tongued, and I understand she's just come into fifty thousand pounds."

The Earl of Palmer got up again, and made a dramatic gesture. "I don't need fifty thousand pounds. I need you, Katherine Mayhew!"

"Precisely how many glasses of Mr. Sledge's brandy did

you consume while you were waiting for me, Freddy?" Kate asked suspiciously.

"You're to give up this governessing slavery at once," Freddy declared, "and run away with me to Paris."

"Lord, Freddy, we'd be at one another's throat by Calais, and you know it. I sincerely hope you're drunk. It's the only logical explanation for this extremely perverse behavior."

The earl sank back down into his chair defeatedly. "I'm not drunk. I just got so wild with boredom waiting for you. That fool Sledge kept looking in every five minutes, asking me if there was anything I needed. He tried to talk to me about those popping new guineas."

"Papua New Guineans," Kate said, correcting him with a smile.

Freddy made a dismissive gesture. "Whatever. Where *were* you, Kate? The concert was supposed to end by nine."

Kate said, "I got back as quickly as I could. I had to take the omnibus, you know, as I hadn't the luxury of the use of your carriage, since you never appeared." She shot him a reproving look, and was bracing herself for more marriage proposals, when she suddenly straightened and added, "Oh, and I nearly forgot. I ran into the most extraordinary scene on my way home. Right outside—right on Park Lane—I saw a man fling a young woman over his shoulder and attempt to stuff her into a chaise-and-four."

The Earl of Palmer stirred in his seat, and his truculent expression darkened. "You're making it up. You're making it up to put me off the subject of marrying me. Well, Kate, it won't work. I'm absolutely determined this time. I even told Mother. She wasn't for it, but she said if I wanted to make a fool of myself, she couldn't stop me."

Kate chose to ignore his last sentence. "I swear to you I'm telling the truth. It was perfectly astonishing. I had to threaten the fellow with the tip of my umbrella before he'd put her down again."

Freddy blinked. "Was he an Arab?"

"Certainly not. He was a gentleman—or at least, he professed to be. He was dressed like one, in any case, in evening clothes, and he had a number of rather dim-witted lackeys about him. He was quite tall, and very broad-shouldered, and had a lot of very wild, very dark hair, and an olive complexion—"

"An Arab!" Freddy cried excitedly.

"Oh, Freddy, he *wasn't* an Arab."

"How do you know? He might have been."

"First of all, he spoke to me in perfect Queen's English, without the slightest accent. And secondly, one of his idiot servants addressed him as 'my lord.' And he had the most extraordinarily green eyes I have ever seen. Arabs have dark eyes. His were light, almost glowing, like a cat's."

Freddy set his jaw. "You certainly got a good look at him."

"Well, of course I did. He was standing not four feet away from me. The fog wasn't *that* thick tonight. Besides, there was light falling from the house."

"Which house?"

"Not two doors down." Kate pointed at the wall to their left.

The Earl of Palmer relaxed visibly. "Oh," he said, rolling his eyes. *"Traherne."*

"I beg your pardon?"

"Traherne. He's taken old Kellogg's place for the season. His daughter's first."

"Yes, the girl he'd been abusing so abominably turned out to be his daughter. A very headstrong young person."

"Isabel," Freddy said, stifling a yawn. "Yes, I've seen her about quite a bit. She's every bit as wild as her father, from what I understand. Made a spectacle throwing herself at some penniless second son of someone or other at the opera the other night. It was excruciatingly embarrassing, even for a jaded observer of human behavior like myself. It isn't any wonder the old man was playing a bit rough with her."

Kate knit her brow. "Traherne? I've never heard of a Lord Traherne. I've been out of society for quite a little bit, I know, but—"

"Not Traherne. Wingate. Burke Traherne's the second Marquis of Wingate. Or the third, or something. How a fellow's supposed to keep track of all that, I still haven't—"

"Wingate? That sounds familiar."

"Well, it should. The man created quite a scandal—though now that I think of it, you were probably in the schoolroom at the time. I was was still at Eton. I remember your mater and pater talking about it once, over dinner with my own ma and pa. Well, things like that can't help but get round—"

"Things like what?" Kate was not fond of gossip, having been the subject of more than a little of it in her time. Still, those eyes weren't easily forgotten.

"The Wingate divorce. It was all anybody talked of for months. It was in all the papers—" Freddy frowned. "Not that I read them, of course, but you can't help glancing at the stories as you tear them up, you know."

"Divorce?" Kate shook her head. "Oh, no. You must be mistaken. The young lady—Isabel—told me her mother was dead."

"And she is. Died penniless on the Continent after Traherne was finished dragging her and her lover through the courts."

"Lover?" Kate stared. She couldn't help it. "Freddy!"

"Oh, yes, it was quite the scandal," Freddy said pleasantly. "Married absurdly young, Traherne did—a love match, with the only daughter of the Duke of Wallace. Elisabeth, I think her name was. Anyway, it turned out to be a love match on his side only. Not a year after Isabel was born, Traherne caught her—Elisabeth, I mean—in a clinch with some sort of Irish poet or something, at a ball in his very own house. Traherne's house, I mean. Threw the fellow out a second-story window, from what I understand, and headed straight for his lawyer's office the next day."

Kate gasped. "Good Lord. Did he die?"

"Traherne? Of course not. I'm certain that's who you saw this evening. He's kept to himself a good bit, understandably—well, no decent hostess'll have 'im at her table—but I suppose he feels he's had to make an entrée back into society, if he ever wants to get that hellcat of his married off."

Kate took a deep breath for patience. Her long acquaintance with the Earl of Palmer had done more to prepare her for a teaching career than any formal training ever could.

"I *meant*," Kate said, "did his wife's lover die, when Lord Wingate threw him out the window?"

"Oh," Freddy said. "No, not at all. He recovered, and married the woman, once the divorce was final. Of course, the two of them couldn't set foot in England again, not after that. Nobody would have 'em, not even their own families."

"And the child?"

"The child? Isabel, you mean? Well, Traherne raised 'er, of course. You'd hardly expect 'im to let his wife do it. Former wife, I mean. I doubt the woman ever saw her daughter again. Traherne would have seen to that. I remember there was a bit of a fuss not too long ago about old Wallace—Elisabeth's father, don't you know—wanting to visit with his grandchild, and Traherne forbidding it. Very unpleasant, I must say."

"Very." Kate frowned in distaste. "What a perfectly horrid little tale."

"Oh, it gets worse," Freddy said cheerfully.

Kate held up a hand, palm out. "I don't care to hear it, thank you."

"But it's quite good. I'm sure you'll enjoy it, Katie."

Kate, lowering her hand, shot him a warning look. "You know I don't like gossip, Freddy. Particularly when it involves members of the *beau monde*. There is nothing duller to me than hearing about the trials and tribulations of the absurdly rich."

Freddy grinned delightedly. "Oh, are we going to have a debate? I dearly love debating with you, Kate. It will be just like old times."

Kate glared at him. "No it won't. Because there's nothing to debate. There can't be two sides to this issue. I'm sick to death of hearing about wealthy, educated people who are incapable of behaving better than . . . than back alley curs."

"You're being quite hard on poor Traherne," Freddy chastised her. "From what I understand, the fellow never recovered from his wife's betrayal. He's turned into a cold, bitter shell of his former vigorous self."

"He looked extremely *vigorous* to me," Kate said, thinking

of the ease with which the man had thrown his daughter—who was no lightweight, being a good few inches taller, and a good many pounds heavier than Kate.

"Oh, he's not wanting for female companionship," Freddy assured her. "Sara Woodhart's the latest, from what I understand. You remember, I told you about seeing her last month in *Macbeth*."

Rousing herself from memories of the marquis's vigorous figure, Kate said, "Yes, that's right. His daughter mentioned something about how he'd rather be with a Mrs. Woodhart than tagging along after her from ballroom to ballroom—"

"Which would be why Traherne's got a slew of chaperones looking out for her. And not very well, either, from what I've observed."

Kate shook her head. "He ought to remarry. It would be cheaper for him, in the long run. And I'm certain in this year's crop of society misses he could find a girl stupid—or greedy—enough to turn a blind eye to his philandering with vapid actresses."

"Except that Traherne's sworn off marriage. Everyone knows it. Says marriage ruined his life, and he won't chance it a second time, thank you very much."

"Oh," Kate said knowingly. "How original. A rich and handsome nobleman who has sworn off marriage. He must have every eligible young lady in London in a dither, trying to dissuade him."

"There, you see?" Freddy, grinning broadly, leaned forward and tapped her on the hand. "That wasn't so bad, was it? You did quite well. I'm prodigiously proud of you."

Kate, after blinking at him for a second, realized what he was talking about, tightened the hand he had touched into a fist, and got up suddenly from her chair.

"That wasn't fair," she said, facing away from him, her back very stiff.

"Of course it was." Freddy did not seem to notice her distress. He yawned and stretched before the fire. "It was a lovely gossip. I feel quite like it was old times again."

"Stop it," Kate said, still addressing the wall, and not him.

In fact, she spoke so softly, Freddy only then noticed she'd left her seat, and looked toward her curiously. "It can never be old times again. You know that."

"Now, Katie," Freddy said, staring at her back with a certain degree of alarm. "Don't go dredging up all of—"

"Freddy, how can I not?" Her voice did not shake, not even once.

"Katie," the earl said gently. "Don't."

"I can't help it. I think about it all the time. The other night I even. . . ."

"The other night you even what?" Freddy asked.

"Oh," she said, shaking her head. Her eyes, however, when she finally turned around to face him, were too bright. "Nothing."

"*Kate,*" he said, with a severity that didn't sound teasing. "Tell me."

She shrugged, but couldn't meet his gaze as she said, "I thought I saw him again."

Freddy blinked at her. "Thought you saw *who*?"

"Daniel Craven." The words, as they fell from her lips, sounded heavy, as if each syllable were a brick, dropping onto the floor. "I thought I saw Daniel Craven."

Freddy was up and out of his chair almost before the words were fully out of her mouth. He strode toward her, and took one of her hands in his. "Kate," he said gently. "We've talked about this."

"I know," she said. Her gaze was on the carpet beneath their feet. "I know. But I can't help it. I *saw* him, Freddy."

"You saw someone who looked like him. That's all."

"*No.*"

Kate snatched her hand from his, and went to the closest window, parting the velvet curtains that covered it. She gazed unseeingly out into the fog-enshrouded street.

"It was him," she said. "I know it was him. What's more, Freddy, he was following me."

"Following you?" Freddy hurried to her side. "Following you where?"

"Right here, on Park Lane. I was with the boys—"

"Daniel Craven," Freddy said skeptically. "Daniel Craven,

whom no one's seen in London in seven years, was following you along this very street?"

"I know it sounds absurd." Kate dropped the curtain back into place and turned back toward the fire. "You think I'm mad. And maybe I am . . ."

Freddy stared after her, clearly troubled. "It's not that I don't believe you, Kate. It's just . . ."

She stood, bathed in firelight, fingering the back of her chair. "It's just what?" she asked, not looking at him.

"Well, so what if it *was* Daniel Craven, Kate? You can't *still* think he had something to do with your parents' deaths, can you? I thought we'd settled all that. What are you imagining?" Freddy shook his head. "That after seven years he's come back to finish you off, as well?"

Kate set her jaw. "Yes. That's rather what I was thinking. I'm sorry if you find it maudlin."

"Oh, now, Kate," Freddy cried. "Don't look at me like that. You know there's nothing, nothing in the world I wouldn't do for you. But all this rubbish about Daniel—you know what people said about it, at the time."

Kate, looking very cross, sank back down into the chair she'd abandoned. "Of course I do. They all thought I made it up. I forgot you were among them," she added, with genuine bitterness.

"Well, Kate, really," Freddy said in gently chiding tones. "You always did have something of an imagination. That isn't a bad thing, not at all. I'm sure it helps a good deal where your little charges are concerned, but—"

"All right," Kate said, closing her eyes tiredly. "All right. I couldn't have seen Daniel Craven. I won't mention it again. But you . . . you've got to stop proposing to me, Freddy. I can't bear it. I really can't. I mean, besides the fact that I'm not in love with you, you know I don't want anything to do with those people—"

"*Those people,*" Freddy echoed. "Polite society, you mean?"

"I never saw anything polite about them," Kate said stiffly. "Nor anything kind or considerate. My God, Freddy, I'm quite sure Cyrus Sledge's Papua New Guineans would have treated me with more compassion than your mother—or all those people who claimed to be my friends—ever did. I'd hardly call a society that spent all of its time whispering about me, *blaming* me, for what my father did, a *polite* society—"

"Bloody hell!"

Now it was the earl's turn to stride across the room. He did so with his fists buried in his trouser pockets.

"I came here to take you out for a nice evening, Kate," he declared, from behind a table heavy with stuffed birds beneath glass bell jars. "So that you could forget, for a little while. How is it that no matter how hard I try to make you forget what happened with your parents, we always manage to come back to it?"

Kate turned on her hard chair to look at him, a little smile playing across her lips. "How? Freddy, take a look around. Isn't it obvious? We're sitting in someone else's drawing room, because I haven't one of my own anymore, and I daren't set foot in yours, for fear of what your mother will say. Freddy, I am living proof of the fact that the gods *do* visit the sins of the fathers upon the children—"

"I thought," Freddy interrupted, "that you hated the Bible. You always said that it didn't have enough female characters in it to be interesting—"

"That wasn't a quote from the Bible, Freddy, for heaven's sake. It was Euripides. Didn't you *ever* pay attention in school?"

Freddy ignored that question. "I feel like smashing something up," he declared loudly.

"Well," Kate said. "Then you'd better go. I can't afford to get the sack on account of your smashing something. The Sledges might be hideously boring, but at least they're kind, which is more than I can say for some of my past employers."

Freddy said, "Bloody hell," again and turned to go, just as the doorknob moved, and Cyrus Sledge, looking extremely nervous, poked his head into the room.

"Oh, my Lord Palmer," he said, waving a fistful of pamphlets. "I see that you're going. Before you do, sir, please take some of these tracts. I mean, if you will. They are extremely illuminating on a subject that I'm sure a young man like yourself will be fascinated by, the unfortunate fate of the Papua New Guineans. . . ."

There was a look on the Earl of Palmer's face that suggested to Kate that her employer would be far better off saving his tracts for another time. She hurried to her feet and hastened to make him aware of that fact.

"Oh, Mr. Sledge," she said, "Lord Palmer isn't feeling well. He has a bit of a headache. Perhaps another time—"

"A headache?" Cyrus Sledge squinted up at the robust figure of the earl. "Do you know how the Papua New Guineans cure a headache, sir? They chew up the bark of a particular species of tree, then spit the masticated bits into a great pot, the contents of which are allowed to ferment for several days in the heat—"

"Kate," Freddy said in a strangled voice.

Kate placed a hand reassuringly on his arm. "It's all right, Freddy," she said soothingly. "If you'll excuse me, Mr. Sledge, I'll just show his lordship to the door."

"He said 'masticate' to me, Kate," Freddy hissed, as she steered him toward Phillips, who waited by the door with the earl's hat, cloak, and cane. "He said 'masticate'!"

"It isn't what you think, Freddy. 'Masticate' means 'chew.' That's all."

"Oh." Looking relieved, Freddy allowed the butler to drape his cloak over his shoulders. "I thought . . . I thought. . . ."

"I know what you thought," Kate said. "Never mind that now." She reached out and took his cane and gloves while he settled his top hat firmly over his short blond hair. "I'll see you next week. Pick me up at seven o'clock."

Freddy nodded. "Yes, that's better. It never works, your meeting me somewhere."

"No," Kate agreed. "Not when you never remember to write the address down. Good night, Freddy." She caught Phillips's eye. "I mean, Lord Palmer."

As soon as the earl was gone, and Phillips had shut the door, Mrs. Sledge poked her head over the upstairs balustrade and asked, her voice warbling, "Did he take the tracts, my love?"

Cyrus Sledge looked sadly down at the pamphlets in his hand. "No, my love," he called back woefully, "he didn't."

Kate, observing their disappointment, couldn't help saying, "Oh, but he did, Mr. Sledge. When you weren't looking, I stuck some of the ones you keep there on the entry table into his lordship's pocket."

Mrs. Sledge inhaled sharply. "Then he's likely to find them tonight, when he undresses!"

Kate did a fair job of keeping a straight face. "Most certainly he will, madam," she said.

"And he'll read them before he goes to bed," Mr. Sledge said happily. "And when he falls asleep, his lordship will dream of the Papua New Guineans! Don't you think so, Miss Mayhew?"

"I can't imagine he'd be able to dream of anything else," Kate said honestly, "after reading those tracts."

Mr. and Mrs. Sledge retired to their room, congratulating themselves at having converted yet another believer in the Reverend Billings's miracles, leaving Kate momentarily alone with Phillips, their butler.

"Miss Mayhew," Mr. Phillips said, as he turned the locks on the front door.

Kate cautiously replied, "Yes, Mr. Phillips?"

"Earlier this evening, when we spoke belowstairs . . ."

Hardly daring to believe the butler was going to apologize for his earlier rudeness, Kate asked suspiciously, "Yes, Mr. Phillips?"

"I forgot to mention one thing." The butler turned to face her. "In the future, will you kindly keep that animal of yours confined to your own room? This morning I found a hairball in one of my shoes."

And without another word, Phillips turned and headed for the baize door.

Kate, suddenly very tired, indeed, leaned back against the wall. Really, she thought to herself. From now on, she was going to spend her evenings off locked in her room with a book.

Chapter Three

*I*t was well after midnight when Burke knocked on the door to Sara Woodhart's apartments in the Dorchester. Still, it oughtn't to have taken her so long to answer. After all, she generally didn't even leave the theater until eleven. She could not possibly be in bed, even though it was—Burke, while he waited, took his pocket watch from his waistcoat pocket, and squinted at it in the dim light of the hotel corridor.

Well, all right, it was past three in the morning. Still, Sara never got to bed before five. And he ought to know. He was the one who'd been keeping her awake these past few weeks.

But when the door finally did open, it wasn't the rouged and powdered face of his mistress that peered out at him, but rather the well-scrubbed and country-fresh face of her maid, Lilly, who said, blinking and rubbing her eyes with rather more astonishment than Burke thought the occasion warranted, "Oh! My lord! It's you!"

"Yes, Lilly," Burke said, more patiently—and more kindly—than he actually felt. "Of course it's me. Who were you expecting, may I ask? Father Christmas?"

"Oh, no, my lord," Lilly said, glancing back over her shoulder, into the darkened apartment. "Of course not. Not Father Christmas, no. Only not you, either. I didn't think . . . I didn't think we'd be seein' your lordship. Not tonight."

"Why not tonight, Lilly? Has Mrs. Woodhart taken ill, or something?"

"Oh, no, sir. Only, when your lordship never turned up at the theater—"

"Yes?"

"Well, we just thought we wouldn't be seein' you tonight, is all."

"Well," Burke said. "You were wrong. Here I am. Now, are you going to let me in, Lilly, or am I to stand out here in this drafty hallway all night?"

Again, Lilly looked back over her shoulder. "Oh, well, of course you can come in . . . only Mrs. Woodhart, she's asleep, you know."

"I assumed as much, Lilly. But I don't think she'll mind if I wake her."

Burke didn't feel he was flattering himself. The velvet box in his coat pocket was his insurance that Sara would not, indeed, at all mind being awakened in the middle of the night— and especially not by Burke Traherne. He had meant to give her the bracelet next month, on her birthday, but thought perhaps to see his jeweler about designing a matching necklace and earrings instead. Diamonds, he had learned over the years, were the surest way to a woman's heart.

"We-ell," Lilly said, stretching the word out to several syllables. "Could you wait, sir, while I see if _I_ can wake her, first? She was feelin' a bit poorly when she come in. . . . Plus you know she always wants to look 'er best for ye. . . ."

Burke said, very slowly, so she'd be sure to understand him, "Why, certainly I'll wait, Lilly. But would it trouble you terribly to allow me to wait _inside_?"

Lilly nodded, but admitted him with obvious reluctance, and only agreed to light a lamp when Burke settled himself onto a couch in the manner of a man who owned the right to. Which of course, he did, since he was the one paying the rent on the apartment. He had paid for the couch, as well.

He was, Burke decided, going to have to speak to Sara about her Lilly. Lord knew, it wasn't easy to find good help these days—Miss Pitt was a prime example. Still, the girl was positively obtuse. Perhaps Lady Chittenhouse could recommend a good ladies' maid. Burke could make out as if he were asking for Isabel. . . .

Burke sat in the semidarkness, glowering to himself. The mere thought of Miss Pitt nearly sent him into an apoplexy of rage. It was all that old woman's fault. If she hadn't given her notice at the last minute like that, he might have avoided spending the majority of his evening arguing with Isabel. Arguing with her? Who was he trying to fool? He'd spent the majority of the evening chasing after her. His new breeches—not to mention his shoes—were ruined from the mud through which he'd splashed in his mad dash after her when she'd slipped from the carriage. The two of them had been forced to return to the house to change before they dared show their faces at Lady Peagroves' which, much to his chagrin, he'd found exactly as that irritating young woman on the street had assured him it would be, a crush filled with hangers-on and country cousins. Not an eligible fellow in the place.

Well, they were *all* eminently eligible. That was the problem. There wasn't a fellow there with whom he'd feel safe entrusting Isabel to dance, let alone marry. Everyone who was anyone, another glum-faced father had assured him, was at Dame Ashforth's.

Well, how was he to have known? A man couldn't be expected to know things like that. That's what he'd hired the chaperone for. Was it his fault that chaperones appeared to be, as a breed, stupid as cats? Besides, he'd come to the conclusion that it wasn't a chaperone he needed for Isabel: it was a bloody long-distance runner. The girl had led him on a merry chase, all through Piccadilly. He'd finally caught her at Trafalgar Square, and only because she'd stopped running to catch her breath, and her white dress had given her away amidst all the whores and flower sellers.

And what had she done when he caught up with her? Laughed! Laughed as if the whole thing were nothing, a merry joke.

A joke! And then he'd had to spend the rest of the evening listening to Lady Peagrove apologize for the fact that there weren't any peers at her cotillion this year, she couldn't imagine where they'd all gone off to, and had Lord Wingate met her cousin Ann, wasn't she lovely, widowed last year, too, poor thing, and stuck out all the way in Yorkshire with those three strapping boys and two hundred head of cattle and no man to keep the place.

Oh, yes. An excellent joke. It had been all Burke could do just to keep from flinging his champagne glass across the room.

Miss Pitt. It was all that Miss Pitt's fault. If she hadn't quit. . . .

And that girl. That girl with the umbrella. It was all her fault, as well. Her and her infernal mouth. Why, if she had kept that mouth of hers shut concerning the Peagroves' cotillion. . . .

Was there an unwritten rule somewhere that chaperones and governesses had to let their tongues run away with them? Was that it? Perhaps he could find one whose tongue had been lost in some sort of tragic accident.

But how effective was a mute chaperone going to be at managing Isabel? He was quite sure he'd run through every last one of Lady Chittenhouse's daughters' chaperones, all of whom had had tongues, and none of them had been the least effective at managing his child. How was he to find another? Was he going to have to advertise? He supposed so. It would take days, and would require the endless questioning of pinch-faced widows and spinsters. And then he'd have to have their references checked, which would take more time. Especially if they'd lied.

And they all lied.

This was not how a man in his prime—and Burke was, most decidedly, in his prime—ought to be spending his time. Between interviewing chaperones and making sure Isabel hadn't snuck out of the house to meet the wretched Saunders—Lord, how Burke would have liked to put a bullet through that gadabout's skull!—he hadn't any time at all to himself. None at all.

It wasn't any wonder Sara had gone to bed. Was he, truly, a man worth waiting up for?

What was he thinking? Of course he was!

Except . . . except that he couldn't help thinking it was a bit strange, this going off to bed so very early. To his certain knowledge, actresses and songstresses tended to stay up until well into the wee hours, generally sleeping until afternoon. Sara had proven no exception to this rule. Well, she was put out with him, because he was so late. It wasn't any wonder, really, that she'd gone to bed. She was a woman—quite emphatically a woman—and, like a woman, she'd taken offense at his tardiness. It was only to be expected, really.

That was when he noticed the boots.

They hadn't really even made any attempt to hide them. Maybe Lilly hadn't known they were there. Tucked into the shadows beside the long draperies that hid the French doors to Sara's bedroom—the French doors through which Lilly had just disappeared—sat a tall pair of gleaming Hessians. Burke didn't have to get up to see that they were clearly men's boots, not a pair of Sara's left carelessly lying about. Sara was a large woman, it was true, but not large enough to fit into a pair of boots which might have fit him.

On the couch, Burke sighed.

Really, this was getting to be too much. If he hadn't known better, he might have begun to suspect that perhaps it was him. There had to be a reason all of these women found it so difficult to remain faithful to him. Was it really, as he'd been telling himself since that wretched evening he'd found Elisabeth and that blackguard O'Shawnessey locked in one another's arms on the landing, that women were entirely fickle creatures, completely incapable of making a commitment?

Or could it possibly be that there was something wrong with *him*, something that drove women away? He'd been accused, in the past, of coldness, of having no heart. Was it possible that was true?

Quite probably. Elisabeth had seen to that. She had ripped whatever heart he'd once had out of his body and thrown it down the stairs that wintry night, sixteen years ago.

Which might have been why, just at that moment, it wasn't hurting him a bit . . . though, considering those boots, it ought to have been.

The French doors were flung open, and the celebrated Mrs. Woodhart, resplendent in a diaphanous negligee he recognized as one he had purchased for her, stood in the lamplight, her midnight-black hair falling about her shoulders, almost down to her waist.

"Darling!" she cried, in the throaty voice that had made her the current toast of London. "*There* you are! Whatever kept you?"

Burke looked from the lovely creature in the doorway to the boots sitting not a foot away from her, but hidden in shadow, he supposed, from where she stood.

He said, simply, "Isabel."

"Oh, no!" Sara shook her head. "Not again. What did she do this time? I hope it wasn't that awful Saunders boy. You know, I hear, Burke, that he is thousands of pounds in debt up at Oxford. Gambling! There's nothing quite worse than a gambler, except perhaps a gambler who can't pay his debts, and I'm afraid that's what our Mr. Saunders is."

Burke had been sitting perfectly still. He had not yet shed his cloak, though he had removed his hat. Now he climbed to his feet.

"You are going to have to do something about that child of yours," Sara said. She was not so large that she could look Burke in the eye when he'd risen to his full height, but she only had to tip her chin up a little to do so. At one time, he'd found the sight of Sara Woodhart's up-turned chin quite charming. Tonight, however, he saw that the black beauty mark Sara painted onto the lower corner of her mouth was smeared, and there appeared to be a red mark on her throat, where the robe to the negligee opened to reveal the ivory skin of her neck.

"Honestly, Burke," Sara was saying. "You allow her to run positively wild. You can't let Isabel hold the reins. You have got to take charge of her, show her that you are in control."

Burke began calmly stripping off his gloves, tugging on each finger individually.

"The problem with these chaperones you keep hiring," Sara went on, not at all shrewishly—never shrewishly. That was part of Mrs. Woodhart's charm—"is that they fear they'll be dismissed if they don't do precisely what the Lady Isabel says. You've got to find someone, Burke, who'll put her foot down, and tell that girl exactly what's going to happen to her if she continues to carry on like a little hoyden."

The gloves completely stripped off now, Burke said calmly, "Stand aside, Sara."

Mrs. Woodhart seemed to remember herself suddenly. She said, with a tremulous little laugh, "Oh, Burke. Didn't Lilly tell you? I'm afraid I've a tickle in my throat. I went straight to bed, after drinking a gallon of tea with honey. You'd best not come too close, love, or you might catch it. Dr. Peters says I've got to rest my voice, or I'll be good for nothing for tomorrow night's show."

Burke slapped the black leather gloves against his palm. He wasn't in a hurry. He had all the time in the world.

"Stand aside, Sara," he said again. "There's something I've got to do, and then I'll be on my way, and you can get your rest."

Sara glanced over her shoulder, into the darkened bedroom behind her. "Honestly, Burke," she said, a little too loudly. "I can't imagine why you'd want to go into the bedroom, when I told you before I'm not feeling my best—"

"There is something," Burke replied unhurriedly, "that I left behind, last time I was here."

Sara turned back toward him, and raised her perfectly molded shoulders in a slight shrug. "Have it your way," she said, in the you-get-what-you-deserve tone she generally reserved for the young men who developed frostbite hanging about the stage door in hopes of catching a glimpse of her.

Burke said tersely, "Thank you." As he brushed past her, he got a sudden whiff of Sara's perfume, a concoction she and a local chemist had come up with and hoped to market as the personal scent of London's greatest thespian. They intended to call the brew Sara. It reminded Burke, strangely enough, of the honeysuckle that had grown outside the stables in which he'd stalled his horse as a boy. Since this was not an unpleasant memory, he quite liked the odor, but wondered sometimes if the horsey undertone was purposeful on Sara's part.

Inside the bedroom, all was dark, except for the faint red light thrown by the dying fire. The great canopied bed was empty, though clearly two heads had been resting against those pillows just moments earlier. Sara, never the neatest of women, had left her garments scattered about the floor. Burke could detect no men's clothing in amongst the garters and crinolines and satin slippers.

Then he noticed a shadow outside the French doors to the terrace. The moon had managed to burn a hole through the fog, and he'd distinctly seen an elbow on the other side of the glassed-in door.

Burke strode toward the doors, and laid both hands upon the latches. Behind him, Sara gasped, and he heard Lilly say, quite distinctly, "Oh, mum!"

He flung open the doors. There, shivering in the spring chill, stood a man with one leg in, and one leg out, of a pair of breeches. He froze—quite literally—when he saw Burke, his eyes going wide as eggs. As Burke stood there, thinking that he didn't know this fellow, but that that wasn't so unusual, since there were lots of people he didn't know in London, the man tore his gaze from Burke's and looked, just once, down, over the balcony railing, to the street several stories below.

And gulped, quite audibly.

Burke laughed, though without any humor. "Don't worry," he said. "I'm not going to throw you off it."

The man—he was more of a boy, really, not a day over twenty-five—stammered, through lips that had gone blue with the cold, "Y-you're n-not, my lord?"

"Certainly not," Burke said. "My days of throwing men through windows and over balconies are quite over."

"Are th-they, my lord?"

"Quite. Rage takes passion, you know, and I haven't felt passionate about anything—certainly any woman—in quite some time. You'll find you feel the same, son, as you get older."

The boy looked immensely relieved. "Oh . . . *thank* you, my lord."

"But just because I'm not in a rage," Burke went on, conversationally, "doesn't mean I shan't be wanting satisfaction from you. I'll expect to meet you tomorrow at dawn—oh, no, I say, that's much too early. Only in a few hours. How about tomorrow at dusk? The far side of the park. You choose the weapon. Pistols or blades?"

The young man's heart—which Burke could plainly see, thumping against the skin of his chest, since the fellow was shirtless—gave a spasmodic shudder. "Oh, sir," the boy said. "I—if you please, sir—"

"Pistols it is, then," Burke said, since he doubted the fellow was much of a fencer. Fencing, long considered a crucial element in the education of a gentleman, seemed to have become a lost art of late, which Burke considered unfortunate. "Bring a second. I'll provide the surgeon. Good night."

He turned, and headed back into the bedroom. There, Sara had flung herself across the bed, and was wailing fitfully.

"Oh, please, Burke!" she cried, lifting her beautiful, tear-stained face from a lace-trimmed pillow. "You don't understand! He forced me! I merely invited him back here for a drink, and the next thing I knew, he'd forced himself upon me!"

Burke nodded, pulling his gloves back into place. He'd thought to use them to strike his rival across the face, but when he'd actually laid eyes on the shivering fellow, he hadn't had the heart. He did wish, however, that he had his horsewhip handy. He'd have applied that, readily enough, to Mrs. Woodhart's generous backside, since it seemed to him she deserved a whipping very badly, indeed.

"Please, Sara," he said. "Histrionics might earn you applause on stage, but they're quite wasted on me. If there was any forcing going on here tonight, I'll wager it was you who did it. Stop crying now, and listen to me carefully."

But Sara was too far into her performance to stop now. She

shrieked, "Burke! Don't you know I could only love you? Only you, Burke!"

Burke sighed. "Listen to me, Sara. The rent on this place is paid through the month, but I expect you to be gone by the first. You understand, of course."

Sara let out a sob. It occurred to Burke that if she'd thrown half this much energy into her performance as Lady Macbeth, she might have pleased the critics better. It was the public who loved her, loved her for exceptionally good looks.

Well, and was he any different, really?

"You can keep the jewelry and the carriage," Burke said. He was, he knew, losing his edge. Just a year ago, he'd have asked for the carriage back. Now he simply didn't care enough to make an issue of it. "And of course all the clothes and hats and whatnot are yours." Was that all? He tried to remember. Had he given her anything else?

No. He was quite safe. She hadn't anything at all of his.

"Well," he said, as he watched the estimable Mrs. Woodhart beat her mattress with her fists. "Good night then, Sara."

He left the bedroom, and retrieved his hat from a wide-eyed Lilly, who said, quite fiercely for such a little country thing, "If you'd only *been* here tonight, instead of off gallivantin' about, it never woulda 'appened, you know, my lord. Her and him, I mean."

Burke raised his eyebrows at this sage piece of advice. "Well, Lilly," he said. "I'm terribly sorry. But I wasn't off gallivanting about, as you so charmingly put it. I had to look after my daughter."

Lilly shook her head, clearly unhappy that her residence in this fine hotel was at an end. "There's folks you can *hire* to look after daughters, you know, my lord," she said bitterly—right before shutting the door in his face.

Standing out in the corridor in front of the door to a hotel suite for which he'd paid, Burke considered the maid's words. "There's folks you can *hire* to look after daughters, you know." Certainly. And he'd hired—how many? He'd lost count of the number of women who'd unpacked their bags in the room next door to his daughter's, only to repack them a few days later and leave—usually in tears. Was there no woman in England with whom Isabel could get along for more than a week? Who could he possibly hire who might satisfy the girl?

He had put that very question to Isabel, the moment they'd returned from the Peagroves' cotillion. She had replied, slamming her bedroom door closed as if to emphasize her words, "Someone like Miss Mayhew!"

Well, Burke decided, there in the hallway outside of Sara Woodhart's door. If Miss Mayhew was who Isabel wanted, then by God, Miss Mayhew was who Isabel was going to get.

Chapter Four

Kate propped Lady Babbie up onto the top of her desk and asked, "What am I do with you?"

Lady Babbie blinked at her with cool green eyes.

"You're going to get us thrown out of here," Kate said. "You've simply got to stop putting headless mice on his pillow. No more stalking his coattails. And no more hairballs in his shoes. You have *got* to stop it. He's making my life a perfect misery."

Lady Babbie opened her mouth and let out an enormous yawn, showing all of her white pointy teeth and her long pink tongue.

"If only," Kate murmured mournfully, "you understood a word I said."

Footsteps outside the schoolroom door. Since Kate had promised Phillips that she wouldn't let Lady Babbie out of her bedroom, she snatched up the creature and thrust her beneath her desk, holding the cat there, spitting and squirming, while she waited to see who was at the door.

But it was only Posie, panting breathlessly from having run all the way from the first floor to the fourth, where the schoolroom was located.

"Oh," Kate said, visibly relieved. She lifted the hissing cat from beneath the desktop. "It's only you. You scared me. I felt sure it was old Fusspot."

"Oh, miss." Posie leaned against the doorframe for support as she attempted to catch her breath. "You won't believe— you won't believe—"

Lady Babbie let out a snarl, and Kate was forced to drop her, or risk getting scratched. "There, you nasty thing," she said fondly, as the cat stalked away, her long striped tail swishing angrily from side to side. "Go on, then. And don't blame me if Mr. Phillips comes after you with the water basin next time you take it into that pea-sized brain of yours to pay him a social call in his private quarters."

Lady Babbie retired to the fireside, and began industriously to clean herself. Kate glanced at the small watch pinned to her blouse. "Are the boys back from their riding lesson already?" she asked. "I'd have thought they'd be another half hour at least. I haven't had a chance to see Cook yet about their tea."

"Not the boys," Posie said, finally managing to gulp a few words out. She kept a hand flattened to her chest, as if to still her too quickly beating heart. "There's a gentleman here to see you, miss. He's waitin' in the library. Fusspot had to put him in the library, since the mistress's got the Ladies' Society fer the Betterment of the Lot of the Popping New Guineas in the front drawing room—"

"A gentleman?" Kate reached up instinctively to smooth back her hair. "What on earth is Freddy doing here, and in the middle of the day? He knows I don't have Tuesdays off. What can be the matter with him?"

Posie shook her head. "No, no, miss," she said, her eyes glittering with what could easily have been mistaken for feverish excitement. "It isn't Lord Palmer. Not a bit! It's a great tall dark man. Big as a mountain an' with eyes just like Lady Babbie's there. I was thinkin he's got to be that man you said you saw abusin' his daughter on the street t'other evening—"

"What?" Kate found herself on her feet before she was even aware that she'd stood up. "Lord Wingate, you mean?"

"That's right." Posie snapped her fingers. "That's his name, all right! Fusspot tol' me, but I forgot it. Wingate. Right."

Kate stared. "Lord Wingate? Here? To see *me*?"

"Yes, miss. That's what he said. He gave Phillips his card and asked if you were at home, just as if you was the lady of the house!" Posie's cheeks were flushed. "You shoulda seen ol' Fusspot's face! Like to 'ave a fit, he was! Went straight to Mr. Sledge an' tol' him, an' Mr. Sledge, he says, 'Well, don't just stand there, Phillips. Go and fetch her!' " Posie shrieked with nervous laughter. " 'Go and fetch her,' he says! To *Fusspot*! You shoulda seen the ol' milksop's face!"

"Good Lord." Kate hurriedly swept cat hair from her skirt. "What could he possibly want?"

"Maybe you poked a hole in his coat with yer umbrella," Posie offered cheerfully. "Maybe he wants to make you pay fer replacin' it."

"Oh, no." Kate froze, even as her foot was on the stairs. "Good Lord, Posie, I can't afford to buy a new coat for that man. His cravats alone probably cost more than I earn in an entire year."

Posie patted her on the arm. "Don't you worry. Just ask him for the coat back, and we'll have Mrs. Jennings stitch that hole right up. You know what a good job she did with the boys' coats that day they took into their heads to pitch those hot chestnuts at one another. It'll be good as new. He won't be able to tell the difference."

Only somewhat comforted, Kate began a slow descent to the second floor, where his lordship waited. There could be only one reason, she knew, why the Marquis of Wingate would deign to call upon the home of Mr. Cyrus Sledge: he was undoubtedly still outraged over Kate's accusations that night nearly a week ago, and had come to demand her dismissal and subsequent removal from Park Lane. When she entered the library, Mr. Sledge would dismiss her on the spot . . . in return for a modest contribution to the Reverend Billings's cause, of course.

But when Kate approached the library door, she found Mr. Sledge hovering about outside it, with Mrs. Sledge and Mr. Phillips in close attendance. All three of them looked up expectantly when she came near, and it was Mrs. Sledge who said, quite kindly, and in a loud whisper, ostensibly so that his lordship would not hear her through the door. "Why, Miss Mayhew! We had no idea you were acquainted with Lord Wingate!"

Kate stared. "I—" she began, but Mr. Sledge cut her off.

"Lord Wingate is an extremely wealthy man, Miss Mayhew." Her employer was trying, Kate could see, to maintain a dignified poise, but his excitement was getting the better of him. "He hasn't the sort of reputation that the Reverend Billings would find desirable in a sponsor—Lord Wingate has somewhat of a checkered past, I'm sure I needn't tell you— but he is so wealthy that even what he might consider a very small donation would keep the Papua New Guineans in prayer books for years to come, and might possibly even pay the salary for someone to teach the poor souls to read them!"

Kate said, "Well, I would think that if Lord Wingate had come to make a donation, he'd have asked to see you, sir, and not me. Perhaps there's been some mistake—"

"There was no mistake," Phillips said majestically, from where he stood by the door. "He asked for you by name, Miss Mayhew."

Oh, Lord, Kate thought. *I'm doomed.*

"Well, whatever he's come for," Mrs. Sledge said, slipping something into Kate's hand and giving her a little push toward the library door, "do see if you could give him these tracts. I understand that Lord Wingate is quite an intellectual. He studied the law for his own amusement, and reads philosophy and things, they say. So he ought to find these quite interesting."

Before Kate could say another word, Phillips had flung open the library door and said, "Miss Mayhew, my lord," and Kate was quite literally propelled into the room by a hand placed very firmly in the small of her back.

She stumbled, of course, over the fringe on the Oriental carpet, and dropped the tracts. When she'd regained her balance, she looked up, and saw the man she'd accosted on the street a few nights before turning around from the fire he'd been staring into.

Only without the fog to soften and blur his extremely hard edges, Kate saw that the Marquis of Wingate was far more intimidating indoors than he'd looked out of them. Over a foot taller than she was, he was nearly as wide as the mantel across the shoulders, though his shape tapered down nicely after that, to a pair of slim hips, and a trim waist without any paunch at all hidden beneath his satin waistcoat. Still, he was far too large for Kate's sense of comfort—too large, and much too direct with his gaze, which once again pierced her with alarming intensity.

So directly, and with so much intensity, that Kate hastily dropped her own gaze, and hoped he wouldn't notice.

"Looking for a parasol, Miss Mayhew," he inquired, "with which to skewer me?"

He'd noticed. She started, though she recognized the voice easily enough. A deep, menacing growl it had been, cutting through the fog and enveloping her with its displeasure. Now there was far more amusement in it than displeasure . . . but it was nonetheless intimidating.

"I assure you," Kate said, looking up, "that I am as handy with a fire poker as I am with an umbrella."

If Lord Wingate was surprised by her temerity, he didn't look it. He said, quite dryly, "Thank you for putting me on my guard. But I'd hoped to survive this interview without having any holes poked through me. Do you know who I am?"

Kate put her hands behind her back, and assumed what she considered a suitably cowed expression. It was one she'd had to work on quite hard in the mirror upon her realization that the only way she was going to survive, after the deaths of her parents, was by her wits. She prided herself that she'd got it exactly right.

"I do indeed, my lord," she said. "You are Burke Traherne, the Marquis of Wingate."

"I am," he rumbled. "I assume you remember reviling me just the other night with some rather startling assumptions. Do you recall them?"

Kate nodded. "Indeed, my lord, I do."

One of his dark eyebrows lifted. "But no apology, I see."

Kate said, "I apologize, my lord, if my thinking you were a vile abuser of innocent women offended you. But I don't apologize for thinking it. You did look suspicious. It was a natural assumption."

"A natural assumption? That there was a—what did you call me?—a vile abuser of innocent women, running around loose on Park Lane? Do you run into that sort of thing often during your rambles about the neighborhood, Miss Mayhew?"

Kate gave a barely perceptible shrug. "*I* was not the one with a screaming woman thrown over my shoulder, sir."

"I explained to you," Lord Wingate said, "that she was my daughter."

"Yes, but why should I have believed you? If you really were a vile abuser of innocent women, you might say anything in an effort not to be caught."

Lord Wingate cleared his throat. "Yes, I see. Well, do you suppose you could set aside your suspicions about the true nature of my character long enough to listen to a proposal?"

"A proposal?" Kate was relieved. It wasn't her he wanted at all. Hallelujah! "Oh, you must wish to speak with Mr. Sledge, then, after all. He is the one, my lord, who is collecting donations in support of the Reverend Billings, who intends to save the downtrodden peoples of Papua New Guinea. Shall I fetch him for you?"

"Certainly not." Lord Wingate was looking at her curiously—quite curiously, she thought, and quite a bit too long. She wouldn't drop her gaze again, but she dearly wanted to. All she could think, when she looked at him, was that he certainly had the arms for throwing another man out the window. His biceps, the outlines of which she could plainly perceive through the finely tailored sleeves of his coat, were massive.

That, and the fact that the deep grooves that ran from his nostrils to the corners of his full, oddly sensitive-looking mouth had probably been put there by his unhappiness over his wife. For a moment, she almost felt sorry for him, in spite of all his money and the fact that he'd treated his wife so abominably. She had to rebuke herself sternly. There was no need to feel sorry for the likes of the Marquis of Wingate.

"I don't care a whit about the Papua New Guineans," Lord

Wingate declared, startling her out of her bemusement. "Are you a great supporter of the Reverend Billings, Miss Mayhew?"

Kate couldn't help letting out a little bark of laughter at that. "Hardly!" she said. "He came here for dinner once, and he—"

She broke off, realizing she couldn't possibly tell this large and intimidating man what the Reverend Billings had done, which was consume the whole of a bottle of claret at dinner and then corner her in the pantry afterward, where he'd attempted to enlighten her on the mating rituals of the Papua New Guineans. Kate had crowned him with a pie dish for his efforts, and he'd left rather hastily after that, without any explanation to his benefactors, who declared his odd behavior a sign of his great genius.

If Lord Wingate noticed she'd left a sentence unfinished, he didn't let on. Instead he said, noticeably relieved, "Well, that's all right, then. What I've come to ask, Miss Mayhew— and you'll excuse me not writing first, but I felt a personal application would be better received, considering our somewhat . . . *unconventional* meeting last week—"

Here he pegged her with such a piercing look that Kate nearly staggered backward, but saved herself just in time by seizing hold of the corner of the wooden stand that held the family atlas.

"I'm wondering," his lordship continued, "whether you might consider leaving your employment here with the Sledges, and come to work for me as chaperone to my daughter, Isabel, with whom you are, I believe, somewhat acquainted."

Kate blinked. Just once. And tightened her grip on the wooden stand.

"I'm quite certain," Lord Wingate went on, "that I can offer at least as comfortable accommodations as you've been afforded here—" He looked about the library distastefully. Though expensively furnished and very well stocked with all the classics, the room had remarkably uncomfortable furniture, and was quite small, besides, being quite the most unused room in the house. "And at twice the salary."

Kate felt her jaw drop. It was perfectly uncouth to stand with one's mouth open—something she'd tried, unsuccessfully, to impress upon the youngest Sledges—but she simply couldn't help it.

The Marquis of Wingate had just asked her to come work for him. It was extraordinary. It was more than extraordinary. It was unbelievable.

Wait until she told Freddy!

"Oh," Kate said, finally managing to lever her jaw back into place. "Thank you kindly, sir, but I couldn't possibly."

It was Lord Wingate's turn to stare, and he did so admirably. Kate felt quite sure he intended to make her feel as if she were as small and insignificant as the tiniest crumb on his table. But she would not allow herself to be cowed. She stood her ground, holding her chin high.

His too bright gaze bored into her with all the intensity of a blaze from a furnace.

"Why," he said slowly, with a patience that was in absolute contrast with the look on his face, "not?"

Kate couldn't help reaching up with her free hand and laying her fingers upon her heart. It struck her as far too dramatic a gesture, of course—he was not able to burn a hole through her chest with his merest gaze, as she rather fancifully imagined—so at the last minute, she played with the cameo at her throat, instead.

She couldn't, of course, tell him. Not the truth. There was no need for that. There were plenty of other reasons she couldn't possibly go to work for him. Besides the fact that he had the worst reputation in the world—only just the other day, she'd heard he'd shot and almost killed a man in Hyde Park, in a duel, it was rumored, over something to do with Sara Woodhart—he was the most physically intimidating man she had ever seen.

Not that he wasn't good-looking. He was attractive enough, she supposed—though he was by no means handsome. Freddy was far better looking, with his fair hair and dimples—a true

Englishman, in both looks and empty-headedness. Burke Traherne, on the other hand, had the look of the gypsy about him.
There was nothing irregular about his features, certainly, but
they hardly seemed to have been arranged with any intention
of pleasing. His face was compelling, she supposed—in a
fierce, almost cruel way—but certainly not anything to swoon
over.

Those shoulders, on the other hand. . . .

"I just," Kate said, swallowing. "Couldn't."

"Then I'll ask again, why?"

Well, *this* was certainly awkward. Why couldn't the man
simply take no for an answer, and go away? But a glance at
Lord Wingate reminded her that he was not a man to whom
the word "no" was uttered very often. A plague take him!
What was she going to do?

She took a deep breath, but before she could say anything,
the marquis demanded, "How much is your current annual
salary?"

Suddenly, Kate saw a glimmer of hope. That was it. She'd
simply be too expensive for him.

"A hundred pounds a year," Kate said at once, pulling from
the top of her head the most outrageously high number she
could think of.

"Fine," Lord Wingate said calmly. "I'll double it."

Chapter Five

For a moment, Burke thought the girl might faint. She was clutching the side of a mahogany atlas stand, and he saw her knuckles go white—as white as her face had been, when she'd first entered the room. Some of the color had returned to her cheeks as they'd talked, but it was all gone again now as her lips moved, and she whispered, like someone in a daze, "Two hundred pounds? *Two hundred pounds?*"

"Yes," Burke said firmly. "That seems a reasonable sum to me."

It didn't, of course. He'd had Miss Pitt and all of her previous incarnations at thirty a year. The girl was lying, of course. There wasn't any possible way that that sniveling mole Sledge could afford her at a hundred a year. Well, he could *afford* her at a hundred a year, but he wasn't the type to spend that kind of money on something as important as his children's education. No, Cyrus Sledge would think nothing of throwing a hundred pounds at that wretched missionary of his. But spend it on insuring that his sons grow to be clear-thinking, well-brought up members of society? Perish the thought!

But it was clear—for whatever reason, and Burke, having come to the conclusion that he would never understand females, wasn't even going to bother himself wondering very much what that reason was—Miss Mayhew didn't want to come work for him. So if he had to pay her two hundred pounds a year, then by God, he'd pay it.

And it would, he'd already decided, be money well spent. He had passed the better part of the past few days observing the much-debated—in his home, anyway—Miss Mayhew, and he had come to the conclusion that she was the ideal solution to his problem. Not as terribly young as he'd first believed—he didn't guess she could be more than few years over twenty—Katherine Mayhew carried herself with an assurance that belied her station in life. In church—yes, he'd even gone to the effort of dragging himself to mass with Isabel on Sunday morning, all in an effort to ascertain Miss Mayhew's worth—she'd kept the four young Sledges, the eldest of whom could not have been more than seven, quiet, a feat at which Burke, who well remembered Isabel at that age, could not help but marvel. On the street, she was greeted pleasantly by everyone she met, and returned those greetings with equal pleasantness, every bit as polite to icemen as she was to duchesses. She dressed soberly, yet attractively, maintaining at all times a neat appearance. And she had already proved that as a chaperone, she was matchless in both courage and resourcefulness: hadn't she attempted to assault him with an umbrella, when she'd believed Isabel to be in danger?

In all, despite her tender years, Katherine Mayhew seemed the ideal employee. It was only her appearance which gave him pause.

He had noted, when she'd accosted him on the street, that she was on the puny side—especially considering the fact she'd thought to fell him with an umbrella.

But what he had failed to realize until the moment she walked into Cyrus Sledge's library was that Miss Katherine Mayhew was absurdly pretty.

Not beautiful, by any means. She was much too small to be labeled any sort of beauty. But Isabel hadn't been at all wrong when she'd declared Miss Mayhew pleasant to look at. In fact, Burke found it rather hard to look away from her. She certainly wasn't the type of woman he normally admired—he preferred dark-haired women to blondes, and liked, on the whole, a more robust figure than the one Miss Mayhew possessed. Yet her honey-colored hair seemed to suit her, the fringe in which it had been cut across her forehead emphasizing the enormity of her grey eyes, the lashes of which were a darker shade than her hair. Her plain, neat dress—a blouse and skirt, entirely suitable attire for a governess—only made one more aware than ever of the narrowness of her waist, and if she hadn't a lot to fill the front of that blouse, what she had was at least perfectly in proportion with the rest of her.

It was her mouth, however, which Burke found difficult to ignore. Miss Mayhew's mouth was, like the rest of her, exceedingly small—smaller than any mouth he'd ever seen, except perhaps on a child. And yet it was an undeniably appealing mouth, the lips delightfully curvy and surprisingly mobile, twisting into all sorts of different expressions in the same manner that a flag twisted in the wind. Currently it was hanging open, as she stared at him in astonishment. He was awarded a glimpse of some straight white teeth and a sharp little tongue, and found the glimpse quite charming. . . .

Then wondered if perhaps he wasn't overtired, since he normally didn't find views of the interior of anyone's mouth charming, to say the least.

"Miss Mayhew," Burke said, since it didn't appear to him that the pretty Miss Mayhew was going to be able to speak again anytime soon, so great was her astonishment over his proposal. "Are you all right?"

Mutely, the girl nodded.

"Can I get something for you? Water, perhaps? Or a glass of wine? Perhaps you ought to sit down. You look quite done for."

The girl shook her head. Burke, perplexed but resolute, went on. "Well, then, I suppose the thing to do would be to make arrangements to have your things brought over. I'll send my footmen, Bates and Perry. How soon do you think you can be packed? Would this evening be too soon? Isabel has some dance or other she insists on going to, and it would probably be just as well if you started right away. In fact, if you like, I can send my housekeeper over to pack for you—"

The little pink mouth snapped shut, as if the girl were a marionette, and the puppeteer in control of her had pulled an unseen string.

"I couldn't possibly!" the girl declared, in tones, Burke couldn't help thinking, of horror. But why should she be horrified? A fanciful imagining on his part. Her tendency to fantasize was contagious, perhaps.

"Well," he said. "I suppose you feel you need to give the Sledges time to find a replacement for you. I quite understand. What was your agreement with them, then? A week's notice? Not two weeks, I hope."

"I—" The girl shook her head. As she did so, strands of dark blond hair that had fallen from the knot atop her head swayed around her face. Not curling—she hadn't a single curl about her—but swaying, like seaweed in water.

"I'm terribly sorry, my lord," she said. Her voice, Burke found, was as pleasing as the rest of her, low in pitch and not at all screechy, as young women's voices often were.

A second later, however, he didn't find her voice half so nice, when she went on to say, "But I couldn't possibly come work for you. I'm very sorry."

Burke didn't move. He was certain he didn't so much as twitch a finger. But suddenly, Miss Mayhew darted behind the atlas stand, as if desirous for some sort of barrier between them. Clutching both edges of the wooden structure, which came up to her chest, she added, "Please don't be angry."

Burke stared at her. He wasn't angry. Exasperated, maybe, but not in the least angry. He had given up anger long ago. His temper was something he'd never had much skill at mastering, and so he'd simply given over being angry about anything. Except Isabel, perhaps, and that young man of hers. The name Geoffrey Saunders was possibly the only thing that could still send him into a rage.

"But I'm not angry." Burke was making an effort to sound calm. "Not a bit."

The girl behind the podium said, "I don't believe you. You *look* very angry."

"But I'm not." Burke took a deep breath. "Miss Mayhew, are you under the impression that I might *strike* you?"

"You have something of a reputation for violence, my lord," she said, readily enough.

Burke felt he really would like to break something, preferably the podium she was clutching so hard. He felt as if he would like very much to rip it out of her hands and hurl it through the hideous stained glass window on the opposite side of the room. But then he remembered he'd given up that kind of thing, and he controlled the impulse.

"I'm afraid I must take umbrage at that, Miss Mayhew," he said instead. "While I certainly haven't made any sort of effort to restrain my inclinations toward force where men might be concerned, I have never in my life struck a woman."

He saw her slim fingers loosen from the sides of the atlas stand. "I'm sorry, my lord," she said. "But the look on your face, when I said I couldn't come work for you—it was rather . . . startling."

"Are you afraid of me?" Burke demanded irritably. "Is that why you won't accept the position? You certainly weren't afraid of me the other night, when you tried to skewer me with your umbrella. Why should you be frightened of me now? Unless. . . ." He experienced another wave of annoyance. It wasn't anger. He refused to call it anger. "Unless someone's been prattling to you about me. About my past."

"Not at all," Miss Mayhew said, too quickly.

"They have." Burke glared at her. "How else would you know about my reputation for violence? Well, you already thought me a vile abuser of innocent women. It must be gratifying to know that you were right."

"How you conduct your personal business," Miss Mayhew said stiffly, "is hardly any of my affair, my lord."

"It oughtn't be," he replied with a grunt. "But I can see that you've already formed an opinion about it. Have you an objection to the fact that I divorced my wife, Miss Mayhew?"

She dropped her gaze.

"I'd appreciate an answer, Miss Mayhew. In matters such as this—business matters, I mean—I find that honesty among all parties concerned is generally best. And so I repeat my question. Do you disapprove of the fact that I divorced my wife?"

"There isn't much about the life men like you lead, Lord Wingate," she said, to the atlas, "that I find worthy of approval."

Burke stared. "Well," he said, after a moment. "That's frank, anyway. I can see that whoever's been prattling to you about me has done a fine job of filling you in on the particulars."

She looked up. "Lord Wingate," she said, and if he hadn't known better, he might have suspected she was angry. "I told you before, your private life really isn't any of my business."

"Oh, I see. And that's what you were doing the other night on the street, when you came at me with your umbrella? Minding your own business?"

Miss Mayhew stuck out her rather sharp little chin. "I *thought* a young woman was in peril," she said, and there was a dangerous light in her grey eyes.

"Oh, of course, of course," he said. "And you were quite convinced you and your umbrella were going to stop a man three times your size and weight."

"I thought I had to try, at least," she said. "Otherwise, I wouldn't have been able to live with myself."

The reply sent a shiver down Burke's spine. He told himself that the absurd physical reaction he felt to her words was actually relief, because she was exactly what he'd been looking for all along in a chaperone for Isabel. It certainly wasn't due to anything else. Certainly not because he thought he'd happened to find—and on his very own street, no less—that rarest of all things in London: a truly good, truly honest person. And certainly not because all that goodness and honesty came wrapped in such irresistibly lovely packaging.

Still, her words took him so by surprise, that he momentarily forgot himself and burst out with a laugh. "Miss Mayhew, what if I were to pay you *three* hundred pounds a year? Would you come work for me then?"

She said, looking quite appalled, "No!"

"Why in heaven's name not?" Then a horrible thought occurred to him. It ought to have occurred to him before. "Are you engaged, Miss Mayhew?"

"I beg your pardon?"

"Engaged." He stared at her. "It isn't such a strange question. You're an attractive young woman, if rather odd. I imagine you must have suitors. Have you impending plans to marry one of them?"

She said, as if the idea were entirely preposterous, "Certainly not."

"Well, then, why the hesitation? Are you in love with Cyrus Sledge? Is it that you can't bear the thought of leaving him?"

She burst out laughing at that. The sound of Miss Katherine Mayhew's laughter had a curious effect on Burke. It made him feel as if thirty-six was not quite so advanced an age, and that there might possibly be more to his future than flannel waistcoats and books by the fire.

Perhaps a madness seized him. There was no other explanation for it, really. His valet was undoubtedly correct, and Burke was beginning to slip into senility. But at that moment, it seemed to him the most perfectly natural thing in the world to cross the room, snatch Miss Mayhew up by the waist, and lay a hearty kiss upon that laughing mouth.

Or at least, that's what he'd intended to do. And he succeeded in most of it, catching her quite unawares, and pulling her easily against him. But when he stooped to kiss her, she brought the atlas up, quite hard, against his forehead. Though the blow didn't hurt, it was unexpected to say the least, and in his amazement, he loosened his hold on her—

And she darted away, flinging open the library doors and leaving him alone in Cyrus Sledge's library.

It wasn't any wonder, really, that he picked the atlas up and hurled it, with all his strength, at the stained-glass window.

Chapter Six

*K*ate didn't stop running until she reached the school-room. Once in its relative safety, she snatched Lady Babbie up from the hearth and began to pace, her face buried in the cat's fur.

Oh, Lord, she prayed. *Please don't let them give me the sack. I am begging you, please, please, please don't let them give me the sack. I haven't anywhere—truly anywhere—else to go.*

It was a prayer not at all dissimilar to the one she'd uttered when the Reverend Billings had assaulted her in the pantry. The only difference, really, was that she'd crowned the reverend with a pie dish because he'd repulsed her, and she'd whacked the marquis with an atlas . . . well, for different reasons.

Posie looked in just as Kate was uttering a silent amen.

"Well?" she asked excitedly. "What did he want, then?"

Kate released the cat, who'd been struggling for some time in her arms. "Oh, Posie," she said with a sigh. "I am utterly wretched."

Posie shook her head. "New coat, then, is it? The bastard. Them titled blokes is all the same, acting like posh gentlemen, when underneath, they're nothin' better than money-grubbers. Well, I've got a bit saved up, if you need a loan, miss. I won't even charge you interest, how's that?"

Kate sank down onto the hearth. "It wasn't the coat, Posie. He wasn't here about the coat at all. He wants to hire me, Posie, to chaperone his daughter during her first season out. For two—no, three hundred pounds a year." Kate took a breath. "And I said no."

Posie was across the room in three strides. She took hold of Kate's wrist and said, "I lied to you. I suspected he wasn't here about the coat. I saw you run up the stairs, and then I heard a dreadful crash from the liberry. I reckon he's broke something, since Fusspot and both the Sledges went runnin' in there. I'll wager he's still there, gettin' the business from Mister and Missus. We can stop 'im afore he gets to the door, and you can tell 'im you've changed your mind. Come on, now. Look sharp, or you'll miss 'im."

Kate snatched her hand from the younger girl's grip. "Posie, I can't."

Posie stared down at her, dumbfounded. "You can't what? You can't live like a queen on three hundred pounds a year? Do you have any idea how much money that is, miss? That's more money than either of us is ever likely to see in a lifetime, that's how much it is!"

Kate winced as Posie's voice rose to a shriek. "Posie," she said weakly. "You don't understand."

"You're right I don't understand! I have to tell you, miss, I like you better'n any of those stuffy bitches they had watchin' the boys before you. But if you don't go an' work for his lordship, I swear to you I'll never speak to you again!"

"Posie." Kate dropped her face down into her lap. When she spoke again, her voice was muffled by her skirt. "I can't work as a chaperone. Not here in London."

Posie glared at her. "And why not?"

She couldn't, of course, tell Posie. She had told no one in the Sledge household of her past. She wasn't sure what they made of Freddy—if they wondered where she had met him, or how the two of them had come to be such friends. No one had bothered to ask. They were a particularly incurious household.

But the fact was that Kate had selected her employers with

care. The Sledges—like all of the families for whom Kate had worked before them—were not, though wealthy, members of the *beau monde*. They were not invited with any regularity to the season's finest balls. They did not even go to the theater, or attend the races. They did not number amongst their acquaintances anyone who might remember the name of Mayhew, or who might have had occasion to own a diamond mine.

And that, as far as Kate was concerned, was just fine. The quieter the lifestyle of her employers, the better her chances at maintaining the comfortable anonymity she'd managed, after seven long years, to attain. Not that, as a governess, she was in much danger of discovery. Occasionally, she was required to escort her young charges to birthday parties and the like. But even there, the chance of being recognized was low, for she invariably encountered only other governesses like herself.

But as a chaperone—and to the daughter of a wealthy marquis—Kate would be thrust into the very same circles in which she had used to travel a lifetime ago. She would visit households in which she'd once been entertained as a guest, encounter persons with whom she'd once shared intimate friendships, meet, after her long absence, old acquaintances . . . not to mention old foes.

And she would be forced to endure, all over again, the snubs, the catty remarks, the suspicious looks, she'd finally managed to escape.

No. She had lived through it once. How, she hadn't any idea. But she had survived it. She would not endure it again. She *could* not.

For she despised them. She quite thoroughly despised the *beau monde*, for their hypocrisy, their snobbery, and their self-serving deceit. Men like the marquis, who thought that because they had money they could treat human beings any way they saw fit. Men like the marquis, who had seen to her father's ruin. Men like the marquis, who had coldly turned their backs when Kate needed them.

All except Freddy. Kind, simple Freddy, who had stuck by Kate, even in her darkest hours.

He had been unwavering in his friendship to her. He was the only one. The only one from the *ton* who hadn't let her down when it had really mattered.

And he was the only one she could now abide.

She couldn't go back. She *wouldn't*. Not for all the money in the world.

"I can't," Kate said, lifting her face from her hands. "Don't you see? I would have to go to dinner parties and balls and the like."

Posie snorted.

"Oh, aye," she said sarcastically. "A fate worse than death. You might even have to drink champagne and eat caviar every night. And get paid three hundred pounds a year for it! It's shocking what people will ask of a girl these days."

"You don't understand," Kate said, with a shake of her head. "It isn't what it seems from the outside, Posie. Those people—the marquis and his friends—they're not like you and me. They're not even like the Sledges. They're horrible. Truly horrible. All of them. They haven't any loyalty, any sort of human decency. All they think about is themselves and their precious money. They can ruin someone's life with just a single well-placed whisper. It doesn't matter whether or not what they say is true. The fact that it was said at all is taken as proof of its veracity."

Posie regarded Kate wryly. "If a bloke gave me three hundred pounds a year, people could say whatever they wanted to about me. With three hundred pounds, what would I care?"

"But you *would* care, Posie." Kate got up suddenly, and paced the length of the schoolroom. "You would care, because it *hurts*. Especially when it isn't true."

"It only hurts," Posie remarked, "if you let it."

Kate stopped pacing and stared down at the younger girl. It was easy, she supposed, for Posie to believe something as trite as that. Posie had never been hurt, not once in her short life. Oh, certainly, the occasional love affair gone wrong, maybe . . . but never *irrevocably* wrong. The eldest of a happy brood of twelve, both of Posie's parents were still living. It was easy, Kate told herself, for Posie to be brave. She had never lost anything she cared about. She hadn't lost *everything* she cared about, as Kate had.

Suddenly, Kate smiled. She couldn't help it. She had never been capable of allowing anything to depress her for long, and now was no exception.

"What's the use?" she asked, spreading her arms wide. "Even if I thought I could put up with it—life in the *ton*— the marquis isn't likely to want me now. I hit him, Posie."

"You *what*?"

"Hit him. Over the head." Kate mimed the action. "With an atlas. He tried to kiss me, just like the Reverend Billings, the conceited dolt."

Posie's mouth, Kate saw, had formed a perfect O of aston- ishment. A second later, she'd jumped up and, clutching Kate by the wrist, tried to pull her bodily toward the door.

"It ain't too late," Posie said. "He might still be down there. Go on and apologize."

"Apologize? *Me?* Posie, are you mad? Didn't you hear me? He tried to—"

"I've got three words for you, Miss Kate," Posie said. "*Three hundred pounds*. Understand me? Now go down there and apologize. On your knees, if you have to. But do it."

"Posie," Kate said, digging in her heels. "Lord Wingate is hardly the type of man to forgive a girl for whacking him on the head." Her grin grew broader. "But if you'd only seen his face when I did . . . though I don't suppose there's anything funny about losing three hundred pounds."

"Can't think of anythin'," Posie agreed. " 'Specially con- siderin' how long a body could live on three hundred pounds, an' never even *have* to work."

Posie's voice rose to a squeal as Kate dropped a hand to her arm and squeezed it, hard.

"Oh," Kate said, through lips that had suddenly lost all hint of color. There was no humor in her voice now. "Oh, God, Posie!"

Posie said, quite calmly considering the pressure on her

wrist, "Change your mind about the unfeelin' rich, did you? I thought you might."

"I didn't think," Kate whispered. "I didn't think . . . I forgot all about her. But three hundred pounds. Three hundred pounds would pay her rent for a long while. . . ."

Posie had no idea what the older girl was talking about. All she knew was that Kate had finally come to her senses.

"And," Posie said, "he's bound to have plenty of atlases, a rich bloke like that. You could just chuck one at 'im, every time he gets fresh. Like as not he'll get the message."

Kate felt as if something cold had clutched her heart. "Do you suppose he's gone?" she asked, through lips that seemed to have gone numb.

"Only one way," Posie said, "to find out."

The two girls tore from the room so noisily that Lady Babbie, who'd retired to the desk, puffed out her tail to three times its normal size, and growled ferociously before settling down again atop the papers Kate had left behind.

The Marquis of Wingate had not, in fact, gone. He was standing in the foyer, making out a note to the Reverend Billings, which was what Mr. Sledge had requested in lieu of compensation for the loss of his stained-glass window. It galled Burke to the core, writing this note—especially since it was for twice what the window was worth—but what else could he do? He'd already attempted the unpardonable—stealing a neighbor's servant. He didn't dare add insult to injury by refusing to pay for something he had broken quite purposefully.

What made it worse was that the Sledges hadn't the faintest idea how he'd broken the window, or even why he'd come to call in the first place. They thought no more of Miss Mayhew than they bothered to think of anyone else outside of Papua New Guinea. Even their own children, who came trooping through the front door just as he was signing his name to the note, inspired no more than a brisk "Wipe your feet before you come in." Not even a peck on the cheek or a "Stop striking your brother with that riding crop."

In fact, it was Burke himself who snatched the crop away

from one of the boys before the lad did any serious damage. His sharp admonishment, "You could put your brother's eye out with that," was met with a sneer, convincing him that Katherine Mayhew must be an angel. How else could she so ably manage Sledge's little beasts?

An angel, or a witch. He was beginning to suspect the latter, since he doubted the former would have left him with the pounding headache he was currently suffering.

And then, as if the very thought of Miss Mayhew summoned her, there she appeared on the stairs. No one else seemed to notice her. Mr. Sledge was still going on, at some length, about the barbaric treatment of dogs by the natives of that ubiquitous country, one more utterance of the name of which was likely to cause Burke to go mad, while his wife was announcing to some women in a nearby drawing room that they needn't get up, it was only the Marquis of Wingate, who frequently stopped by to call upon her husband. The butler very glumly passed by, carrying a dustpan filled with broken shards of brightly colored glass, and the children kicked at one another with their muddy riding boots.

And yet, somehow, above it all, Burke was able to hear Miss Mayhew's voice call from the stairway, which was as near to him as she could get, with all the people in the entrance hall: "Lord Wingate, I'll gladly come, if you'll still have me."

Burke Traherne had been quite rightfully accused of many things in his day, but stupidity was not one of them. He hadn't the slightest idea what had caused the girl to change her mind—though he had a suspicion that the redhead in the maid's uniform standing behind her might have had something to do with it, especially since she seemed to be poking Miss Mayhew quite forcefully in the back.

But he wasn't about to stand there and question her decision.

Oh, he was not at all charmed by the way she'd rebuffed his advances. He was insulted and a little chagrined. But she was, after all, only a servant, and undoubtedly knew no better. His father had always warned him not to dally with the help, advice Burke now saw as quite sage.

The girl was clearly a man-hater. That was the only explanation for it, really. Burke had never in his life been rebuffed
by a woman, so the experience had been particularly demor-
alizing . . . and unique.

But a man-hater, while irritating, would make a splendid
chaperone for Isabel, and so he gave a low bow, and said, his
deep voice carrying easily over the tumult around them, "Miss
Mayhew, I'm honored. May I send my footmen this evening,
then?"

She nodded mutely. Indeed, she couldn't have spoken if
she'd wanted to, since the din in the entranceway had risen to
such a level that no one, not even Burke, would have been
able to hear her if she'd tried. He cast her a final, appraising
glance—really, but she was uncommonly pleasant to look at.
It was a shame about the man-hating thing. Then he retrieved
his own cloak and hat, since the butler seemed busy, and there
was no footman that Burke could see, and left the house, satisfied that he had just purchased not only peace of mind for
himself, but a bright future for his daughter. And all for the
bargain price of three hundred pounds.

Of course, there was also the matter of the sizable welt on
his forehead. But he had a feeling that that was best left ignored. He'd behaved ignobly, and Miss Mayhew had very
properly let him know it. It wouldn't happen again.

Or, if it did, he'd see to it there weren't any heavy books
lying about.

Chapter Seven

$\mathcal{K}$ate dashed up the stone steps, her heart hammering in her ears, her throat constricted so tightly with fear, she could hardly breathe. *Please*, she prayed. *Let it be unlocked. Please let it be unlocked. Please—*

The front door swung open, however, before she even had a chance to touch the handle. Vincennes, Lord Wingate's butler, looked down at her quizzically. "Miss Mayhew," he said, pleasantly enough. "How do you do? Did you—"

But Kate hadn't time for pleasantries. She pushed past him, seized hold of the door, and shut it behind her.

Vincennes, to his credit, looked as if this extraordinary behavior was perfectly normal, and said only, "I do hope you managed to get to the post office before it closed, miss."

Kate hardly heard him. Rushing into the drawing room just off the foyer, where a fire had not yet been lit for the evening, she went to one of the large casement windows, and parted the drapes.

"Mr. Vincennes," she panted, gazing out onto the street. "Do you see that man out there? Standing on the corner, in the light from the gas lamp?"

The butler obligingly peered over her shoulder. "Indeed, I do, miss," he said.

So! It hadn't been her imagination! Not this time.

"Pardon me, miss," the butler said, as the two of them stood in the darkened room, staring down at the rain-soaked street. "But do you have reason to dislike Mr. Jenkins?"

Kate's breath fogged the pane through which she was peering. She reached up to rub at the spot. "Mr. Jenkins? Who is Mr. Jenkins?"

"The gentleman we're looking at."

Kate squinted astonishedly up at the butler. "You *know* him?"

"Certainly, miss. He's a physician. He frequently pays calls in this neighborhood. . . ."

Kate, feeling her cheeks heat up, let the curtain drop. "I'm such a fool," she confessed sheepishly. "I thought . . . I thought he was someone else."

"Perfectly understandable, miss," Vincennes said kindly, "in fog like that."

But Kate could not so easily dismiss her mistake. Freddy, she thought dejectedly to herself, as she made her way up the wide, curving staircase to her room, had been quite right. She did have too much imagination. What on earth would Daniel Craven be doing, standing on a street corner—in the rain, no less—in London, when no one had seen or heard from him in seven years? She was being ridiculous. Worse than ridiculous. Hysterical, even.

But when she approached the door to her bedroom, and saw that it was slightly ajar—when she had most definitely closed it when she'd left—she grew suspicious. Surely Vincennes would have told her if someone had come calling for her. And he certainly wouldn't have allowed the visitor into her room! No, it had to be one of the maids, or—

Kate flung open the door and was more than a little surprised to see the Lady Isabel Traherne—lying on her stomach with her feet in the air—stretched out across Kate's bed, petting Lady Babbie.

"I didn't know you had a *cat,* Miss Mayhew!" Isabel cried, when she noticed Kate upon the threshold.

So much for keeping Lady Babbie's presence a secret, Kate thought to herself. All that trouble she'd taken, smuggling the indignant cat into the house in a basket, had been for naught.

And good thing to know that in the future, if she didn't care for visitors, she'd best keep her door locked.

Aloud, however, Kate said, "Be careful. She bites, when she's in the mood."

Lady Babbie, probably just to be contrary, allowed Isabel to scratch her ears without the slightest protest, however.

"Listen to her purr!" Isabel sighed. "I always wanted a cat, but Papa always said I was too irresponsible to take care of a plant, let alone an animal, and he'd never let me have one. What's her name, Miss Mayhew?"

Kate cleared her throat uncomfortably as she undid her bonnet strings. "Lady Babbie," she said.

"What was that? I didn't hear you."

"Lady Babbie," Kate said, a little more loudly.

Isabel looked at her curiously. "What a strange name. Did you call her after someone you know?"

"Not exactly," Kate muttered, as she removed her hat, and went to the mirror to adjust her coiffure. Then, noticing Isabel's dissatisfied expression, she explained reluctantly, "I've had her since I was ten. At the age of ten, I'm afraid the name Lady Babbie struck me as inexpressibly elegant. That's all I can say in my own defense."

"Since you were ten," Isabel said, giving the cat a wondering stroke beneath the chin. "She must be *ancient* now."

"Only thirteen," Kate said, not without some indignation.

"So you're twenty-three?" Isabel, quickly losing interest in the cat, rolled over onto her back and stared up at the filmy white canopy, sprigged here and there with pink and green florets. "That's quite old. I thought you were much younger."

Kate went back to work arranging her books on a shelf near the fireplace, a task she'd left an hour earlier to post a letter. "Twenty-three," she said, a bit defensively, "isn't so very ancient."

"It is not to have been married already." Isabel rolled over and propped her hands up on both elbows, then dropped her chin into them. Dressed only in her underthings and a silk robe, her hair tied up in strips of rag, she put Kate in mind of Posie, who'd often visited her in a similar ensemble of an evening. "Why haven't you been married before, Miss May-hew? You're such a pretty little person. I can't imagine why someone hasn't picked you up and put you in his pocket and kept you. Hasn't anyone ever asked?"

Kate said, looking down at the spine of the book in her hand, "Asked if he could put me in his pocket? Certainly not."

"Well, to marry him, then."

"No one with whom I was in love."

"Really? Did he marry someone else, then?"

Kate slid the book into place on the shelf. "Did who marry someone else?"

"The man you loved, of course."

Kate laughed. "Not hardly. I've never been in love with anybody."

Isabel sat up, quite shocked. "*What*? *Never*? Miss Mayhew! I'm only seventeen, and I've been in love *five* times! Twice in the past year alone."

"My goodness." Kate reached into the box Phillips himself had brought over from the Sledges', so great was his delight in seeing her gone, and retrieved another book. "I suppose I've been far too discerning, then, in my affections."

"I should say so," Isabel declared. "Did Papa tell you who I'm mad about lately?"

Kate placed the book on one shelf, saw that it didn't quite fit, and transferred it to another. Since she had not seen Lord Wingate—not even once—since that afternoon in the Sledges' entranceway, she could not exactly say that yes, she'd had a lengthy conversation with him about his daughter's romantic life. In fact, it had been well over a week since she'd last seen the marquis. Mr. Sledge had thrown quite a tantrum upon learning she intended to leave his family, and Mrs. Sledge had taken to her bed for a full forty-eight hours. Kate had felt it only right to remain until they found a replacement for her, and sent a note explaining as much to the marquis. She'd received a letter back, but not from the marquis. It had been from his lordship's housekeeper, Mrs. Cleary, urging her to take all the time she needed.

And while it had been gratifying to learn that the Sledges

valued her as an employee—Mrs. Sledge, in particular, had been extremely liberal in heaping abuse on the marquis for stealing her away—it had also been lovely beyond words to bid adieu forever to that cramped, overfurnished house. Posie was the only person Kate supposed she'd miss—Posie and, surprisingly, the four littlest Sledges, who'd wept quite bitterly when she'd broken the news to them, and refused to promise, though she asked them very seriously, not to torment the new governess with thorns in her sheets and snails in her tea.

Kate might have been perfectly content with her decision had it not been for Freddy, who'd been so appalled upon hearing of it the next time she'd seen him, he'd been struck dumb for several minutes, a circumstance Kate could not remember ever happening before, not in all the years she'd known him.

"Lord Wingate?" Freddy had said, when he'd finally found his tongue. And by that time, they'd been twice around the park in his new phaeton, in which he'd insisted upon taking Kate driving, though she'd have preferred to spend their time together in a nice tea shop, and not whipping about in an open carriage.

"Lord Wingate?" Freddy had repeated. "Burke Traherne, you mean? The one you poked with your umbrella?"

"Yes," Kate had replied. "That's the one. Do watch where you're going, Freddy. You nearly ran over that dog—"

"You're going to go and live in Traherne's *house,* and look after his *daughter*?"

"Yes, Freddy. That's what I said. For three hundred pounds a year. Although I don't imagine I'll be there a year, since if the Lady Isabel is any bit as amiable as she is rich, she will probably be married by the end of the season, anyway. Freddy, *must* we go so fast?"

"But I told you about him, Katie! I told you all about him, didn't I? About how he divorced his wife, and threw—"

"And threw her lover out a window, yes. Lord Wingate seems to have a propensity for throwing things out windows. He threw an atlas out the window, you know, when I said I wouldn't work for him."

"The devil he did!"

Kate was beginning to regret having mentioned it at all. She'd *had* to tell him, of course—he'd have found out eventually. She'd had to tell him. Only she couldn't help wishing he would be a bit more understanding.

"I don't like it," Freddy said flatly. "Besides the fact that you'll be living with *him*"—his dark expression explained, only too clearly, who *he* was—"you'll be putting yourself in an impossible position. Think about it, Kate. You'll be taking that girl places where just a few years ago, you were an invited guest. Only now you'll be going as someone's *servant*—"

"A few years ago," Kate said with a sniff. "Try *seven* years ago, Freddy. No one will remember."

"The devil they won't! Kate, you were all anybody talked about for—"

"Seven *years* ago, Freddy. I'm an old lady now. Why, I found a grey hair the other day."

Freddy scowled. "You may think you've changed, Katie, but believe me, you haven't. They'll recognize you—"

"Nobody notices a chaperone." She hoped.

"—and then there'll be those awkward questions you hate so much, and possibly even some pitying looks. All of those old biddies you so despised will talk of nothing else. 'Would you believe who showed up at my place last night, Lavinia? The Mayhew girl. Only she was *working*, and as a *chaperone*, poor little thing.'"

Kate said, "You know, Freddy, I never realized it before, but you're quite a fine mimic. That was Lady Hildengard, am I right?"

"The point," Freddy said fiercely, "is that you're going to hate it. You know you couldn't stand those women—"

"Freddy, you are missing the point. Three hundred pounds is a lot of money. I can bear all the Lady Hildengards in the world for three hundred pounds. You know Papa left me nothing but debt—"

"*You* aren't responsible for the debt your father left behind," Freddy reminded her.

"No, but I can't help but feel responsible for the *people* he left behind. You know Nanny hasn't got a cent."

"Nanny!" Freddy burst out. "Is *that* what this is about? Your old *nanny?*"

"Yes," Kate said calmly. "Three hundred pounds could pay the rent on Nanny's cottage for years to come. There's no possible way I could say no, Freddy."

"There's no possible way you're saying yes," Freddy declared, pulling his horse to a violent stop. "Kate, you're not going to work for Burke Traherne. I won't have it!"

"Oh," she said tartly. "And I suppose *you're* going to pay the rent on Nanny's cottage, then?"

"I said I would, if you'd only let me."

"I won't." Kate shook her head. "I shall take care of Nanny myself."

"I'll find her address," Freddy threatened, "and write to her and tell her what you're doing. Then you'll be sorry."

Kate laughed at that. "Oh, and what will you tell her, Freddy? That I've accepted a position that pays me *nine times* what I was earning before, for less work? I'm going to be working as Lord Wingate's *daughter's chaperone*, Freddy. It's a perfectly respectable position. Even Nanny would agree. It isn't as if," she added, "I've agreed to be his *concubine*, or something."

"Damn it, Kate!" Freddy reached over and found one of her hands, then pressed her fingers, quite hard, with his own. "The man's got a temper to beat the devil. Why, last week he put a bullet through some poor fellow over that Woodhart woman. He's a profligate bounder, besides. He's probably only hired you so he can have his fun debauching you, and then turn you out when he's tired of you. He hasn't a heart, you know."

Kate blinked up at him astonishedly for a moment, then burst out into peals of laughter. Freddy did not share her amusement, and glared at her disapprovingly. But Kate couldn't help it, and was gasping for breath by the time she'd calmed enough to ask, "Oh, Freddy, do you really think so? I've always wanted to be debauched by a profligate bounder! And he's *paying* me for the honor, besides. However did I get so lucky?"

Freddy scowled. "It isn't funny, Kate. I'm warning you, Traherne—"

"Yes, yes, yes." Kate pulled her hand from his and patted him with it. "He's an awful, dreadful man. Freddy, I know all that, believe me. And I shall be on my guard."

"On your guard? Kate, it isn't a matter of being on your guard. What if—"

"Besides, Freddy, it isn't as if Lord Wingate has expressed the slightest interest in me *that* way." She hadn't dared, of course, to tell him that actually, the opposite was true. "He has Mrs. Woodhart to entertain him. What could he possibly see in me when he has her?"

Freddy said something, but under his breath, so she could not make it out.

"And while Lord Wingate very well might be a profligate bounder," Kate went on, as much to convince herself as him, "you have to admit he cares a good deal for his daughter's happiness. And how terrible can a man who loves his daughter be?"

"Kate—"

"And as for debauching me, Frederick Bishop, the marquis's whole purpose in hiring me, as near as I can tell, is so that he can have his evenings free to go out and carry on with his debauching without his daughter finding out. Now what have you to say to *that*?"

Freddy slumped defeatedly against the phaeton seat. "Kate, won't you just marry me? It would make everything so much simpler."

Kate blinked at him. She so enjoyed Freddy's company that she sometimes quite forgot that he considered her more than just that—a companion. She felt a pang of guilt as she realized she probably ought not to be accepting his invitations to tea and carriage rides. It wasn't fair of her, she thought all at once, to continue to meet with him. It raised false hopes.

And yet he was the best—and only—friend remaining from her former life. She couldn't see herself without him.

Unfortunately, she also couldn't see herself with him . . . not the way he wanted her to be.

She sighed gustily. "Oh, Freddy," she said. "It *wouldn't* make things simpler. It really wouldn't."

Because, though she didn't feel she needed to remind him of the fact that moment, there was no place for her anymore in Freddy's world—a world in which she had once traveled with grace and ease. How could she possibly return to it, knowing, as she did, what people had said—were doubtless *still* saying—about her father? Ignorant hypocrisy, fatuous rumor-mongering. Lord, no. She'd sooner die than go back.

And of course, even if she could bring herself to embrace that world from which she'd fled—or rather, been banished—all those years before, she could not, in good conscience, have married Freddy. Not when she knew perfectly well she didn't love him. Supposing—just supposing—she married Freddy, and then realized, as Isabel's mother had, that she was actually in love with someone else. How horrible! She couldn't do that to Freddy—not what Elisabeth Traherne had done to the marquis. Why, look how disastrously *that* had turned out for everyone.

A sweeping glance across the room she stood in told her it hadn't turned out badly for *everyone* involved, however. This was the prettiest bedroom she'd been in since before her parents' death—certainly the prettiest bedroom she'd had since she'd begun hiring herself out as a governess. The walls were covered in paper that matched the material that made up the canopy of her bed, white with pink and green bouquets. There was a matching set of deep green velvet armchairs before the fire, and a white dressing table with gilt knobs and a massive gilt-framed mirror above it. The room was nothing like the cubicle in which she'd frozen at the Sledges', due to Phillips's stinginess with the çoal.

As for the rest of the house . . . well, Kate could not remember a time she'd been in a more elegant, yet eminently comfortable, home. Everything, from the paintings on the walls to the candles in their holders, was of the finest quality, and most pleasing design.

And she was being paid three hundred pounds a year to live in this luxury!

"I can't," Kate said now, to the girl stretched out on her bed every bit as languidly as Lady Babbie, "say that your father's mentioned your gentleman friend to me."

"Gentleman friend," Isabel echoed, with a smirk. "Geoffrey would laugh if he'd heard you call him that. I say, Miss Mayhew, have you actually *read* all those books?"

Kate looked down at the crate at her feet. "Yes," she replied. "Of course.".

"Why do you keep them?" Isabel wanted to know. "I mean, if you've already read them."

"Because." Kate lifted a well-used copy of *Pride and Prejudice*. "Some books are so good, you want to read them over and over again. You become attached to them. They become . . . well, they become like family."

"Family?" Isabel echoed.

"Yes. When you've read them so many times, you can't help but start to think of them as relations—dependable, loving relations, who won't ever let you down. Opening them again is like paying a visit to a favorite aunt, or . . . or crawling into the lap of a beloved grandfather." Seeing that Isabel's expression remained skeptical, Kate said, with a little laugh, "Well, I suppose to you, Lady Isabel, it may not sound like much, but you, after all, have a father who loves you, and I daresay some grandparents, too, who dote upon you. My books are all the family I have left." She did not mean to sound melodramatic, and, realizing that her words might have been mistaken for being so, added jokingly, "Besides, the advantage of having books for your relations, instead of real people, is that they never borrow money from you, or drop by unexpectedly. The only real danger lies in accidentally leaving one on the omnibus, which I'm ashamed to admit I've done once or twice in the past. . . ."

Isabel wrinkled her nose. "Miss Mayhew," she said. "It's a very good thing you're so pretty. It makes up for the fact that you are *quite* odd." She looked up at the ceiling. "Besides which, *I've* never read a book like that. A book I cared to read more than once, I mean."

"Haven't you?" Kate held up *Pride and Prejudice*. "Have you read this one?"

Isabel squinted at the cover. "Oh" she said, disgustedly. "Papa is always trying to get me to read that."

Kate said, "You ought to. You'd like it. It's about girls your age, falling in love."

Isabel lifted her face from the fist against which she'd sunk it. "Really? I thought it was about a war."

"A *war*? What in heaven's name made you think it was about a *war*?"

"Well, it's called *Pride and Prejudice*, isn't it?" Isabel said obliquely. But she actually got up off the bed and strode over to where Kate stood, took the book from her hand, and flipped through it, which Kate supposed was a start, anyway. "Besides, Papa's always reading books, and they're usually about wars, or the law, or something even more boring."

Kate reached back into her crate. "Oh?" she asked casually. "Your father likes to read, then?"

Isabel grunted. "It's all he ever does, practically. I mean, besides entertain women like that horrid Mrs. Woodhart."

Kate coughed, but unfortunately, Isabel did not take the hint.

"I swear, Miss Mayhew," she went on, with a sigh, "sometimes I think if it wasn't for women like Mrs. Woodhart, Papa would never leave the house! Back at home—Wingate Abbey—he never lifts his face out of whatever book he's reading, except to go riding once in a while. It's embarrassing."

Kate straightened. "Embarrassing?"

"Well, nobody *else's* father does that. The girls I visited back when I was at school, *their* fathers would go out every day and hunt, and fish, and things like that. Not *my* father, though. *My* father is always home, *reading*. I tell him all the time that it isn't natural, that he should go out more. I mean, he isn't getting any younger, Miss Mayhew. He just turned thirty-six. He's *never* going to meet someone at this rate, and settle down."

"But I thought he *had* met someone," Kate said innocently. "You mentioned a Mrs. Woodhart."

"But he can't marry Sara Woodhart," Isabel cried. "She's an *actress*. Papa can't marry an actress. It wouldn't do. Besides, she's already married."

Kate raised her eyebrows. "Oh."

"The fact of the matter is, Miss Mayhew, there isn't much time left. Soon Geoffrey and I are going to be married, and Papa will be left all by himself."

"Really?" Kate's eyebrows rose even further. "You and Geoffrey?"

"Yes. I must find Papa a nice woman, Miss Mayhew, so he won't be lonely when I'm gone. Not a woman like that Mrs. Woodhart, either. A *nice* woman"—Isabel's gaze slid slyly toward her—"like *you*, Miss Mayhew."

Kate had to stifle a peal of laughter. The idea of a man like the Marquis of Wingate stooping to marry his daughter's chaperone was so preposterous that she wished she had someone to share it with. It was too bad Freddy was taking the whole thing so badly.

Reminded of Freddy's remark that the marquis had sworn never again to marry, after his first disastrous match, she thought it might be best to change the subject before Isabel warmed to it too thoroughly.

"Has, um, Mr. Saunders actually *asked* you to marry him, Lady Isabel?"

The very mention of the name Geoffrey, it appeared, was enough to distract Isabel from any subject.

"Not yet," she said, with some heat. "But he hasn't exactly had a chance, with Papa breathing down my neck everywhere we go." She awarded Kate another of those sly, sideways glances. "But maybe now that *you're* here, Miss Mayhew. . . ."

Kate had already sucked in her breath to inform the Lady Isabel—though not in so many words—that it would be a cold day in hell when she'd go against the wishes of the man who was paying her so generously to look after his only child when the man himself suddenly appeared, tapping on the door which Kate had left open.

"Ah, Miss Mayhew," Lord Wingate said. He was, Kate

saw, actually holding one of the very books his daughter so disparaged, his index finger tucked inside it to mark the place where he'd left off reading it. "Pardon me for interrupting. You and Isabel have a function to attend this evening, I believe?"

Kate nodded, hastily averting her gaze so that she did not have to look into those too bright green eyes. Burke Traherne had passed his jade irises on to his daughter, but somehow, in Isabel's paler complexion, they were not nearly so discomforting.

Then again, maybe it wasn't the marquis's eyes that were making Kate so nervous, but the fact that almost the last time she'd looked into them, she'd been hurling an atlas at his head. And the time before that, she'd been pointing the business end of her umbrella at his heart. Truly, they had not had the easiest time of it, getting to know one another.

"Yes, my lord," Kate managed to say, briskly enough. "Lady Allen's for dinner, and then a ball at Baroness Hiversham's—"

"Then breakfast at Lord and Lady Blake's," Isabel interrupted, checking off invitations on her fingers as she recited them in bored tones, "and shopping with their odious daughters. Then lunch with the Baileys, followed by more shopping, or perhaps some calls to find out who has got engaged and who still hasn't yet, then home to change for dinner with Lord and Lady Crowley, after which there's the opera, then a card party at Eloise Bancroft's, then a few short winks of sleep, and it's off riding the Ladies' Mile with those awful Chittenhouses, then breakfast again, I swear I don't remember where—"

"Isabel," Lord Wingate said mildly, "perhaps you'd prefer to be back at the Abbey."

Isabel broke off and stared at him. "Back at the Abbey? Wingate Abbey, you mean? Certainly not. Whatever would I do *there*, when Geoffrey is *here*?"

"Well, judging from your tone of voice just now, you seem to be finding London a bit dull."

Isabel dropped her hands to her sides. Kate was standing

close enough to her to see the slim fingers ball into fists. "Oh, you'd like that, wouldn't you?" The Lady Isabel tossed her head, sending her rag curls bouncing. "Anything to stop me from seeing Geoffrey!"

Kate didn't think it was her imagination that had Lord Wingate looking bemused. "On the contrary," he said. "I was thinking perhaps you feel the need for a respite in the country, in order to restore you to your characteristic ebullience."

Isabel let out a frustrated shriek, then strode furiously for the door, slamming it—apparently for dramatic emphasis—behind her.

And leaving Kate and her employer alone in her bedroom.

Chapter Eight

Kate, appalled, stared at the closed door, as if looking at it long enough might open it again, and restore some propriety to the situation.

Lord Wingate, however, seemed to feel no such discomfort. *Well*, Kate thought with disgust. *He wouldn't.*

He immediately sank into one of the green velvet armchairs by the fire, and began to gaze moodily into the dancing flames.

"You see, of course," Lord Wingate said, in his deep voice, never shifting his gaze from the fire, "what I am up against. Young love. It is a considerable adversary, Miss Mayhew."

Kate swiveled her head from the door to Lord Wingate and back again. *Well, isn't this cozy?* she thought. *Supposing Mrs. Cleary, the housekeeper, happens by, and hears his lordship's voice coming from the new chaperone's bedroom?* Or worse, Mr. Vincennes, the butler. So far, Mr. Vincennes did not appear to despise Kate, in spite of what he must have undoubtedly thought her very peculiar behavior. But Vincennes didn't know about Lady Babbie—not yet. And he certainly didn't know his lordship had invited himself into Kate's room for a little teatime tête-à-tête. . . .

"Isabel," Lord Wingate went on, as casually as if they were discussing the weather in Bath, "has convinced herself that she is in love with this young man, this Geoffrey Saunders. It is, of course, an impossible match. Mr. Saunders is a second son, without a cent to his name, except that which his elder brother doles out to him. He is supposed to be a scholar, but has been run out of Oxford by the numerous individuals to whom he owes money lost at playing cards. How he makes his living now, I haven't the faintest idea, but one must suppose philandering to be involved." Finally, he turned his face from the fire, and pinned Kate with his steely gaze. "Isabel is to be kept from him at all costs."

Riveted where she stood by those emerald eyes, Kate swallowed. She had fancied the twin armchairs before her hearth were quite large—she had sunk into their deep cushions with a good deal of room to spare. But Lord Wingate's enormous frame dwarfed the furniture, making Kate quite painfully aware of a fact she'd been hoping to forget . . . that Burke Traherne, the third Marquis of Wingate, was truly a remarkable figure of a man.

Unaccountably, Kate recalled that Mrs. Cleary had, just that afternoon, handed her a check for fifty pounds. "An advance," the plump old lady had informed Kate, "against whatever costs you might incur changing positions."

And though she hadn't asked for an advance, Kate had gratefully accepted it, then hurried to her bank, and then to the post office, where she'd mailed the entire sum to her nanny in Lynn Regis. At the time, she hadn't stopped to wonder why his lordship might have paid her two months' salary in advance. She'd supposed it was so that she could purchase what she might need in order not to shame her employer with her shabby dresses at the society functions she'd necessarily be attending. But she still fit quite nicely into her gowns from her own first season out. They had proven to be quite serviceable once they'd been well aired, and needed only to be slightly altered by the skillful Mrs. Jennings, so that the skirts were not quite so full, according to the new fashion, and the necklines not quite so daring—daring necklines not being at all the thing for chaperones. The gowns had had to be dyed, too, since the majority of them were white. At twenty-three, Kate knew she was entirely too old to wear white.

But now she had a new and somewhat disturbing idea what

the advance had been for. It was so that she couldn't quit, not without owing the Marquis of Wingate a considerable sum, a sum she could never hope to repay. He had obviously learned a lesson from Isabel's past chaperones, and was intent that this one, at least, would not get away so easily.

And flight was the first thought that entered Kate's head the moment Lord Wingate's sea-green gaze fell upon her. In fact, she started toward the door, following in Isabel's footsteps.

Only when she laid a hand upon the latch, the marquis's deeply rumbled, questioning, "Miss Mayhew?" brought her back to herself.

Good Lord, what was she thinking? Kate Mayhew didn't run from anything—well, except for shadowy figures on the street whom she mistook for Daniel Craven. But certainly not authoritative marquises, no matter how piercing their gaze, or how thoroughly they managed to fill a chair.

And so instead of fleeing, she took a steadying breath, then merely opened the door and swung it wide, so that anyone passing through the corridor outside could see that the master of the house was only paying a social call upon his newest employee.

"I quite understand," Kate said in a calm voice, turning round to face him, and even managing to meet his gaze without blushing. "You have objections against the young man. That is only natural. You love your daughter, and want the best for her. Only I wonder, my lord, if forbidding Lady Isabel from seeing Mr. Saunders is quite the best way to handle the situation."

Lord Wingate peered at her from round the back of the chair in which he sat. He looked quite uncomfortable, twisted in his seat that way, and Kate, taking momentary pity on him, moved round to the matching chair, though she didn't sit down in it.

"I beg your pardon," the marquis said, in tones of some incredulity. "But I believe I know how my own daughter ought to be handled."

"And I'm almost certain that's what Juliet's parents were

thinking, when they forbade her to see Romeo."

Lord Wingate raised a single dark eyebrow, an unreadable expression on his face. "It's been some time since I had the Bard thrown in my face during the course of a conversation."

"Then you shouldn't mind," Kate said, "my reminding you of the tragedy of Abelard and Heloise. I'm quite certain Heloise's uncle Fulbert felt the same way about her relationship with Abelard that you feel about Mr. Saunders."

The marquis said, with a chuckle, "You know, I have a good deal of sympathy for Fulbert. It wouldn't bother me a bit to see Mr. Saunders meet the same fate as that rascal Abelard—"

"My point," Kate interrupted flatly, "is that Romeo and Juliet and Abelard and Heloise all met with tragic fates due to parental interference in their romances—"

The marquis glowered. "Damn it, Miss Mayhew. Isabel isn't about to kill herself, let alone run off to any convent. Though frankly, I'd prefer the convent over matrimony to that gadabout."

"Lord Wingate," Kate said. "Both history and literature teach us that forbidding a child from something lends it a certain mystique that it otherwise wouldn't hold. Your dislike for Mr. Saunders might be exactly what Lady Isabel finds so appealing about him."

"Then what do you suggest I do, Miss Mayhew?" Lord Wingate snapped. "*Allow* her to throw herself at this jackanapes?"

Kate spread out her arms. "What harm could come from a few dances with him? The more time she spends with him, the more likely she is to notice his failings."

"And supposing she doesn't?" Lord Wingate inquired. "Supposing she falls even harder for him, and the next thing I know, I'm a grandfather?"

Kate flushed. She was grateful that she was standing near enough to the fire for any change in color to be reasonably blamed on the intensity of the very strong blaze.

"I highly doubt it will come to that, my lord," she said. "Isabel seems to me to be a girl of uncommon good sense, and a very strong character. She would never allow herself to be compromised."

Lord Wingate snorted, and sank deeper into the chair. "You don't know very much about young girls, do you, Miss Mayhew?"

"Because I used to be one, you mean?" Kate couldn't keep a trace of dryness from her tone.

Lord Wingate pinned her once again with that emerald gaze. "I would imagine that you, Miss Mayhew, were quite a different sort of girl than Isabel."

Kate glared at him. "Your daughter might be in possession of greater wealth and status than I was, but I assure you, my lord, I was every bit as—"

She broke off in confusion when she saw that Lord Wingate was laughing. She had never really heard him laugh before— he had always seemed, since the evening she'd first met him, to be in a singularly foul mood. But now, laughter poured out of him, making him look quite a bit younger than his thirty-six years. It also made Kate uncomfortably aware that his cravat was loosened. When he threw back his head to laugh, his shirt collar opened to reveal his throat, at the base of which she spied a good number of coarse black hairs. Kate, her gaze instantly drawn to those silky curls, found herself completely unable to look away. Whatever, she wondered idly, was the matter with her?

When Lord Wingate stopped laughing long enough to look at her again, she sincerely hoped he didn't notice her unaccountable attraction to his open shirt collar, or that her blush was now a fiery glow that had spread over most of her face and neck.

"I wasn't referring to your lack of wealth and status, Miss Mayhew," he said, still smiling. "I was referring to the fact that you are quite obviously more attractive than my daughter ever will be, and you likely were when you were Isabel's age, as well. Attractiveness more than makes up for lack of wealth. Unlike Isabel's, your beaux, Miss Mayhew, could not have been after you for entirely pecuniary reasons."

Quite suddenly, Kate wished she'd kept the door closed

after all, and *not* because she didn't want Lord Wingate's assumptions about her supposedly impoverished childhood overheard. She hurried across the room and pulled the door shut, saying over her shoulder, "Shhh! Supposing she hears you?"

"So what if she does? Isabel knows she isn't pretty. Unfortunately, she inherited my looks." He pulled a pocket watch from his waistcoat and began to wind it. "And," he muttered, "her mother's brains."

"It's perfectly dreadful of you to disparage your own child in such a manner," Kate said, quickly crossing the room to stand beside his chair. "Lady Isabel is quite lovely—"

"She has animal spirits," Lord Wingate corrected her. "Which is different from physical attractiveness. People are drawn to her because she is vivacious. Though I've sent Isabel to the best schools, she has retained nothing, as far as I can tell, aside from a few dance steps. Whereas you, Miss Mayhew, were blessed with good looks and intelligence, far more than can be said for my daughter. So surely you can see," he said, putting his watch away again, "why I don't believe that a comparison between your girlhood and Isabel's is necessarily appropriate, under these circumstances."

Then, as if noticing for the first time that she was standing and he was sitting, he rose, looking quite bothered about it, and said, gesturing to the chair across from his, "I've quite forgotten my manners. Do sit down."

Kate glanced at the closed door. "I don't think—"

"Sit!"

She started at his abrupt tone, and quickly sat, folding her hands in her lap and staring warily across the short piece of space between them.

"That's better," Lord Wingate said, lowering himself back into his seat with some satisfaction. "You are very small, Miss Mayhew, and yet I was getting a crick in my neck, looking up to you."

Not at all certain how to respond to that, Kate chose instead to worry the subject they'd originally been discussing. "I really believe, my lord, that Lady Isabel ought to be allowed to see this Mr. Saunders, at least in my presence. What possible mis-

chief could they get up to, with me there in the room with
them?"

"Miss Mayhew," Lord Wingate said severely. "How is it
that on the night we met, you were sufficiently suspicious of
my perfectly innocent behavior to want to turn me in to the
police, and yet you are naïve enough to believe that a chaperoned couple cannot—" He broke off, after sending her
another of his piercing looks, then suddenly shifted uncomfortably in his seat. "Well. Never mind. But suffice it to say,
Miss Mayhew, that I myself was only slightly older than Isabel
when I first began courting her mother. Allow me to assure
you that there is all kind of mischief a chaperoned couple
can—"

Kate interrupted quietly. "Perhaps that's the problem."

Lord Wingate flashed her a look of annoyance. "What is
the problem, Miss Mayhew?"

"Perhaps you fear that your daughter is going to make the
same mistake you did."

"Well, *of course* that's what I fear, Miss Mayhew." He eyed
her oddly. "And I must say I find it . . . singular, to say the
least, to be sitting here discussing my marriage with the
woman I've hired to act as my daughter's chaperone."

"And yet you're overlooking an important point, Lord Wingate."

"What point?"

"That however ill-advised you think your marriage to Isabel's mother might have been, it produced something you care
about very much. You can hardly blame your daughter, sir,
for refusing to heed her father's warnings, when she's perfectly aware that if you had heeded your own father's, she
might never have been born."

He leaned back in his chair with enough force to cause it
audibly to creak. His expression was no longer inscrutable. He
looked positively astonished. Kate, suddenly aware that she
might have gone too far, looked at the carpet. Three hundred
pounds, she said to herself. *Three hundred pounds.*

"My lord—" she said, an apology already on her lips, but
Lord Wingate cut her off.

"Miss Mayhew," he said, and Kate braced herself. Was he going, she wondered, to throw her out the window? She had three in her room, looking out over a lovely garden two stories below. She imagined that, thanks to the spring thaw, the ground just might be soft enough to break only a few bones, not kill her outright.

"You make your points," the marquis went on, in his deep voice, "with astonishing clarity, whether you are wielding an umbrella, an atlas, or simply *le mot juste.*"

Kate felt the blood that had drained from her face returning with a vengeance. "Lord Wingate—"

"No, Miss Mayhew," he said, climbing to his feet. "You are perfectly correct. Forbidding Isabel from seeing Mr. Saunders has not cooled her ardor for him one iota."

Kate got up from her chair. "Lord Wingate . . ." she began, but her voice trailed off a second later when she realized she was addressing the silver buttons of his waistcoat. Burke Traherne was so much taller than she was that she was obliged to crane her neck if she wanted to look up into his face.

And then the minute she did so, she regretted it. Because even though it had been nearly a week since that embarrassing incident in Cyrus Sledge's library, everything she'd felt then came back in a rush: the shock at the hardness of his chest, the incredible strength in those muscular arms; the stimulating scent of him—a scent that shouldn't have been the least arousing, since it was only a combination of soap, and the fainter odor of tobacco; the sight of those sensual lips, so out of place in such an otherwise masculine face.

But most of all the intense heat that emanated from him, which had produced in Kate the oddest desire to give in to that warmth, to press herself against it and forget everyone and everything else, to lose herself in all of that intoxicating masculinity. . . .

And then, of course, the horror that she could even think such thoughts, and about someone like *him,* coupled with the indignation that he'd *made* her think them, which in turn had caused her to reach for the atlas. . . .

And here she was, days later, suddenly as aware of his

physical presence as she'd been when she'd stood in his arms. Only this time they weren't even touching, his arms weren't even around her. . . .

Abruptly, Kate sat back down, her knees having suddenly given way beneath her.

The marquis, however, did not move from where he stood. Kate wasn't certain, since she found herself perfectly incapable of looking at him, but she believed he was looking down at her.

And then, as if his thoughts had been traveling along the same lines as hers, he said, in a somber voice, "I believe I owe you an apology, Miss Mayhew, for that unfortunate incident in the Sledges' library."

Kate, certain she'd gone scarlet all the way to her hairline, kept her face turned resolutely toward the fire.

"We owe apologies to one another," she said stiffly. "Let us consider those apologies said, and the matter done with."

But that didn't seem to satisfy Lord Wingate. "I am afraid that won't do, Miss Mayhew. I was the one who behaved abominably. You had every right to repudiate me."

"But I ought," Kate said, now speaking to her lap, "to have repudiated you in a gentler manner. And it is for that that I apologize."

Lord Wingate cleared his throat. "Nevertheless," he said. "I feel an obligation, as your employer, to assure you that it will never happen again."

She risked a glance at him then, surprised as much by his words as by his tone. Why, he actually sounded sincere! But that, of course, was impossible. Sincerity was not a virtue held in any sort of esteem by the *haut monde*. He was only parroting what he thought a gentleman ought, under the circumstances.

Wasn't he?

But he certainly *looked* as if he meant it. Was it possible that there existed a nobleman who was *not* a two-faced parasite?

No. And if so, it certainly wasn't this one. She would not soon forget how he'd treated her that afternoon in the library, as if she'd been put on earth exclusively for the purpose of providing him with a bit of lascivious entertainment.

Still, Kate stood up again, unwilling to let him think she was incapable of letting bygones be bygones. She stuck her right hand out toward him, and, looking him straight in the eye, said, as his large warm hand closed over her much smaller, and significantly cooler, fingers, "And I shall do everything in my power to see that you do not become a grandfather before you're ready, Lord Wingate."

A strange expression passed over the marquis's face. As it was similar to the one he'd worn the moment before he'd tried to kiss her that day, she took a wary step backward.

But he merely shook her hand, and then turned to go, muttering something about how she had better hurry up and dress, as she hadn't much time before the carriage pulled round.

Before he left the room, however, Lord Wingate was stopped in his tracks by the sight of Lady Babbie stretching luxuriously, all of her claws extended, on Kate's bed pillows.

"Good Lord," he said.

Kate felt all of her short-lived self-assurance drain away. Before she had a chance to begin apologizing for the animal's presence, however, Lord Wingate asked, "That cat's not female, is it?"

Kate raised her eyebrows. "Yes, she is. Why do you ask?"

"Well, it explains why I saw Vincennes's ginger tom sniffing around this floor earlier. You had better keep this door closed, Miss Mayhew, unless *you* want to be a grandparent."

And with that, the marquis left the room without another word.

Chapter Nine

It hardly seemed possible, but after six interminably long weeks, Burke Traherne finally had an evening to himself, to do with exactly as he chose. He almost didn't dare believe his good fortune.

Since Isabel had been released from school, Burke had been harassed and harangued at every turn. He had cajoled, threatened, and finally punished, all to no avail. Storms of weeping had become a commonplace occurrence. Remonstrations were hurled hourly. Burke had found himself using language he had not employed since his own days at school, when the headmaster's whip had brought swift retribution for every curse, and finally cured him of the habit. All it had taken, however, was a seventeen-year-old girl's first season out to bring them back to the tip of his tongue.

And now, quite suddenly, silence. Perfect, undisturbed silence.

It was an exceedingly odd sensation. Burke was still a bit incredulous. Under Miss Mayhew's firm but gentle guidance, his daughter, Isabel, had actually left the house without a single tear or recrimination. She had even kissed him goodbye! Kissed his cheek and laughed, saying, "Good night, you silly old thing. And thank you for letting me see Geoffrey. Enjoy your silly old book."

She was a changed creature, and Miss Mayhew hadn't been

in the house twenty-four hours yet. Could it be that if he had only given in to Isabel's demands that she be allowed to see the wretched Saunders, he might have had this silence weeks earlier?

No. Impossible. Because with the other chaperones, everything had been a battle, from deciding on which dress to wear to how Isabel ought wear her hair. But tonight, none of it. The dress had been agreed upon without acrimony, and Isabel's hair had never looked less blowzy—doubtlessly the work of Miss Mayhew.

Oh, there was no doubt about it. It was Miss Mayhew. It had to be. There was no other explanation for it.

And now he was free. Free to enjoy his "silly old book" at last.

And Burke had settled down to do just that—enjoy his silly old book, which was just that, a work by Mr. Fenimore Cooper that he ought to have read as a boy, but was only just now getting to. He sat in a deeply cushioned, hugely comfortable chair by a fire that hissed every so often from the rain that was pouring steadily outside. He had a glass of his favorite whisky resting on the small table beside him, and he had left instructions with Vincennes that he wasn't to be disturbed, not by reports from his various properties overseas—he had holdings in both Africa and the Americas—not by petty household difficulties, and, most especially, not by Mrs. Woodhart.

For Sara Woodhart, in her continuing effort to win back his affections, had lately taken the habit of sending missives marked *Important* at all hours of the day and night, and instructing the messenger to wait for a response, thus inconveniencing the entire household until Burke either sent the letter back unopened, or penned a laconic reply. The missives were not, actually, all that important, since they contained only long and tearful—in some cases, the ink with which they'd been written was smeared, as if by actual tears—appeals to Burke's better nature, begging his forgiveness.

But there was nothing, in Burke's opinion, for him to forgive. He ought, he sometimes felt, to thank Sara for her inconstancy. Because of it, he had been driven to the desperate act that had resulted in his securing the peace he was currently enjoying. He did not regret, not for a minute, the sum of money he was paying in order to insure it, either. Though to some, three hundred pounds was a staggering sum, three hundred pounds to a man who had a few hundred thousand more than that was nothing.

And yet it had bought him something he'd thought beyond price:

Quiet.

Luxuriating in his solitude, Burke dove into his novel, beginning where it was proper, with the preface, which he normally skipped. He was in no hurry, after all. He had all night. He had, in fact, an endless calendar of nights, since he had not yet found a replacement for the estimable Mrs. Woodhart. He was in no rush to find a new mistress. Mistresses were fine things, it was true—as fine as this whisky that rolled so smoothly over his tongue when he sipped it—and yet, like the whisky, too much of any fine thing was not necessarily good.

Perhaps, he thought, lifting his gaze from his book, and staring into the fire, he would not find a new mistress at all, but try celibacy for a change. It was a novel thought, and yet it seemed to fit in with his new mode of restful quietude. He had never, after all, given celibacy a try. Even during those horrible months after he'd discovered Elisabeth with her wretched Irishman, when he'd torn about the Continent in a drunken haze, he'd still had a need to slake, and he'd slaked it readily enough, with ballerinas and the occasional soprano.

But the truth of it was, he was tired of mistresses. Oh, they were pleasant enough, he supposed, in their way. And his appreciation for a finely turned ankle and ivory shoulder had not waned in the least. But there was no denying that aside from their obvious usefulness in relieving pent-up . . . er . . . tension, mistresses were a bit of a nuisance.

Perhaps this was a natural result of the fact that their affections were of the purchased variety. And while actresses like Sara Woodhart were fairly good at feigning an interest in the buyer, the dancers and singers hardly even bothered. They were far too used to being worshiped themselves to know how to worship others. And it seemed to Burke that if he were going to spend good money on a woman, she ought to at least *act* as if she liked him.

And there was, of course, the uncomfortable fact that he was not the most even-tempered of men. Invariably, mistresses—perhaps by the very nature of their position in a man's life—drove him to some act of violence, whether it be dispatching some rival for her affections—such as they might be—or defending himself from various members of her family, who felt outraged by his refusal to marry their sister/daughter/cousin/niece or, in one memorable incident, mother. Burke's reputation for possessing a volatile temper was bad enough. He did not need to have it constantly tempted.

It was factors like these that cemented Burke's resolve to avoid mistresses for the time being.

He took another sip of whisky, replaced the glass, and neatly turned to page two of the preface to *Last of the Mohicans*. He was, he decided, going to enjoy his newfound peace and quiet.

Peace and quiet, at long, long last.

Only now that he had it, Burke found that he couldn't help thinking perhaps it was a bit *too* quiet.

Not that he missed Isabel's tantrums. Nor did he miss having chaperones fly into the room and give notice ten minutes before an engagement was to begin. Good Lord, he did not miss those things at all.

But he did find that he'd grown rather . . . well, *used* to them. To having at least *some* noise about the house. Isabel had been a noisy baby, who'd grown into a rambunctious child. His life after the divorce had been filled with considerable upheaval, but one thing had always remained constant: Isabel, and her incredible capacity to fill a house, no matter how large, with her presence. How often had he railed at her to be quiet? How many nurses had he given the sack for failing to keep her that way?

And now that he'd finally gotten his wish—a quiet house— he found himself missing the screams, the bickering, the occasional explosions.

It was suddenly so quiet, he could hear the clock above the fire ticking. It actually ticked quite loudly. Perhaps there was something wrong with it. A clock shouldn't tick so noisily.

And the rain. It was making quite a noise against the windowpanes. Surely they had to be experiencing some sort of hurricane, for the rain to be pounding down so heavily.

Isabel, he reflected, since her absence had brought her to mind, had been so delighted by his sudden reversal on the Geoffrey Saunders issue that she had almost—just almost—looked pretty. In one of the dozens of white ballgowns he'd purchased for her, she'd flitted into his room and thanked him, while Miss Mayhew waited by the door, holding on to her young charge's wrap. A Miss Mayhew whom, Burke had noticed immediately, looked quite different from the Miss Mayhew with whom he'd shared such an . . . interesting conversation just an hour earlier. That Miss Mayhew had been fetching, but no more, in a plain white blouse and tartan skirt. This Miss Mayhew looked radiant in silk—grey silk, to be sure, but extremely well cut, and quite obviously designed with the intention of bringing out the wearer's assets, which in Miss Mayhew's case included an extremely narrow waist and a small though pert bosom.

The gown had not been at all indecently cut—in fact, it hadn't allowed even a hint of décolletage—and yet, Burke realized, it didn't really matter what a woman like Miss Mayhew covered her body with: men were always going to picture her naked. Well, men like himself, anyway.

Not, of course, that he had the slightest intention of ever again acting on his attraction to her. He had quite lost his head that afternoon at the Sledges'. It wouldn't happen again. He couldn't afford to allow it to happen again, not if he valued his newfound peace and quiet.

And yet, it had to be admitted that it did rather bother him, the thought of Miss Mayhew out and about in a silk dress—even a grey one. If Burke found her attractive in it, it was only natural that other men would, too.

Burke shook himself suddenly. What was he doing? Meditating on his daughter's chaperone's figure, rather than enjoying his evening alone!

Duncan was quite right: he was getting dotty in his old age.

Burke turned resolutely to the third page of the preface to the book he was reading. It was quite interesting, the preface. He'd have to remember to read the preface from now on. It had obviously been put into the book for the express purpose of being read. Why was he always skipping it?

Why was that bloody clock so loud? He'd used to think Isabel maddeningly loud, but now, well, now he knew what loud was. He'd have Mrs. Cleary send the clock out for cleaning upon the morrow. It was surely defective.

Chaperones, Burke knew quite well, didn't dance at balls. They sat behind the mothers and the widows and the spinsters no one wanted and watched their charges, making sure no improper advances were made against them, and kept them from slipping off with their partners into a garden or upstairs bedroom. Burke had never heard of a chaperone dancing at any function to which she'd escorted a charge.

But it occurred to Burke that there was no real convention dictating that a gentleman *couldn't* ask a chaperone to dance. Miss Mayhew was certainly young enough that she might not be taken for a chaperone at all. Supposing—just supposing—someone at this ball she and Isabel had gone off to happened to notice the fair-haired young woman in the grey silk dress?

And what if this someone took it into his wretched head to ask her to dance? It would be rude of Miss Mayhew to say no, when it was clear she was otherwise unengaged. But Burke had never taken offense at Katherine Mayhew's rudeness to him—and she had been very rude to him, indeed. Why should any other man be different? Her rudeness, in fact, might be exactly what was so appealing about her.

Her rudeness and, he had to admit, that absurdly small, pink-lipped mouth.

She might, of course, tell the fellow that she could not possibly dance with him because she'd been employed by the Marquis of Wingate to chaperone his daughter. That was precisely what she was there to do, after all, not dance with whey-faced young men who happened to spy her from the ballroom floor. That would be quite the proper thing for her to do, Burke decided.

And Miss Mayhew was very proper. She had made sure that her bedroom door was open almost the entire time Burke had been in there with her, hadn't she? There weren't many women, Burke knew, who'd have bothered with such propriety. Especially when it involved a rich and titled fellow like himself. Many a woman, he knew from experience, would have quite thrown herself at him, under the same circumstances.

But not Miss Mayhew. Not at all. In fact. . . .

In fact, if he hadn't known better, he might almost have suspected Miss Mayhew of harboring a dislike for him.

But that wasn't possible. She had quite forgiven him his moment of weakness in Cyrus Sledge's library. She had shook hands on the matter. Miss Mayhew's handshake had been all that was warm and generous. She did not dislike him. Not a bit.

Except. . . .

Supposing the fellow wasn't whey-faced? The fellow who asked her to dance, that is. Supposing he was some Italian count, debonair and charming, and Miss Mayhew, obviously no sophisticate—she had thought Burke some sort of flesh-peddler, hadn't she, the first time she'd seen him—fell for him? It would be quite easy for a wealthy gentleman with an accent and a handsome face to win the affections of a girl like Miss Mayhew, if he went slowly enough. The girl must surely be looking for any opportunity to escape her slavish existence as a paid companion to spoiled society brats. Why, even now, this very second, some nefarious hanger-on might be trying to wheedle himself into Miss Mayhew's good graces, promising her moonlight and grappa. . . .

Burke threw down his book and went to the hallway to call for Duncan to lay out his evening clothes.

It was ludicrous, he knew. He was being exactly what Isabel had called him, a silly old thing. Miss Mayhew was not about to run off with any count, Italian or otherwise.

But Burke knew enough about his own sex to know that it would not be for lack of trying. If Miss Mayhew escaped this or any other function without falling prey to some reprobate, it was only because she had slightly more sense than the average female. She had made it this far through life, it was true, without his help. But she had doubtlessly never traveled before in the circles she was about to enter. She could have no way of knowing just how unscrupulous the gentlemen of the *beau monde* could be when it came to a fresh new face. And since he was the one who was forcing her to enter this exalted sphere, it was his duty to protect her. A chaperon for the chaperone, so to speak.

He would, he told himself later, as he waited for his phaeton to be brought round, just pop in for a moment to take a peek at how she was faring. If she seemed to be doing all right, he would go to his club. He had tucked the copy of *Last of the Mohicans* into his coat pocket, just in case.

And if it looked as if she needed him, well, he would be there.

And he'd have the added advantage of checking to see whether her theory about Isabel and young Saunders was correct. On the whole, he decided, as his phaeton swung round, it was promising to be a most profitable evening.

Chapter Ten

$\mathcal{K}$ate was perfectly aware of the gentleman staring in her direction. She had felt his gaze boring into her ever since she'd entered the ballroom.

But she refused—she absolutely *refused*—to imagine that it was Daniel Craven. No. Once in one night was entirely enough. She would not make a fool of herself a second time. It was bad enough that he'd haunted her dreams for so long, the mere thought of him seemed to turn her into a quivering mass of jelly. She simply could not go around thinking she was seeing him while she was awake, as well. Not unless she wanted to be pegged a madwoman.

The man who was staring at her, she decided, was probably just someone who thought he knew her. Well, she'd known it would happen. Try as she might to stay well away from the dance floor, she'd spotted at least a dozen faces she recognized. She'd managed to avoid them by ducking behind pillars and potted palms, but it was only, she knew, a matter of time before someone pulled aside the palm fronds, and cried, "Why, Kate Mayhew! Whatever are *you* doing here? Wasn't your father the one who . . . ?"

Kate moved her seat a little nearer to the grey-haired dowager in front of her. Not because she fancied the old woman would deign to engage her in conversation—a mere chaperone? Perish the thought!—but because she hoped the woman's towering coiffure might offer her camouflage.

Isabel, she was not happy to see, catching a glimpse of her charge through the assorted heads in front of her, was behaving as disgracefully as could be. She had been a perfect nightmare through dinner, hardly saying a word to the eligible—and quite good-looking—gentlemen on either side of her. Her heart, she'd explained to Kate later, had been too full to allow her to speak, she was *that* excited at the prospect of being allowed to see Mr. Saunders. Kate had pointed out that it was all well and good to look forward to seeing Mr. Saunders, but when there was a duke at one elbow and a baron at the other, she might at least deign to ask them how they were enjoying their pheasant.

And then when they'd arrived at the baroness's, Isabel had quite literally thrown her wrap at Kate and made a mad dash for the ballroom, where she immediately latched onto a tall, fair-haired gentleman, whose side she had not left—not even once—for the entire evening. This gentleman, Kate supposed, was Geoffrey Saunders.

He was not unprepossessing, as young gentlemen went. Kate supposed he'd have to have *some* charms, or Isabel would not have been interested in him. She was not certain, but she thought she recognized him from her own season out—unless, of course, she was mistaking him for his elder brother, whom, she'd heard the dowager in front of her whisper, was rumored to have twenty thousand pounds a year.

The younger Mr. Saunders appeared to be about Kate's own age, and was everything that was dashing, from his raffishly curled blond mane to the shiny sword he wore at his hip—an affectation, since he was not in the army, or at least was not in uniform. She could quite see how a young and inexperienced girl like Isabel might fall for a Geoffrey Saunders. Especially since, from what Kate could see, no other gentlemen seemed at all interested in her—unless, of course, her marked preference for Mr. Saunders had already driven everyone else away.

She was going to have to have a talk with Lady Isabel,

Kate decided, the moment they were alone again. The girl simply could not continue to carry on in this manner. She was making a fool of herself in front of everyone. It wasn't any wonder her father had forbidden her from seeing the young man, if this was an example of how she behaved around him. Why, even now she was playfully pulling at that ridiculous sword. And this was supposed to be the daughter of a marquis!

Well, the daughter of the most notorious marquis in London, she amended. Perhaps that was why no one, not even the dowager beside her, was lifting an eyebrow at Isabel's scandalous behavior. They seemed to expect it from a girl whose own parents made such spectacles of themselves with their scandalous divorce.

"Well," came a deep voice at her shoulder. "Are you planning on ignoring me all night, then, Kate?"

She turned quickly in her seat. "Freddy!"

He gave a gallant bow. "The very same. I've been trying to get your attention for the past ten minutes. Why did you keep looking away? I know you saw me."

Kate blushed. She couldn't, of course, tell him the real reason—that she'd thought he was Daniel Craven. He'd only tease her some more. Then, realizing the dowager and her friends were paying close attention to their conversation, Kate got up, and taking the earl's hand, let him guide her through the sea of mauve and silver skirts.

"I saw you," Kate confessed, when they'd made it out of what she had scornfully called Spinsters' Corner, when she'd been Isabel's age. Little had she thought then that she might one day end up amongst their silver-haired ranks!

"That is," Kate went on, "I knew *someone* was staring at me. But I never imagined it was you. What are you doing here, Freddy? I thought you despised this sort of thing."

"You know I do," he said, tugging irritably on his white gloves. "Mother made me come."

Kate looked around nervously. "She's here? Oh, Freddy, should we be seen together? You know how she feels about me."

"Pish posh." Freddy shrugged his shoulders. "I'm not afraid of her."

"You should be," Kate said, dryly. "She controls your purse strings, doesn't she?"

"Only till I'm thirty," Freddy said. "Then I can do what I like with Grandpapa's money."

"I don't know what I'm worried about," Kate said with a shrug. "It's not as if she'd recognize me. I swear to you, Freddy, it's exactly as I told you. I've run into a half-dozen girls I used to know and they honestly haven't recognized me."

Freddy looked at her skeptically. "Sorry, Kate. I think they recognized you, all right. Recognized you and just preferred not to become reacquainted. You haven't changed a bit, you know. You're still the prettiest girl in the room."

"Oh, Freddy." Kate gave him a good-natured shove. "Go on." Then she let out a little shriek. "Good Lord," she said, staring out across the dance floor. "Is that who I think it is? Emmaline St. Peters? Hasn't she gotten herself a husband yet?"

Freddy followed the direction of her gaze. "Old Emmy? Of course not. No one good enough for 'er, and all. What is this? Her eighth season out?"

"Tenth," Kate said emphatically. "She was two years ahead of me in school. Oh, Freddy, we mustn't gossip about her. It's too wicked. But how *can* she wear white?"

"Which reminds me," Freddy said. "Haven't I seen this gown you're wearing before, only in a different incarnation?"

Kate dragged her attention from the spectacle of the aging debutante and looked down at herself. "What do you mean?"

Freddy took her by both hands and held her at arm's length. "Dame Ashforth's," he said, running a critical gaze up and down the length of her dress. "June twenty-seventh, eighteen hundred and sixty-three. You had only a single dance with me, and told Amy Heterling that I trod upon your toes. I was crushed when I heard about it."

Kate's jaw dropped.

"Yes," Freddy said, releasing her hands. "You see, I love you quite madly. I liked it better when it was white. And what have you done to the front of it, there? All the little interesting bits are gone."

Recovering herself, Kate said flatly, "The 'interesting bits,' as you call them, have been covered with an insert. It doesn't do, you know, for the chaperone to show more bosom than her charge."

Freddy sighed. "It's a burning shame to butcher a Worth in that manner."

"Speaking of burning," Kate said lightly, "I would think Mr. Worth would be delighted this dress has turned out as well as it has, considering its history. You can hardly even smell the smoke anymore."

A look of horror appeared on Freddy's handsome face. "Kate," he cried. "I'm so—I'm so sorry. I didn't mean to—"

Kate gave him a playful tap on the shoulder with her fan. "Freddy! What's wrong with you? I'm only joking."

"I know," he said, looking miserable. "Only it wasn't a joke, really. I mean, I'm sure all of your things smelled horribly after . . . after—"

She snapped the fan open, and laid it over his mouth, effectively keeping him from continuing.

"No more," she said, with mock authority. "You know better than to speak of such things on a dance floor. It offends Bacchus."

When she lowered the fan again, Freddy looked sheepish. "Allow me to make amends, then, to the god of revelry," he said, "by asking you for this dance."

Kate looked horrified. "Are you mad? Do you want to get me into trouble my first night out? I'm supposed to be keeping an eye on Lady Isabel, not cavorting with my former beaux."

"What do you mean, former?"

"You know what I mean." Kate heard a scream, and, recognizing Isabel's voice, quickly turned back toward the dance floor. Geoffrey Saunders, she saw, had snatched his sword back from Isabel, and was pretending to run her through with it. Kate quite sympathized with his feelings, but really, she could no longer tolerate this sort of behavior.

"Excuse me, Freddy," she said, her mouth tightening. "I'm afraid I've got to go and commit a murder."

Freddy caught her by the arm, however, before she took a single step. "Whoa, now. That's not the way."

Kate hissed, "What do you mean? Freddy, I can't let her go on like that. She's making a scene."

"But it will be worse if her chaperone suddenly strides up and cuffs her on the ear." He nodded his head toward the dance floor. "I know a better way. Come on. You approach from the left. I'll create a diversion on the right."

Kate hadn't the slightest idea what he was talking about, but she moved in the direction he'd pointed. Isabel was at the center of a large group of young people, and if she wasn't the prettiest girl in the group, she was certainly the most animated, and Kate knew that high spirits tended to make up for even the plainest face.

When Isabel spotted Kate, she half expected her to run— Kate was quite certain her disapproval must have been easily readable on her face. But instead of fleeing for cover, Isabel darted forward and seized Kate by the hand, then dragged her, despite her protests, into the center of the group.

"Geoffrey," Isabel cried, hauling Kate up before her beau like a prize salmon she'd caught. "This is she, Geoffrey! The lovely Miss Mayhew who made it possible for me to be able to see you again! Isn't she the veriest angel, Geoffrey? So little and precious! I simply adore her, and you must, too."

To which Mr. Saunders replied, "Your wish, as always, Lady Isabel, is my command."

And to Kate's horror, the young man stooped down, lifted her hand, and laid a kiss upon her knuckles.

Kate was quite glad supper had taken place so many hours before, or she was quite certain hers would have come up again.

"Isn't she a love, Geoffrey?" Isabel asked. "Oh, Miss Mayhew, I'm so awfully glad you came to live with me. Really, I must be the luckiest girl in the world!"

Mr. Saunders hadn't yet released Kate's hand. He was looking down at her very intently, and she could not help but notice that his eyes were extraordinarily blue—something that must have contributed to his irresistibility, as far as Isabel was concerned.

Kate knew what he was going to ask before he said it. In fact, she might almost have said the words along with him, they were so familiar to her.

"Don't I know you from somewhere, Miss Mayhew?" he asked.

"I fail to see how that would be possible, Mr. Saunders," Kate said, managing a queasy smile. She gave her hand a tug, and Mr. Saunders released it at once. Turning to Isabel, Kate whispered, "Lady Isabel, I need a word with you, if you please."

Isabel whispered back, quite audibly enough for everyone on that side of the crowded room to hear. "Not *now*, Miss Mayhew."

Kate reached out and laid a hand upon the back of Isabel's arm, right where her upper arm met her elbow.

"No," Kate whispered. "*Now*, my lady."

Isabel yelped. Kate was putting steady pressure on her funny bone. Not hurting her, exactly, but not causing her any great pleasure, either.

At that moment, Freddy sauntered up, and slapped Geoffrey Saunders rather hard upon the back.

"Saunders, old bean," he shouted. "Good to see you. Been a while, hasn't it?"

Geoffrey grew noticeably paler behind his mustache. "Lord Palmer," he said, losing a good deal of the bravado he'd exhibited in front of Kate. "How nice to see you again."

"Listen, Saunders," Freddy said, swinging an arm around the younger man's neck. "I'm not sure if you remember the last time we met. It was at old Claymore's country place. It rained all weekend, and we were all forced to stay indoors and play at bagatelle. Coming back to you now? In fact, if I recall correctly, you ended up owing me quite a tidy little sum by Monday morning. . . ."

Their voices trailed off as the earl dragged the younger man away. Isabel, glumly watching them go, no longer protested as Kate quickly led her off to a quiet corner of the room.

"Lady Isabel," Kate said brusquely, as she reached up and adjusted a few of the girl's curls. "You are entirely too free with your affections where that young man is concerned. You must learn to be more guarded."

Isabel, her eyes still on her lover's back, murmured, like an automaton, "I'm not."

"You are, Lady Isabel." Kate tugged on her charge's bodice, which had slipped down even lower than it was supposed to. "It doesn't do, you know, to let a young man be so sure of your affections. If you want to win him, the best way to do it is to keep him guessing about whether or not you like him."

Isabel's bright green eyes, so like her father's, fastened onto Kate's face. "But if he doesn't know I like him, he won't come around," she said plaintively.

"On the contrary," Kate said. "He'll come around more."

Isabel's lower lip began to jut out petulantly. "That's rot," she declared. "If you like someone, you should let him know it."

"Certainly you should . . . *after* he's declared himself."

"But how's he going to know to declare himself," Isabel asked, "if I don't give him any encouragement?"

"You're going to give him encouragement," Kate explained gently. "You should encourage all of your beaux equally, however. It's far too early in the season to be singling one out from all the others."

"But Geoffrey's the only one who ever really pays any attention to me, Miss Mayhew!"

"Because you've made it perfectly clear to everyone else that Mr. Saunders is your favorite, and that you have no interest in anyone else. But you can't tell me he's the only man who asked you to dance tonight."

"Well," Isabel said, looking down. "No. But he asked for all my dances as soon as he saw me, and so then when Sir William asked—"

"You hadn't any dances left." Kate nodded. "In the future, you should reserve the first and last dance for Mr. Saunders, but leave the rest open for other young men who might ask."

"But Miss Mayhew——"

"Do you want Mr. Saunders to ask you to marry him?"

"Oh, yes!"

"Then you must be *different*. You must not make it so easy for him. If he thinks he's already won you, he'll grow bored. And then he'll move on to someone he feels represents more of a challenge."

"Bored?" Isabel cried, paling visibly. "How horrid!" She scissored a glance in the direction in which Mr. Saunders and the earl were returning. "I couldn't stand for Geoffrey to grow *bored* of me. . . ."

Freddy, Kate saw, was still chattering amiably, but Mr. Saunders looked exceedingly glum. As he sauntered to her side, the earl gave Kate a comical leer, even as he slapped the younger man on the back and said cheerfully, "Well, I'm glad that's settled, then. Just a little misunderstanding between friends. Happens all the time, don't it, Kate?"

Kate gave him a very sour look. "I'm certain, *Lord Palmer*," she said, pointedly avoiding his Christian name, and wishing he would do the same, "that I don't know what you're talking about."

"Bah!" Freddy turned to Isabel, who was looking up at Geoffrey Saunders with an expression on her plump face that could only be described as worshipful. "Ho there, little lady," Freddy said, in a voice so boomingly loud that Isabel actually jumped a little. "What do you say you and I take a turn about the room? I feel like doin' a jig or two."

Isabel's green eyes went very wide as she looked from Freddy, to Geoffrey, to Kate, and then back again. "Oh, but . . ." she stammered. "Oh, but I promised——" Her gaze landed on Kate, whose mouth suddenly got very small.

"Oh," Isabel said, looking down again. "Oh, yes, thank you, Lord Palmer. I should be delighted."

Kate had the pleasure of seeing Geoffrey Saunders's jaw drop as the earl whirled Isabel off onto the dance floor. He did not look hurt so much as he did perplexed. Feeling quite pleased with herself, Kate opened her fan, and began applying it with a good deal of energy.

"Beastly hot in this room," she commented. "Wouldn't you say so, Mr. Saunders?"

Geoffrey Saunders was a handsome boy—there was no denying but that he was a pleasure to look at—but just because he looked like an angel, Kate soon discovered, didn't mean he was one. Because when he'd collected himself enough to speak again, what actually came out of his mouth were the words, "Look, here, Miss Mayhew," and those he uttered quite testily.

Kate, pretending to be taken aback, raised her eyebrows. "Yes, Mr. Saunders?"

"Well." Geoffrey Saunders's blue eyes, she saw when she raised her gaze to meet his, were ringed with golden eyelashes that were extraordinarily long for a man. And, she noted, Mr. Saunders knew how to use them. He fluttered them quite innocently. "I was thinking. You're different from Lady Isabel's other chaperones. I mean, aside from being younger—and quite a bit better looking—"

This last was said with a swift appraising look out from under the eyelashes that, Kate knew from experience, was supposed to make her blush with pleasure. What it actually did, however, was make her apply her fan even harder to her burning face, as she thought furiously, *The cheek! The insolent cheek!*

"—you've got a brain or two in your head, I can tell. Well, as it happens, I've got brains, too." Geoffrey paused, as if expecting her to say something like, "But of course you do, Mr. Saunders. Anyone could see that." But Kate, perversely refusing to give him any satisfaction whatsoever, said nothing.

"What I'm trying to say," Geoffrey went on, "is . . . well, there's money to be made here, Miss Mayhew. Quite a lot of it. And if we two were to put our heads together, Miss Mayhew, I'm quite sure we could come up with a plan that would make us both quite . . . comfortable."

Kate said, "Oh, really?" in a noncommittal tone.

"Really." A footman passed by, and Mr. Saunders seized a

glass of champagne, one for each of them. Kate declined the one he offered her, however, and with a shrug, Mr. Saunders downed them both. "Might I ask your salary, Kate? May I call you Kate?"

Kate said tartly, "You most certainly may not. Nor do I see any reason why I should reveal my salary to *you*."

Undaunted by her rudeness, Mr. Saunders went on. "Well, I can tell you what it is. Twenty-five pounds a year. Am I right?"

Kate watched as Freddy expertly whirled the Lady Isabel about the room. Isabel actually appeared to be enjoying herself. The color had come back into her cheeks, and occasionally she giggled with pleasure at something the earl said.

"Twenty-five pounds a year," Mr. Saunders repeated, ignoring Kate's pointed silence. "Do you have any idea how much the Marquis of Wingate is worth, Miss Mayhew? Any idea at all?"

Kate said, "I haven't, but I feel quite sure you're going to tell me."

"Damned right I am. Nearly half a million pounds." Mr. Saunders deposited the empty champagne glasses on the tray of a passing footman. "He has properties in the West Indies, Africa, and South America, holdings that have taken in, at last count, half a million pounds, Miss Mayhew. Out of which you are earning a piddling twenty-five a year. Doesn't that make you angry, Miss Mayhew?"

Kate watched as, the set ending, the earl bowed low to the Lady Isabel, who curtsied quite prettily.

"What makes me angry, Mr. Saunders," Kate said calmly, "is your impertinence."

Mr. Saunders, rather than taking offense at her manner, seemed delighted by it. "I say, Miss Mayhew," he said admiringly. "You've got spirit. I like a girl with spirit. You and I should get on *capitally*."

It was on the tip of Kate's tongue to tell Mr. Saunders that they were not going to get on at all, capitally or otherwise, since she hadn't the slightest interest in pursuing an acquaintance with him. She was kept from imparting this information, however, by two events, which, occurring simultaneously, soon wiped all other thoughts from her head.

The first was Freddy, having swept Isabel back from the dance floor, suddenly seized Kate by the waist and spun her around, declaring loudly to one and all, "Dancing is in my blood, I swear it! You simply *must* have this next waltz with me, Katie!"

She was about to tell him not to be a fool when, from the corner of her eye, she caught sight of a tall, dark man striding quite purposefully toward her. Assuming that here, at least, was one old acquaintance who recognized her, despite the primly cut dress, she struggled out of Freddy's grasp, then turned to meet her accuser.

But her voice dried up in her throat. Because while it *was* an acquaintance who stood before her, their relationship was not of such long standing. For it was, of course, the Marquis of Wingate.

Chapter Eleven

$\mathcal{L}$ord Wingate."

She said it so faintly, she didn't think Freddy could have heard her, especially over the strains of the orchestra the baroness had hired.

But Freddy must have heard her, since he let go of her so abruptly, she staggered. Though she righted herself quickly, she had to reach up and push some of her hair from her eyes, and when she could see again, she realized she must have missed something, because Freddy was glaring at Isabel's father . . . and Isabel's father was glaring right back.

"Bishop," Lord Wingate said, in a cool voice.

"Traherne," Freddy said right back, in an identical tone.

Kate wasn't at all certain what made her suddenly insinuate herself between the two men. But she did so, and with an irregularly beating heart, although when she spoke, she sounded entirely cordial.

"Why, Lord Wingate! What a surprise. We weren't expecting you here tonight."

"That," the marquis said, staring over the top of her head—at Freddy, evidently, "is perfectly obvious."

Kate went on, aware that she was prattling, but unable to stop herself. "I believe you know Mr. Saunders. But I wasn't aware you were already acquainted with the Earl of Palmer."

"Indeed," the marquis said. "Lord Palmer and I have shared

many common. . . ." He paused, and then said, as if thinking better of his original choice of words, "*Adventures*."

Freddy, to Kate's astonishment, laughed. "Adventures," he said, with a chuckle. "Well, that's one word for it, anyway." Then he stuck his right hand out, right past Kate. "Pleasure to see you again, Traherne," Freddy said.

"The pleasure," Lord Wingate said, his gloved hand swallowing Freddy's in a grip that looked, to Kate, a good deal more painful than friendly, "is all mine."

An uncomfortable silence ensued after the two men dropped their hands. Kate, aware that Lord Wingate's eyes were on her, but incapable, just then, of meeting his gaze, opened her reticule and began to dig through it, thinking furiously to herself as she did so, *Oh, God, I'm going to kill Freddy, really kill him! This is all his fault. I told him chaperones don't dance. And now Lord Wingate's going to give me the sack, and I'll have to pay back the money he advanced me. Well, I jolly well know where that fifty quid is coming from, and if Freddy says one word about that wretched mother of his complaining about his spending, I'll just remind him about how he lost me a perfectly good job with his stupid tricks. . . .*

It was Isabel who broke the silence by saying animatedly, "Papa, did you know that Lord Palmer has *two* horses running at Ascot this year?"

Lord Wingate, Kate saw when she looked up, bore this news with admirable calm. "Does he?" he inquired politely.

"Indeed he does," Isabel said. "They're both American bred."

"I presume, then," her father said, not taking his gaze off Kate, even though all she did was pull a watch from her bag, and scrutinize its face, "that Lord Palmer has something against English horseflesh."

"Most definitely not," Freddy cried. "Only it happens that I know a particularly fine breeder in Kentucky, and he's supplied some of my friends with a few real high-steppers, so I thought—"

"Oh," Isabel interrupted, turning her jade-green gaze upon

Mr. Saunders. "Weren't you telling me that you just purchased a high-stepper, Mr. Saunders? Is he from Kentucky, too?"

"Actually," Geoffrey Saunders drawled, with far more self-assurance than Kate thought wise, considering whom he was addressing, "I prefer Arab bred myself."

"*Arab?*" Freddy cried. "You must be joking."

Saunders stuck out his perfectly sculpted chin. "I beg your pardon, my lord, but I am not."

An argument naturally ensued as to who bred the finest horses, the English, the Americans, or the Arabs. Kate, grateful to Mr. Saunders—and Kate was not insensible of the fact that this was a startling turn of events, her being grateful to a man like Geoffrey Saunders—took advantage of the diversion to slink away, in search of some champagne with which to fortify herself against the ride home, which, she was certain, was going to prove very unpleasant.

But Lord Wingate, as it happened, hadn't the slightest intention of waiting for the ride home. No, he apparently chose to rebuke her right there in the ballroom, in front of God and everybody.

She felt the hard fingers close around her arm, and of course didn't have to turn to know to whom those fingers belonged. She merely sighed and slowed her steps. *Really*, she thought. *I'm going to* kill *Freddy.*

"Lord Wingate," she said, turning around to face him. "I can explain. It was just a rather childish moment of—"

But Lord Wingate wasn't even looking at her. He was staring in Freddy's direction. "Miss Mayhew," he said. "Has that gentleman been bothering you?"

She followed his gaze. Yes, it was most definitely Freddy he was looking daggers at. Trying not to think so much about the fact that his fingers were still cutting off the blood circulation in her arm, she said, "Well, not really. You see—"

"I *do* see," the marquis said. "And I was very much afraid something like this might happen."

And then he suddenly let go of her arm, and quite methodically began stripping off his gloves.

"Lord Wingate," Kate said, in some alarm. "I believe you misunderstand me—"

"Oh, I understand," the marquis said, working his fingers from the constricting white cotton, "and I can only hope you'll accept my apologies, Miss Mayhew, for the insulting treatment you've received at the hands of that particular gentleman. I would have hoped that his reputation where the fairer sex is concerned would have prevented any hostess in London from admitting him into her home, but I can see that the baroness, being a foreigner, must not have heard of his latest scandalous entanglement. . . ."

Kate's eyes widened, both with astonishment at the idea of Freddy having any sort of entanglement, scandalous or otherwise, and at the idea of the Marquis of Wingate, of whom she'd heard nothing but shocking rumors, referring to someone else's behavior as reprehensible.

"Really?" she said. "With someone here in London?"

The marquis made an impatient, dismissive gesture, as if the discussion had suddenly grown tedious. "A Viennese soprano."

Kate threw a startled glance in Freddy's direction. Viennese soprano? Viennese soprano? When he was perpetually professing his love for *her*? And all the time it turned out that he was making love to some Viennese soprano?

No. It was too incredible.

"Oh, really," she said, shaking her head in bemusement. "You must have mistaken him for someone else, my lord. You can't possibly mean *Freddy*."

The marquis paused, the second glove halfway removed.

"Freddy?" he echoed.

Too late, Kate realized her mistake.

"Oh," she said, through lips that had gone suddenly dry. "I meant Lord Palmer, of course."

The marquis stared at her. There were, Kate supposed, worse things than being stared at by the Marquis of Wingate. Just then she couldn't think what those things might be, but she was certain there were worse things. There had to be.

But having those eyes, like twin coals glowing in the embers of a dying fire—although what sort of coal burned green, Kate hadn't the slightest idea—boring into one was surely the most uncomfortable sensation in the world.

"You said"—the marquis did not seem to notice her discomfort, or, if he did, he was enjoying it, since he did not look away from her, or even so much as blink—"Freddy. I heard you, quite distinctly. It is true that it is unbearably loud in this infernally hot room, and"—this part he added quite dryly—"I *am* advancing in years, I know, but my hearing is still perfectly good. And I'd like to point out, Miss Mayhew, that you indicated to me, back in the Sledges' library that day, that you were unattached."

Kate blinked at him, perfectly perplexed as to the direction in which this conversation was heading. "Well, yes, of course I did, Lord Wingate. Because I *am* unattached."

Lord Wingate cast a glance in Freddy's direction. And quite suddenly—and not without a distinct sinking sensation—she knew *exactly* where the conversation was headed.

"Oh," she said quickly, hoping if she behaved casually enough, he might let the subject drop. "You mustn't mind Freddy, my lord. He was only being foolish. I thought he could be useful in convincing your daughter that Geoffrey Saunders isn't the only young man in the world. That was before, of course, I knew anything about this—ahem—reputation you mentioned—"

"There it is again," Lord Wingate interrupted, with the air of a man who hears a faint buzzing noise about his head, but can't quite trace the source.

Kate actually looked about for a fly, and not seeing one, asked, "There's what again, my lord?"

"That name." His voice dropped to a growl. "You called him *Freddy*, Miss Mayhew. I heard it, quite distinctly, twice. And yet you tell me that you are unattached."

"I *am*," Kate insisted. "I—"

"So there is no entanglement whatsoever between you and Lord Palmer?"

"Not on *my* part, Lord Wingate," she blurted, then regretted it immediately, when the marquis said, "Ah," in a tone that suggested she'd confirmed a suspicion he'd been harboring.

"Then there is a possibility," Lord Wingate said, "that the earl entertains romantic feelings toward you?"

Furious at herself for having said anything at all—but more furious with him, for having made her do so—Kate declared, "I would never presume to claim knowledge of anyone's innermost thoughts and desires, my lord. I can only answer with certainty about my own. And, as I stated before, my own consist of nothing but the affection one naturally feels for an acquaintance of very long standing. I've known the earl since I was a child. My parents were quite good friends with his. When you walked in, Freddy was just roughhousing with me, as we used to during our school holidays, which I frequently spent at Palmer Park. . . ."

Her voice trailed off. She could tell by the marquis's expression that he did not believe a word she was saying. She felt stung, not so much because he thought she was lying—she was quite certain that a man whose wife had done to him what Lord Wingate's had would expect nothing but lies from a woman—but by the fact that he'd somehow goaded her into saying anything at all. What was she doing, telling this man the intimate details of her life? Indeed, she hadn't wanted him to know, and had been relieved that, as yet, he'd asked her no questions about her family, her past. It was such a sad story . . . such a *stupid* story, in its way. If it were a novel, she would not have finished reading it, because it would have struck her as too depressing, the players in it too pathetic. She hadn't any intention of telling him—not unless she had to. But judging from his expression, an abridged version might be necessary.

But before she could utter another word, Isabel came hurrying up to them, the ends of her sash, which had come undone, streaming behind her.

"Oh, Miss Mayhew," she cried breathlessly. "Can you fix this awful thing? It keeps coming undone, and people are trodding on it." She turned her back toward Kate, who reached up and began automatically to tie the sash in place again.

"Isn't this a lovely ball, Papa?" Isabel asked her father, as

Kate worked behind her. "I'm having such a lovely time. Aren't you?"

Kate kept her eyes on the bow she was forming, and so did not see Lord Wingate's face as he replied, in tones of perfect dryness, "Splendid."

"Only it doesn't seem to me, Papa," Isabel went on, "that you are being very polite, standing there like a stick while Miss Mayhew hasn't a partner for this set. You ought to ask her to dance."

Kate gave the sash a tug that was perhaps more forceful than necessary. "That's quite all right, Lady Isabel," she said, trying to keep her tone pleasant. "I'm not here to dance, after all. I'm here to look after you."

Isabel ignored her. "You had better ask her soon, Papa," she informed her father, "or all her dances will be taken."

Kate gave Isabel's sash a wrench, and said, "Honestly, I can't think where you come up with this nonsense."

"Well, first Lord Palmer," Isabel said matter-of-factly, "and now that nice-looking gentleman over there." Isabel nodded her head at a man who was standing some feet away, gazing quite unabashedly in their direction. "He's been staring at you for the past five minutes, I swear. He must admire you awfully, Miss Mayhew."

Kate looked in the direction Isabel indicated . . .

. . . and froze.

She found she could not move. Not one inch. Her heart, in the bodice of her gown, was the only part of her that retained mobility, and it began moving much too rapidly for comfort, pounding so hard in her ears that it drowned out even the strains of the orchestra across the room.

She wondered, dimly, if she was going to faint. She had only fainted once in her life, and, interestingly, the face she was staring at now had been the last thing she'd seen back then, just before she'd lost consciousness. At least, she'd always thought so. Afterward, when she'd regained consciousness, those who were gathered round her insisted she was wrong. Daniel Craven, they'd said, had been nowhere near the scene, had had nothing to do with the fire that had killed both of Kate's parents.

That's what they'd said, anyway. And even now, seven years later, she didn't have any reason to disbelieve them.

Except, of course, for what her own eyes had told her.

But smoke, like fog, she had been assured, could play tricks on the mind. The shadowy form she'd sworn she'd seen when she'd flung open her bedroom door that dreadful night, to find the hallway leading to her parents' bedroom consumed in flames, hadn't been there at all — or, if it had, it had only been a figment of her imagination, struggling to come to grips with the horror of what she was seeing.

Smoke. Smoke and flame. That was what she'd seen. Thick, cloying smoke, which had choked her as she'd screamed for her parents, desperate to find them in the heat and haze. And red-hot flames, shooting higher and higher, forming a solid wall of fire between Kate and her parents' bedroom door.

She hadn't been able to get to them. Instead, she'd fallen, coughing uncontrollably, to the floor. Even then, she'd crawled, until something stopped her, just before the wall of smoke and flame. Something . . . or someone. Someone who knew her name, and said it, turning her over, and lifting her away from the heat. Daniel Craven. She was sure it had been Daniel Craven.

But Daniel Craven, they told her later, hadn't even been in England at the time—his name had been on a passenger list for a ship that had left for South Africa the week before—and couldn't possibly have rescued her that night.

No one, however, had been able to explain how it was that she'd managed to get from that smoke- and flame-filled hallway to the servants' stairway, where she was found by the household staff as they ran for safety.

She'd never know. She'd told herself long ago that she'd never know, and it was better, in the end, not to wonder.

Except. . . .

Except that there were those who whispered things, horrible things, about that night. Things Kate would never believe, things Kate knew in her soul weren't true.

The one thing no one whispered—no one but Kate—was Daniel Craven's name.

And here he stood in front of her, staring at her as if she, like the mythological phoenix, had risen up from the ashes. . . .

"Oh, look," Isabel said. "He's coming this way. He's jolly handsome, Miss Mayhew. Who is he? One of your old beaux?"

"Not exactly," Kate said weakly.

Chapter Twelve

$\mathcal{W}$ell, if it isn't Kate Mayhew."

That *voice*. A shudder of revulsion ran through her. How *could* he? How could he saunter up to her—Daniel Craven always sauntered. He was much too lazy to walk at anything but a leisurely pace—and say her name, as if nothing—nothing at all had happened since the last time they'd met ... Where had it been? A dinner party, she thought. A dinner party, in her very own house, a few nights before the fire. ...

"They told me you had moved away, or something," he said, in that voice that turned her stomach. "But here you are, looking, I must say, as delectable as ever." He leaned down and kissed her on the cheek, his lips cool.

She said nothing, but inwardly, her mind raged. It *had* been him. It *had* to have been him, all those times she'd thought she'd seen him. He had been following her. He *had*!

Kate, who stood with her gaze downcast, could not see Lord Wingate's expression, but she supposed he must have looked taken aback, since Daniel said to him, in his flippant way, "Oh, don't worry. Kate and I are old, old friends. Aren't we, Kate? Here, introduce me to these nice people, like a good girl."

Kate did look up then. She looked up, right into his pale blue eyes, and said, in a voice that surprised even her with its coldness, "I didn't know you were back in England, Mr. Craven."

"Oh," Daniel said, with a shrug. He was a big man, almost as English-looking as Freddy, though Daniel's hair was a trifle darker blond, and he wore no mustache. Still, he had the same loose-limbed lankiness, a sort of rawboned quality that made him look out of place in a ballroom. His place, quite obviously, was on a horse, pursuing foxhounds, or possibly in the wilds of Africa, hunting rhino. It was a deceiving quality, however, for as much the sportsman as Daniel looked, he was a shrewd businessman . . . and an even shrewder observer of human behavior.

"Yes, well," he said, with the same easy smile that, seven years ago, had sent so many heartstrings humming—including, briefly, Kate's. "I only just got back. From Botswana, I mean. Miserably hot country, Africa. Simply horrid."

Geoffrey Saunders, who had come up behind Isabel, their dance being over, asked, having overheard the last part of Daniel's statement, "South Africa, you mean? Whatever were you doing there?"

That smile grew—to Kate's eye, at least—distinctly reptilian. Yet the gaze Daniel turned upon her wasn't without warmth. That, Kate knew, was the most dangerous thing about Daniel Craven. He appeared, to the casual observer, to be human, capable of experiencing such emotions as compassion and remorse.

Kate, however, knew better.

"Diamonds," he said. "Or, rather, a diamond mine." The look he gave Kate was apologetic. "There really was one, Kate," he said. "All along. Not where I originally thought, but not far off—not far off at all."

She nodded. Of course. Of course the mine existed. Close to the one in which Daniel Craven had convinced her father and all of his friends to invest . . . but just far enough from it that the diamonds in it did not, technically, belong to them. Oh, no.

"But whatever are you doing here, Katie?" Daniel asked, reaching out and seizing both her hands. "It *is* still Katie, isn't it? I shouldn't be miladying you, should I? I know how persistent that young fellow—Whatever was his name? That young earl who was so besotted by you. Surely you and he must be married by now—" He broke off, looking down at her questioningly. "Why, Katie, whatever is the matter? You've gone white as a sheet. And are you *shaking*?"

To Kate's utter surprise, Lord Wingate reached out and pried her fingers gently, but firmly, from Daniel's hands. "Miss Mayhew is unwell, as you can plainly see. Please excuse us."

Daniel looked startled. He had noticed Lord Wingate's presence surely, but had apparently dismissed it though how anyone could dismiss a presence as formidable as the marquis's, Kate could not begin to guess—and now, he seemed taken aback.

"Just a moment—" He blinked a few times. "I mean, Kate and I were just—"

But the rest of what he said was lost to Kate's ears as Lord Wingate steered her from the ballroom. He did it quickly, with the ease of a man long practiced in escaping crowded rooms. It was a good thing, Kate thought, that he kept a hand on her elbow, or she might have stumbled, he was moving that swiftly.

He threw open a door, and she felt a rush of cool air on her face. They were, she saw when she lifted her head, on a stone terrace, overlooking a night-shrouded garden. Crickets chirped in the dark, but so softly that they were nearly drowned out by the strains of the orchestra back in the ballroom.

Crickets, Kate thought, finding the discovery, in some detached part of her brain, hilarious. In the middle of London. Crickets!

Her knees suddenly too weak to support her anymore, she dropped down onto a rough stone bench, where she sat with her head bent, taking in the fragrant air, hoping she didn't sound as if she were gulping, or worse, sobbing.

Roses. She smelled roses. There must have been a vine of

them, climbing along the terrace wall. The rain had stopped, but the bench beneath her was still damp.

"Here." Lord Wingate thrust a glass of something beneath her nose. "Drink this."

"No, really," Kate said. "I'm feeling much—"

"Drink it."

It was a voice she didn't dare disobey. She took the glass, and brought it to her lips. Claret, rich and warming. She drank it all.

"That's better." He took the glass from her and set it aside. Then, before she knew what he was about, he'd peeled off his coat and settled it about her shoulders.

"Oh," she said, startled by the sudden weight, not to mention the sudden heat. "No, I couldn't—"

"Nonsense." He sat down on the bench beside her, careful, she noticed, to keep about a foot of distance between her crinoline and himself. "You're trembling."

She was, of course, but she'd hoped he hadn't noticed. Still, much as she didn't want to admit it, the warmth his coat provided was very welcome, indeed—even if it did smell of *him*, mingled odors of freshly laundered shirt and, more faintly, tobacco, odors Kate recalled only too well from that embarrassing moment in the library, when he had embraced her. . . .

Not, she imagined, that *that* was likely to happen again. He was bound to give her the sack anyway, after this. It wasn't enough that Daniel Craven had ruined her life once. No, he had to keep on doing it, again and again.

She sat there in abject misery, thinking this, listening to the crickets and the occasional shriek of laughter from inside the house. Isabel's voice was clearly audible, even at this great a distance. Hearing it, Kate tensed, preparing to get up again, and at least attempt to perform the duties for which Lord Wingate had hired her. . . .

But he laid a restraining hand upon her arm, saying, "Isabel will be all right with Mr. Saunders for a moment or two. As long as we can hear her, we know she's not up to anything too mischievous. And frankly, I think we have more important things to worry about, you and I."

Kate said, all in a rush, "I can't pay back the fifty pounds you advanced me, Lord Wingate. I already spent it."

The look he cast her—she could see his face quite plainly in the light thrown from the glass panes in the French doors that led to the terrace—was inscrutable. He said, "I don't recall asking for your advance back."

"But if you're going to dismiss me—"

"I don't recall saying I was going to dismiss you, either."

She blinked up at him. Inside the ballroom, Isabel could be heard to shriek, "Oh, I *never!*"

Kate stammered, "I just . . . I just assumed, after. . . ."

Lord Wingate said, "I admit I would be interested to know, of course, how it is that a young woman such as yourself, whom I imagined had led something of a sheltered life, comes to be acquainted with so many gentlemen in a single gathering—"

"Not so many," Kate interrupted. "*Two.* Two gentlemen. And I explained to you that one of them—Lord Palmer—was an old family acquaintance. . . ."

"Ah, yes." The marquis nodded. "So you said. And the other?"

Kate, who hadn't been expecting him to put the question so bluntly, found herself murmuring, "He . . . he was a business partner. Of my father's."

"A business partner," Lord Wingate said carefully. "Of your father's." At Kate's vigorous nod, he added, "A business partner of your father's, at whom you were staring as if he were a ghost."

Kate swallowed. "It . . . it's been some time since he and I. . . . I hardly expected to see him here. He's been out of England for quite a while—"

"So I understand. In South Africa, I believe he said. Looking after a diamond mine." Lord Wingate's tone was as dry as when he'd addressed his daughter on the subject of whether or not he was enjoying the ball. "Your father must be spectacularly well connected, Miss Mayhew, if he is acquainted with earls and owners of diamond mines."

Stung, Kate hurried to her feet, even though, truth be told, her knees were still shaking. How stupid she'd been. How could she have thought, even for a moment, that he wasn't like the rest? She had been duped by his kindness, by a single glass of claret and the loan of his coat. Well, she would not make the same mistake again.

"I'll thank you, Lord Wingate," she said, with all the dignity she could muster, "to refrain from using that sarcastic tone of voice with me. I am not, as you seem to think, a liar. If you choose to believe so, that is your—"

"Sit down, Miss Mayhew," the marquis said, in a bored voice.

"I won't," Kate said. She was so close to tears that she could feel them gathering at the corners of her eyes, but she went on, as haughtily as she could. "I don't choose to remain in the company of people who doubt my word—"

"I don't doubt your word, Miss Mayhew," the marquis said. "On the contrary, I think it entirely possible that the parents of a chaperone—who was, after all, a governess when I first met her—might possibly have been friends to an earl."

She must have looked incredulous, since he added, "Well, I assume that, like yourself, Miss Mayhew, your father is an educator, and that in that capacity, he would certainly know many of the parents of the boys whom he teaches. But," he added, "from the look on your face, apparently I am wrong in that assumption."

Kate, feeling a little ashamed of herself—and surprised that, after everything she'd gone through in the past few years, she still cared what anyone thought of her anyway—said, in a voice that was considerably less haughty than the one she'd used a few moments before, "No, you are not wrong. At least"—she shrugged—"not so wrong as to make it worth mentioning."

"That's gratifying to know." Lord Wingate climbed to his feet. "But what it doesn't explain is the look of utter terror that appeared on your face when that gentleman approached you back there."

Kate felt her cheeks heat up. Now that she was safely out of Daniel Craven's presence, she was able to chide herself for having behaved so foolishly in front of him. It was ridiculous, utterly ridiculous, this idea that he had been following her, that he had been in her home the night her parents died, that he was somehow responsible for their deaths. Now that his pale blue gaze wasn't on her—wasn't anywhere in sight—she was able to see how silly she'd been even to think it. Daniel Craven was a swindler, certainly. He was also a flirt and a skirt-chaser. But he was no killer. Why, he was far too lazy for something so complicated as *murder*.

"It . . ." Kate struggled to come up with an explanation, any explanation, that might sound plausible. Since anything other than the truth—that she thought him a cold-blooded killer—was that, this was no great difficulty. "It's only that I haven't seen him—Mr. Craven—since before my parents died. To speak with, I mean. He and my father were very close, but he . . . Mr. Craven did not even bother to come to the funeral. So I thought it impertinent of him to speak to me the way he did—so familiarly. And then to have done it in front of you . . . I was sure you'd dismiss me on the spot, particularly after what had happened with Freddy, and I got . . . well, I got nervous."

The marquis frowned. "Nervous," he echoed. "I was not under the impression that you were a nervous sort of person, Miss Mayhew." But the way he was looking at her, with those too green eyes, was making her very nervous, indeed. "I am, however," he said, "hardly the ogre you evidently think me. I'm sorry, Miss Mayhew, to hear of the loss of your parents. When did they pass away?"

She said faintly, "Seven years ago."

"And may I ask how they died?"

"There was a fire."

There was a fire. Four fairly simple words, none above a syllable. And yet to Kate, they were the four worst words in the English language, words that would always cause a shiver to go up her spine. In fact, she gripped the lapels of the coat he'd draped across her shoulders a little tighter, as if to shield herself from a sudden dip in temperature.

And then, rather to her confusion, she felt the fingers of the marquis's ungloved hand slide along her jawbone, then take hold of her chin, and lift her face so that he could look down into it.

"That," he said, so quietly that it was almost as if he were speaking to himself, "is one I haven't seen before."

Kate, not having the slightest idea what he was talking about, but nevertheless instantly paralyzed by his touch, asked, "I beg your pardon?"

"You have a strangely expressive face, Miss Mayhew," he said, his voice still no more than a murmur. "And, I've noticed you've a marked inability to hide your emotions. You appear to be quite cheerful by nature, and so when you mentioned the fire. . . . Well, I was surprised by what I saw in your eyes."

Kate, completely unable to tear her gaze from his, asked softly, "And what did you see in my eyes, Lord Wingate?"

She didn't mean to be provocative. She asked because she was genuinely curious. Had she looked frightened? She hoped not. Kate could not abide cowardice, though she knew she hadn't acted with any great bravery when Daniel Craven had appeared so suddenly.

Or had she merely looked sad? There were times when Kate's loneliness for her parents—for anyone, really, with whom she had a shared history, someone besides Freddy with whom she could talk about her life before the fire that had changed it so irrevocably—seemed almost more than she could bear. How had she looked? What had he seen in her eyes?

But she was never to know. Lord Wingate was just opening his lips to reply, his fingers on her face very warm—a warmth that, like his coat about her shoulders, ought to have been reassuring, but which caused Kate's heart to slip into a rhythm that was certainly less than even—when the French doors burst open, and Isabel, her face very flushed, cried, "*There* you are. I've been looking all over! It's time for the Sir Roger. Are you coming?"

The marquis had dropped his hand the second Isabel started speaking, and Kate, for her part, had turned quickly away, already allowing his coat to slip from her shoulders. As Isabel stood there, looking at them expectantly, Kate said, passing the garment back to its owner, "Thank you for the use of your coat, Lord Wingate. I'm feeling much better now."

Lord Wingate took the coat without a word, but Isabel was not so tactful.

"Oh, you needn't worry, Miss Mayhew," she said, "about that man who made you so pale. He left straight after Papa took you away. Who was he, anyway? Someone who used to be in love with you? He was very handsome. I don't know why you didn't marry *him*."

"He wasn't anyone," Lord Wingate said, before Kate had a chance to reply. Shrugging back into his coat, he took his daughter by the arm, and continued. "An old business acquaintance of her father's, whom she hadn't seen in quite some time. Now, what's this about the Sir Roger?"

"It's starting," Isabel said, "in five minutes. Everyone's got to take part, or it won't be any fun. You and Miss Mayhew have got to join. Will you, Papa? Miss Mayhew? Will you, please?"

Kate, who'd been revived by the claret—but even more so by the heat Lord Wingate's touch had quite inexplicably sparked within her—said, with something like her normal no-nonsense tone, "You know very well, Lady Isabel, that I can't join you. But I shall be delighted to sit and watch you and your father dance."

Isabel made a face as they reentered the ballroom. "Me? And Papa? Dance? No, thank you. Geoffrey's already asked me. Papa, if Miss Mayhew won't dance with you, you'll simply have to find your own partner."

Lord Wingate, Kate saw, smiled a bit enigmatically. "I shall see what I can do," he said.

And then they were swallowed up in the crush of bodies that crowded the ballroom. Isabel, soon finding Mr. Saunders, hurried away, and Lord Wingate, Kate saw, was directly accosted by a large, heavily jeweled woman who spun around when he inadvertently brushed against her in an effort to get by.

"Wingate," she bellowed. "I didn't know you were here! I

saw the lovely Lady Isabel, but not you. When did you arrive? How could you have come out and not looked for me?"

How the marquis bore being greeted by this overbearing woman Kate did not wait to find out. Their conversation on the terrace—the whole evening in general—had made her quite uncomfortable, to say the least, and it was with great relief that she slipped away, hoping that her employer would be too distracted by his admirer to notice that Kate had gone.

But when a few minutes later she had slunk back to her seat in Spinsters' Corner, she caught sight of him again, and found that the marquis's penetrating gaze had followed her, despite the gaggle of splendiferously dressed women who'd gathered round him. He looked at her over the heads of his admirers—admirers who did not seem in the least concerned about the Marquis of Wingate's reputation, violent or otherwise—and raised a hand.

Kate, staring at that hand, felt a sudden and curious rush of emotion. And then she blushed at the absurdity of her reaction. Because it was only a *hand,* of course, casually raised to let her know that she had not, in fact, escaped unnoticed, that the marquis had been perfectly sensible of her disappearance, and that he had troubled himself to discover where, exactly, it was that she'd slipped off to.

And yet to Kate, it was more than just a hand. It was an indication that, for the first time in a very long time, she was not alone. Well, she had certainly never been *completely* alone . . . after all, she had Freddy. But though Freddy had always been a good friend, he had not necessarily been the most reliable—and now that she knew about his soprano, she saw why. He had certainly not been someone who, lost in a crush of admirers, would think to seek out Kate, wherever she happened to be in the room, and wave to her.

Which caused Kate to wonder what, in fact, Lord Wingate was doing at the ball in the first place. She had been under the impression that he couldn't stand these sort of events. So what was he doing at this one? Certainly he could not be here because of Isabel. That was *her* duty, looking after Isabel. Had Lord Wingate harbored some doubts about Kate's ability to handle his daughter? Had he come to the ball to see how well she fared at it?

Or was there some *other* reason he'd come all this way, in all this rain?

I was very much afraid something like this might happen. Those had been his words when he'd first taken her aside. Had he been afraid that she would be tempted to desert her post, as it had surely looked as if she had, when he'd first walked in and found her in Freddy's arms?

Yet he had not rebuked her for it. He had, in fact, apologized for Freddy, believing the earl had taken a liberty.

And when Daniel Craven had accosted her, the marquis had been almost protective in the way he'd steered her from the room, sensing she was unwell. . . .

I was very much afraid something like this might happen.

Good God. Kate straightened in her seat, almost as suddenly as if she'd leaned back upon a pin someone had carelessly left upon the chair back. That was *it*. That *had* to be it.

Lord Wingate was looking out for her.

He was doing it this instant, right before her eyes. For though he had lowered his hand, his gaze still alighted upon her, every so often, even as he casually shook hands with acquaintances, and sipped a glass of champagne. He was keeping an eye on her. He kept an eye on his daughter, too, but. . . .

But he was also looking out for her chaperone.

It was ridiculous, of course. Ludicrous, even. Here was a man who had the worst reputation imaginable: he had divorced his wife, and tried to kill her lover; he had kept the product of their union from her in an effort to punish her for loving another man; he'd dueled with Lord knew how many men, and had had affairs with women all over Europe, and had even, shortly upon making her acquaintance, attempted to make love to her. . . .

And yet, here Kate sat, feeling a rush of warmth and gratitude and—she might as well admit it—*liking* for her employer.

How could she? How could she possibly like a man like that? How could she, Kate Mayhew, whose head was planted so firmly upon her shoulders, possibly like a man like Burke Traherne, who was, in every way imaginable, so thoroughly lacking in morality? What was the matter with her? What was she *thinking*?

But she knew exactly what she was thinking. And what she was thinking—what she couldn't *help* thinking—was that it had been a terribly long while since anyone had troubled themselves to look out for her, even a little.

Oh, certainly Freddy did, when he remembered to, which tended to be whenever his mother was out of town. But the marquis had come down, on his own accord, for the express purpose of seeing how Kate was faring. He had even apologized to her for what he had perceived as a slight against her by one of his set.

And it had been a long time—a very long time—since anyone had apologized to Kate for anything. The fact that the marquis had done so made her feel . . . well, it made her feel as if she belonged.

It was a little thing, a ridiculous thing. But there it was. She felt as if she belonged . . . not necessarily to some*one*, but to some*thing* . . . a family. And not the pages-and-binding variety, which she had only just a few hours earlier explained to Isabel was the only kind of family she had anymore. But a real family, of flesh and blood.

She had never felt as if she belonged to any of the other families with whom she'd lived since the deaths of her parents—not the Piedmonts, or the Heathwells, or, God forbid, the Sledges. It didn't do, Kate knew, for someone in her profession to get to feeling too close to her charges. Children grew up, and then there was no need for a governess—or, in this case, a chaperone. It had already happened to Kate several times, even in her relatively short career. The only thing for it, really, was to put on a brave face, and sally on to the next assignment. What else was there for her to do?

Oh, she could marry Freddy, she supposed. She could always marry Freddy . . . providing, of course, she could put up with his mother.

And the soprano, of course.

But Kate wasn't ready to give up, and if she married Freddy, that would be precisely what she was doing. Somewhere out there, she was convinced, was the man for her, and even though, at twenty-three, she was advanced in age for the marriage market, she wasn't going to allow herself to surrender without a fight. After all, she'd known girls of eight and twenty—even over thirty—years of age, who'd found love and marriage. Why shouldn't she?

So there was nothing for it, really, but to carry on, and work to earn her keep, and face each day as another opportunity at finding the love she was certain was waiting for her. For everything she had ever read had assured her that love came to those who were patient, and good at heart. And she trusted that she was both things. Love was surely just around the corner for Katherine Mayhew. She simply had to find the right one.

Corner, that is.

But in the meantime, it seemed, she had found a family. A fractured one, to be sure, but still, something to which she felt she belonged.

And that feeling of belonging was what was making her feel so warm. It was a feeling she hadn't experienced in quite some time. It was a feeling she quite liked.

It was a feeling she very much feared she could get used to.

Chapter Thirteen

No," Lady Isabel Traherne said petulantly. "That isn't what I asked for. I asked for sugared *orange* slices, not *peach*." She fell back against the pile of pillows behind her, raised a lace handkerchief to her red and running nose, and moaned, "Oh, take it away. Just take it away."

Brigitte, Lady Isabel's personal maid, shot Kate, who was sitting a few feet away, an aggrieved look. Brigitte was taking her mistress's illness quite hard. She had been working ceaselessly at trying to find ways to amuse and cheer the invalid.

Kate, on the other hand, found it exceedingly difficult not to laugh at Lady Isabel's theatrics. She managed to keep a straight face this time only because she'd had some little practice over the course of the past week, during which Isabel's cold—and it was, the physician had assured them, *only* a spring cold—had gone from bad to worse.

Kate's belief that she had finally found a place in which she belonged had not lessened, even as her charge grew more and more irritable, and less and less likable, as her cold progressed. For now that they were not constantly at the opera, or a ball, or a card party; not attending the races, or a luncheon, or hopping from milliner shop to milliner shop in quest of the perfect bonnet, Kate had come to know the rest of the household quite well, and had developed a thorough liking for almost all of the inmates of 21 Park Lane.

The housekeeper, Mrs. Cleary, was a clever and sensible woman, who seemed to worship Kate for her ability to discipline the headstrong Isabel—whom, Kate learned, had run quite wild before she'd taken up residency. The butler, Vincennes, was everything that Mr. Phillips had not been, and a good hand at chess, besides, and was forever hovering about, asking Kate if she had time for a game. Even Brigitte, the French ladies' maid, whose head was filled with little more than giggles and gossip, was a thoroughly pleasant companion, though Kate suspected the only reason she'd taken so to her mistress's chaperone was that Kate spoke a little French, and Brigitte, missing her mother tongue, enjoyed conversing in it once again.

Really, the only person at 21 Park Lane about whom Kate had any misgivings whatsoever was her employer . . . and that was only because she saw him so very rarely. For a man who—according to his own daughter—loved nothing more than a good book, it seemed to Kate as if Lord Wingate was never at home to enjoy one. Kate had been forced to spend much of her time during Isabel's illness trolling her father's library for material with which to amuse her, and never once had she encountered him there. She had seen him a good deal oftener before Isabel's illness, when she'd looked out from Spinsters' Corner, and glimpsed him in the crowd, one eye invariably on his daughter, and the other inevitably turned in her direction.

Which she hadn't minded. She hadn't minded it a bit. Truth be told, running into Daniel Craven the way she had that first night had thoroughly unnerved her. She could not say why, precisely. The rational part of her mind told her that Daniel could in no way have had any part in the tragic deaths of her parents. But another, deeper part of her insisted that he had. It was a thought she routinely pushed down, but it had a tendency to rise now and then . . . especially in her dreams, which, since seeing him again, had tended more and more often to revolve around the fire.

She had thought herself done with nightmares. They had haunted her almost every night for the first year after her parents' deaths. But after seven years, they had ceased almost completely. Until, that is, she'd thought she'd seen Daniel Craven on Park Lane . . . and then actually had seen him, across a ballroom.

Now the nightmares returned, not with any regularity, but more than just occasionally. And in them, she was once again trying frantically to reach her parents, trying to cross that burning hallway, and once again, something—someone—pulled her back. In her dreams, she never saw who that someone was.

Waking, however, she knew. The name Daniel Craven, Daniel Craven, Daniel Craven, echoed through her head every morning like church bells, ringing out the time.

Fortunately, after that first night, she did not see him again. She looked for him—she would always look for him, now that she knew he was back in England. But fortunately, it appeared he was not invited to many of the same parties as the daughter of the Marquis of Wingate. Which suited Kate just fine. Though she had not, she felt, handled their first interview at all well, she did not feel anxious to prove herself in another. The farther Daniel Craven stayed from her, the happier she felt.

This was not the way she felt, however, about another gentleman who seemed to be avoiding her. She knew perfectly well that she ought to have kept her mouth shut over Freddy's soprano, but somehow, one night, it had simply slipped out. They had been standing about, watching Isabel whirl across the ballroom on the arm of a boy who was not Geoffrey Saunders—which had consequently caused Mr. Saunders, who was standing close by, to complain, "I don't understand it. She promised *me* all her dances, first thing when she arrived this evening, and then every time I look, some other bloke's got her."

Pleased to see the young man so discomfited, Kate had remarked, lifting a glass of champagne from the tray a footman offered her, " 'A woman is always a fickle, unstable thing.' "

Freddy had flicked an amused glance in her direction. "Surely not the Bible, Kate?"

"Good Lord, no." She took a sip. "That was Virgil."

"I say, Kate," Freddy said, moving closer to her. "There's Traherne, over there by that potted palm, lookin' right at you. What's *he* doin' here, I wonder? I wouldn't think this was his sort of thing. Is he here to spy on you, d'you think?"

Kate said, with a shrug, "I rather fancied it was you he was staring daggers at. After all, you're the one who's always dragging his daughter off to turn a reel, aren't you?"

"Only because *you* won't turn one with me," Freddy said, wounded. Then, as if it had only just occurred to him: "I say, Kate. Did he say anything to you about me that night he caught the two of us dancin'?"

"About you manhandling me, you mean?" Kate asked.

"Yes. I'm sorry about that. Don't know what came over me. I was caught up in the moment, and all. I don't suppose I've a head for dancin'."

"No," Kate said. "His lordship didn't say anything about your manhandling me."

Nor had Kate said anything to Freddy about Daniel Craven being back in town. Freddy hadn't noticed him that evening at the ball, having become embroiled in another heated argument over horses with the young Mr. Saunders. Which was, Kate figured, just as well: Freddy had been one of the many people who'd believed her insistence that she'd seen Daniel Craven the night of the fire a symptom of the smoke inhalation she'd suffered, a sort of a hallucination. Her practically fainting at the sight of the man seven years later would only have confirmed Freddy's belief that her antipathy for Daniel Craven was ill-founded. After all, what had he done at the ball, but greet her with perfect civility? And she'd gone and fainted.

Instead, she said, mischievously, "Lord Wingate did, however, wonder what you were doing there, and ventured that she must have been busy that night."

Freddy stared down at her. "That who must have been busy that night? My mother, you mean?"

"Certainly not." She took another sip of her champagne. "Your Viennese soprano, of course."

Freddy's jaw had dropped. He'd shot a look in the marquis's direction that, had he noticed it, might have caused Lord Wingate some little discomfort.

"That devil," Freddy had said quite vehemently, beneath his breath. Then, to Kate, he'd said, "Listen to me, Katie. She means nothing, I swear it. She was just a way to . . . Well, it isn't as if you've been giving me any encouragement and . . . and . . ." Freddy had darted a murderous look in the marquis's direction. "I'll kill him," she'd heard him murmur. "I swear I will." To which Kate had responded by striking him lightly on the arm with her fan.

"Oh, Freddy, stop it. I'm delighted to hear that you don't spend every moment you're away from me pining for my company. It's a blow to my ego, I'll admit—and I'm disappointed you never told me about her, since I thought we shared everything with one another"—*well, not quite everything*, she'd amended guiltily to herself—"but I suppose I'll live."

Freddy had been much too appalled to say another word. And his effrontery over what she'd considered merely lighthearted bantering must have been extreme, since Kate heard mighty little from him after that. He seemed to avoid all of the functions at which he thought she might be in attendance, and he certainly never came calling for her of a Sunday, her only day off.

Kate, surprised, supposed the soprano had meant rather more to Freddy than he'd let on.

And, strangely, even though his daughter was ill—a trifling illness, surely, but an aggravating one, nonetheless—Lord Wingate was rather scarce himself, and from his own home, no less. Oh, he peered in first thing after breakfast, to see how Isabel had fared the night, and occasionally looked in at the end of an evening out, but nothing more than that. Kate supposed he had found a replacement for Mrs. Woodhart, with whom, she understood from Isabel—who knew far more than was good for her about her father's romantic life—he'd split. But this idea Isabel dismissed with much disgust. He had not found a replacement for Mrs. Woodhart, and would not, if he knew what was good for him. It was time he married, and the sooner the better, according to Isabel, since Geoffrey Saunders was bound to propose any day.

But the likelihood of the marquis marrying, however fondly his daughter might wish it, was viewed with a good deal of skepticism by the rest of the household. He had been heard more than once to disparage the entire idea of marriage, and usually, upon any servant announcing an intention to form such a union, tried to counsel them out of it. If the hapless individual refused to abandon his or her quest for the altar, the marquis was known to sigh sadly and hand over a gold crown, with his sincere wishes that said individual find happiness, in such a tone that suggested such happiness was extremely rare.

And, Kate eventually learned from his lordship's valet, the marquis had most recently been spending all of his time not in pursuit of a new mistress, but down at his club. Or at least, that was where Duncan was frequently sent with deliveries of fresh shirts.

Not that Kate had taken to listening to kitchen gossip. Only it seemed that whenever his lordship's name was mentioned, she could not help but listen. Mrs. Cleary's story, for example, of a time when it had snowed so hard one Christmas Eve at Wingate Abbey that the housekeeper—a Catholic—had resigned herself to forgoing mass, for fear of slipping on the way. Imagine her surprise when she'd awakened Christmas morning to the sound of scraping, and looked out her window to see the master of the house—he had given his staff the day off—shoveling a path for her through the deep white stuff.

"And wouldn't take a thank-you," Mrs. Cleary had informed Kate, over tea one evening, after a sniffling Isabel had fallen into a restless sleep. "Wouldn't hear a word of it. And him not even a churchgoer! But he was always like that, since he was a wee little one, Master Burke. Always putting others ahead of himself, but doing it on the sly, like, so you would never know it, unless you caught him at it. I've heard there's some as put his lordship down as having a violent temper." Here the old woman's voice dipped conspiratorially, "And I'll not lie to you. He's got the devil's own. But only when he's vexed, miss. Only when he's vexed. The rest of the time, he is the best of men. The best."

Kate might have thought Mrs. Cleary was exaggerating a little, as elderly ladies—particularly housekeepers—were wont to do, especially when speaking of their employers, except that she heard similar stories from all of Lord Wingate's other servants, as well. Isabel's father, it seemed, was generous to a fault, kind beyond all comparison, and generally perceived to be exactly what Mrs. Cleary had insisted he was: the best of men.

Except, of course, for his temper, which all agreed was extremely volatile. Kate was advised to steer a wide berth around any subjects that might engender the master's wrath, and was even offered a list of those subjects, which included, among other things, matrimony and flannel.

Though Kate memorized the list, she thought it highly unlikely that an opportunity for bringing up any of these offensive subjects was going to rear itself, since she now saw so little of him. In fact, she'd lived in his home for nearly a month before she happened actually to sit down to a meal with him, and that had been a distinctly uncomfortable affair at which the marquis, who had clearly been expecting to enjoy his breakfast in solitary perusal of the newspaper, had attempted to find a subject upon which they might converse with one another, and failed, finally leaving the table with a hasty excuse.

Kate would, of course, not have been a woman if this had not irked her. It was obvious to her that Lord Wingate was avoiding her, just as it had been obvious to her before that he'd been following her. Strangely, his avoiding her dismayed her a good deal more than his following her ever had. She did not flatter herself that Lord Wingate was in love with her, despite what had happened in the Sledges' library, but she had thought that he rather *liked* her, at least a little.

But that, apparently, had been a false impression, his lordship having proved that his time was better spent elsewhere.

Other men, however, were not so fickle with their affections. Mr. Geoffrey Saunders had remained a constant admirer, as Brigitte now proved, by taking away the offensive sugared peaches, and revealing, instead, a letter upon a silver salver.

"Perhaps," Brigitte said, her French accent very thick. "Perhaps this will make her ladyship smile, then. It came just now, in the post. Another love letter, I think."

Isabel groaned, her eyes closed. "Oh, how my head pounds! I haven't the strength to read it. Put it on the table with the others, Miss Mayhew, would you?"

Kate put aside the book she'd been reading aloud—*Our Mutual Friend*, by Mr. Dickens, *Pride and Prejudice* having been finally disposed of the day before—stood up, and removed the letter from the silver salver the maid held out to her. Recognizing the handwriting on the envelope, Kate said airily, "Oh, look, another from Mr. Saunders."

Isabel sat up with as much energy as if someone had suggested her bedclothes were aflame.

"From Geoffrey?" she cried. "Is it really? Oh, give it here, Miss Mayhew! Please give it here!"

Kate surrendered the letter, and Isabel fell upon it with savage eagerness.

"Oh," she cried, reading happily. "Oh, he misses me, Miss Mayhew! He says he is *pining* for me."

Kate said, "As he ought."

"But supposing he does a harm to himself, for missing me so much? He says here he might. He says he can't promise he won't. Oh, mayn't I answer this one, Miss Mayhew?" Isabel looked up pleadingly. "*Please* mayn't I answer this one?"

"I don't know." Kate furrowed her brow, pretending to think. "How many is that this week?"

"*Four*, Miss Mayhew! Surely I may answer him after *four* letters begging to know why I haven't sent a reply to any of his others, and threatening to do himself a harm if I don't reply to this one."

Kate sighed. "I suppose," she said, "you may send him a brief note, explaining that you are ill, and—" Then, seeing that Isabel was scrambling out of bed and toward her writing desk, Kate broke off, and cried, instead, "Where do you think you're going, my lady? Get back beneath those blankets. You heard what the doctor said."

"How can I care what the doctor says," Isabel wailed, struggling against Kate's detaining hands, "when my darling Geoffrey is *pining* for me?"

"You'll care a good deal," Kate said tartly, "if you catch something worse than a cold, and are kept from him that much longer. Think what a harm he'll do to himself then."

Isabel stopped struggling immediately. "Oh," she said, sinking back against the pillows. "You are right, Miss Mayhew. Darling Miss Mayhew, where would I be without you? For you are always right."

Kate, tugging at her sleeves—which Isabel had frightfully wrinkled in her frantic struggle to get out of bed—said, "I *am* always right. It would help if you'd remember that, my lady. Now stay put, and I'll go and fetch some stationery. And at your peril you spill ink on the sheets again."

But she had hardly taken two steps toward Isabel's desk when Brigitte's startled voice stopped her.

"Oh, miss!" she cried, as a grey-and-white blur streaked past her skirts, and into the hallway beyond the door she held open. "*La chatte! La chatte!*"

Kate was up and running before the words were fully out of the maid's mouth. Isabel had all but adopted Lady Babbie as her own, and the feline had fallen for her constant offerings of creamed herring and milk, and had taken to sleeping on her bed instead of Kate's. Kate did not mind, since she knew as soon as Isabel was well again, she would forget all about Lady Babbie, who would then return to Kate's room.

But in the meantime, it was a challenge to keep the animal contained in the sickroom, since the door to it was left continuously open, allowing Lady Babbie to escape and explore sections of the house not necessarily welcome to her. This time, Kate saw, as she ran after the fleeing animal, she was headed for the door to Lord Wingate's private chambers, rooms which Lady Babbie had expressly *not* been given permission to enter. Her heart rate speeding up, Kate careened after the fleeing animal, and just missed seizing her at the room's threshold.

Kate did not hesitate. The door had been left partly open, most likely by the valet, who'd been conducting an inventory of his lordship's waistcoats, having decided that morning that one appeared to be missing. It being made of flannel, it was supposed that Lord Wingate had disposed of it himself, but Duncan left nothing to chance, and had decided to make that determination for himself by conducting a thorough search of his master's closets.

Kate pushed the door all the way open, then peered about the room, hoping to spy Lady Babbie right off, and spirit her away before Duncan happened to notice her presence.

The valet, however, was not in sight. And as it was the first time Kate had had an opportunity to enter the room, she was struck momentarily by the sheer immensity of the place, and could only stand there, panting and blinking, Lady Babbie completely forgotten.

The chamber was three times as large as her own, containing a massive fireplace, before which there was a comfortable arrangement of leather chairs and a sofa, and above which hung a crossed set of rather wicked-looking swords. At the opposite end stood an equally massive bed. Dark blue curtains fell from all four of its posts, sweeping the floor of the raised dais on which the bed stood. Matching dark blue material curtained the fourteen-foot windows that looked out across the park, and the carpet below Kate's feet was also that same deep blue.

It was a very grand room—a very grand room, indeed—and yet, as Kate stood there looking at it, she was struck with a feeling of pity for him. Because it was a terribly large room to have all to oneself, and it seemed to Kate that the marquis must be very lonely in it, which was undoubtedly why he spent so much time out, away from it.

It was as she was standing there, thinking this perfectly ridiculous thought, that she became aware of the sound of vigorous splashing from behind her. Turning, she saw a half-open door, behind which stood a standing mirror.

"Duncan?"

Kate's blood froze in her veins. It was Lord Wingate's voice.

"Duncan, where have you got to with the towels?"

And then, to Kate's horror, she glimpsed something so disturbing that, without another thought, she turned and bolted from the room. She did not stop running until she reached her own chamber, into which she flung herself, locking the door behind her.

Nor did she unlock it until some time later, when she was forced to, in answer to an irritated, "Miss Mayhew? Miss Mayhew, are you in there?"

Collecting herself as best she could, Kate went to the door and undid the lock, then opened it a fraction of an inch. His lordship's valet stood in the hallway, holding an extremely irritated and rather damp Lady Babbie in his arms.

"Miss Mayhew," Duncan said, with wounded dignity, as he thrust the cat toward her. "May I ask that in the future, you restrain this creature? I found it a moment ago, lapping water from his lordship's bath."

Kate took the cat silently and started to close the door, but the valet stopped her with a concerned, "Miss Mayhew? Are you quite all right? Do you want me to fetch Mrs. Cleary for you? Because if you don't mind my saying it, you look as if you had seen a ghost."

But it was not a ghost Kate had seen. It had been quite the opposite of a ghost, being very much alive. So alive, in fact, that the sight of it had burned itself into her memory, and Kate was quite certain it was never, ever going to leave.

Now she could only smile at the valet in a sickly fashion and say, "Oh, no. I'm quite well," and then close the door, and lean upon it some more, perfectly unconscious of the fact that Lady Babbie was struggling frantically to escape her arms.

For what she had seen, of course, was Lord Wingate, in the *flesh*. . . .

Chapter Fourteen

The two of them were back in the Sledges' library. They were wearing very much the same things they'd had on the day Lord Wingate had first made his extraordinary offer. The sun was filtering weakly through the stained-glass window in much the same manner. And, as had happened that day, Lord Wingate suddenly, quite without any warning, seized her about the waist, and pulled her against him.

Only this time, Kate didn't stop him. She didn't lay a finger on the nearby atlas. She didn't so much as glance at it. Instead, she threw her arms about Lord Wingate's neck, and raised her face toward his in a perfectly scandalous manner. . . .

And she didn't care. She didn't care a bit what happened. And when what happened was that Lord Wingate lowered his mouth over hers, well, that was just fine. More than fine, as a matter of fact. It seemed to be exactly what she'd been longing for him to do all these weeks.

And when he tightened his strong arms around her, and she found herself molded to every contour of his lean, muscular body, his heat seeming to singe her through her clothing, well, that felt right, too. So right, in fact, that it seemed perfectly natural for her to run her hands along those rippling muscles, first the ones she felt beneath the sleeves of his coat, and then the ones beneath his shirt, along that hardened, thickly haired chest, and then the ones that made up the deeply ridged wall of his stomach, until finally she sunk her hands even lower, low enough so that she could feel the firm flesh of his thighs beneath his breeches. . . .

Only now, conveniently, he was bereft of those breeches. Lord Wingate was perfectly naked, and so was she. A second later, they were sinking down upon Cyrus Sledge's cracked leather couch, their limbs and tongues entwined. . . .

It was at this point Kate woke up. Woke up panting, and with her hand between her legs.

And that was not all. Not only was her hand there, pressed up against the part of her which was throbbing so tenderly, but when she brought that hand away, it was *damp*.

And even as she sat there, trying to catch her breath, she realized that she was damp *all over*. There were rivulets of sweat between her breasts, not just between her legs.

She looked around her dark bedroom. Everything looked exactly as it had when she'd gone to bed a few hours before. But there seemed to be something different, something not quite right.

And then she remembered. Yes, of course. The difference was with *her*.

It wasn't any good, of course. Try as she might, Kate could not get the image of what she'd seen in Lord Wingate's bedroom out of her head. How could she? She had never in her life seen a naked man, except in paintings, and the occasional statue. And frankly, in her newly enlightened opinion, paintings and statues did not even *begin* to tell the story. Statues had no hair, for one thing, and paintings . . . well, all Kate could think was that most painters were men, and that when presented with a model who looked like Lord Wingate, they'd undoubtedly—out of sheer jealousy, if nothing else—underplayed the sheer immensity of . . . *things*, conscious that their own was nothing to it.

Or so Kate supposed. There really was no other rational explanation for it. The *thing* had been huge. Lord Wingate was a big man—she had always known he was a big man. But she had seen plenty of paintings and sculptures of big men, and their *things* had never been as big as Lord Wingate's.

And that hadn't been all. It had been enough, of course, but it hadn't been all. Because Kate had seen the whole man—with the exception of his head, the mirror having cut off his reflection at the neck. But then, she already knew what Lord Wingate's head looked like, so what did she care about that? It was what she'd seen below his neck that she found impossible to stop thinking about.

His back had been to her, but the mirror had reflected everything she might otherwise have missed. Nothing was left to the imagination, from that broad expanse of chest, covered thickly all over with crisp dark hair; the flat, copper-colored nipples hidden within that hair; the firmly ridged abdominal muscles along his flat stomach; the concave indentations on either side of his smooth white buttocks; even the thick patch of hair between his legs, from the center of which hung that appendage that had Kate so thoroughly convinced artists throughout the ages had been sadly lacking in worthy models.

It was the sight of the *whole* man to which Kate kept returning in her mind's eye—and now even in her dreams—despite her efforts to expurgate all memory of it. A few quiet hours of reading to the invalid Isabel had done nothing to drive it from her head. Even as she was pronouncing Mr. Dickens's words, she kept thinking, *Why, his shoulders were every bit as big as I imagined.* And, *I suppose I shouldn't wonder at his thighs looking so very strong. After all, he rides every day. I wonder if he fences, too. He certainly* looks *as if he might.*

Several times, Isabel had to call for Kate's attention, and point out to her that she seemed to have skipped a page. Which, in her distraction, it appeared she had.

"Are you quite all right, Miss Mayhew?" Isabel wondered.

"Certainly," Kate replied, too quickly. "Why do you ask?"

"You don't seem at all yourself. Your cheeks are very pink."

Kate pressed her hands to them. Her fingers did, indeed, feel refreshingly cool against her hot face.

"Oh," she said. "It's nothing. It's quite warm this evening, and the windows are closed against your catching a greater chill."

"Perhaps you are becoming ill, as well," Isabel said, sounding quite delighted at the prospect. "Oh, and then I shall have a chance to nurse you, Miss Mayhew. Won't that be excellent fun?"

Kate found the idea of being nursed by the Lady Isabel Traherne highly amusing. But she managed to keep herself from laughing, and only said, "How very charitable of you, my lady."

Still, later, before she climbed into her bed, Kate looked at her reflection in the mirror, and thought that Isabel was correct. Her cheeks *were* flushed, her eyes unnaturally bright. *Bright with newfound knowledge*, Kate thought wryly to herself. How was she ever, she wondered, to look Lord Wingate in the face again, knowing as she did how his chest hair fanned out in a wide furry arc across where he was broadest, then tapered down as it neared his belly, thinning to the merest ribbon of hair beneath his navel, before flaring out into a thick nest between his thighs? How was she ever to sit across that vast plane of a dining table and attend to his polite attempts at conversation, while picturing him as she'd seen him last? How was she to keep herself from thinking of the smooth tanned skin stretched so taut over the swell of each of his biceps, or the obvious strength, so tightly controlled, of his broad back?

Impossible situation!

And now a few hours later—though it seemed only minutes to Kate, who, despite the disturbance of her thoughts, had fallen asleep almost as soon as her head hit her pillow—she'd awakened feeling as hot as if she'd been running, and almost as out of breath. Her bedclothes were twisted about her sweating body, and she had, she saw, flung off her nightdress at some point during the night.

But none of that was as disturbing as her dream—or the fact that when she'd taken inventory of her limbs after waking, she'd found that hand tucked between her legs.

Even more horrifying was the fact that, when she hastily jerked that hand away, a throbbing tenderness remained where it had been. Worse, the tenderness turned to an ache with every passing second she did not return her hand there.

Sitting up, her hair falling in sticky tendrils about her shoulders, Kate shook her head, trying to clear it.

Then something struck her windowpane, and Kate almost shrieked in surprise.

The glass didn't break, but when another projectile rattled against it a second later, she realized that it was this sound that had awakened her in the first place. Her first thought, given the hour and the time of year, was bats. Her second, more rational thought was, *Why, someone is throwing stones at my window!*

And she instantly leapt up to see who that person was.

It was only at the last possible minute she remembered the fact that her nightdress lay in a puddle by one of her pillows. She flung it over her head, then went to another window which, due to the warm weather, she'd left open.

All three of her windows looked out toward the back of the house, over a small garden that contained not only well-tended and beautiful flower beds, but also a gazebo and a small fish pond, complete with a fountain. It was a restful place to enjoy breakfast or casual tea, and Kate had taken to spending no little amount of time there when her charge had no need of her.

Which was why it didn't come as a complete surprise to her when she leaned out and saw a fair-haired man standing to one side of the small pear tree by the gazebo. It wasn't surprising, but it was unnerving, to say the least. Kate, having spied him, immediately drew away from the window, her heart thumping unevenly.

Because, of course, though she couldn't clearly make out his features, she assumed it had to be Daniel Craven.

Well, who else could it have been? All of her other acquaintances—well, her *only* other acquaintance, Freddy—would have contacted her in the traditional manner. Who but Daniel Craven, uncertain of his reception after her reaction when she'd run into him that night all those weeks before, would have reason to throw pebbles at her bedroom window? How Daniel had known the window was hers, or even how he had happened to find his way into Lord Wingate's London garden, she didn't stop to think. All she could think, as she stood there, clutching the neck of her nightdress, her mouth gone dry, her heart stuttering, was that he had found her. He had found her out.

And it went without saying that now that he'd found her, he'd find a way to ruin her, somehow.

She could not say how she was so certain of this. After all, her own personal dealings with Daniel Craven had always been pleasant ones—up until, of course, the day he'd run off with all that money.

And the night of the fire, of course.

What did he want? What did he want from her? There had been a time—very brief indeed, and seven years ago—when she, as well as several of her friends, had rather admired her father's handsome young business partner, and had giggled about him with one another. And at the time, Kate had fancied that Daniel, flattered by her schoolgirl crush, had quite enjoyed flirting with her.

Was that why he had sought her out again? Did he think that, seven long years later, he could take up flirting with her again, as if nothing had happened?

If so, he was in for a shock. Kate had not only ceased admiring him, she suspected him, in her weaker moments, of being her parents' murderer. . . .

That could not, she told herself, be what he wanted. Daniel Craven was a manipulator, and what possible use could she be to him now? She hadn't any money, not like seven years ago. Was it possible he planned on duping Lord Wingate, the way he'd duped her father, and hoped to be able to use her to do so?

Well, if that was what he was thinking, he had something else entirely coming. . . .

Another stone rattled against the glass, this one louder than the others. Kate started at the noise, thinking it was bound to wake other members of the household . . . even Isabel, right next door. What could she do? If Lord Wingate found out, he would have no choice but to sack her. It didn't do for one's daughter's chaperone to have gentlemen paying midnight calls. . . .

Another stone smacked against the window, this time with enough force nearly to break the glass.

That was it. She hadn't any choice now. If she didn't go down and see what he wanted, he'd wake the entire house. Swallowing hard, Kate turned around and went to fetch her peignoir and slippers. Flinging both on, she opened the door to the hallway and looked out. No one was about, of course. It had to be after three in the morning. With any luck, she'd be able to get rid of him, and get back to bed before anyone awoke. . . .

There were two sets of doors leading out into the garden. The first was in his lordship's library, the second in the breakfast room. Kate used the library door, since it was the first she came to. Though the entire house was dark, she hadn't needed a candle, since enough moonlight shone through the windows to light her way. She moved past the gloomy shadow that was Lord Wingate's desk, and unlatched the French door that led to the garden steps. She could see the fair-haired man quite clearly now through the panes of glass, and what she saw caused her to hesitate.

Because, of course, it wasn't Daniel at all, but. . . .

"Mr. Saunders!"

Kate stood in the moonlight, her hands on her hips, glaring down at the young man who, even as she watched, was drawing back his arm to launch another volley of pebbles at her window. Startled at the sound of her voice, he dropped the stones, and stared up at her.

"Miss . . . Mayhew?" he whispered. "Is that you?"

"Of course it's me."

Her relief was like cool water on a hot summer day. *It isn't Daniel Craven,* was all she could think. *Thank God, it isn't Daniel Craven at all.* Her heart returning to something like its normal rhythm, she berated herself for having thought it was Daniel Craven in the first place. Daniel Craven had no reason—no reason at all—to seek her out, and wouldn't. Not ever again.

Geoffrey Saunders, on the other hand. . . . Now, what was *his* reason for this midnight visit?

Kate came down the stone steps to the garden, her diaphanous robe billowing out behind her like a lace-trimmed sail. "Mr. Saunders, what in heaven's name do you think you're doing?"

He gaped at her. He was a handsome man, but gaping, he looked as foolish as anyone.

"I. . . ." he stammered. "I. . . ."

"If you're looking for Lady Isabel," Kate said, keeping her voice low, "I must say your aim leaves something to be desired."

He looked up at her windows. "Oh," he said, recovering himself somewhat. "Did I get the wrong room, then?"

"You most certainly did." Kate might not have been so short with him had she not initially mistaken him for Daniel Craven—and he had not happened to wake her from the particular dream she'd been having at the time his pebbles struck. As it was, however, she was now in an extremely impatient state of mind, and not in any mood to be trifled with by handsome young ne'er-do-wells.

"Mr. Saunders," she said imperiously. "I confess myself ashamed of you. How dare you come sneaking onto Lord Wingate's property in the dead of night, like some kind of thief?"

He grinned at her, a bit foolishly, but charmingly, nonetheless. He was a very charming young man.

"What can I say?" He shrugged his broad shoulders. "I am a man in love, Miss Mayhew. I throw myself upon your mercy. It's been nearly a week since I last heard from her. Am I forgotten, Miss Mayhew? Am I to be cast aside like a soiled glove?"

Kate snorted. "You'd have done better to have confessed to drunkenness, Mr. Saunders. Spare me your poetic meandering. The Lady Isabel has been abed with a cold for the past five days."

His face lit up. "A cold? The deuce you say, Miss Mayhew. Oh, it was good of you to let me know, and not lead me on, as other women might have." His grin grew crooked. "I told

you we'd make an excellent team, you and I, Miss Mayhew."
His blue eyes roved over her peignoir. "And might I add that
I find your current ensemble simply smashing. It's too bad
you didn't wear *that* to the baroness's. You'd have had to beat
all the fellows off with a stick."

Kate thought about slapping him. Instead, she coldly folded
her arms across her chest, since it appeared to be her décolletage toward which his gaze was straying. She had had inserts
sewn into all of her ballgowns, but it had never occurred to
her that anyone might see her in her nightclothes, and that
they would ever be considered too daring for a chaperone.

"Mr. Saunders," she said. "Leave this property at once. If
I ever hear of you attempting to contact Lady Isabel in such
a manner ever again, I shall go straight to Lord Wingate."

"Not, I hope," Mr. Saunders said, "dressed as you are. Otherwise, I fear Lord Wingate would be quite as incapable as I
am of attending to your words. . . ."

"Perhaps," Kate said, lowering her arms, her cheeks flushed
hotly, "you'll attend to *this*, then."

On the word "this," she trod as hard as she could upon the
young gentleman's foot. And since she happened to be wearing slippers with a pointed heel, she had the satisfaction of
seeing Mr. Saunders gasp and seize his booted toes.

"Consider that, Mr. Saunders," she said, with as much
haughtiness as she could muster, "just a sample of what you're
likely to receive from Lord Wingate, should he happen to hear
of your behavior here tonight. More likely he'll put a bullet
in that thick skull of yours, and I, for one, shan't weep a drop
at your funeral."

She spun around and headed back up the steps to the French
doors. Behind her, Mr. Saunders hopped about, keeping from
crying out with pain with an effort that must have cost him
plenty. Once Kate was safely indoors again, the latch secured
against his following—had he been of a mind to do so—she
watched his painful writhing for several moments. She wanted
to believe that she had instilled enough fear of Lord Wingate's
wrath in him that he would climb back over that garden wall
he'd evidently scaled. On the other hand, a desperate man did

not always make the wisest choices. She would keep watch, she decided, until she was certain he was going away. . . .

It was just then that Kate heard the knob to the library door turn. She whirled around, and a second later, Lord Wingate, holding a candelabrum, strode into the room.

Chapter Fifteen

ord Wingate," Kate said, when her tongue came unglued from the back of her throat, where it had flattened itself the moment she'd seen him come through the door.

Lord Wingate threw her a startled glance. He had not seen her, and Kate realized belatedly that she might have escaped unnoticed, if only she'd kept her mouth shut.

On the other hand, if he had noticed her, and she hadn't yet made her presence known, he might have thought she was trying to hide something.

Which, indeed, she was.

"Miss Mayhew?" Lord Wingate's vision, unlike her own, was not accustomed to the moonlight, and he had to hold the candelabrum aloft before he could make her out, standing before the French doors. When he did so, his eyes widened perceptibly, and his hand fell away from the doorknob, which up until that moment he'd still been holding.

"Miss Mayhew," he said, in a tone of such astonishment that it almost seemed to suggest that, despite the fact that she'd been an inmate in the house for the past several weeks, he had never actually considered that a possibility might arise wherein they would encounter one another by chance within it. "What . . . ?"

Are you doing in my library at three o'clock in the morning, was how he'd undoubtedly meant to finish that question. He was, however, obviously much too surprised to go on, and could apparently only stand there and stare at her. It was, of course, an awkward meeting, considering how they were dressed, Kate in her peignoir, and Lord Wingate in a dressing gown. But Kate couldn't help thinking that her employer's extreme incredulity was quite out of proportion for the situation. After all, it was not as if she were *naked*.

This thought, of course, reminded Kate of the last time she'd seen Lord Wingate, and this, in turn, caused color to flood her face. Good Lord! Her dream! She'd quite forgotten her shameless dream. And here they stood, the two of them, in a library—not the same library they'd stood in during her dream, but a library just the same. Worse, they were wearing a good deal less clothing than the last time they'd stood together in a library. No wonder the man was so flummoxed— although he couldn't have had the same dream, nor could he have known about hers. . . .

Kate, realizing with a start that her employer was waiting for an answer of some kind from her, said the first thing that came to mind, which was, "My cat."

Lord Wingate looked, if such a thing was possible, even more perplexed. "Your cat, Miss Mayhew?"

She remembered herself, and replied, as lucidly as she was able, which was not very, "Yes, my cat. I heard cats fighting in the garden, and I thought Lady. . . ." Her voice trailed off as she remembered she'd never told Lord Wingate her pet's ridiculous name, and that there really wasn't any reason for her to do so now. She cleared her throat. "I thought my cat might have gotten out."

In the glow cast from the candelabrum, Kate saw Lord Wingate's dark eyebrows lift. It had never occurred to her before, but she realized suddenly that her employer had a slightly diabolical look about him, with his dark complexion and sharp features. When he raised his eyebrows in the candle-light, she was put in mind of paintings she'd seen of Lucifer.

"And?"

Lord Wingate's commanding voice shook her from her

imaginative musings. "What?" she stammered stupidly.

"And," Lord Wingate said, with an impressive degree of patience, "was . . . it . . . your . . . cat?"

Kate glanced over her shoulder, and had to stifle a groan. The idiotic Geoffrey had actually sat down upon a stone bench, pulled off his boot, and was scrutinizing the toes she'd trod upon, looking, she hadn't any doubt, for breaks. Fool! Did he *want* to have his head blown off? Because that was surely what would happen if the Marquis of Wingate found him there. . . .

"Oh," Kate said with an airy laugh, turning her face away from the glass panes. "Oh, no, it wasn't, after all. But what"— she moved away from the French doors, hoping to distract Lord Wingate's attention from what was going on just outside them—"brings you to the library at such a late hour, my lord?"

The marquis's gaze, as she'd hoped, followed her. He was staring at her as warily as if he was convinced she was demented, and might at any moment make a sudden dash for a fire iron, with which to skewer him.

"I came down," he said cautiously, "because I was having trouble sleeping, and the book I'm currently reading was not proving particularly . . . restful."

"Oh?" Kate, still not comfortable about his proximity to the garden, sidled up to him, and glanced at the book he'd removed from the pocket of his dressing gown. "Oh, *Last of the Mohicans*. Yes, I can see what you mean."

Lord Wingate's gaze seemed riveted to her face—a fact which Kate, under the circumstances, did not mind a bit. He cleared his throat. "I'm having a bit of trouble getting into it. I can't seem to get much past the preface."

Kate wrinkled her nose. "Preface? What are you bothering with the preface for?"

It seemed to her that Lord Wingate looked more astonished than ever upon her uttering those words. But, convinced she now had him thoroughly distracted from the French doors, she didn't care if he thought her a plebeian for eschewing prefaces. In fact, she reached out and took the book from him, saying kindly, "What you need, my lord, is something to put you to sleep. And you know, I have just the prescription. Where do you keep the *s*'s?"

He continued to stare down at her. His eyes, in the candle-light, looked greener than ever. "The what?"

"The *s*'s." She pointed at the book-lined walls. "They are arranged by author, I assume?"

"Oh." He nodded toward the wall to the right of the fire-place. "Over there."

"Excellent." Kate thrust her hand into the crook of his el-bow—a bold move, certainly, but under the circumstances, a necessary one, she thought—and began to steer him in that direction. He did not resist, and Kate began to think that the evening might possibly end without a murder after all.

"Let me see," she said, squinting at the titles before them, which were stacked on shelves that ran from floor to ceiling. "Hold the light a little higher, would you, my lord?" He com-plied instantly, and she said, "Oh, that's better. Now, what have we here? *Sab*, *Sal*, *Saw* . . . Ah, here we are. *Sc*. Way up there. Oh, dear. I see we shall have to do some climbing."

She took her hand from his arm, and reached for the wheeled ladder, which someone had left conveniently close at hand. Passing Lord Wingate his copy of *Last of the Mohicans* with a polite, "Will you hold this a moment, please," Kate lifted the hem of her nightdress and began to climb the bottom rungs without further consultation.

"Miss Mayhew," Lord Wingate said, in some alarm, hastily tossing the book away and reaching for her elbow. "Miss May-hew, I assure you, I am perfectly capable of finding my own reading material—"

"Oh, I don't mind, my lord," Kate said. From her new, lofty position, she sent a furtive glance through the arched window above the French doors, and saw, to her relief, that Mr. Saun-ders had pulled his boot back on, and was currently occupied in adjusting his hat. Stupid man. She turned back to the books before her. "I'm not a bit afraid of heights," she assured her employer.

"I can see that," Lord Wingate said, very dryly. He had not let go of her elbow, only she was so high up now that he could only hold on to it with some effort. "Nevertheless, I would feel a good deal better if you would allow me to—"

"Ah." Kate found what she was looking for, and pulled it from its place on one of the higher shelves. "Here we are." She held the book at an angle so that he could see the title from where he stood upon the ground. "*Ivanhoe*," she said. "Sir Walter Scott. Guaranteed to put anyone to sleep. The bits with Rebecca are good, but everything in between is just one terrific yawn."

"Yes," Lord Wingate said, a bit impatiently. "I've read it, Miss Mayhew. Now come down from there, before you fall down."

Kate glanced once more toward the garden. Mr. Saunders, she saw, was gone at last. She sighed with relief. Why she should have tried to protect that silly boy, she hadn't the slightest idea. But if it got about that the Marquis of Wingate had shot his daughter's lover in his London garden, she knew better than anyone how the gossip-mongers would never stop wagging their tongues, and there was enough tongue-wagging about the marquis already. . . .

Not, of course, that Kate cared a whit what anyone said about her employer. It was his daughter she was thinking of. Whatever wrongs her father may have committed, Isabel should not have to suffer for them. It wasn't Lord Wingate's welfare Kate was thinking about at all.

Or so she told herself.

"All the better," she said, beginning to climb back down the ladder. "That you've read it before, I mean. It will put you to sleep the sooner that way."

"Thanks very much for your concern," Lord Wingate said. His grip on her elbow tightened. "Do watch your step, Miss Mayhew, you nearly trod upon your . . . er . . . robe just then—"

"Oh, but I didn't," Kate assured him lightly.

And then she very promptly did, and completely lost her footing.

She made a grab for the upper rungs, but since she didn't want to drop the book, which looked to her like an original edition, and therefore quite expensive, she could not reach out with both hands, and missed. Her heart flew into her throat, and she had just time enough to think, *Well,* this *is embarrassing. I do hope I don't land with my nightdress up over my head,* since of course she wasn't wearing anything beneath it, before she fell.

Only she didn't fall. Because at the last possible minute, Lord Wingate thrust aside the candelabrum, and caught her.

The silver candleholder fell, with a loud clatter, to the parquet. The impact doused the flames. Plunged suddenly into darkness, Kate had to wait a moment for her vision to adjust to the much subtler moonlight filtering in from the windows. Not that there was much to see. After all, her face was pressed up against Lord Wingate's chest—the same chest that, some hours before, she'd stood dumbly admiring when she'd seen it reflected in a mirror. Now, up close, it proved ten times as interesting. True, she couldn't see, but she was all too capable of *feeling,* and what she *felt* was every bit as appealing as what she'd seen.

Lord Wingate was wearing a dressing gown, it was true, of a rather sturdy satin. And beneath it, he appeared to be wearing some sort of shirt of an equally soft fabric. Neither garment was particularly thick, however, and Kate could feel through them the hair which she'd seen carpeted the marquis's chest.

And it was every bit as crisp as it had looked in the mirror. Not only that, but beneath it, she could feel the steady beat of his heart. It was slamming against the wall of warm muscle she could also feel beneath her cheek, muscle that was every bit as hard as it had looked. The arms that she'd been revering for so long were around her, keeping her aloft, but also proving with the restrictiveness of their embrace that they were every bit as strong as she'd suspected. Why, he was holding on to her as if she weighed no more than an eiderdown.

And that wasn't all she felt, either. Because if she moved her leg—ever so slightly—she could feel, through the thin material of her peignoir, the long line of the marquis's thigh—just as hard and unyielding as it had looked to her in the mirror. But just beyond that thigh, slightly farther to the left, was something that wasn't anywhere near as hard as the rest of him. She knew because she'd accidentally brushed her leg against it when she'd been struggling to find a foothold, not yet aware that the marquis had a firm hold on her.

And yet this soft thing gave off an amount of heat that was astonishing, since she could feel it all the way through the material of both their nightclothes. The only thing hotter, really, than this appendage, was Lord Wingate's breath, which she could feel on her forehead. She looked up, finding that she could see better than she'd thought. So well, in fact, that she was rather startled to find the marquis's lips not even an inch or two from hers.

No sooner had she made this realization than she made another, which was that it was quite light enough in the room for her to look up into Lord Wingate's eyes.

And the moment she did that, she was lost.

Quite thoroughly lost. Because she became convinced then that he was going to kiss her. He was holding her in his arms, after all, and their bodies were pressed together quite as closely as two bodies could be. All she had to do, really, was lift up her legs and wrap them around his waist, and it would be precisely like her dream, only they weren't yet naked. . . .

Good Lord! What was she thinking? She felt heat rush into her face, and hoped the moonlight wasn't bright enough to reveal the fact that she was blushing. How could she have remembered that wretched dream at a time like this? She had to think. He was going to kiss her. She was perfectly convinced he was going to kiss her. Should she let him? There weren't any atlases about, and he knew it. He *had* to kiss her. He just *had* to.

Even as she was thinking this, a curious thing began to happen. That mysterious throbbing sensation she'd felt between her legs when she'd first wakened from her dream returned, all in a rush. Such a rush, in fact, that she felt damp there, again.

And she was not the only one affected in such a manner. The heat emanating from that area of Lord Wingate that had most attracted her suddenly rose a few degrees . . . and the temperature wasn't all that was rising. He seemed to swell against her, that part of him that seconds before she'd thought the only soft area on a body otherwise hard as rock. Now she could feel his arousal pressing solidly against her hip.

Suddenly, it appeared to Kate as if her dream had every likelihood of coming true, and for a moment, she could not decide whether or not this was something she wanted. A part of her—that traitorous part between her legs—wanted it very much. But . . .

But then it became a moot issue when Lord Wingate, without a word, set her down upon her feet and released her.

"Are you quite all right, Miss Mayhew?" he asked politely.

Quite all right? Kate's brain muzzily sorted through the words. *Quite all right?* Her body, everywhere that it had come into contact with his, seemed to be aching. *Quite all right? You were going to kiss me. You were going to kiss me, and then you didn't. No, I am not all right!*

"Yes," Kate replied. "Perfectly all right, thank you."

"You really oughtn't," Lord Wingate said, "go about climbing ladders in such an ensemble."

Kate could only blink at him. "No," she said. "I really oughtn't."

"Well." He plucked the book she was still clutching out of her fingers, then stooped to lift the fallen candelabrum. "I thank you for the reading suggestion. And now I think we had both better be getting back to our rooms. It's very late. Or early, as the case may be."

Kate could only nod dumbly, then move along when he gestured for her to go ahead. She made her way back to her room, although she didn't know how. Lord Wingate, it appeared to her, made small talk the entire way, complimenting her on the improvements he'd seen in his daughter's behavior, and asking her how she liked the house, and if there was anything she needed.

Yes, Kate replied, in her head. *You.*

"No," she replied, out loud. "Thank you."

And then she was in her own room, with the door shut, and

he was gone. She was alone—well, except for Lady Babbie, who lay curled in a ball at the end of her bed.

Moving mechanically, Kate untied her peignoir, and let it slip off her shoulders. Then she made her way back to bed, shedding her nightdress, too, along the way. Climbing back between the cool sheets, she lay there for a moment, wondering what on earth—*what on earth*—had come over her. How could she have so forgotten herself? How had she stood there—or rather, lain there, because, after all, she'd been completely supported by Lord Wingate's arms—and wanted him so very badly? He was a profligate bounder who thought nothing of breaking women's hearts. Hadn't Freddy assured her of that?

So what had she been doing, lifting her face like that, almost daring him to kiss her? Had she gone insane?

Most likely. Driven insane, actually. Driven mentally insane by the sight of his nude body. That was what had done it. She'd been perfectly all right up until this afternoon. Then one glimpse at what lay beneath those satin waistcoats and trim-fitting trousers, and calm, cool Katherine Mayhew was now a quivering mass of feminine longing.

What's more, she wasn't even very sure she *liked* him.

Well, all right. She *liked* him. But she certainly wasn't in love with him. She only wanted him.

With a disgusted sigh, Kate threw the sheet up over her head. Sleep, she knew, was going to be a long time in coming.

Chapter Sixteen

⌒

She's just lovely, my lord." The baroness lifted her lorgnette, and peered through it. "Really, quite the loveliest girl in the room."

Burke, looking in the same direction as the old woman, could only nod. It was true. She *was* quite the loveliest girl in the room. And it wasn't just this room, either. It proved true wherever they went. Inevitably, she was always the loveliest girl in the room.

"Such grace," the baroness said. "Such charm. She won't stay unattached for long, mark my words, Lord Wingate."

As if he didn't know it.

"And you know," the baroness said, "I can't help thinking, my lord, that my son, Headley, might be just the right boy for her. To be perfectly honest, you cannot accuse either one of them of being intellectuals. I highly doubt either of them have opened a book since they left school."

Burke threw the woman a startled glance, then realized, with a feeling of ridiculousness, that she had been talking about Isabel, and not Kate Mayhew. Well, and why not? Kate Mayhew, as she ought, was keeping to herself to one side of the room. A woman like Baroness Childress would hardly bother speculating over possible matches for a chaperone. It was Isabel, whirling away on the dance floor, about whom she'd been speaking all along, Isabel, whom she'd declared the loveliest girl in the room.

The woman was evidently quite mad.

Not that Burke begrudged his daughter some degree of charm. But the baroness was blind—or else he himself was mad—if she could not see that the only woman in the room deserving of such accolades was his daughter's chaperone.

"I think them," the baroness was saying, "most eminently suited. And you needn't worry, Lord Wingate, that I entertain the same old-fashioned notions as some of my less enlightened peers. I think divorce, in your case, was quite the sensible line of action."

No. It was quite definitely he who was mad.

It had been coming on slowly, this madness, but it had taken quite a firm hold over him. Why else would he be at this dreadful soirée were it not for madness? He had hired Miss Mayhew, after all, to escort Isabel to functions of this sort. So what was he doing, trailing after the two of them? It was the madness, the madness which had begun that rainy night he'd first ventured out to make sure she was not being harassed by members of his set. A useless errand, because of course all he had learned from it was that he was not the first man to have admired her. Nor was he likely to be the last.

"My husband, of course, has other ideas, as I'm certain you are aware. I thought I would venture to let drop, however, the fact that I fully support Headley in all of his ventures, and that the baron will come around to my way of thinking presently."

Burke would have thought that he'd have felt gratification that first night, upon finding his worst suspicions confirmed. After all, the entire reason he'd ventured out into that loathsome rain had been to assure himself that Miss Mayhew was not, in fact, in any danger of being taken advantage of by one of his peers.

The fact that his worst fears had been realized—that he'd had to stop not one, but two "gentlemen" from harassing her—was no reason, no reason at all, for him to have felt such unmitigated rage.

But there it had been, without question, that all too familiar sensation that if he didn't strike someone, he might spontaneously · combust. It was not simple gratification that, once again, he'd been right in supposing the worst of his fellow man. No, this had been white-hot rage, the sort he hadn't felt in ages.

And why he should have happened to feel it upon finding that Miss Mayhew was every bit as attractive to the rest of his sex as she was to him, he did not venture to wonder. Not then. Then, he'd simply told himself he was angry because she was his daughter's chaperone, and how much chaperoning could she possibly do, while she was being pursued by every randy buck in London?

"Oh, Lord Wingate." The baroness laid a hand upon his arm, as if sensing he was not lending her his full attention. "Allow me to tell you about Headley's inheritance. He's got three thousand pounds a year from my poor late father. Now, I know that isn't much, but the baron intends to settle a certain amount upon him just as soon as Headley chooses a *sensible* bride. And your daughter, of course, being eminently sensible. . . ."

Was it possible that she had been telling the truth that night, when she'd insisted Bishop was merely a friend of the family? It didn't seem to him that Katherine Mayhew was the type of woman who would ever stoop to lying. And yet it was perfectly incredible, her claim that her parents—who could only have been tradespeople, or, at the most, educators of some kind—could have been acquaintances with an earl. Burke, a marquis, had no acquaintances whatsoever outside his own circle.

The fact that he had very few within that circle, as well, did not occur to him.

And the other fellow . . . Craven, he thought he'd heard her call him. A business associate of her father's? Ludicrous. Why had she paled so upon merely being greeted by a former business associate of her father's? There was something else going on there, Burke was convinced. And he was going to get to the bottom of it. See if he didn't.

In the meantime, he flattered himself that he had sussed out the truth behind Miss Mayhew's relationship with the Earl of Palmer. Bishop was a friend of the Mayhew family, that was certainly true. But only because he had somehow insinuated himself into their circle, undoubtedly drawn there by the sight of Miss Mayhew's fetching lips.

Burke himself had done everything he could think of to distract himself from the temptation of that mouth. He had stayed, as much as he was capable of staying, away. He had spent whole days—and even some nights—at his club, which he had never appreciated before, having always possessed a marked aversion to the sort of club that would accept a man like himself.

But it kept him, at least, from being at home, where he was all too likely to run into Miss Mayhew. Miss Mayhew who, in some way he could not understand, seemed to draw him to her, the way fire was drawn to air.

About the only thing Burke hadn't tried was quenching that fire.

And it wasn't for lack of offers, either. Sara Woodhart was as persistent as ever in her efforts to win him back. And there were several other women—the wife of a certain MP, a ballerina, even a princess of questionable virtue but undoubtedly noble Russian blood—any of whom he could, at any moment, have had, any number of ways. But for some reason, he simply wasn't interested.

It was this lack of interest in the more carnal pleasures in life that worried him more than anything. Because it wasn't that he didn't want a woman. It was that he only wanted *one* woman.

And the woman he wanted was the one woman he couldn't have.

Burke was perfectly aware that even a man of his low character and wretched reputation could not go about debauching his daughter's chaperone, however tantalizing she might look in a nightdress. And that was the only reason, he was quite convinced, that he wanted her so badly. She was simply so absurdly attractive. That was all.

It hadn't anything to do with her *personally*. It was her

looks. It certainly wasn't because she was kind. Kindness was hardly considered an important character trait in young women anymore—though apparently no one had told his daughter's chaperone, since he had observed her, on numerous occasions, slipping coins or a soft word to ragged children on the street, and even, to his horror, helping the elderly with their burdens.

Nor was it her seemingly endless patience with all living things, from the Sledges—who, in Burke's opinion, ought to be shipped off to Papua New Guinea and forced to stay there—to his own child, whom he'd been tempted more than once to horsewhip, but to whom he'd never heard Miss Mayhew utter a harsh word.

And it hadn't anything to do with her manners, which were faultless—she was as polite to the other servants as she was to his neighbors, amongst whom ranked a duke.

Nor was it her engaging frankness. It certainly wasn't because she was at all times sensible and practical, and never screeched or threw tantrums, unlike every other female with whom he'd come into contact during his lifetime. It wasn't her laughter, which sometimes, especially when he was most trying to avoid her, came floating down from Isabel's room.

And it certainly wasn't because, when he spoke to her, he actually believed she was listening, or that when she replied, it was with that rarest of all things, honesty.

That he couldn't believe. Not after so many years of having been lied to, by so many women, starting, first and foremost, with his own wife.

No. It was her looks, pure and simple. Yes, he'd never before found himself attracted to anyone so small or so blond or so . . . well, virginal. But there was something about her that had made him want her more than he had ever wanted any woman he had ever known.

Most likely it was her mouth. Certainly, most days, he could not get that mouth out of his thoughts. On the other hand, the fact that she seemed to have a tendency to run about his house in the middle of the night in diaphanous, lace-trimmed wrappers and practically transparent nightdresses did not hurt, either. How he'd ever managed to keep himself from throwing her across his desk and violating her ten different ways then and there, he still hadn't the slightest clue. He must, in spite of everything, still be in possession of some shred of self-control.

But it hadn't been easy. It had taken everything he had to set her down again, after she'd landed so miraculously in his arms. When that mouth—that mouth that, from the very first time he'd laid eyes upon it, had never been very far from his thoughts—had ended up so very close to his own, he'd very nearly satisfied the wish that had, over the course of just a few weeks, become almost an obsession, and kissed her.

And she had wanted him to. He was certain of it. She'd been holding a book—a big, solid edition of something by Scott—and she hadn't even tightened her fingers on it. She'd been fully prepared to let him kiss her.

And yet he hadn't. At the last possible second, he'd drawn back, and let her go.

Why?

Because he was mad. That was all. Simply, utterly, irrevocably mad.

"And you needn't worry, my lord," the baroness was saying. "It's true we have run into some financial problems of late—well, the baron *would* invest in those African diamond mines a few years back, and we all know what happened with *that* but any amount you would settle on your daughter would, of course, remain hers. We are quite forward-thinking. Why, even the baron is beginning to come around to the idea that women are quite capable of handling their own finances . . . well, with the help of an accountant, of course."

Burke turned his head and said, "Baroness Childress."

She smiled up at him confidently. "My lord?"

"If your son—Headley, did you say his name was? Headley, then. If Headley sets so much as a foot near my daughter, Baroness Childress, I will personally rip out his liver. Do you understand me?"

The baroness paled beneath her face powder. "Lord Wingate. . . ." she stammered, but he didn't stay to hear more. He moved around the edge of the dance floor, elbowing his way through the crowd.

Because, of course, he had noticed that Miss Mayhew was no longer sitting alone. A fair-haired young man had joined her. And not, he saw, to his disappointment, the Earl of Palmer, whose face he would sincerely have enjoyed rubbing into the parquet floor beneath their feet. No, it was the other one, Craven, the one who'd distressed her so.

Burke didn't know the fellow, of course—had never even heard of him, which wasn't unusual, since Burke didn't know many people anyway, and made a habit of paying no heed whatsoever to gossip, having been the object of a considerable amount of the stuff himself—and knew he would not have as much fun frightening him away as he might have Bishop. Still, he fully anticipated having an enjoyable time intimidating the fellow, who seemed, if the amount of color that had waned from her face was any indication, to be making his daughter's chaperone very nervous, indeed.

"Oh, yes," Miss Mayhew was saying, in that curiously throaty voice of hers that seemed much too low for someone of her size, and had caused, on more than one occasion, the hair on Burke's arms to stand up. The voice did not reflect any of the unease its owner appeared, judging from her lack of color, to be feeling. "Lady Babbie survived. They found her, I understand, hiding in a closet the day the fire was finally put out."

Craven noticed him first. He said, with too much enthusiasm, "Why, hullo, there. What a surprise. Look, Katie. Your friend has joined us. Again."

"Katie" turned in her chair with surprising quickness. "Oh," she said. Suddenly, as Burke stood there watching, all of the color that had drained from her face returned in a rush, flooding her cheeks hotly. Burke watched in amazement, rendered quite speechless by the sight. He had never seen anything like it.

Kate climbed hastily to her feet, and stood twisting the silken cord to her reticule around and around one finger.

"Oh," she said again. "I . . . I . . ."

Burke ignored her—inasmuch as he was capable of ignoring Katherine Mayhew—and, thrusting his right hand past her and toward a laconically smiling Craven, said in a hearty voice, "As this seems to be becoming a habit, I suppose I ought to introduce myself. Burke Traherne, Marquis of Wingate."

Craven stuck out his own hand, grasping Burke's in a grip nowhere near as strong as his own.

"Daniel Craven," he said with a pleasant smile. "Esquire." Then, drawing his hand back again, and with a wink in Kate's direction that infuriated Burke even more than the fingers the blighter had been resting against the back of her chair, he said, "Moving up in the world, Katie? Why settle for an earl when you can get yourself a marquis, eh?"

All of the color that had blossomed in Miss Mayhew's cheeks disappeared. She appeared, for a moment, to sway a little upon her feet, as if his rudeness had physically rocked her. But before Burke could draw back an arm and send it crashing into the blighter's face, she was saying, faintly, "Lord Wingate is my employer, Daniel. I'm chaperone to his daughter, Lady Isabel."

Craven, looking from Kate's ashen face to Burke's curled fist, said, "Oh, I say. No offense meant, my lord. Katie and I are old friends. I was only teasing her a bit."

"I don't believe Miss Mayhew appreciates your teasing, Mr. Craven," Burke said woodenly. "And I know I don't. I think it might behoove you to find someone else to tease, in the future."

Craven was not a small man. He stood fully as tall as Burke, and only a dozen or so pounds lighter. In a fight between the two of them, it would be hard going saying who'd emerge victorious. Except, of course, that Burke had never lost a fight in his life, and the mere suggestion of him doing so was ludicrous. He rather hoped Craven would take that first swing, even though a fistfight in Lady Tetmiller's ballroom was hardly the best way to secure an appropriate husband for Isabel. Still, it might go a long way toward relieving some of this tension that seemed to have been building up in him over the past few weeks. . . .

But Craven didn't lift so much as a finger. Instead, he said, looking quite apologetic, "Oh, I *am* sorry. I didn't know. Please excuse me if I seemed rude, won't you?" And then, with rather fortuitous timing, he apparently spied someone in the crowd whom he knew. "Oh," he said. "There's Barnes. Do forgive me if I rush off—"

And then he did so, to Burke's disappointment.

But Kate did not look at all disappointed. She looked positively relieved to see him go. So much so that Burke could not help demanding, rather sharply, "Miss Mayhew, who *is* that man to you?"

The relief in her eyes wiped clean away, and was replaced by anxiety again a fraction of a second later.

"I told you," she said. "He was a business—"

"Associate of your father's," Burke finished for her. "Yes, yes, so you said." Realizing that was all the information he was going to get on the subject, he said, "Well, if he bothers you again, Miss Mayhew, kindly let me know."

Kate's eyes were very wide as she echoed, "Let you know? But what can *you* do about it?"

He merely smiled at her naïveté. "Leave it to me," he said.

But she was not so naïve as he supposed. "You can't kill him, my lord," she said, with some asperity.

He eyed her. "Can I not? And why not? I hope you're not going to say you're in love with him, Miss Mayhew, and could not bear to see his blood shed, when it is perfectly obvious the man frightens you witless."

"He doesn't," she said, her chin sliding out stubbornly. "And that isn't why you can't kill him."

"Oh?" He couldn't help noticing how much even a look of intractability became her. Really, considering the number of young girls in roses and lace that were flitting about the place—not to mention their elder sisters and mammas, in rubies and velvet—it did not seem at all likely that the prettiest woman in the room would be a former governess, a mere chaperone, in a simple grey silk dress, wearing no lace or jewelry whatsoever.

And yet it was undeniably true. Well, there might exist men who'd try to deny it, but frankly, Burke cared for no one's opinion but his own. And in his opinion, Kate Mayhew was the prettiest woman he had ever seen.

Which was why, that night he'd first met her, that night she'd first accosted him with her umbrella, he ought to have run, run far, far away.

"Why can't I kill him, then?" he asked.

"Because it would only cause a scandal," she said, with some impatience. "And then your daughter will have no choice but to marry Geoffrey Saunders, as he'd be the only man willing to have her."

Burke considered this while beside him Kate seemed suddenly extremely interested in the contents of her reticule, which she began to rifle through with some energy. It was, Burke realized, their first meeting since the incident in the library almost a week ago, and he supposed she was somewhat unnerved by his presence. Which was only natural, considering that she was very young, and very inexperienced. It was up to him, he supposed, to try to instill some normalcy into the situation, to let her know as far as he was concerned, nothing had changed between them.

Well, nothing much.

"I presume," Burke said, observing Miss Mayhew pull a small gold watch from her bag, and scrutinize its face rather more closely than necessary, considering the brightness of the light from the chandelier over their heads, "that Isabel is all right. She is not tiring herself out by dancing too much?"

"Oh, no." Miss Mayhew dropped the watch back into the depths of the bag, and, still without meeting his gaze, replied, "She is quite well. The surgeon declared her perfectly cured this afternoon. I'm afraid she's back to worshiping Mr. Saunders up close, rather than from afar."

"I see," Burke said.

He wished she would look him in the eye. He couldn't stand this accursed awkwardness. If only he hadn't given up

on *Last of the Mohicans* that night. If only he'd stayed in his
room. He'd have never encountered Miss Mayhew in her
nightclothes, and he'd never have known, as he did now, that
the corset she was currently wearing was a needless frivolity.
Her natural waist was slender enough on its own. And that
those breasts, hidden now beneath all that silk, were, though
small, as close to perfect as any he'd ever had the privilege
of seeing. And he'd not only gotten a fairly good look at
them—really, what kind of chaperone went about in virtually
transparent nightwear?—but he'd felt them through the fabric
of his dressing gown. Her nipples, hard as little pebbles, had
seemed to burn holes through the black satin lapels of his robe.
How they might feel against the palm of his hand was a question Burke had been asking himself ever since.

Kate, who had found a loose thread on one of her gloves,
was now apparently using it as an excuse to avoid his gaze.
Was she angry with him? Or merely embarrassed? Was it possible he had been flattering himself when he'd fancied she'd
wanted him to kiss her?

But she'd never been kissed before. He was as certain of
that as he was of her virginity. What Burke wasn't certain
about was how, precisely, one proceeded to seduce a virgin.
He didn't want to frighten her. There was no use, of course,
thinking back to how he'd managed it with Elisabeth, since,
of course, he had found out on his wedding night that Elisabeth hadn't been as virginal as one might have expected, considering the fact that she'd worn white, after all, to the
ceremony.

Burke said, coming to a sudden decision, "Miss Mayhew,
all I'm saying is that if that man—or any other—bothers you,
I will be more than happy to see that he puts a stop to it."

She stared up at him in the manner of one who is quite
convinced a companion is mentally deficient.

"Lord Wingate," she said. "I told you. Mr. Craven is nothing to me, merely an old family—"

Burke ground his teeth. He couldn't help it. "That may be
true," he said. As he stooped to speak into her ear, since the
room was so noisy, he could barely hear himself think, Burke

couldn't help but notice that Miss Mayhew's ear was quite a charming one, very small and quite clean, like the rest of her. "But I believe his intentions toward you are a little more than friendly. . . ."

Before she could open that delightful mouth to reply, someone had begun tugging on his sleeve.

"Lord Wingate?" a familiar voice asked.

He shook his head, not willing to let his conversation with Miss Mayhew be interrupted, however intent the rest of the world might be at doing so. But the woman at his elbow persisted.

"My lord?" More tugging. Then the soft, inviting, "Burke?" that he'd heard her utter so many times, generally from the middle of a tangle of sheets and pillows.

He felt his blood go cold in his veins. What was *she* doing here? Surely she hadn't been invited. She did *not* belong at a debutante ball. On the other hand, some hostesses were so desperate for their parties to be perceived as a success, they invited just about anyone who might be remotely construed as society.

Even actresses.

"Aren't you going to introduce me to your new little friend, Burke?" Sara asked, her voice dipping to a kittenish purr, as she snaked a hand through the crook of his arm.

Burke looked down at her. Sara was, as always, exceedingly well made up, and exquisitely dressed. One could hardly believe, to look at her, that underneath that generous bosom— much of which was on display just then—there beat a heart that, she kept insisting, in letter after letter to him, was permanently broken by what she insisted was his cruel desertion.

Burke did not, in fact, believe it. And in answer to her question, he gave a curt, "No," and removed her hand from his arm.

Sara blinked her kohl-rimmed eyes, looking wounded as a fawn. It was a look she'd perfected by practicing it for hours on end in front of a mirror. Burke knew, because there'd been a time when he'd delighted in watching her do it.

"Lord Wingate," she said, her voice now sounding childishly hurt. "Is that any way to treat an old friend?"

Before Burke could reply, Miss Mayhew said, "No, of course it isn't, Mrs. Woodhart. But you see, I'm not Lord Wingate's new little friend. I'm Miss Mayhew, his daughter's chaperone."

Although the hurt left Mrs. Woodhart's beautiful face, it was replaced by a new emotion. Burke recognized it as suspicion. "Oh," she said knowingly. "The *chaperone*."

"I saw a poster of you as Lady MacBeth a few months ago, Mrs. Woodhart," Kate went on to say. "Which is how I recognized you."

"Indeed," Sara said. Both of her eyebrows were raised, stretched to their limits. This was not a good sign, Burke knew. It meant she was going to say something impertinent. To spare Miss Mayhew, and avoid any embarrassment to himself, he quickly reached out, and seized the actress's plump upper arm.

"Mrs. Woodhart," he said, with some desperation. "May I have the pleasure of this dance?"

"Certainly, Burke," she said.

But Burke did not manage to steer her away quickly enough, because as they stepped out onto the dance floor, Sara said, in an insinuating tone, "Well, I can see now what's been occupying all of *your* time these past few weeks, Burke."

Kate heard, of course. Everyone heard. That was what Sara wanted. She considered herself the injured party, no matter how many times Burke pointed out that she was the one whom he'd caught with another. He had always prided himself on the fact that all of his past relationships—with the exception of his marriage—had at least ended amicably. His breakup with Sara Woodhart, however, was destined to be an acrimonious one.

Just how acrimonious, however, he hadn't anticipated. Not until the crack of her outstretched hand striking his face, seconds after he'd informed her, as they waltzed, that there was no longer any place for her in his life, and that if she ever spoke to him again at a function he was attending in the company of his daughter, he would personally see to it that, whatever particular production she happened to be in at the time, all its financial backing would be dropped.

Most of the guests, and most likely the hostess, saw the slap, or at least heard it, and everyone saw Sara storm from the ballroom, the skirt of her gown swaying angrily from side to side as she walked.

Including, of course, Kate Mayhew.

Chapter Seventeen

~

$\mathcal{G}$eoffrey," Isabel said dreamily, from the corner of the carriage she was slumped in, "says he has something to ask me, Miss Mayhew."

Kate, seated in her own corner of the carriage, said nothing. Her mind was too full to attend to Isabel's prattling.

"Did you hear me, Miss Mayhew?" Isabel leaned forward a little. "I said that Geoffrey says he has something to ask me."

"Mr. Saunders," Kate corrected her automatically. "Addressing young men by their Christian names is vulgar, unless they are related to you."

"Fine, then. *Mr. Saunders* says he has something to ask me, Miss Mayhew."

"Well," Kate said. Her mind was full, it was true. One might even say she was troubled . . . perhaps even deeply troubled. But it wouldn't do, she knew, to let her charge know that. And so she asked, "Why didn't Mr. Saunders ask his question tonight then, if it was so important? It wasn't as if he hadn't the opportunity. How many dances did the two of you have?"

"Four," Isabel said, in the same dreamy voice.

"Well," Kate said again. "Then he had plenty of opportunity. Sometimes I can't help thinking young Mr. Saunders is a bit lacking in intellect."

Isabel took not the slightest offense at this slander against her love. "I suppose," she said, "he didn't ask me tonight at the ball because he wanted a more romantic atmosphere. Lady Tetmiller's was sadly lacking in that, don't you think, Miss Mayhew?"

Kate did not reply right away. The atmosphere of romance—or lack thereof—at Lady Tetmiller's was hardly foremost in her mind. No, it was what had happened directly before they'd left the ball that Kate could not get out of her head: the memory of Daniel Craven, who'd left her alone for the whole of the evening after Lord Wingate's warning suddenly stealing up and seizing her hand, then dragging her behind a pillar and asking, worriedly, "Katie? Is everything all right? I got the feeling from Lord Wingate that perhaps. . . ."

She'd been more prepared this time than she'd been an hour before, when he'd come toward her from out of nowhere and begun chatting amiably about their mutual acquaintances. This time she did not even pale, but said, calmly tugging on her shawl, which she'd collected already from the cloakroom, "Everything is fine, Mr. Craven. Only I wish—"

"Mr. Craven?" He had looked crestfallen, and had plucked up one of her hands to squeeze. "I remember a time when it used to be Daniel."

Looking down at their joined hands, Kate had said, "I remember that time, too, Mr. Craven. But that was some time ago. Before the fire, remember . . ."

"Blast the fire," Daniel had burst out vehemently. "Can a bloody fire have changed things so much, Kate, that you don't have time anymore for your old friends?"

She'd blinked up at him in astonishment. "But of course it can, Mr. Craven," she'd said. "The fire changed everything. You ought to know that. You were there, after all."

Daniel had dropped her hand as if it, like her past, had suddenly burst into flames.

"What do you mean?" he'd asked too quickly, his pale eyes fixed to her face. "What do you mean by that? I wasn't there, Kate. I wasn't anywhere near—"

Kate hadn't heard the rest of what he'd said, because Isabel had begun calling for her, frantic over the apparent misplacement of a glove. But now, jolting along in the carriage home, Kate could only wonder at herself. Why on earth had she said that about his having been there that night? What could she have been thinking? He hadn't been there. He *hadn't*.

"Well," Isabel said, bringing her back round to the present. "Well, Miss Mayhew? Don't you agree with me? About Lady Tetmiller's being so lacking in romantic atmosphere?"

Kate, recovering herself, said with a laugh, "Romance? I'm hardly qualified to answer that question, being, according to you, far too old to entertain any hope a man might ever want me."

"Oh," Isabel said, waving a hand airily. "I know of at least one man who wants you very much, Miss Mayhew. But we're talking about me, now. I believe Geoffrey's going to ask me to marry him."

"And what," Kate inquired, "does he propose the two of you will live on? Moonbeams and morning dew? Mr. Saunders owes far more money than he makes, you know."

"I shall simply have to convince Papa to pay off his debts," Isabel said, with a shrug. "And then the two of us will start fresh."

"Your father would far sooner approve your marrying a Papua New Guinean than Geoffrey Saunders," Kate said.

Again the airy hand wave. "I shall take care of Papa. I expect he'll do whatever I say after that embarrassing scene tonight."

Kate looked pointedly out the window of the chaise. "I don't know what you mean," she lied.

"Oh, Miss Mayhew, don't pretend you didn't see it. Mrs. Woodhart slapped him hard enough to be heard all the way to Newcastle. I've never been so mortified in all my life. I mean, really. All my friends think he said something lascivious to offend her."

Kate couldn't help glancing over at her charge, her eyebrows raised. "Lascivious?"

"Yes. Isn't that a delicious word? I learned it from one of your books. I forget which one."

Kate turned her face back toward the window. "I'm sure,"

she said, after a moment's silence, "that they only quarreled. Mrs. Woodhart is an actress, and is probably prone to dramatic gestures like the one tonight. I'm certain there wasn't anything *lascivious* involved."

"They weren't quarreling," Isabel said knowingly. "Papa dropped her months ago. He hasn't had a mistress since you came to stay with us, Miss Mayhew."

Kate pretended to be absorbed in admiring a passing barouche. "How you come to know these things," she murmured, "I will never understand."

"Oh, that's simple enough. Duncan told me."

Kate shook her head. "You shouldn't be listening to servants' gossip, Lady Isabel. You know better than that."

"Oh, pooh. It's perfectly obvious to everyone in the entire house, if not all of London by now, that he's in love with you, Miss Mayhew."

Now Kate had to tear her gaze away from the window and stare, horrified, at her charge, while color flooded her cheeks. "Lady Isabel!" she cried, her voice cracking.

"Well, it's true." Isabel, looking a bit like Lady Babbie after catching a particularly fat mouse, curled up on the seat opposite Kate's, and all but purred. "Surely you've noticed how he avoids you when we're at home. But then he pops up wherever we go, sure as clockwork. He can't help himself. I believe he wakes up each morning and says to himself"—she performed an uncannily accurate imitation of her father's deep voice by dropping her own several octaves—" 'I shall be certain to avoid Miss Mayhew today.' But then by evening, all his resolve is gone, because you really are irresistible, Miss Mayhew. Like chocolate."

Kate said, with all the sternness she could muster, "Lady Isabel, you *must* stop teasing. It isn't respectful of your father, and it is unkind to me."

Isabel ignored her. "Even Mrs. Cleary said something the other day. She said, 'It's not like his lordship to miss his supper. But I don't believe he's been home for it these past three months.' And three months is how long *you've* been here,

Miss Mayhew. He's avoiding you, probably because the very sight of you sends him into a frenzy of lust."

Kate, realizing that the more she protested against this subject, the longer Isabel was going to continue to worry it, said only, "Wherever did you pick up *that* phrase? It certainly wasn't from any book of *mine*."

"Three months is the longest Papa's ever gone between mistresses," Isabel went on. "Once he went six weeks, but that was only because of a riding injury. As soon as he was back in top form, out he went to find another one. He must really be in love with you, Miss Mayhew, or he'd have found a replacement for Mrs. Woodhart by now."

Kate said, her voice constricted, "Oh, look. Here we are on Park Lane." *Thank God.*

"Perhaps," Isabel said thoughtfully, "we could have a double wedding. You and Papa, and Geoffrey and I. Wouldn't that be lovely, Miss Mayhew? We'd be such an attractive wedding party. You and Papa look very well together, because you have such little, smiley lips, and Papa's are so big and growly."

Kate could ignore the topic no longer. "Lady Isabel," she burst out. "I hope you aren't serious. You can't possibly think a man in your father's position would ever entertain the notion of marrying someone in mine."

Isabel did not look, however, as if she were anything but serious. "Why not, Miss Mayhew?" she demanded. "It's not as if you're an actress, or"—she shuddered—"a ballet dancer."

"*Marquises*," Kate said, severely enough that she hoped it would put an end to the conversation, "*do not marry their daughters' chaperones.*"

Isabel lifted her nose into the air. "They do," she said, "if the marquis in question is my father, and the chaperone is *you*, Miss Mayhew."

The carriage pulled to a halt. Kate nearly catapulted from her seat in her haste to leave its confines—and Isabel's heartless chatter.

She could hardly meet the footman's gaze as he handed her down from the vehicle. *Good Lord*, she kept thinking. *Does*

Bates think Lord Wingate is in love with me? And in the foyer, when Mr. Vincennes came forward to ask if there was anything her ladyship required before retiring, Kate couldn't help saying to herself, *Surely Mr. Vincennes knows better than to think so!* And when she was safe in her own room, peeling off her dress, and heard the giggle of Isabel's maid from the next room, she thought, *Oh, no. Not Brigitte, too.*

Crawling naked into her bed—she had given up wearing nightdresses since the day she'd first spied Lord Wingate coming out of his bath; she invariably woke with whatever she'd worn to bed twisted about her hips, so she'd decided to make matters simpler by wearing nothing—she asked herself, for the thousandth time, why she didn't just chuck it all in and marry Freddy. Everything would be a good deal simpler if she did. True, she didn't love him, but she was beginning to think love wasn't such a pleasant thing, after all. Of course, he hadn't exactly renewed the invitation lately—their relationship seemed to have been permanently strained by the introduction of that Viennese soprano—but Kate was fairly certain Freddy wouldn't say no, if she introduced the topic.

The problem with the plan—besides Freddy's mother, of course—was that, while it would certainly *physically* remove her from Lord Wingate, it wasn't guaranteed to remove him from her mind, where he'd been dwelling, nonstop, for the week that had passed since that fateful night in the library. It wouldn't be at all fair of her to marry Freddy knowing she was in love with someone else . . . if, indeed, love was what she felt toward the marquis. Kate wasn't completely convinced "love" was the word for it. Isabel's phrase "frenzy of lust" might be more apt.

Sleep, which had become very elusive of late, came to her rather quickly that night. As usual, she was dreaming of her employer—this time, they were *both* on the ladder in the library, naked, of course—when she was wakened suddenly by a sound she recognized. Sitting up at once, she turned incredulous eyes toward the window.

There it was again. That rattle of pebble against glass. That idiot boy was up to his same tricks again. After all her threats, he was doing it again, come, no doubt, to ask Isabel that infernal "question" she'd been chattering about.

Well, he'd regret it, this time. She'd get Lord Wingate. See if she wouldn't.

Throwing back the sheets, Kate hastily pulled on her nightdress and wrapper. No sooner had she set foot into the hallway, however, than she'd realized she couldn't possibly wake Lord Wingate. It would mean a duel, since a man with the marquis's temper was highly unlikely to be satisfied with a mere verbal lashing. And news of a duel was likely to get out, and the inevitable rumors would spread like wildfire, until Kate was quite certain people would be going about saying Isabel's father had found Mr. Saunders in his daughter's room, and thrown him out the window. . . .

No. She wouldn't wake the marquis. She'd handle the situation herself. She'd give Geoffrey Saunders another reminder of just how very nasty she could become when adequately motivated.

But when she flung open the French doors to the garden steps, she found that she'd been mistaken. Not about how nasty she could be when motivated, but about the identity of the man in the garden.

For it wasn't Geoffrey Saunders at all. It was, in fact, Daniel Craven.

"Oh, there you are," he said, lowering the hand that held another fistful of pebbles he'd evidently been intending to hurl at her window. "Thank God. I was worried I'd got the wrong window."

Kate, completely speechless, could only stare at him. He must, she decided, in some distant part of her brain, be drunk. There was no other explanation for it.

"I hope you aren't angry, Kate," he said, dropping the pebbles, and brushing his fingers off upon his trouser leg. "I asked that boy, the one with whom your little Lady Isabel is so besotted, about the best way to get in to see you—past that ogre of an employer of yours, I mean—and this is what he recommended. You aren't miffed at me, are you, Kate?"

Kate shook her head—not in response to what he'd asked,

but because she could not quite believe what she was seeing. "What," she whispered hoarsely, "are you *doing* here?"

"Isn't that obvious, Kate?" He smiled at her—she could see the smile plainly in the moonlight. She knew it was a smile meant to reassure her, but all it did, actually, was send a shiver of fear up her spine. "I had to come. After what you said tonight. . . ."

She blinked. "What I said? What on earth could I have said that would induce you to do something this . . . this stupid?"

"Stupid?" He didn't look as if he liked the sound of that. The smile disappeared. Kate was rather thankful for that. "What's stupid, Kate, about my wanting to see you?"

"You can see me in the morning," Kate said. "Like a normal person, by calling at the front door. But this . . . this is madness, Daniel. I happen to need this job. You of all people should know how much I need this job. Do you want me to be given the sack?"

He seemed to relax a little. "Of course not," he said. "How could you even think such a thing? It's just that you heard him—your Lord Wingate—tonight. He doesn't seem to like me very much. I wasn't at all sure he'd let me see you the normal way. What can you have been thinking, Kate, agreeing to work for a man like that?"

Kate said truculently, "He's a very kind man, and I'll thank you to keep your opinions on the matter to yourself. And it isn't as if I had a lot of choice in the matter, you know. Some of us have to work to earn our keep. We don't all happen to own diamond mines."

He flinched as if she'd slapped him. "Kate," he said, in a voice she supposed he meant to be tender. She cut him quickly off.

"Truthfully, Daniel," she said, "I think it would be best if you left."

He looked even more hurt. "Kate," he said, spreading his arms wide. "How can you say that? We have so much catching up to do, you and I. Why, I still have never gotten to say how very sorry I am about what happened—you know, between your father and me. It wasn't true, Kate, what he told everyone about me. I mean, it's only natural you'd take his word over mine, but really, Kate, I swear I didn't take anyone's money. I don't blame him for looking for a scapegoat, but—"

Kate only stared at him coldly. "Are you suggesting my father took it, then?" she asked.

"Lord, no, Kate. I don't know what happened to it. I swear I don't. I suppose it was cowardly of me to leave the way I did, but I . . . well, it seemed the best thing to do, at the time. I've regretted it since. You don't know how much. Just like I've regretted not being there for you, you know, after the . . . well, after the fire. That terrible fire. Your father was a great man, Kate. A very great man, despite what . . . well, what anyone else thinks. You and I, Kate, know the truth."

Kate noticed that as he'd spoken, he'd been taking slow, cautious steps toward her. She, in her turn, had been backing away, until the French door was at her spine, and she could go no further.

"I think," she said carefully, "that you had better go, Daniel."

"I felt so terrible," Daniel said, ignoring her request. "I had no idea your poor father had taken things so hard. I mean, he never seemed to me to be the type to kill himself, let alone take your poor mother with him. . . ."

It was on the tip of Kate's tongue to shout at him her suspicion—the suspicion she'd harbored since that awful night. In fact, she had even inhaled, and was preparing to make her accusation, even though reason and every rational fiber in her being told her she was wrong, she *had* to be wrong, when she saw all the blood in Daniel's face drain away.

A second later, he turned around and started racing for the back wall. She couldn't for the life of her think why he'd given up so easily—or looked so frightened all of a sudden—until she felt the latch of the French door behind her move, and then heard her employer's deep voice ring out, in tones of unmistakable anger:

"*Miss Mayhew*. May I have a word?"

Chapter Eighteen

$\mathcal{M}$y lord," Kate said with a gasp, turning quickly around. "I can explain. . . ."

But she never got the chance. Her voice trailed off as she got a look at his face. The marquis had never struck her as a particularly handsome man, in the strict sense of the word, despite her attraction to him. She had never seen him looking the way he looked just then, however. While anger supposedly became some people, that certainly wasn't true of the Marquis of Wingate. His face had become a livid mask, his lips curled back into a snarl, his nostrils flared, his eyes—those jade-green eyes, which Posie had declared glowed like a cat's—in truth seeming to shine out of the darkness in which the library was swathed, since this time, he held no candle.

Kate made a noise—not a word, but a sort of gulping sound—and then, before she could entertain another rational thought, something came shooting out of the darkness that surrounded the marquis, and locked around her wrist. Too late, Kate realized that the something was Lord Wingate's hand, and that if she'd had the slightest bit of sense, she'd have followed Daniel Craven, and run for her life.

But she'd been completely distracted by the fact that Lord Wingate, though still in his evening clothes, had loosened his cravat and undone most of the buttons to his shirt, so that his wide, thickly furred chest was in plain view. Kate, standing there stupidly, had been wondering what it might feel like to run her fingers across the flat, muscular plane of his stomach, when suddenly she found herself with a closer view of it than she'd bargained for as the marquis yanked her nearly off her feet, and dragged her into the darkness with him.

Kate, who'd never before had the slightest trouble finding her tongue, seemed perfectly incapable of using it at this point. It might have been because, once she was inside the library, the marquis kicked the door to the garden closed, then took her by both shoulders, and spun her around to face him. The fury in his eyes was rather out of proportion, Kate couldn't help thinking, for the situation.

"Was that your *cat* I saw out there with you, Miss Mayhew?" he demanded harshly. "I'm sorry, but I'm afraid that excuse won't work this time. I saw him, quite clearly, so don't insult my intelligence by attempting to lie."

She stared up at him. That he'd been drinking was clear from the fact that she could smell whisky on his breath. Whether or not he was drunk was another question entirely. He didn't seem drunk. He wasn't slurring his words, nor did he seem the least unsteady on his feet. But why, then, was he behaving like a jealous husband?

"You ought to have let me know you were lonely for male companionship, Miss Mayhew," he snarled. "While I might not have Lord Palmer's devastating good looks, I'm a bit more convenient, you know, considering the fact that you needn't sneak out into gardens after midnight to meet me. My room's just a few yards down the hall from yours, you know."

Slowly, comprehension dawned. Lord Wingate thought that had been *Freddy*, not Daniel Craven, in the garden just now. He'd seen Kate speaking to a blond man and assumed . . .

Oh, dear.

Kate had just enough time to wonder, *But he's in such a passion, even if I told him the truth, would he believe me?*, before Lord Wingate, with a sound that seemed to Kate very much like a moan, dragged her forward and crushed her mouth beneath his.

Kate had spent more hours than she liked to admit fantasizing about this exact moment. But none of her dreams had prepared her for the real thing. Because in her dreams, the marquis didn't have sharp whiskers that stung the soft skin of her face. And in her dreams, the marquis's lips weren't so hard, so insistent on hers. And when, in response to this insistence, Kate relaxed her own lips so that he could do to them whatever it was he seemed so badly to want to, his tongue didn't come darting into her mouth. Not in her dreams.

And certainly, in her dreams, the marquis had never held her quite so tightly, causing her to be crushed against his unyielding chest. His hands had never roamed up and down her back and sides, stroking her through the silky material of her peignoir. And never, not even once, had one of those hands come up to close over one of her breasts.

That was the thing about dreams, though. Sometimes reality was most definitely preferable.

The moment Kate felt the marquis's fingers on her breast, her eyelids, which had drifted closed when he'd first started kissing her, sprang open. What, she wondered, is he *doing*?

The answer, of course, was quite evident, or should have been, to the dimmest of individuals. He was making love to her—hard, violent love.

And she was liking it. She was liking it quite a bit.

Kate had been kissed before. Not like this, of course. But then, nothing she'd ever experienced had been quite like this. But never had she allowed a man to touch her the way the marquis was touching her . . . never had she *wanted* a man to touch her that way. It was perfectly shameless how much she wanted him to touch her. Why, no sooner had his fingers closed over her breast, than she'd risen to her toes, and thrown her arms as far around his neck as they would reach, thrusting her nipple more deeply into his palm. And no sooner had his tongue found its way into her mouth than she was meeting it with her own. What kind of girl let a man do these things to her? What kind of girl *liked* it?

Kate Mayhew, apparently.

Oh, well, Kate thought. And then she couldn't think at all, because the fingers that had been cupping her breast moved, and suddenly, Kate's peignoir was a filmy puddle on the floor. And then *both* the marquis's hands were on her breasts. Considering the fact that he was kissing her at the same time, so deeply, so intrusively, that his tongue seemed to be intent on exploring every crevice of her mouth, she found it rather hard to breathe all of a sudden, or even to stand up, since he was so tall, and she had to rise practically to the tips of her toes just to keep on kissing him. . . .

But that turned out to be no problem at all, because Lord Wingate, apparently recognizing her distress, suddenly reached down, and, cupping her buttocks in the hands that had been cupping her breasts just seconds before, lifted her against him. It seemed only right to Kate at that point to slip her legs around his waist, since that was what she'd done in her dream.

Only in her dream when she'd done this, she had wakened before she'd encountered the extremely hard thing thrusting against the front of his trousers. Now it seemed perfectly natural to press herself against it, and she did so enthusiastically. And when doing so elicited from him another one of those sounds, halfway between a whimper and a moan, she thought that encouragement enough to do it some more.

She couldn't see, of course, where it was he was taking her, since her entire field of vision was filled with him. But when she felt something flat and hard beneath her, she realized he'd set her down upon the edge of his desk. Not, she thought, where they'd made love in her dream, but she was beginning to think her dreams terribly pallid when compared to the real thing.

Especially when the marquis, still kissing her, seemingly with no intention of ever letting her mouth alone, reached out and slipped her nightdress up over her head.

And then, much to her disappointment, he did stop kissing her. The sound of their mouths tearing apart was loud in the darkened room. Still, there was enough moonlight for her to see that he was simply standing there, staring at her, as he held the nightdress in one limp hand. She ought, she supposed, to have tried to cover herself—she was completely naked, after all. But she figured she'd already had the advantage of having seen him without any clothing, so she ought to extend a similar courtesy for him.

Besides, she rather liked the way he was staring, as if he couldn't look away. And so she leaned back against the heels of her hands, and let him look, until, with another one of those moans, he dropped the nightdress onto the floor and came back to her, this time fastening his mouth not to her lips, but on the tip of one of her breasts.

This was something Kate had not been expecting, and it caused her nearly to leap from the desk in astonishment . . . not out of offended propriety, but because of the way the heat from his mouth on her naked breast made her feel, which was unlike anything she'd felt before. The aching sensation between her legs that she'd come to recognize returned with a vengeance the moment his tongue began circling first one nipple, and then the other. Sinking her fingers into his dark hair, she closed her eyes and let her head fall back until her long hair trailed across the desktop. Really, but this was just too deliciously wicked. . . .

But that was nothing compared to how she felt when the marquis's fingers suddenly moved between her legs. Again, she nearly bolted from the desk. But he had wrapped a hand around her neck when she'd leaned her head back, and he kept her in place by kissing the column of her throat, pressing his fingers on the exact spot Kate had been pressing for nearly a week now. She was so startled by his expertise in this area, thinking she had somehow communicated this desire with her mind, that she opened her mouth to express her astonishment. But he silenced her once more with his lips and tongue, and she decided that it probably wasn't that important anyway.

What did seem important, however, was that she feel the skin on those shoulders she'd been admiring for so long. And so she reached out and ran her fingers beneath the fabric of his shirt. What she felt surprised her. His body was as strong and as hard as she'd always known it would be, but where it wasn't covered in coarse black hair, his skin was smooth, almost as smooth as her own. He seemed to recognize her curiosity, and obligingly ripped his shirt and coat off, with enough force for her to hear fabric rend.

But he didn't seem to care about that as he wrapped her in his naked arms and drew her against him for another of those sense-shattering kisses. Now what pressed between Kate's thighs was not his fingers, but the full force of his erection. She could feel it behind the fabric of his pants, straining to be set free, and it seemed to her only fair that she release it. Only she hadn't the slightest idea how men fastened their trousers. She laid light fingers against the front of his pants, looking for some sort of opening, but apparently, she hurt him, since he jerked away, and then looked down at her for a few seconds, as if she had shocked him.

She could not see his expression, since his back was to the moonlight that was spilling in through the windows and French doors. His eyes were shaded in darkness, his features cast into planes of grey and black. But there was enough light for her to see his hands move, after a moment. And then, miraculously, his trousers were gone, and when he came back to her, that part of him which had been yearning to be free *was* free . . . and singed the inside of Kate's thigh with its heat.

And then that ache Kate had been feeling—that sensation of emptiness she'd been experiencing since she'd first dreamt of the marquis—suddenly made sense. Of *course*. She ached because she needed him to fill her. And if her fingers, which she put out to touch that part of him pressing so insistently against her, did not deceive her, he was more than capable of handling the job. He should be able to fill her quite nicely.

In fact, there might be . . . well, a bit *more* than she needed there. She didn't suppose there was any way he could maybe make himself a little . . . *less*.

But when she raised her head to inquire about this possibility, his lips came down over hers again, making speech an impossibility. And then to Kate's very great astonishment, he seemed actually to *grow* in her hand. She wouldn't have thought it possible, since he'd seemed impossibly large before, but there was no denying it. The hot flesh around which her fingers was curled was actually *growing*.

And then before she knew what was happening, the marquis's hands were cupping her buttocks again, and he was sliding her up to the very edge of the desk, right up against that burgeoning flesh. He kept on kissing her, his tongue invading her mouth the same way that other part of him was invading the area between her thighs. And for a few seconds, Kate welcomed the weight of him, the width of him, the heady sense of finally, finally being filled. . . .

Until a white-hot burst of pain caused her to tear her mouth from his with a gasp and sink her fingernails into those shoulders she'd admired for so long. She had to bite her lower lip to keep from crying out.

But it was too late. She was broken. She was as sure of it as she was sitting there. He had broken her in half, and now she was probably dying. She clung to him, feeling tears spill from the corners of her eyes. She was going to die, right there, in his arms.

Well, she supposed she'd asked for it.

But then a second went by, and the pain seemed to ebb a little, and the marquis said, his breath hot in her hair, "Miss Mayhew."

For some reason, this made her laugh. Although it was difficult to laugh, with him filling her like that.

"I believe," she said, "that at this point, you had better call me Kate."

"Kate, then," he said, and lifted his head to look down at her. He must have seen the tears, since he cupped her face in his hands, and with his thumbs, wiped them away. "Beautiful Kate," he whispered, lowering his head again, until his forehead rested against hers.

Then, simply, "Kate," the third time with a note of desperation in his voice. And then, as if he couldn't help himself, as if he were trying to stop himself, but couldn't, simply couldn't, he plunged even more deeply into her. . . .

And it no longer hurt. Kate realized it all in a rush, just as his hands, still cupping her face, brought her mouth up to his, as if to silence whatever protest she might make. But she made none, not even as his lips and tongue began another one of their calculated assaults upon her senses. Because it no longer hurt. In fact, it felt good, having him inside her. More than good. It felt right, as if he were something she'd been missing all her life, and his being there made her suddenly whole.

Maybe, just maybe, she wasn't dying after all.

No, she decided, a moment later, when he began to move, slowly at first, and then with mounting urgency, within her. Definitely not dying. Unless she had already died, unbeknownst to herself, and was now ascending some kind of celestial ladder to heaven.

Because that's how it felt, his filling her so completely. Like she was heading for paradise. She'd wrapped her legs around him again, and now she held on to him as if he were the only stable thing in an otherwise topsy-turvy world, pressing herself as closely as she could to him, not letting him go, no matter how hard he thrust within her. And he was driving himself into her with no little force, using his hands to cushion her spine as he bent her body farther and farther back. . . .

And that's when it happened, that thing that had been happening to her all week, whenever she'd pressed her hand between her legs and thought of him. Only it had never happened exactly like this. No, never quite like *this*.

Suddenly, it seemed as if that celestial ladder Kate had been climbing exploded into a thousand shards of gold, and she was falling . . .

. . . but a delicious, languorous fall, with the pieces of the ladder, glowing like stars, falling with her, and landing on her, and kissing her skin all over, as if she were being brushed by thousands of angel's wings. . . .

And then she opened her eyes, and she was on Lord Wingate's desk in the library, and he, breathing very heavily, indeed, had collapsed on top of her.

A small voice inside her head said, *Oh, no.*

Chapter Nineteen

❦

"You will, of course," Lord Wingate said, from across the pillow, "give up chaperoning Isabel at once."

Kate blinked at the dark blue canopy above her head. It looked extremely far away. The ceiling in Lord Wingate's bedroom was very high, and the canopy over his bed very nearly reached it, unlike the canopy over her own bed, which came nowhere near the towering height of the town house's ceilings.

"I will?" Kate asked. "Why?"

It was a question she had been asking herself for several hours, ever since she'd realized what she'd done. But this time, she didn't mean, *Why did I just let that happen?*

"Well, don't you want to have your evenings free?" Lord Wingate asked, his voice the same lazy drawl it had been ever since the first time they'd made love, several hours earlier. "To spend with me?"

"Oh," she said. "Of course."

"There's so much," the marquis said, "I want to show you."

He was lying beside her, his head propped up on one hand, supported by his elbow. With his other hand, he kept stroking the smooth white skin over her hip. He hadn't stopped touching her in one way or another—fingering her hair, caressing her face, holding her hand—since that moment downstairs when he'd lifted his face from her neck, where he'd buried it when passion overcame him, and said, under his breath, but still audibly, "Mine."

That was all. Just that single word: *Mine*.

Not that Kate had been expecting a marriage proposal, or a declaration of love, or even a thank-you. She wasn't precisely a woman of the world, but she wasn't completely naïve.

Still, it seemed an odd thing to say. Even odder, he said it with so much savage conviction—really, the way she imagined some sort of conquering barbarian would exult over spoils he'd earned in battle. Only the Marquis of Wingate, despite the fact that he seemed fairly to exude masculinity, was not what any person would call a barbarian . . . well, not unless that person had seen him heave something—or someone—out a window.

Still, Kate did not necessarily consider herself spoils.

Not that she didn't understand why he might feel a certain amount of *satisfaction*. *That* she could understand. She was feeling a lot better herself. Well, physically, at least.

Emotionally, however, she was convinced she'd just made the worst mistake in her entire life.

Lord Wingate seemed to have no such misgivings. In fact, from the moment he'd so triumphantly declared her his, he'd begun talking, rather wildly, she thought, about their future together. A future, she quickly ascertained, in which she would no longer be in his employ as his daughter's chaperone. No, that position appeared to be lost to her forever. Now there was a new, and much better paying opening for her to fill:

That of the marquis's mistress.

"First thing after breakfast," he said, his fingers still tracing patterns on her hip, "we'll go and start looking at properties. I think I heard there were some lovely town houses for let over in Cardington Crescent. Would you like to live there?"

"Why," Kate asked, "can't I go on living here?"

"Well, because people will talk, Kate. And we don't want Isabel to find out, now do we?"

Kate looked back up at the canopy. It rather hurt her to look at him, naked as he was. He was still so powerfully attractive to her, despite the fact they'd made love . . . oh, so many times, she'd lost count. If anything, she was more attracted than ever to the marquis. For he wasn't only a highly skilled, thoroughly enthusiastic lover. He was also extremely kind—every bit as kind, it turned out, as Mrs. Cleary had sworn he was. After he'd muttered that mysterious "mine," he'd lifted Kate from the desk as gently as if she were a baby, and then carried her all the way up the stairs, to lay her, not in her own bed, as she'd thought he would, but in his.

Then the marquis himself—well, it wasn't as if he could call a servant to do it, since it was after three in the morning—had heated her a bath, and made her get in it, and tenderly washed away, with his own hands, the evidence of their crime . . . though almost as soon as he wrapped her in a towel they committed that crime again, this time in his lordship's massive bed.

Well, how was she supposed to help herself, when he kept on touching her the way he did, and saying that she was beautiful, and kissing her . . . God, how he kissed her! As if he couldn't stop himself, half the time. As if her mouth had been put on earth for the express purpose of being kissed by the Marquis of Wingate. How was she supposed to resist? How was any woman supposed to resist anything, however sinful it might be, so utterly delightful?

But this . . . this was not delightful. *This*, she felt, she could resist without any trouble at all.

She rolled over onto her stomach and said, to the ornately carved headboard, "Then you're saying. . . . What you're saying, Lord Wingate, is that I'm not to see your daughter anymore?"

"For heaven's sake, Kate," he said, lifting a strand of her long blond hair, and passing it across his lips. "Call me by my name. Call me Burke."

She said it, though it felt strange. "Burke, then. Not even to visit? Not even for an afternoon?"

But he wasn't listening anymore. The sound of his name on her lips had a stirring effect on him, and he was reaching for her again, pulling her against him to kiss her some more. Kate's mouth felt bruised by the ravaging it had already undergone that night, and yet she still couldn't bring herself to stop him, because it was something, to be kissed by him. It was certainly something.

When he let go of her, however, just so that he could look at her a little more in the candlelight, she said, "So I'm not to speak to your daughter again. Is that it?"

He said, running a finger along her throat, "Well, I hardly think it appropriate, under the present circumstances. But you needn't worry about Isabel. I'll find her a new chaperone, so that you and I"—he put both hands on her shoulders, and playfully pushed her back against the mattress—"will have our evenings free for *this*."

Kate didn't have to ask what he meant by *this*, since he showed her, by lowering his mouth to one of her nipples, and caressing it with his tongue.

Kate, staring up at the canopy again, her fingers in his thick dark hair, said, "So I'm to sit all day in my new town house, and wait for you to come see me in the evening?"

He said something that sounded very much like "Hmmm," but it was hard to tell, since he was speaking with his mouth full.

Kate said, "I should think I'd get bored. Not to mention lonely, living all by myself in a town house."

He lifted his head and smiled down at her. It was a smile that made her heart ache, it was so beautiful. Men weren't supposed to have beautiful smiles, and Kate supposed that to anyone else, Lord Wingate's would not be. But to her it was, and she had to look away, because it dazzled her eyes.

"Lonely?" he echoed. "You won't be lonely after I hire you the best ladies' maid in London. Not to mention cook, and butler, footmen, drivers. . . . I can see you, Kate, circling the park in a black phaeton, with yellow trim. Would you like a phaeton, Kate? With a matched pair of greys, to go with your eyes?"

She said, "I suppose so. I shan't have anything else to do."

"Is that what's bothering you?" He chuckled, and kissed her again. "You shall have plenty to do, young lady. I'll see to that. You have an obligation, you know, to keep me as happy as you've made me tonight, and that will be quite a time-consuming job. And as for being lonely, I shall pretend you didn't say that, since I told you I shall be with you every chance I can. But"—he touched the tip of her nose—"if it really bothers you so much, all of this boredom you're supposedly going to have to endure, I suppose I could set you up in a little shop. A flower shop, perhaps. Or better yet, a bookshop! I know how you love books. Would you like that, Kate? Would you like to own a bookshop? To be a business woman?"

She looked at him. She couldn't answer him honestly, of course. If she had answered him honestly, she would have said, "No, thank you, I don't care to be a business woman at all. What I would like to be is your wife."

But of course she couldn't say that, because he hadn't the slightest intention of marrying her. Not now. Not ever.

And it wasn't as if she hadn't known that, either. Freddy had told her months ago that the Marquis of Wingate had sworn off marriage, that he intended never again to risk his heart—and his good name—in marriage. She had known it, known it perfectly well.

What's more, even if the marquis *had* proposed, she could not have said yes. How could she?

And yet she'd still gone and done the stupidest thing— really, the stupidest thing—she had ever done. The stupidest thing, perhaps, that any woman in the world had done, ever.

And she didn't mean making love with the Marquis of Wingate. Oh, no. That was nothing.

What she'd done was far, far worse than that.

What she'd done was fall in love with him.

Stupid, stupid girl!

For years now, she'd been convinced she was incapable of falling in love. She had even doubted such a thing—love— existed. Oh, certainly, she had loved her parents, and she loved Freddy, too, she supposed, in her way. And she, like all girls, had suffered from the occasional crush, when she'd admired someone—like Daniel Craven—more than any other man in her acquaintance, for a time.

But this swoony, moony sensation Isabel was always professing to feel . . . this feverish compulsion to write page after page of dreary poetry, or worse, to compose a song. . . . No, Kate had been quite firmly convinced: other people, maybe. But not her. Not Kate. Her feet were planted too firmly on the ground. She was far too sensible, far too old at twenty-three to bother with such nonsense.

Oh, yes, certainly, it happened in books. But love? True love? Never in real life, except possibly to the very lucky. . . .

But now it had happened to her, and she didn't consider herself lucky at all. In fact, she considered herself the most unlucky woman of all time.

"So very grave," the marquis said, this time touching her lips with the tip of his finger, as he smiled down at her thoughtfully. "Such a serious expression. I don't think I've ever seen you look quite so stern before, my love. What are you thinking?"

But she couldn't tell him. She was much too much of a coward. Because she knew that if she told him that she couldn't stay with him, couldn't do what he asked, he would only try to convince her . . . and it wouldn't take much convincing, either. All he'd have to do was kiss her again. She was convinced she'd do anything in the world for his kisses.

Fortunately, she was spared from replying at all, when he said, "How stupid I am. You must be exhausted. Are you wondering if I'll ever let you sleep? Well, I will. Here." He sat up, and extinguished the candle. Then, leaning back down again, he gathered her to him, spooning his body around hers, until she lay with her back curled to his front, in a cradle he formed of his arms. "Sleep now," he said, kissing her, but this time without the intention to arouse, on the top of her head. "There's so much we have to do tomorrow, you and I, Kate."

She lay with her cheek against the silken skin that covered his bicep—that bicep she'd so admired, yet never dreamed might someday serve as a cushion for her head—but she did not close her eyes. Not even when, moments after she'd thought he'd fallen asleep at last, he pulled her even closer, and whispered her name again, and gently kissed her cheek.

Just her name. And the softest of kisses imaginable on her cheek. And yet it made Kate want to cry—silently, so as not to wake him. But enough so that tears spilled out, and she was quite certain he was going to notice the wetness on his arm, and wake up.

But he didn't. His breathing grew deep and even, and when, after nearly twenty minutes had passed, she lifted his heavy arm, to see if he would snatch her back to him, he did not, she slipped away, and padded, quite naked, since she couldn't find her nightclothes, back to her own room.

It was close to dawn, and Cook woke at dawn, to begin preparing the elaborate breakfast his lordship liked, ham and bacon and kippers and scones and coffee and cream. Kate knew she hadn't much time. She dressed hurriedly, and packed only what she could carry. She would send for the rest of her things. Lady Babbie, of course, was not the least bit happy about being stuffed into a basket, nor was she particularly calm when Kate lowered the lid of that basket down over the cat's head. But there wasn't much Kate could do about that. She only prayed no one would hear the cat's caterwauling as she made her way downstairs.

At the threshold of her room, she turned, and looked back. She had left a letter—just one letter, addressed to Lady Isabel Traherne—on the bed she hadn't slept in that night. She supposed Isabel would find it, when she came bounding into Kate's room to discuss whatever plans they had for that day. The thought caused Kate's eyes to fill again, and she quickly stepped out into the hallway, and closed the door behind her.

Out on the street, though it wasn't quite five o'clock, there were plenty of people up and about, and Kate hadn't the slightest trouble flagging down a hansom cab.

Part Two

Chapter Twenty

*B*urke sat down at his usual place at the head of the table, and reached for the newspaper Vincennes had left for him, neatly ironed and turned to the sporting pages, the only section the master of the house bothered reading. The news was generally depressing, and he preferred, for the most part, not to know it.

Only today, he felt he might actually be able to face it, and had flipped to the front page and was perusing it without the slightest qualm, when Isabel came into the room, and flopped into her chair at the opposite end of the table.

Burke waited a beat, expecting Kate, as was her usual custom, to follow his daughter into the breakfast room, and take her place in the chair at the long table's middle section. But when, after a minute passed, and Isabel, looking more particularly grumpy than she usually did of a morning, petulantly inquired why there wasn't any haddock, he couldn't help asking, "Miss Mayhew is sleeping in this morning?"

Nor could he keep from smiling as he asked it. Because, of course, it was his fault that Kate was so tired . . . his fault, and he wasn't the least sorry for it. Nor did he imagine that she was, either.

"I wouldn't know," Isabel said coldly. "Miss Mayhew's not here."

He nearly choked on the sip of coffee he'd been in the act of swallowing.

"Not here?" he echoed, when he could speak again. "What do you mean, she's not here?"

Isabel eyed the plate of haddock Vincennes presented to her with a flourish. "Precisely what I say. She isn't here. She's been obliged to leave us. No, I don't want haddock. I'll take the eggs."

Burke, the newspaper forgotten in his hands, stared at his daughter in utter perplexity. "Obliged to leave us? Whatever can you mean, Isabel?"

Isabel looked up from the eggs the butler was piling onto her plate. "Didn't she leave you a letter, then? She left *me* one."

"No," Burke said, beginning to feel a bit uneasy. "No, she did not leave me a letter."

Nor had he expected her to. When he'd awakened alone in his room, he had assumed that she'd slipped off to her own, in order to avoid inviting gossip from the staff. It had never occurred to him . . .

Well, and why should it? How could she simply have left? It was impossible!

"Oh." Isabel took a bite of eggs, made a face, and put her fork back down. "Well, in her note to me, she explained that she was obliged to leave us for a bit, as she'd just got word that a relative of hers was quite ill. Though," Isabel said, lifting her fork again, and this time using it to skewer a piece of ham, "how she contrived to get word of a sick relative before the first post, I haven't the slightest idea."

Burke glanced at his butler. "Vincennes, did any messengers arrive this morning, with a letter for Miss Mayhew?"

The butler did not look up from the tea he was pouring into Isabel's cup. "No, my lord," he said.

"What's even odder," Isabel said, "is that Miss Mayhew never mentioned having any relatives to *me*. She told *me* her only family was her books."

"Her what?" Burke said.

"Her books. She told me she hadn't anyone left in her family who was still alive, and so her books were her family. Where this sick relative came from, I haven't the slightest idea. Isn't there any milk, Vincennes? No, I don't want cream. I want milk."

Burke said, with a calmness that frightened him a little, "Did Ka—Miss Mayhew say when she expected she'd return from, er, visiting this sick relative?"

"No," Isabel said. She bit into a piece of toast. "But I don't expect it will be anytime soon. She took Lady Babbie with her."

Confused, Burke asked, "Lady whom?"

Isabel looked at him, then rolled her eyes. "Oh, really, Papa," she said. "Don't you know Miss Mayhew at *all*?"

He raised his eyebrows. Was there anything that he did *not* know about Kate Mayhew? Certainly he knew everything that was important to know about her. He knew how, when she addressed him, it was invariably with that sweet archfulness— bordering on the edge of impertinence, but never crossing fully into it—that had drawn him to her in the first place, despite the umbrella she'd been poking into his chest. How, when she raised her gaze to meet his, he could read in those soft grey irises of hers the secret promise of embers needing only the slightest stoking before bursting into flames of heat and passion. He knew how, when he kissed her, those lips, which had fascinated and bewitched him for months, fell open in the most inviting manner imaginable. And how, when he entered her, she sucked in her breath, gasping each time anew at the size of him, and yet generously taking all of him into her much smaller frame. . . .

And he knew how, when she said his name, it caused him to forget everything: everything he had ever known, everything he had ever been, everything he had ever hoped to be, except a seemingly insatiable desire to hear her say it again. . . .

"Lady Babbie," Isabel continued, thankfully oblivious to the carnality of her father's thoughts just then, "is Miss Mayhew's cat, of course. And if Miss Mayhew's taken her cat with her, well, then I expect that she'll be away for quite a while.

And I can't say that I blame her. I'm very certain you were horrid to her."

That remark shook Burke from his pleasant memories of his activities with Miss Mayhew the night before. In fact, it sent his sense of uneasiness escalating to full-fledged alarm. He shook his head, trying to rid it of a sudden buzzing sound that had begun between his ears. "*When? When* was I horrid to her?"

"Last night, of course. When you frightened away Mr. Craven, and then shouted at her for it. But it wasn't *her* fault he came throwing pebbles at her window, the way he did."

"Mr. Craven?" Burke threw down the newspaper and stood up, leaning his fists upon the table, for fear he might use them for something else. "Daniel *Craven*? What the devil has *Daniel Craven* to do with any of this?"

"Papa," Isabel said, shaking her head until her black curls swayed. "You know perfectly well. I heard the whole thing. Those pebbles he was throwing woke me, too. But really, she told him straightaway to leave. You know she doesn't like him, Papa. I'm sure it was very wrong of you to shout at her the way you did. He couldn't have been up to any good, slipping round here like that—"

"*Daniel Craven?*" Burke kept his fists exactly where they were. Otherwise, he was quite certain he might put them through the back of his chair. "That was *Daniel Craven* in the garden last night with Miss Mayhew?"

"Yes, of course," Isabel said. "Who'd you think it was?"

Abruptly, Burke felt as if all the marrow left his bones. Either that, or his skeleton had suddenly turned to jelly. He sat down quickly, because for a moment, he was quite convinced he was going to fall down.

Daniel Craven. Daniel Craven. All this time, he'd thought it was Bishop who'd been out there in the garden with Kate. But it hadn't. It had been *Daniel Craven.* He'd accused her . . . well, he wasn't certain exactly what it was he'd accused her of. That part of the evening was a bit of a blur. But he'd accused her of doing something, and of doing it with the Earl of Palmer.

When all the time, it hadn't been Bishop at all. No, not at all. It had been Daniel Craven, a man whose very glance, if Burke wasn't mistaken, terrified her to the core. And he'd had the blockheaded audacity to accuse her of—

Not that she had blamed him for it. That much he did remember. No, she hadn't resented the implication, or even mentioned it again, once he'd started kissing her. . . .

But he'd accused her of something. Something dreadful. Something of which she was perfectly innocent.

And now she was gone. And no wonder.

"You needn't look like that, you know," Isabel said.

He blinked at her. She was sitting with one elbow on the table, her chin balanced in her hand, stirring her tea with a silver spoon as she gazed at him, a kind smile on her face—the kindest smile Burke had ever seen on his daughter's face.

"I'm quite certain that whatever you said last night to Miss Mayhew," she said, "she'll forgive you, Papa. Some mornings, I'm perfectly horrid to her, and she's always forgiven *me*."

Burke found he had no reply to make to that. What could he say? He felt as if someone had just reached into his chest, pulled out his heart, and tossed it to the floor.

And up until the night before, he hadn't even been aware he still *had* a heart.

"Miss Mayhew will be back soon," Isabel said confidently. "After all, she left her books."

But Miss Mayhew did not come back soon. Certainly she did not come back that day. Nor did she send notice of where she'd gone, or any word of explanation as to how long she'd be obliged to stay there. All day, Burke waited at home for the post. And each time Vincennes presented him with the silver salver containing the mail, there was no letter, nor even a note, from Kate Mayhew.

Nor did the post bring any word the next day. Or the next.

It was then that Burke, who had been baffled and hurt before, began to grow angry.

He did not know why he was angry. After all, it was not as if Kate had stolen from him, or betrayed him by running off with some other man. No, nothing like that. She had merely disappeared. Disappeared without a word, and after a night such as the one they had spent together. A night such as Burke had never experienced in his life, and he was a man who was no stranger to such delights.

But never, never in his thirty-six years, had he spent such a night as the one he'd spent with Kate. How any woman could simply walk out after having spent a night like that, he could not fathom. He could not fathom why she had left, or what he could possibly have done to drive her away. Certainly he'd been wrong about Daniel Craven—stupidly, idiotically wrong. But she'd forgiven him that. He was quite certain she'd forgiven him that the moment their mouths had met. So why? *Why*?

He had been, he was convinced, the most careful of lovers, conscious all the time—well, all right, not *all* the time. But *most* of the time, after that first initial thrust, that thrust that he'd felt destroy the thin fabric of her maidenhead—of her inexperience, her innocence. He had, he felt, exerted iron self-control, keeping even his climaxes, the most powerful he had ever known, in check, as much as he was able, for fear of either hurting or frightening her. She was so very young, and so very small, he'd been afraid of breaking her.

And yet, incredibly, that delicate vessel, which he had lifted as easily as one would lift a child, and held aloft with a single arm, had contained a spirit more genuinely sensual, more passionate, more giving, more *everything,* than any woman he had ever known.

And now she was gone, in spite of the pleasure they'd shared, in spite of the care he'd taken, even in spite of his offer of a town house and carriage, even—what could he have been thinking?—his promise of purchasing for her a bookshop. Never had he been so generous with any of his other mistresses.

But never, it had to be admitted, had he felt this way about any of his other mistresses. Or even, truth be told, his wife.

It was on the fifth day of Kate's absence that Burke summoned the servants to him, and quizzed them, one at a time, on the chaperone's possible whereabouts. But though their concern for the missing young woman was quite genuine, not a single one of them could tell him where Miss Mayhew might have gone. No, she had never mentioned an ill relative in their presence. In fact, she had stated quite plainly that all of her family was dead. Burke's next move was to send Mrs. Cleary to the Sledges, and put to them—and to their servants—the same questions. It was absurd, he knew, to go canvassing the neighborhood for news about one of his own staff, but he did not see any other way to go about it. Cyrus Sledge might think it strange, but Burke didn't give a whit what Cyrus Sledge might think. All he wanted was to find Kate Mayhew.

He did not, of course, wish to alarm his daughter, and so he kept from her, as best he was able, his concern over her chaperone's disappearance. And Isabel, quite preoccupied with her romance with Geoffrey Saunders, only periodically said things like, "I do wish Miss Mayhew would hurry up and come home. I've got so many things to tell her," and "If only that horrid relative of Miss Mayhew's would hurry up and die so she could come back to us." The only thing for which Burke could be grateful was that in Miss Mayhew's absence, Isabel had not much interest in attending the dozens of functions to which she'd been invited, and did not ask her father to accompany her. It was no use, she said, going to balls without Miss Mayhew to help her with her hair. Geoffrey would quite go off her if he happened to see what a rat's nest was growing on her head.

It was on the tenth day after Miss Mayhew's abrupt and mysterious departure that Burke was pacing the upstairs hallway, and happened to pass by the door to her room, and notice that it was open. There were sounds of activity from within it.

With a myriad of emotions in his chest—relief that she was finally home; bitter outrage that she'd left him so coldly; and a certain amount of salacious delight at the prospect of once again hearing his name pronounced by those adorable lips—he stepped into the room, but saw only Mrs. Cleary there with one of the footmen, lowering Kate's books into a crate. At the sound of his footstep, Mrs. Cleary looked up, and then, incredibly, blushed. Burke, who had never before seen the old woman blush, could only stare.

"Oh, my lord," the housekeeper said, all in a rush. "I'm so sorry if we have disturbed you."

He stared at the crate. He stared at the books in the footman's hands. He stared at the blush on his housekeeper's face.

"Where is she?" he asked.

He did not shout it. He did not hit anything as he said it. He merely asked it, in what he considered a quiet, reasonable voice.

"Oh, my lord." Mrs. Cleary rose from her knees, and, wringing her plump, dimpled hands, cried, "I only just received the letter this morning. I would have shown it to you straightaway. . . ."

He said, again in what he considered an utterly calm voice, "Yes?"

To Mrs. Cleary, however, he did not evidently sound so calm, since she hastily thrust a hand into her apron pocket, and drew out a piece of foolscap.

"Here it is," she said, hurrying toward him. "Right here. It's not from Miss Mayhew, you see. But it does say she does not believe she will be able to return to London anytime soon, and begs to inform you, my lord, that you had best engage a new chaperone—"

Burke took the letter from his housekeeper's fingers and perused it.

"I only hesitated to tell you, my lord," Mrs. Cleary went on, "because I knew how much it was going to upset poor Lady Isabel. She was so very fond of Miss Mayhew—and I'm quite sure the feeling was mutual. Miss Mayhew never had a harsh word to say for my lady, and you know, my lord, as well as I do how she can be . . . trying. Well, young girls are trying, I suppose, by nature. But I've never seen anyone improve as much as Lady Isabel improved once Miss Mayhew came to stay. Almost like she was a different person."

But Burke had come to the part of the letter where an address was given, to which Mrs. Cleary was asked kindly to send the remains of Miss Mayhew's belongings. He stared at this address for nearly a full minute while Mrs. Cleary chattered on.

"Lady Isabel's going to take this news very hard, I'm afraid," the housekeeper went on. "Very hard, indeed, my lord."

But Burke hardly heard her. Because he had already turned around, and was heading out the door.

Chapter Twenty-one

The maid who answered the door stared very hard at the card Burke presented to her.

"Lord Wingate," she said, "to see Lady Palmer. Yes, my lord. I'll just go and see if her ladyship is in."

Then off she scampered, her apron strings flying behind her. Burke, left standing in the morning room, briefly entertained the thought of tearing the house apart, stone by stone, until he found her. But he thought that might not ingratiate himself to his hostess.

A door was flung open a few minutes later, and an elderly, but by no means frail, woman entered the room, her neck and hands heavily bejeweled, her gown a season out of date. But then, when one had reached one's seventies, fashion was not necessarily one's primary concern.

"Lord Wingate," the Dowager Lady Palmer said, coming toward him with only the lightest taps of her ivory-handled cane. "I hardly believed my eyes when Virginia handed me your card. You have some gall, young man, to come paying social calls this late in the game. You are still in disgrace, you know, from polite society, for divorcing that pretty young wife of yours. Some bootlickers might be willing to forget such an affront, especially when it happened so long ago. But not me. I consider divorce a sin, young man. A mortal sin. I don't care how many lovers she had."

Burke's lips parted. What came out from between them was more of a growl than anything else.

"*Where is she*?"

"Where is who?" The dowager waved her cane at him. "I don't know what you're talking about."

"You know very well what I'm talking about." Burke thought he would have liked, despite the woman's age and sex, to wrap his hands about her wobbly neck and choke her to death. "Katherine Mayhew. I know she's here. I've seen the note instructing that her things be sent to this address. Now I demand that you let me see her."

"Katherine Mayhew?" The dowager looked geuninely shocked. "Can you be so stupid as to think, just because I receive a man like yourself, who is as base as base can sink, that I would admit to my home the daughter of the man responsible for driving my husband into an early grave? You must be mad, Lord Wingate. You certainly look it. I've never seen any gentleman look quite so scruffy as you do at the moment. How long has it been since you shaved?"

He said only, "I know she's here. If I have to, I will rip this place apart until I find her. But I will find her."

The dowager snorted. "We shall see about that. Virginia! Virginia!" The pretty maid poked her head in. "Fetch Jacobs at once. I want this madman removed from my house."

No sooner, however, had the maid closed the door, than it opened again, and the Earl of Palmer strolled in, looking annoyed.

"What's all the infernal shoutin' about, Mother?" he demanded. "I can hardly hear myself think." When his gaze fell upon the marquis, his eyes widened.

Burke did not hesitate. He was across the room like a shot, his fist plunging into the younger man's face with all the force of a blow from a blacksmith's hammer. The earl went down, taking a small table, and the vase of flowers that had been sitting on it, with him. The dowager screamed, then promptly joined her son upon the floor in a dead faint. But Burke paid not the slightest heed. He reached down and seized Bishop by his lapels, then dragged him back to his feet.

"Where," Burke demanded, giving him a shake, "is she?"

But the earl had only been dissembling unconsciousness. He swung round his right fist and caught Burke in the jaw with it, a full, roundhouse punch that sent the marquis staggering backward, into a sideboard filled with porcelain shepherdesses, all of which slid to the parquet with a crash.

"She isn't here, you bastard," Bishop said. "And even if she were, you would be the last person I'd admit it to."

Burke, rising up from the wreckage of the Dresden shepherdesses, threw a solid punch to the younger man's nose. It hit home, and blood flew, in a bright red arc, from the middle of Bishop's face, and onto the pale blue sofa.

"She *is* here," Burke said. He was breathing heavily by now, but he was by no means through. He might have ten years on the earl, but he was still in top fighting form. "My housekeeper had a letter from you this morning, directing that her things be shipped to this address."

"Certainly," Bishop said. He circled the marquis warily. "Because just this morning, I got a letter from Kate, asking me if I'd be so good as to allow her to keep her things here for a bit—"

"A likely story," Burke said. There was an ottoman separating him from the earl, so he kicked it out of the way. It landed in the fireplace. Fortunately, as the weather was warm, there was no fire burning in the hearth. "I imagine you'd say just about anything, wouldn't you, to keep her to yourself."

Bishop was still backing up, holding the ends of his cravat to his streaming nose. "I would," he said. "In fact, I'd say anything, if I thought it would keep a brute like you from her."

This assertion earned the earl another wallop to the head that sent him tumbling back over the pale blue sofa already spattered with his blood. Burke followed, but wished he hadn't when Bishop kicked his legs out from under him, and he landed, with a thunderous crash, on his back beside the earl.

"The truth of the matter," Bishop said, scrambling to throw himself astride Burke's prone body, and then wrap his hands around the marquis's neck, "is that she isn't here. You're mad to think it. My mother would sooner allow Attila the Hun to spoil her guest linens than Kate Mayhew."

Burke, struggling to break the slighter man's grip, paused in his efforts to ask, "Why?"

"Why?" Bishop was gritting his teeth as he tried to choke the marquis to death. "How can you ask why? You know why."

Burke, tired of the game, clubbed Bishop in the temple with his fist, knocking him against the wall, where Bishop collapsed, bleeding profusely, and breathing rather noisily. Burke, less injured, but still sore, crawled toward him, and eventually sank down to lean upon the wall beside him

It was while the two men were slumped there, attempting to catch their breaths, that a side door was flung open, and a butler, followed by two enormous footmen, entered the room.

"My lord," the butler said, after he'd taken in the wreckage that had once been his mistress's morning room. "Are you in need of assistance?"

Bishop looked at Burke. "Whisky?" he asked. Burke nodded. "Whisky, Jacobs," Bishop said.

The butler nodded and, with one last glance at the broken shepherdesses, heaved a shudder, then withdrew, the footmen following him with the dowager's unconscious body cradled between them.

"Why," Burke asked, when his breathing had grown more regular, "does your mother hate Kate?"

"You are such a fool," Bishop said disgustedly, as he dabbed at his nose with his coatsleeve. "Do you even know Kate at all?"

"Of course I know her." Burke was tempted to tell the younger man just how very well indeed he knew Kate, but decided that would be ignoble. And so he only said, "I know all I need to know about her."

"Well, I would have thought you'd look into her background a little more before you hired her."

Burke blinked at the younger man. "If you are going to tell me that Kate is a thief," he said, feeling anger, white-hot and liquid, course through his veins again, "then all I can say is, you're the one who doesn't know her at all."

"Of course she isn't a thief," Bishop said. "Her father's the thief."

Burke stared at him. "Her *father?*"

The door opened again, and this time the butler entered alone, carrying a silver tray on which rested a cut-crystal decanter filled with amber liquid, and two glasses. Observing that, in their tussle, they had overturned all the tables in the room, the butler knelt down upon one knee, and placed the tray on the floor beside the earl. Then he unstopped the decanter, and carefully poured out two fingers of whisky in each glass, handing one to Bishop, and one to Burke.

"Thank you, Jacobs," Bishop said. "Is my mother all right?"

"Fainted, my lord," Jacobs replied. "We carried her to her room, where her maid is applying smelling salts."

"Very good," Bishop said. "That is all, Jacobs. You may leave the tray."

"Certainly, sir." The butler, climbing back to his feet, left the room, closing the door quietly behind him after a final glance at the headless shepherdesses.

"Kate's father," Burke prompted, after he'd swallowed most of the contents of his glass.

"Oh," Bishop said. He sipped more cautiously than Burke, having, apparently, some loosened teeth. "Right. You mean to tell me you don't know who her father was?"

Burke leaned his head back against the flowered wallpaper. They were sitting below a window, and outside it, he heard a bird begin to sing. "No," he said.

"Well, does the name Peter Mayhew sound familiar?"

Burke said the name experimentally. "Peter Mayhew? Yes, actually. For some reason, it does."

"For some reason." Bishop rolled his eyes. "The reason it sounds familiar, Traherne, is because it was on everybody's lips about seven years ago. At least as much as yours was, a decade before that."

"Why?" Burke stared at the other man sarcastically. "Did

he divorce his cheating wife and throw her lover out the window, as well?"

Bishop looked disgusted again. "Certainly not. Peter Mayhew was a prominent London banker. He lived with his wife and daughter in Mayfair."

"Mayfair?" Burke said, his eyebrows raised.

"Yes. Mayfair." Bishop looked a bit smug. Well, as smug as a man with a recently broken nose could look. "On Pall Mall. Right next door, as a matter of fact, to this house."

"So," Burke said. He tried to tamp down an unreasonable desire to take the earl's face and grind it into the floor. "You and Kate really did grow up together."

"Correct." Bishop reached over, unstopped the decanter again, lifted it, and poured more whisky into Burke's glass. "Her father handled a number of substantial accounts, including my parents'. Eight years ago, Mayhew had the misfortune to meet a young man who claimed to own a diamond mine in Africa. The only reason, according to this young man, that he had not tapped this mine was that he lacked the financial backing to do so. I did not meet this gentleman—if he was one, which I very much doubt—but Mayhew seemed to believe in his claim, strongly enough to encourage his friends and neighbors to invest in his mine."

"Which," Burke said, "did not exist."

"Of course not. Mr. Mayhew's fine young gentleman took all of his clients' money, which included most of Mayhew's own fortune, and absconded with it. Or at least, that was Mayhew's story."

"There was reason to doubt it?"

"Let's just say there was enough reason to doubt it that several of the men who'd lost money—including my own father—felt the appropriate course of action was to take Mayhew to court."

Burke licked his lips. They tasted salty. He realized that was because one of them was bleeding. "And?"

Bishop looked surprised. "What do you mean?"

"I mean, who won?"

Bishop blinked. "You don't know? Kate didn't tell you?"

Burke inhaled deeply. One one thousand, he counted. Two one thousand. Three—

"No," he said, when he was certain he could keep himself from lunging at the younger man again. "Kate did not tell me."

"Well," Bishop said. "The case never went to trial. Because the person named in it—Peter Mayhew—died the day before it was to have begun—the trial, I mean."

"Died?" Burke dabbed at his bloodied lip with his shirt-sleeve. "In the fire, you mean?"

Bishop eyed him. "Kate told you about that, did she?"

He nodded. "She said both her parents died in it."

"That's right," Bishop said with a nod. "They did. I wasn't here that night, you know—I was away at university. But some of the servants here still speak of it. Flames shot twenty, thirty feet into the sky. It's a wonder anyone lived, but everyone did, with the exception of Kate's parents. Every single servant, and Kate herself, got out. Even that damned cat of hers survived it. The fire was contained to only one part of the house, you know—you can't see it from the street, and the new owners have done wonders rebuilding. Just Kate's parents' bedroom was destroyed. Rather uncanny that, don't you think?"

Burke knit his eyebrows. "What do you mean?"

"Well, a fire that hot, you'd expect it to take down the house, but it burned rather slowly after that initial explosion of flame. They were able to put out the flames rather handily—"

"What are you saying?" Burke glared at him. "I haven't time for games, you know, Bishop. If there's something you're trying to say, just come out and—"

"All right." Bishop made a face. "You always were a bit of a stick in the mud, Traherne. What I'm trying to say is that afterward, there was a certain amount of suspicion that the fire had been set deliberately. There was a strong smell of kerosene, more than if a simple lamp had been knocked over—"

"You're saying," Burke said slowly, "that someone murdered Kate's parents?"

"Good God, no." Bishop shook his head. "No, the feeling

at the time was that Peter Mayhew set the fire himself. To avoid the humiliation of a trial."

Burke stared at the younger man. "Suicide?"

"Well, murder-suicide, to be technical about it. I mean, I doubt his wife had any say in the matter. They found her still abed—well, what was left of the bed, anyway. It's doubtful she ever woke. . . ."

"Good God," Burke said, through lips that had gone numb, but due to neither Bishop's knuckles nor his whisky. "I . . . I had no idea."

"No." Bishop, apparently tired of sipping his whisky from a glass whose rim kept interfering with the cravat he was holding to his nose, chose instead to unstop the decanter, and drink directly from it. "You wouldn't, I suppose. It was in all the papers, but. . . ."

"I read only the sporting section," Burke confessed.

"Ah. Well, then, you'd have no way of knowing. And Kate wouldn't have told you. She never speaks of it . . . understandably, I suppose. But also . . . well, I think she'd prefer to forget it. And who wouldn't? I doubt a single one of her employers— and she's had a few—know who she is, or that there was a time when she enjoyed the very same privileges as a good many of her charges."

Burke took the decanter from him, and poured a generous amount of whisky into his mouth.

"She was never the same afterward, really. The servants found her, quite unconscious, in a stairwell, and someone carried her to safety. What Kate was never able to say was how she got into that stairwell. There are those who believe her father put her there, before even starting the fire, in order to ensure she got out. But Kate . . ."

Burke eyed him. "Yes?"

"Kate has always insisted it happened a bit differently. Well, you can't blame her, really. It can't be pleasant, the thought that your own father would kill himself and his wife simply in order to avoid some prison time—and public humiliation, of course. So Kate concocted this story that I believe, to this day, she still considers the truth of what happened that night."

"Which is?" Burke asked, though he thought he knew the answer already.

"Well, that the young man—the one who invented the diamond mine—came back in the dead of night, and set the blaze himself in order to keep Peter Mayhew from testifying. Because of course Mayhew and his attorneys were determined that they could prove his innocence, if only they could find that young man who'd run off with all the money. . . ."

Daniel Craven. Who else could it have been? What had Kate said, when he'd asked her why she seemed so discomfited by Mr. Craven? That she was put out with him for having skipped out on her parents' funeral? Lord, what a fool he'd been. She suspected him of having killed her parents. No wonder she went so pale every time he came near. . . .

And he, the great, dunderheaded fool that he was, had accused her, that night in the garden, of fraternizing—a polite word for what he'd thought she'd been doing—with such a man. The man she thought had burned her parents alive.

Burke stared at the earl. He was, he knew, quite drunk by now—it was, after all, only just noon, and he had consumed most of a quart of whisky. Still, that could not explain the maudlin thought that kept creeping, uninvited, into his brain.

"So," he said, enunciating carefully, since he knew he had a tendency to slur his words when he was this besotted. "Strictly speaking, Kate's father was not, in fact, a thief."

"No," Bishop said. "Just a fool."

"A fool," Burke said. "But also a gentleman."

"A foolish gentleman."

"But still," Burke persisted. "He was a gentleman. Which would make Kate a gentleman's daughter."

"Yes," Bishop said, after some consideration. But the word came out sounding like "yesh." "But what difference does it make? Gentleman's daughter or not, a man's got an obligation to treat a woman honorably."

Burke eyed him. "Are you saying I did not? Treat Kate honorably, I mean? Is that what she told you, in her letter?"

"No. Only that she couldn't stay in London anymore, and would I be so kind as to forward her things to her." He snatched the decanter from Burke, and took a long pull at it. "That's all I am to her, you know. An address, at which she can store her things." Then the earl narrowed his eyes. "And what, precisely, do you mean by calling her Kate? It should be Miss Mayhew to you, Traherne. Unless there's a reason I don't know about for why she quit your place so suddenly."

"And where," Burke asked, in a tone he fancied was slyly without emphasis, "does she require you to send her things?"

When Bishop lowered the bottle, he was giggling. "Do you think I'm a fool, Traherne? You think I'd tell you? Even if she hadn't stipulated—very explicitly, I might add—that I wasn't to tell you, no matter how hard you hit me?"

Burke laughed along with him. "But of course you're going to tell me," he said, "because we're quite good friends now, you and I, and you know that I only have Kate's best interests at heart."

"But you don't," Bishop said. "I know perfectly well that you don't. You have the same interest in Kate that I have. The only difference, of course, is that *I* want to marry her."

He glared at him. "How do you know I don't want to marry her, too?"

"You?" Bishop guffawed. "Marry Kate? Impossible!"

"Why?" Burke demanded, bristling. "Why is it impossible?"

"Everyone knows you swore off marriage forever, after your divorce, Traherne. Even Kate knows it."

Burke looked at him carefully. "And how precisely does Kate know it? I never told her any such thing."

"You didn't have to. I told her. I told her you would probably only debauch her and then give her the boot when you tired of her." Bishop nearly dropped the decanter as he turned to stare accusingly at his new drinking companion. "That's not why she ran off, is it? Did you debauch her, you bastard?"

Burke could think of no answer to this. He had, in fact, debauched her, although it hadn't seemed like debauchery at the time. And that was, clearly, why she'd run off. But he certainly wasn't going to admit as much to the Earl of Palmer. He couldn't, he suppose, blame the earl entirely for what had happened, since he had been an active participant, as well . . . after all, he had quite enthusiastically outlined for Kate the details for their future in sin together. When what he ought to have been doing, of course, was making wedding plans.

But how was he to have known? She had never said a word about where she'd come from. How was he to have known she was a gentleman's daughter?

That was no excuse, of course. He oughtn't to have treated any woman the way he'd treated Kate, gentleman's daughter or not. But he hadn't even entertained the idea of marriage for seventeen years. How was he to have thought of it that night?

He ought to have thought of it. If he had, he wouldn't be sitting here amidst the wreckage of a morning room, drinking whisky straight from the decanter on a Monday afternoon, wondering how a man who had no heart could be so certain his was breaking.

Chapter Twenty-two

D̶ear Lord Wingate, the note read.

Well, of course. What had he expected? That she'd call him by his Christian name? She had done that only once, and only because he'd asked her to. She wasn't likely to do it in a letter telling him why she could never seen him again.

Dear Lord Wingate, it read.

> I know you are probably angry with me, but I felt I had to leave. I'm afraid I cannot be your mistress. I would very much liked to have tried to be, but I know that I am just not cut from that sort of cloth, and should have made both of us unhappy in the end. I hope you will forgive me, and that you won't mind my sending this letter to Lord Palmer to give to you. I feel it would be far better for me if I didn't see or hear from you for a while. Please give Isabel my love, and try to make her understand why I had to leave, without, of course, telling her the truth. And do keep her from eloping with Mr. Saunders. He mentioned trying something of the sort to me once.
>
> I can only add, God bless you, and please know that I am, and shall always remain, very truly yours,
>
> Kate Mayhew

Burke, after having read the whole letter, looked up to the top of the page—hardly even a page, really. Half a page, written on a piece of foolscap, the kind that could be purchased in any village shop. Well, Kate wasn't stupid. She wasn't going to write him on a piece of hotel stationery, which might be easily traced—and read it again.

But no matter how many times he read it, the words remained the same.

No recriminations. Never, anywhere in the text, did she curse him. Nor was there any sign that she'd wept while writing it. The ink was nowhere blotched. He wondered how many drafts she'd written before settling on this one. She had cleverly kept from dropping a single clue as to where he might find her. And she never expressed the slightest hope—however unconsciously—that he might endeavor to do so.

Well. It was more than he deserved, he supposed. He hadn't expected a letter from her at all. And he hadn't quite believed his eyes when Bishop slapped it into his hand as he'd been taking his—rather bloody and drunken—leave that afternoon. In fact, he'd thought it a hastily drawn bill for all the damage he'd done to the dowager's morning room.

"It's from Kate," the earl had said, his voice muffled beneath the cloth he held to his still-dripping nose. "She sent it, along with my letter. I wasn't going to give it to you at first, but . . . well, looking at you now, I think you better have it."

Instinctively, Burke had flipped the note over, checking the seal. Bishop, still quite drunk, had let out a bitter laugh.

"Don't worry," he said. "I didn't read it. Didn't want to. Whatever the hell happened between you two. . . . Well, to tell you the truth, I just don't want to know."

Burke quite agreed with him. He didn't want to know, either. He wanted to forget. He wanted to forget everything that had happened since that foggy night he'd first encountered her. Which was why, six hours later, he was sitting in his study— not the library. He had not been able to bring himself to go into the library since the night he and Kate . . . well, that was another thing he was trying to forget.

He sat there, drinking his own whisky, reading and then rereading her letter. This activity, he knew, was not particularly conducive to forgetting her, but he could not seem to put the letter down, since it was the only thing he had of hers with which to remember her. Well, with the exception of her nightdress and peignoir, which he had rescued from the library floor before they could be found by one of the maids, and which he now kept balled beneath his bed pillows.

Sentimental? Yes. Insufferably maudlin? Quite so.

And yet he would not part with them, or the letter, for all the money in the world.

It was as he was reading her letter for what had to be the hundredth time, hoping some line in it would change, that the door to his study was thrown open.

"Excuse me," Burke rumbled, without looking up. "But I closed that door for a reason."

"And I opened it for a reason." Isabel, dressed in her evening wear, stood before him with tears glittering in her eyes. Her hair was too tightly pulled back, and then burst into some kind of explosion of curls at the back of her head. It was not a flattering look. It was not a hairstyle Kate would have allowed her to leave the house wearing.

"I walked into Miss Mayhew's room a moment ago," Isabel said, her voice filled with something that was just barely suppressed, "to return a book of hers I borrowed, and what do you think I found there? What do you think I found?"

Burke lifted his glass to his lips and drained it. Never mind. He had plenty more whisky in a bottle right at his elbow.

"She's gone!" Isabel's voice throbbed dramatically. "Papa, she's gone! The books are gone! Miss Mayhew is *gone!*"

"Yes," Burke said, pouring himself another drink. "I know."

"You know?" Isabel cried. "You *know*? What do you mean, *you know*?"

Burke said, in a toneless voice, "Miss Mayhew has found that her relative—the one that was ill—needs her more than she feels we do, and so she has regretfully tendered her resignation."

He glanced at her to see how well this lie had worked. It seemed to have gone over well enough. Isabel was pale, certainly. And tears were gathered beneath her long black lashes.

But she did not look angry. At least, not just then.

"But I don't understand." Isabel shook her head. The explosion of curls at the back of her head trembled. "Papa, Miss Mayhew had no relatives. She told me so. Who is this ill relative of hers?"

Burke sipped his drink. There was something about whisky. It numbed one so pleasantly. And when he woke in the morning with a headache, all he would need to do was drink more of it. Headache gone. If he could just ensure that a steady supply of whisky was poured down his throat, morning, noon, and night, he might be all right.

"Wait a minute." Isabel's green eyes narrowed dangerously. But he was too drunk to see the danger. At least just then.

"Wait a minute," Isabel said again. "You're lying."

Burke lifted an eyebrow. "I beg your pardon?"

"You heard me. You're lying to me, Papa. Miss Mayhew isn't with any sick relative."

Burke said, "I don't know what you're talking about, Isabel. She wrote you herself—"

"She was lying, too," Isabel declared. "No one writes in a letter that a *relative* is sick. They write 'my aunt,' or 'my cousin,' or 'my grandfather's brother's wife.' They don't say '*my relative*.' Miss Mayhew was lying, and so are you."

Burke leaned his head against the back of his leather chair, and sighed. "Isabel," he said.

"Tell me," Isabel said. "You must tell me. I am not a child anymore. I am a grown woman, practically engaged to be married—"

"You are *not*," Burke said emphatically, "practically engaged to be married. Not until *I* say you're practically engaged to be married."

Isabel said, "Fine, then. I'm not engaged to be married. But I am still an adult, and I demand that you tell me. Where is she, Papa?"

Burke studied the ceiling. "I don't know," he said simply.

Isabel's voice rose. "What do you mean, you don't know? Where were her books sent?"

"To Lord Palmer's," Burke said to the ceiling. "He's sending them on to her, wherever she is."

"What do you mean, wherever she is? You don't *know* where she is?"

He shook his head. "No, I told you that. She won't say." Then, looking at her finally, and seeing her stricken expression, he added, holding his hand out toward her, "I'm sorry, Isabel."

"You're *sorry*?" Isabel's voice rose another octave. The emotion which had been suppressed now broke through the surface, and overcame her. That emotion was, as near as Burke could tell, hysteria. "You're *sorry*? What did you do to her, Papa? What did you *do*?"

He couldn't tell her, of course. He could only shake his head some more. Then, to his surprise, Isabel flung herself down upon her knees before his chair, and let out a heart-wrenching sob.

"*You* did something," she said, pounding on his thigh with a fist. "The night in the garden, when Mr. Craven came, *you* did something to Miss Mayhew. You lost your temper. You lost your temper with her, didn't you? *You're* the one who made her go away. *You're* the one. *You* did it." She shook her head with such violence that the explosion of curls came tumbling down about her shoulders, just as tears were tumbling down her cheeks. "How *could* you, Papa?"

Burke stared down at her miserably.

"Isabel," he said. "I'm sorry. I said I was sorry."

She reached up and wiped away her tears with a bent wrist—a gesture that so reminded Burke of her childhood that he had to blink, thinking, for one drunken moment, that she was four years old again. "Of course you are," Isabel said, in a more reasonable tone. "Poor Papa." She sniffled a little, then blinked at him. "Are you very sad? You *look* sad."

What he was, of course, was very drunk. But he couldn't tell her that. Much as he couldn't tell her the real reason behind Kate's sudden departure.

"I am very sorry for you, Papa," Isabel said, reaching up to stroke him on the cheek. But she quickly pulled her hand away again, as if she had burned it. Which, in a way, it turned out she had.

"Papa," she said chidingly. "How long has it been since you shaved?"

Burke said, "I don't know."

"You are very untidy." Isabel reached up to adjust his cravat. "And how did you get that cut upon your eye? Papa, have you been fighting again?"

He shrugged. "Yes."

"You are a very bad papa," Isabel said, drawing a handkerchief from his waistcoat pocket, and applying it gently to the cut. "Very, very bad, not to take care of yourself. What would Miss Mayhew think of you, if she were to come back?"

Burke said, "She isn't coming back, Isabel."

Isabel made a sound with her tongue. "Now, Papa, you don't know that. She says that now, because she's angry with you—deservedly so, I'm sure. You can be very wicked, indeed, when you get into a temper. But Miss Mayhew loves you, Papa. Of course she will be coming back."

Burke leaned forward, and eagerly grasped her by the shoulders. "Did she tell you that? Did she tell you she loved me?"

"No," Isabel said, and then, when he let go of her, and slumped back into his chair, added, with a little laugh, "Silly Papa. She didn't have to tell me she loves you. Anyone with any sense could have seen that she did. Almost as much as you love her."

Burke eyed her from the depths of his chair. "What makes you think," he asked carefully, "that I am in love with Miss Mayhew?"

Isabel rolled her eyes. "Oh, Papa," she said. "Of *course* you love her. Everybody knows it."

"Who," Burke asked suspiciously, "is *everybody*?"

"Oh, for heaven's sake," Isabel said. She tossed the bloodied handkerchief aside, lifted the hem of her gown, and climbed back to her feet. "Are you trying to tell me you're not in love with Miss Mayhew? Because if you are, I'll be more than happy to point out to you the dozens of instances in which you made it perfectly obvious that you were, starting with the fact that you were willing to pay her so much just to get her to come here in the first place—"

"That," Burke said, hurling himself from the chair, and placing a good distance between himself and his daughter's accusation, "was because you were driving me to distraction with your constant nagging!" He raised his voice in mocking imitation of hers. " '*I want Miss Mayhew as my chaperone. Why can't I have Miss Mayhew as my chaperone.*' You left me no other choice!"

"And how," Isabel said, folding her arms across her chest, and observing him with a slight smile upon her lips, "do you explain the fact that after you hired her, you continued to attend all of the balls and parties you'd claimed to hate so much, just so you could stand in a corner and spy on her?"

"That," Burke declared, from the window to which he'd strode, "wasn't spying. I was concerned for her safety. Miss Mayhew possessed a glaringly obvious naïveté concerning men."

"Please, Papa. Just admit it. You love her. That's why you've been going about like a bear since she left, growling at everyone, and practically snapping their heads off. That's why you haven't shaved, or washed, or even changed clothes since the morning we discovered she was gone. That's why you've been getting into fights, and drinking so much. You love her, and you know it's entirely your fault that she left, and your heart is breaking."

"It isn't," Burke said, with as much dignity as he could muster, being, as she'd claimed, unshaved, unwashed, unlaundered, and considerably drunk. "My heart cannot be breaking, because I have no heart."

Isabel rolled her eyes. "Yes, yes, I know. You have no heart, because Mamma broke it seventeen years ago. I've heard the rumors, too, Papa. Only unlike you, I do not believe them. You have a heart, and it's hurting you very much right now, and deservedly so, since I am sure you were very wicked. But Papa, I assure you, from the bottom of my *own* heart, Miss Mayhew will be back. She *has* to come back."

Burke looked at his daughter curiously. "Why?"

"Because," Isabel said with a shrug. "If she loves you anywhere near as much as I do, she won't be able to stay away."

Then, with a brilliant smile, Isabel turned, and left the room, leaving her father alone with that completely unsatisfying consolation.

Chapter Twenty-three

$\mathcal{F}$rederick Bishop, the ninth Earl of Palmer, was quite fond of his club. It was a highly prestigious club, admitting only highly prestigious individuals. Only titled peers—those of the finest discretion, and oldest families—roamed the heavily paneled halls, and partook of the roast beef luncheon. Politicians and intellectuals were strictly banned, so that the conversation never strayed from the subjects of sport, cigars, and . . . well, sport. Membership was so selective, in fact, that Freddy could take a seat in one of the deep leather chairs by the fire in the main room, and not be disturbed by a single soul for hours at a time.

For a man who lived with a woman like his mother, this was not something to be taken for granted.

Which was why he was so surprised when one of the club's staff members approached him, bowing obsequiously, and whispered, "I beg your pardon, my lord, but there is a man in the hallway—"

Freddy, conscious that he had become the recipient of a number of unpleasant looks from his fellow club members, whispered back quickly, "Well? What has that to do with me?"

"The man, my lord, insists upon seeing you. He says if he does not see you, he will light fire to the place. He has already struck down three employees I sent out to get rid of him. He is quite insistent, my lord . . . and I might make free to mention, a little drunk, I think."

Freddy, curious to see who could possibly have struck down three club employees—all of whom had been hired for their enormous girth, one of the most important functions of an exclusive club being its exclusivity—and wondering, as well, why on earth such a person should insist upon seeing him, rose from the comfortable chair in which he had been dozing, and followed the manservant to the club foyer.

There, he saw the Marquis of Wingate methodically destroying the place, primarily by lifting club employees by the throat and pounding them against the walls. Portraits of the club's prestigious founders swayed. There was a baronet crouched behind the elephant-foot umbrella stand, and a duke behind a potted fern, both apparently hoping to escape the marquis's notice.

"For heaven's sake," Freddy said disgustedly, as Traherne lifted a six-foot-two footman and tossed him over a banister. "Is it really necessary, Traherne, for you to make a scene everywhere you go?"

The marquis looked up.

"Good Lord," Freddy burst out. "Is that even you, Traherne? You look utterly wretched. Put that boy down, and step in here—" Upon noticing the startled expressions of the club employees, Freddy said sourly, "Yes, yes, I know 'im. You wouldn't believe it to look at him now, but he's actually a marquis, and usually quite a bit better groomed. Put 'im in here, and for God's sake, one of you fetch some whisky."

The Earl of Palmer's orders were quickly carried out. Burke was escorted into a small private office, where club members usually sat to draft their monthly checks to their stewards, mistresses, and cigar-makers. There, Burke was directed to take a seat, which he did, feeling suddenly rather exhausted. The sofa was a leather one, and very soft. It seemed to envelop his body, embracing him in its buttery confines. Burke told himself not to give in to the couch's comforting embrace. It was all a ruse, no doubt, to get him to forget his purpose in being there.

"Here, now," Palmer said, after messing about with a bottle and some glasses one of the cretinous club waiters had brought in. "Drink this down."

Burke looked suspiciously at the balon the earl held out toward him. "That's not whisky," he said.

"No, it's brandy. But what in the hell do you care? It's still alcohol, old man. And you look as if you need it rather badly."

Grudgingly, Burke took the oversized goblet, into which had been poured only the tiniest amount of liquid, and pelted it down. Brandy. Oh, yes. He'd had brandy before. He used to have brandy quite a lot, as a matter of fact, back before his life had become a blur of whisky hangovers. A reassuring warmth rose up from his gullet.

Well, Bishop had been right about one thing. It was still alcohol. He held out the empty glass.

"All right, all right." Bishop refilled the balon. "Not so fast, now. They charge me by the bottle, you know, and this stuff's twenty years old."

Burke downed more of the stuff, feeling it burn a familiar path down his throat, straight to his gut.

"I hope you don't mind my saying so, old man," Bishop said, taking a seat in the leather chair opposite Burke's couch, "but this bursting into places and throwing people about is getting rather old. I thought we'd settled all this, anyway, last time we saw one another. What was it, two months ago now, wasn't it? You'll see the old proboscis has recovered nicely." Bishop turned to give him a profile. "You notice the lump, of course. Everyone notices the lump. But you know, I rather like the lump. I think my face was frightfully feminine, you know, before you broke my nose. Really, Traherne, you did me a favor. Rather disappointed to see I wasn't able to cause you any permanent scarring whatsoever. But you look wretched enough that I'm willing to overlook it." He took a sip from his own balon. "So. I assume you're going to tell me why you're here. Only don't, I beg of you, ask me to tell you where Kate is. She still hasn't given me leave to say."

"She's gone," Burke said. And as he said it, he felt as if his heart constricted to half its usual size inside his chest. It was as if some kind of internal fist kept gripping him round his vitals, and squeezing. Squeezing until he hadn't any air to breathe, or blood to his head.

Bishop cleared his throat. "Well, of course she's gone, old boy. We went over that last time we saw one another, you know."

"Not Kate." Burke spoke in short, grunting bursts. It was the only way he could get out what he had to say without knocking anyone's face into the wall. "Isabel."

"Isabel?" Bishop's jaw dropped. "*Lady* Isabel? Your daughter?"

"No." Burke flung himself from the too comfortable couch, and strode toward the hearth, upon which a merry fire was crackling, although it was not cold outside . . . at least, insofar as he'd been capable of feeling the weather. "No," he said again, with barely suppressed rage. "Lady Isabel the dancing ice monkey, you fool. Of course my daughter. She's gone. She's left me."

Bishop let out a low whistle. "They seem to do that a lot on you, don't they, old boy? Leave, I mean."

A second later, he regretted both the whistle and his flippancy, when the marquis seized him by his coat lapels and hauled him out of his seat and up into the air.

"You're going to tell me," Burke said, enunciating carefully, so the earl would understand, "where she is."

Bishop's feet were several inches off the ground. He looked down at them regretfully, as if he missed the floor. "Uh, Traherne," he said, enunciating just as carefully as the marquis. "How in hell would I know where your daughter ran off to?"

"Not Isabel," Burke said shortly. "Kate."

Bishop coughed. "But, um, really, Traherne, I don't see—" He broke off with a strangling noise as Burke tightened his grip.

"She's run off." Burke's voice was now nothing more than an extremely menacing growl. "Isabel's run off with that bastard Craven."

"*Craven?*" Bishop burst out. "*Daniel* Craven?"

"You know any other?"

"But—" Bishop shook his head, truly flummoxed. "What about Saunders?"

What *about* Saunders? Even as he stood there holding two hundred pounds of earl in midair, Burke was traveling back, in his mind's eye, to the night before, when Isabel had confronted him in his study. He'd been slumped before the fire, as had become his nightly custom, a glass of whisky in his hand, a bottle of the stuff placed at a convenient distance from his elbow. He'd heard her step on the threshold, but he hadn't thought to prepare himself for the confrontation that was to follow.

Isabel had been nothing if not sympathetic during the weeks that had gone by since Kate's cruel—that's how Burke perceived it, anyway— desertion. He'd expected her to utter some soft words of encouragement, or maybe suggest, as she had once or twice, that he get his hair cut. He had not expected her to launch into him as if he were an errant message boy.

"Drunk again," Isabel had said in disgust when she'd come close enough to get a look at the bottle, which was very nearly empty no matter, though, since Vincennes would bring him another whenever he rang for it.

"Is this," his daughter demanded, "how it's going to be from now on, then? You're going to drink yourself to death? Is that the plan?"

He looked up at her through bloodshot eyes. "That," he said, "is all I've come up with so far. Do you, perhaps, have some other suggestion?"

"Yes," Isabel said. "Actually, I do. Why don't you get up off your ass and go look for her?"

Burke eyed her disapprovingly. "Don't," he said, "use language like that in my house."

"Or what?" Isabel, dressed to go out, shook her head. "What will you do to me?"

"Turn you over my knee."

Isabel laughed. It was not a pleasant laugh. It was quite scornful, as a matter of fact.

"I should like to see you try," she said. "I doubt you could lift a mouse, in your present condition. When's the last time you ate a decent meal? Or got some fresh air?"

Burke only scowled into the fire. There was no use, he knew, in telling her that to him, all food tasted like sawdust, and that the air, indoors and out, smelled fetid. Instead, he said, "I'm still whole enough to cut off your allowance."

"Certainly you are," Isabel agreed dryly. "But I'll only go through your wallet the next time I find you insensible from drink. Which, if the level of what's in that bottle there is any indication, should be in about a quarter of an hour."

"Isabel," Burke said impatiently. "What do you want? Is it money you want? You're going out, I take it."

"Indeed, I am. By myself, I might add. I've become quite the scandal of the season, going about chaperoneless, as I have been recently, thanks to you."

"Thanks to yourself," Burke corrected her. "I am not the one who spent three months throwing myself at that young jacka—"

"Do not," Isabel said, holding up a gloved hand, "disparage Geoffrey. I am perfectly aware of your feelings toward him."

"Are you? And yet why do I get the feeling that you are still seeing him, behind my back?"

"Come out with me tonight," Isabel said, "and see for yourself. I think you'll be happily surprised. I no longer have an interest in simple little boys like Geoffrey. I think you'll be pleasantly surprised when you see who I'm keeping company with now."

Burke looked at her. She did not look as well as she had back when Kate had been supervising her wardrobe and hair. Left to their own devices, seventeen-year-old girls sometimes made ill-advised fashion decisions. Tonight's was a fringe of frizzed hair over Isabel's forehead that had not been there, near as Burke could remember, last time he had seen her. It might have been all the rage as far as London coiffures went, but on Isabel, it looked ridiculous. He wondered if it was her real hair, and was tempted to reach up and tug on it. But that, he decided, would require too much effort.

Quite like going out.

"No, thank you," he said, and turned back to the fire.

"Oh!" Isabel cried, with a stamp of her slippered foot. "Really, Papa! What's happened to you? I remember a time when you would not sit idly by and allow a woman to treat like you this. I don't understand why you simply don't go to her and—"

"Because," Burke interrupted, through gritted teeth. "I don't know where she is."

"Oh, and a man of your wealth and connections hasn't the means to find out?"

He hissed, to the fire, "I fail to see the point in searching for her, when she's made it perfectly clear she doesn't care to see me again."

"Papa, she was angry when she wrote that. I am sure, now that she's had time to reflect, she doesn't still feel the same. She's probably sitting there, wherever she is, thinking *you* don't care to see *her* again."

"And," Burke said, taking a healthy sip of whisky, "she'd be perfectly correct in thinking so."

"No she wouldn't. If Miss Mayhew walked through the door right now, Papa, you'd fall down and kiss her feet." Isabel tugged on her glove with a disgusted expression on her face. "Though I highly doubt she'd think much of you, seeing you as you look now, so untidy and scratchy-faced. And I wouldn't blame her. You've turned into a perfect beast. Why, Daniel says—"

"Daniel?" Burke peered at her through his murky, alcoholic haze. "Who is *Daniel*?"

"Daniel Craven, of course," Isabel said.

Suddenly, Burke was on his feet. And suddenly, he did not feel a bit drunk. And he wasn't mooning over Kate anymore, either. Anger had a delightful way of taking over, and making everything else seem to matter very little, when compared to the object of one's wrath.

"You go near that man again, Isabel," he said, "and I'll snap your neck in two."

"He's not what you think, Papa," Isabel insisted. "He's not what Miss Mayhew thought, either. Why, he's everything that is perfectly charming. He's just dreadfully misunderstood. Why, he's quite sorry for—"

"You're not to go near him," Burke raged. "You're not to speak to him, or dance with him, or so much as *look* at him, do you understand?"

"I don't need your permission to see him, Papa," Isabel said coldly. "I'm of age. If I wanted to, I could marry him. And we needn't worry about posting any banns, either, not when all we have to do is cross the border and—"

He took a quick step forward. He had never in his life struck his daughter, and he had no intention of doing so now. But she didn't know that, and she stumbled backward.

"Isabel," he said menacingly. "I'm warning you. If you go near that man again, I'll kill him. First him, and then you."

Isabel tossed her head. "Daniel said you would react this way. I told him he was wrong, but it appears now that he was quite correct. I think you are being too horrid for words. I love him, Papa, and I am going to marry him, with or without your permission."

He came as close to hitting her as he had ever come. What he hit, instead, was the window, and what he hit it with was the whisky glass he'd held. The glass in the window shattered first, and then, a few seconds later, the whisky glass broke, as it struck the street below. Isabel, who had ducked, straightened, then stared at him. The look she gave him was one he would never forget, no matter if he lived to see a hundred. It was a look of utter contempt, mingled with such abject pity, that Burke felt as if someone had sunk a fist into his gut.

"Isabel," he'd said desperately.

But it was too late. She'd turned and, without uttering another word, left the room.

He did not see her again. The next morning, Mrs. Cleary, tears streaming down her face, brought him the note. Isabel had gone, with Craven, to Gretna Green. She would return, she asserted, a married woman. And if he had any care at all to see his grandchildren, he would do nothing to try to stop them.

"I say." Bishop, who'd listened quite patiently to Burke's

abridged version of this story, while continuing to hang in midair, spoke rather dryly. "That *is* a bit rough, old man. Why don't you put me down now, and together we'll try to think this through."

Burke did set him down, and not very gently, either. "I've thought it through," he said, running a hand through his overlong hair. "And the only solution is that I've got to find Kate. Kate's got to go with me to Scotland. Isabel won't listen to me, but she'll listen to Kate."

Bishop shrugged his shoulders. Burke's manhandling of him had apparently done something to the lining of his coat. "Well, I'm sure that's true, old bean," Bishop said. "But you're forgetting one rather important thing. Kate doesn't want me telling you where she is. You do remember that, don't you?"

"But this," Burke said, "is an emergency."

"Well, I'm sure it is, old man. To you, anyway. But you have to understand, it isn't in my best interests—or, I'm convinced, Kate's—for you to find her."

Burke blinked at him. "Right," he said, through bloodless lips. "You want her for yourself."

"Well, rather," Bishop said. "I mean, she doesn't feel that way about me, of course, but given time—"

"And your soprano?" Burke asked politely, since he was not in the least interested in the earl's romantic life.

"Yes, well, she is a bit of a complication, and all of that. But Kate's a very understanding woman—"

"Not," Burke said, "as understanding as you might think."

Bishop threw him a speculative glance, and said, "Well, you might have a point there. I don't know what to say, old man. I really do feel my hands are tied. I mean, I gave her my word I wouldn't tell you anything."

Burke took a deep breath. He said, "Bishop. My daughter is an inexperienced seventeen-year-old girl. She has thrown herself into the arms of a coldhearted bastard who, at the very least, is a thief, and who could possibly have burned two people alive in their bed. And *that* is to be my son-in-law. *That* is the type of man who will father my grandchildren."

Bishop frowned. "It's hard luck," he began, but Burke interrupted him.

"Think of Kate," he said, with one last, desperate attempt to make the younger man understand. "Think of what Kate would say, if she knew. If she knew Isabel had thrown herself into the power of Daniel Craven, what would Kate say? What would Kate want you to do?"

Bishop's face, which had been wearing a slightly intractable expression, changed. He unfolded his arms and said, "By God. By God, you're right. Sorry, old bean. I'll tell you. Of course I'll tell you. Katie would never forgive me, I'm sure, if, under the present circumstances, I *didn't* tell you." He took a deep breath. "She's in Lynn Regis. Her old nanny rents a cottage there. White Cottage, I think it's called. I don't have the exact address on me just now, but if you'll wait a moment, I'll send a boy . . ."

Bishop's voice trailed off, because he found he was speaking to an empty room.

"Well," was all he could think of to say, after that.

Chapter Twenty-four

White Cottage was the last house at the farthest end of a road that seemed traveled primarily by sheep . . . which was pleasanter, Burke supposed, than most of the roads in Lynn Regis, which seemed to him to be packed with people, in spite of a storm of rainclouds that were gathering out over the sea, and appeared to be closing in on land rather quickly.

White Cottage itself was just as it was named, a pleasant enough looking structure, very much on the small side, with numerous vines of late-blooming roses crawling about it. It was beneath an arbor of these enormous blooms Burke was forced to stoop in order to cross the yard to the front door. Had he been in a less agitated state of mind, he might have stopped to admire the tidy garden and cheerful window boxes, filled with chrysanthemums and other autumnal blossoms. As it was, however, it was all he could do to keep himself from knocking the door down with his shoulder.

He did manage to pause before knocking, and run a hand through his hair. He had given in to his valet's demand that he shave before leaving London, but had eschewed the haircut Duncan had insisted he needed. There wasn't time, and it wasn't as if, he'd told himself, Kate cared how he looked. She could only hate him—quite deservedly so. And so what possible difference could a haircut make?

Except that now that he was seconds away from seeing her

again, he wished he'd at least let Duncan give him a trim.

But as this was the least of all the regrets he was carrying about with him, it was easily cast aside. He raised a fist, and thumped upon the door.

A voice—not Kate's—from deep within the cottage called, "Coming," but it was nearly a full minute before the speaker actually reached the door. A minute during which Burke kept turning and looking back at the driver of the carriage he'd just left. The driver, alert to his master's every command, kept looking questioningly back, thinking there was something the marquis wanted. But what Burke wanted, his driver could not supply.

The door opened, and an old woman, leaning heavily on a wooden stick, squinted up at him. "Oh, it's you," she said, after her milky blue eyes had taken in Burke, his overlong hair, and the chaise-and-four behind him. "You must be here for Katie."

Burke felt as if the fist, or whatever it was inside of him, had loosened a little, his relief was so great. He said, "Yes. Yes, I am. Is she here, madam?"

"Madam." The old woman smiled. It was a kind smile, made more appealing by the fact that, mercifully, she still had all of her teeth. "No one's called me 'madam' in ever so long. Hinkle's the name, you know."

Burke uttered a silent prayer that God deliver him from this old woman's presence without incident of violence.

"Yes," Burke said, trying not to sound as impatient as he felt. "Mrs. Hinkle, might I trouble you to tell me whether Miss Mayhew is at home? You see, it's very important that I—"

"Oh, it's *Miss* Hinkle," the old woman said, with a sparkle in her eye, for all she had to be half-blind. "And I'll have you know I'm still turning a head or two, young man, down in the village of a Sunday morning."

Burke felt the fist inside of him tighten until he thought his heart was going to explode from the pressure.

"Miss Hinkle," he managed to say in a normal enough voice. "Where might I find Miss Mayhew?"

"Out back," the old woman said, pointing in a direction

that might have been behind the cottage. "Taking in the wash. It's going to rain, you know. I'd have done it myself, only my foot's been acting up again, and . . ."

Her voice trailed off. Not because she'd stopped speaking, but because Burke had walked away from her, going through the garden, and then around the side of the house. Behind White Cottage was rolling field, and beyond the field, the sea, churning slate-grey and ominous beneath the approaching storm cloud. Not far from the cottage, in the middle of one of these fields, stood a gnarled and twisted tree, from which a line ran, twenty or so feet away, to another tree. From this line hung half a dozen white sheets, some pillowcases, and other linens, all of which were fluttering violently in the wind. Behind these sheets, Burke could see the slim silhouette of a woman, a basket by her feet. Her skirts, all that he could really see of her, were plastered to her legs by the wind. Her arms were lifted over her head as she reached up to undo the pins that held the laundry in place. Occasionally, she had to rise on tiptoe to do it.

But although he couldn't see her face, Burke knew without the slightest doubt that here, at last, was Kate.

Burke strode up to the laundry line, oblivious to wind and sea, and stood on one side of an undulating sheet. Just behind it, Kate was struggling with a particularly stubborn clothespin. When she'd finally wrooted it from the corner of sheet it held, the white material fell away.

She hadn't changed. If anything, she was more beautiful than he remembered. The wind had brought out the color in her cheeks, and even the shock of seeing him standing there couldn't drain that healthy bloom entirely away. If he'd been hoping that she had suffered as he had in the months since they'd last seen one another, then he was disappointed. She was still slender as ever, but there was a newfound buoyancy to her figure, a fresh softness to her face, an added lustre to those gentle grey eyes. And her lips—those lips which had been haunting him in his dreams for what seemed like forever—were fuller, and—if such a thing were possible—even duskier, and more kissable.

Those lips finally parted, after she had stared at him for nearly a minute, and that low voice he knew so well said, "You look terrible."

He blinked. The whole of the interminably long ride from London, he'd been imagining what they would say to one another when at last they met again. He had pictured everything from her throwing her arms around him, and pressing those lips he'd missed so much to his, to her picking up blunt objects and hurling them at his head.

He had never, however, imagined her matter-of-factly commenting on his looks.

He found that he could not form a reply. It was as if suddenly he had forgotten how to speak. He stood there, struggling to think of something—anything—to say, and could not come up with a single thing. He could only stand there and stare at her, taking in every detail, from the fact that she wore a dress he had never seen before, a blue and white cotton one, with a green woolen shawl thrown across her shoulders, to the way the wind picked up long strands of her blond hair that had escaped from the knot at the top of her head, and sent them waving about her face.

"Well," Kate said, after another minute, reaching up to sweep one of those strands from her eyes. "Don't just stand there. It's going to rain soon. Help me get the laundry in."

And then she started tugging on the pins holding the next sheet down.

He might not have been able to speak, but he found that he could move. And so he did, helping remove the pins she could not reach and then aiding her in the folding process by holding the opposite corners of each sheet. This was a tricky business, considering all the wind, and occasionally, their fingers touched. Each time, they carefully avoided the gaze of the other.

And yet each time—to Burke, anyway—it was as if some kind of explosion occurred at the ends of his hands, he was that sensitive to her slightest touch. It was a weakness, he knew. An insufferable weakness that went along with the insufferable way he felt about her. And yet there was nothing he could do about it. Nothing except pray that she felt it, too.

Which, he saw, with an explosive feeling of relief a few seconds later, she did. She had to. Why else were her fingers shaking as if the wind, which wasn't warm, but was not particularly cool, either, had dipped down to arctic temperatures? She was, he saw, only feigning this complete lack of feeling. She felt. She felt very much, indeed.

Only how to get her to admit it? That was the question.

She's angry, he said to himself. She's angry, that's all. Her letter—her letter, which had been without acrimony, without recrimination . . . which had been sweetness itself, at least in closing . . . had not reflected what she now felt, which was anger. And she had a right to be angry, he supposed. He had, after all, insulted her. More than insulted her. Humiliated her, with his asinine assumption that she'd welcome a chance at becoming his mistress. Not to mention what he'd thought about her and Craven.

She had a right to be angry.

"I am perfectly capable," she said, when he bent down and took the laundry basket from her, when it was finally full, "of carrying my own washing."

He held on to the basket. "Not," he said, "with your fingers shaking like that, the way they're doing now."

She hid them, crossing her arms over her chest, and tucking her hands from his sight. "I'm cold," she said defensively.

"Would you like to borrow my coat?"

She met his glance, and then looked hastily away, as if remembering, as he was, another time when he had loaned her his coat. She said, "No," in a faint voice. "That isn't necessary. Thank you."

He didn't think he could stand it, this cold, indifferent Kate, even if it was only an act.

"What did you do, anyway, to get Freddy to tell you where I was?" she asked huskily, her gaze on the ground. "Threaten to tell his mother about that soprano of his, or something?"

He shook his head. "I told him the truth," he said. "That I need you."

He ought, of course, to have stopped right there. Because

there was a perceptible softening in those eyes, which she'd seemed determined to keep every bit as cold and flat as that sea just beyond the cliffs.

But he was too new at love, and had been rubbed too raw by it to consider what that softness might mean. Instead, he lumbered clumsily on, saying, "It's Isabel, you see."

The softness turned to alarm. "Isabel?" she echoed. "What about her? Is she all right?"

He shook his head. "She's run off, Kate."

She stared up at him, seemingly unconscious of the fact that the wind had picked up a stray curl of her hair, and was buffeting it against her cheek. "Run off," she said. "Run off? Where to?"

"To Scotland," he said. "With Daniel Craven."

Her lips fell open. *"Daniel?"* she echoed, in tones of, if he was not mistaken, horror. "But how? What happened to—"

"You've got to help me, Kate," Burke interrupted desperately. "Only you can convince her to come home. I know I haven't any right to ask it of you. . . . Only I didn't know what else to do. You've got to help me. For Isabel's sake."

She dropped her gaze. He could no longer see what she was feeling. He only barely heard her murmured, "Yes. Yes, of course."

And then she was walking past him, hurrying toward the cottage.

But all he was aware of was the fact that she had agreed to come with him. He didn't see what she took haste to hide from him, which was a sudden smarting at the corners of her eyes, which could, she told herself, be easily blamed on the wind. Well, and what had she been expecting, after all? It had taken him nearly three months to come after her, and then he'd only done so because Isabel was in trouble.

Grave trouble, too, from the sounds of it. Daniel Craven. God help her. Daniel Craven.

What on earth could he want with *Isabel*?

Falling into step beside her, Burke held on to the laundry basket and thought, *She's angry. Of course she's still angry. But I can explain it all. It isn't too late. It isn't too late until she marries Bishop. Until then, I've still got a chance.*

Nanny Hinkle, however, apparently didn't think so.

"So you're the one," she said, ten minutes later, as Burke sat across from her at the kitchen table. Kate had gone upstairs to "get a few things together," as she'd said to the old woman. "Lord Wingate and I will be going away for a few days, Nanny," was Kate's brief explanation of things. "Just a few days, on an urgent errand. And then I'll be back."

She'd added this last with a quick glance at Burke, as if he might be tempted to dispute it. And, indeed, he had drawn in a breath to do so. Because the only way she was coming back, he'd decided during their walk from the washline, was for the occasional visit, maybe with their children, after they were married. He hadn't the slightest intention, now that he'd found her again, of ever letting her out of his sight.

But he couldn't say this out loud. Not when Kate was still in such high dudgeon. So instead, he'd said to Nanny Hinkle, whom he felt might like a more detailed explanation than Kate had offered, "Miss Mayhew is trying to be discreet. But this is a secret I feel I can safely share with you, Miss Hinkle. It's my daughter, you see. She's run off with a man, and I need Miss Mayhew's help in convincing her to come home."

"Oh," Nanny Hinkle had said. She had put a pot of tea on the fire and a plate of scones in front of him the minute he'd followed Kate through the door. It was almost as if the old woman had been expecting him. But that, of course, was impossible.

As soon as Kate had slipped upstairs, the old woman pinned him with her milky stare, and said, "It won't work, you know."

Burke had let his tea go cold in front of him. He hadn't had a drop of whisky in twenty-four hours, but that did not mean in its place he was prepared to start sipping the type of beverages favored by elderly women.

At first he thought to dissemble, and pretend he hadn't the slightest idea what the old lady was talking about. "I'm afraid I don't know what you mean," he said politely.

"I think you do." Nanny Hinkle had spooned four heaping spoonfuls of sugar into her own cup, and now, much to

Burke's disgust, she was sipping the steaming brew as if it tasted delightful. "I raised Katie from a baby, and was with her until she was sixteen. And I never in my life met a stubborner person."

Outside, lightning flashed. Then, off in the distance, thunder rumbled. Burke glanced around the cottage. It was a pleasant enough looking place, though the raftered ceilings were a bit low for someone his height. He rather liked the idea that this, contrary to all his wild imaginings, was where Kate had been all the time they'd been separated. It was a good place to be, he thought. A safe place. Though this old woman . . . she was not the kindly nanny she appeared to be, that was certain.

"I think you'll find, Miss Hinkle," he said, when his gaze fell on a familiar-looking tabby cat who'd draped herself across the clean sheets in the laundry basket the moment he'd lowered it, "that I can be quite stubborn, as well."

"Not as stubborn as *her*," Nanny Hinkle said, with another glance at the ceiling, "or you wouldn't be here."

Burke watched as the cat let out an elaborate yawn, then began kneading the sheets with her front paws. "Maybe not." Burke couldn't help pointing out, a bit smugly, "But she's coming with me, isn't she?"

"For the sake of your daughter." The old woman bit into one of her scones. When she spoke again, she sprayed crumbs in his direction, without seeming to care in the least. "That's all."

Burke, irritated, and not just because of the crumbs, said, "I don't believe that's all. I don't believe she's only doing it for Isabel."

"That," Nanny Hinkle said, with a shrug of her spindly shoulders, "is your prerogative, of course, my lord."

He stared at her. "You can't put me off her, Miss Hinkle," he said. "You can go on telling me how stubborn she is, and I'll go right on nodding politely, but you won't be able to put me off her."

"Won't I?" She looked at him, then grinned. "No, I can see

that I can't. Well, that's a shame. You'll only be disappointed."

Kate's voice came floating down the narrow staircase, sounding suspicious. "Nanny," she called. "What are you telling him?"

"I'm not telling his lordship anything at all, my sweet," the old woman shouted, at a volume that belied her fragile looks. Then, dropping her voice, she said to Burke, "I remember when your divorce was in all the papers."

Burke stiffened. He said carefully, "Oh?"

The old woman waved a veiny hand in the air. "Quite the scandal, that was."

"Are you trying to imply, Miss Hinkle," he said, "that I am not good enough for Kate?"

She looked at him steadily. "You know about her parents, of course."

Surprised at the blunt way she'd introduced this new topic, he nodded.

"People called that a scandal, too," Nanny Hinkle said. "And it made all the papers, like your divorce." She sipped her tea. "Their friends—grand people, like yourself—dropped them. None of them could go anywhere without being followed by jeers and whispers. Jeers and whispers from them that had once called themselves friends. It can scar you, something like that."

"Certainly," Burke agreed, not certain where, precisely, the old woman was headed.

"It scarred you," she said. "But in a different way than it scarred Katie."

"What," Burke demanded, losing patience, "are you trying to tell me?"

"She won't go back." The old woman regarded him unblinkingly.

Burke assumed, then, that the old woman knew what he'd done, what he'd tried to make Kate. Which was embarrassing, certainly. But it was also a moot point. Because he fully intended to right that wrong.

Accordingly, he leaned back in his chair, and said, "I think you underestimate me, madam."

The old woman snorted. "I think you underestimate Kate. But what is the point of telling you that? Why would you listen to me? I'm an old woman. And no one listens to old women."

Kate appeared on the stairs, carrying a valise and dressed in traveling clothes. "I do," she said. "Now, Nanny, are you going to be all right while I'm gone? I'll stop at Mrs. Barrow's on the way out of town, and ask her to look in on you. And there's the meat pies from Saturday in the larder, don't forget. And the milk comes tomorrow. . . ."

Nanny Hinkle's face changed when Kate came back into the room. She became once again a sweet old nursemaid, rather than the sharp-eyed inquisitor she'd been when in the sole company of the marquis.

"Ah," she said, as Burke rose, and hastily took hold of the valise Kate held. It was, he discovered, disconcertingly light. "But there's one thing you've forgotten, my love, haven't you? What about Lady Babbie?"

Kate, busy with her bonnet strings, said, "Oh, Nanny, I'll be back in a few days, I'm sure. No longer."

Nanny Hinkle shot Burke a look he construed as triumphant. It wasn't until Kate had kissed the old woman goodbye, and accepted a bundle of hastily wrapped scones that she pressed upon her, that Burke stooped to kiss the old woman's hand.

"We'll be back," he said with a hearty confidence that, in truth, he only half felt. "For the cat."

"*She'll* be back," the old woman said, with a shrewd glance at Kate, who'd already stepped outside.

"I don't think so," he said.

"Then you," the old woman said, "are in for a good deal of heartache."

Chapter Twenty-five

T̃hen you—the old woman's words kept echoing through his head—*are in for a good deal of heartache.*

A few hours later, Burke was still hearing those words, over and over again. Well, what did *she* know about it, anyway? So she had known Kate forever. So what?

True, he did not know how much Kate had told her nanny about what had actually transpired between herself and her employer. But that didn't mean he was destined for failure. Because there was plenty he knew about Kate that Nanny Hinkle didn't.

He knew, for instance, that when her lips were pressed together—as they had been for most of the time he'd been sitting across from her in the enclosed carriage, several hours of hard riding, and very little conversation—that she wasn't necessarily angry. In fact, sometimes it merely meant that she was thinking about something.

He felt it most likely that she was thinking about Daniel Craven. She had asked for an account of events leading up to Isabel's elopement, and had listened quite patiently while he gave them—well, an abridged version of them, anyway, since he could not tell her what Isabel had said concerning his relationship with her former chaperone. Kate had nodded, expressing her confidence that in Isabel's revealing in her note that they were headed to Gretna Green, she was surely hoping they find her before the wedding took place. "Why else," Kate asked, "would she have mentioned where they were going?"

It was a strategy for how, precisely, she was going to handle Isabel in the face of this crisis, he assured himself, that Kate was concocting at that very moment. He could see her face quite plainly, though the storm clouds overhead had rendered the sky above the carriage as dark as if it were dusk, even if according to his pocket watch, it was only just past four o'clock. She was dressed—quite becomingly, in his opinion—in a plain brown cloak, and matching bonnet, against which her blond hair looked very light, indeed. And her cheeks, though they were well out of the wind, were still very pink. As, of course, were her lips.

It seemed possible to him that she might keep those lips of hers closed for the entirety of their journey. She had never been a chatterbox, but nor had she ever been this quiet.

She's angry, he told himself, again. *And she has every right to be.* It was all his fault, this silence. He had to do something about it. He had to do something about it or go mad.

He said, speaking loudly enough to be heard above the rumble of the carriage wheels and rhythmic clopping of the horses' hooves, "I'm sorry, Kate."

She wrenched her gaze from the passing landscape, upon which it had been fastened, and said, obviously startled, "I beg your pardon?"

"I'm sorry. For what happened. That last night in London. I didn't realize . . . I thought it was Bishop in the garden with you. I didn't know it was Daniel Craven—"

No sooner were the words out of his mouth than he wished them unsaid. He had sworn to himself he wasn't going to mention anything that might give her cause for pain.

Her cheeks seemed to go up in flames. She looked quickly away, and said in a voice that sounded strangled, "Please just forget it."

"I can't forget it," he said, wishing she would look at him. "How can I forget it, Kate? It's all I've thought about ever since. Why didn't you say anything?"

She shook her head, her gaze locked on the window. "It wouldn't," she said, "have made any difference."

"What do you mean? It would have made all the difference in the world. Kate, if only you'd told me some little part of your past. . . ."

She did look at him, then. She turned her head to look at him with eyes shadowed beneath her bonnet brim. "But I did," she said. "I told you about the fire."

He was up off the seat opposite hers and onto the one beside her before the words were fully out of her mouth.

"But not," he said, reaching for her hand, "the whole story. Not about what happened, who you were—"

"What would have been the point?" she asked, tugging on her fingers.

"Because if I'd known who your father was—"

Her mouth popped open, and he was offered a tantalizing glimpse of her tongue before she remembered herself, and shut it again.

"Are you telling me," she said, "that if you'd known my father was a gentleman, you wouldn't have—"

"No," he said hurriedly. "No, I'm quite certain we still would have . . . but Kate, if I'd known, I'd have done then what I intend to do now."

She eyed him. "And what's that?"

"Well, ask you to marry me, of course."

Every bit of color drained from her face. Then she gave her hand a wrench, trying to pull it from his. "Let go of me," she said, in a voice he didn't recognize.

He tightened his grip. "No. Listen to me, Kate—"

"I heard you," she said, and he realized then that the reason he didn't recognize her voice was because it was filled with tears. "Please let go of my hand, and go back to your seat."

"Kate," he said, trying to speak gently, "I know you're angry with me, and you've a right to be. But I think—"

"If you do not let go of my hand," Kate said, sounding as if she were choking now, "and get back to your seat, I shall tell the driver to drop me at the nearest crossroad."

"Kate. I don't think you understand. I—"

"No, *you* don't understand," she said, her voice shaking every bit as violently as her fingers had shaken when they'd been taking in the laundry. "I will open that door and jump, so help me God, if you don't do as I ask."

He felt, for a moment, that *he* might like to open the door and jump. Or at least throw something through it. But since this would accomplish nothing whatsoever, he did as she asked instead, and retired to the opposite seat, where he sat, his arms folded across his chest, staring at her perplexedly.

What in God's name was wrong with her? Here he'd tried, to the best of his ability, to rectify the situation, and she had reacted as if he'd . . . well, as if he'd suggested that she become his mistress again. She had a right to be angry at him for that, God only knew. But why was she angry with him for asking her to marry him? It was his understanding that women considered marriage proposals worth more than diamonds, and prized them accordingly. Was she miffed, perhaps, because his hadn't been accompanied by a ring? Well, he hadn't exactly had a chance to stop and get one yet. He was in the act of trying to stop his daughter from eloping with a scoundrel, and hadn't time to think these things through.

Across from him, Kate had wedged herself as tightly into her corner of the carriage as she could, and turned her face as far from him as she was physically able, to keep him from seeing her tears. The rain had started, a hard, pelting rain, accompanied by a good deal of lightning, and thunder that grew louder with each clap. Raindrops streaked the glass in the window. But as she was incapable of seeing anything, thanks to her tears, this hardly mattered. What she was doing instead was thinking, *What have you done? Kate, what on earth have you done? The man asked you to marry him— something you've been waiting to hear him ask for the past three months, and you say no to him? Why? Why?*

She knew why, of course. Because she was a perfect fool, that was why. She'd been a perfect fool to accept a position in his household in the first place. She'd known from the start it was a bad idea. Look at him! Just look at him! Wasn't he everything she had come to despise? Wealthy and arrogant and entirely sure of himself. . . .

And she'd been right. Look what had happened.

The worst. The only really sensible thing she'd done in the past six months, she told herself, was leave him before her feelings for him became too impossibly tangled for her to extricate herself.

Not that she was extricated even now. When she'd pulled down that sheet and found him standing there, it was as if no time at all had passed since she'd last seen him—except, of course, that he looked so very different now, so deliciously vulnerable and hurt.

But that, of course, was due to worry over Isabel, not, as she'd initially thought, with the first flicker of hope she'd allowed herself since the night she'd left, because he'd been heartbroken over her abandonment of him. It had taken all the strength she had to keep herself from throwing her arms around him, and kissing him a thousand times, as she'd fantasized every single night since she'd left London.

But then she'd remembered.

When she'd first shown up at Nanny Hinkle's door, the evening after that sleepless, heavenly—but in the end, utterly wretched—night with the Marquis of Wingate, she had felt only sorrow. But when the days crawled by, and formed into weeks, and then the weeks formed into months, and he didn't come . . . well, that was when she realized how extremely fortunate she'd been, how narrowly she'd escaped something that, in the end, would have only turned out wretchedly.

And then he had appeared. As suddenly as if the wind had blown him to her.

But it hadn't been the wind. It hadn't been the wind at all. It had been Daniel. Lord, what could Daniel be thinking? He couldn't possibly be in love with Isabel. Men like Daniel were incapable of feeling love for anyone but themselves. So what was he up to? What could he be hoping to accomplish? The girl had money, yes, but then, so did Daniel, now that his mine had paid out. So if he hadn't stolen Isabel for love or for money, then *why*?

Something cold was gripping her heart, had been gripping it since Burke had first uttered the words "Daniel Craven" back there, by the washline. Because Kate had a terrible feeling that she knew what Daniel was up to. She hoped she was wrong. She hoped against hope she was wrong.

But no other explanation made sense.

She wouldn't, however, share her fears with Burke. No, he had enough to worry about. Better that he think Daniel really intended to marry his daughter, than that he knew the truth. . . .

Lord. The truth.

He'd found out the truth—one truth, anyway—and now he wanted to marry her. Because he had found out who her father was. Because he had found out she was a gentleman's daughter, he wanted to do what he ought to have done no matter *whose* daughter she'd been.

Well, it wasn't going to happen. She couldn't—*wouldn't*—allow it.

The only problem, of course, was that it wasn't going to be easy to keep that in mind. Even now, as he sat opposite her, his jade-green gaze fixed unblinkingly on her, she couldn't help noticing the backs of his hands, which were bare. The backs of the Marquis of Wingate's hands were covered with the same coarse black hair that covered the rest of him, the parts only she—well, and half the actresses in London—had ever seen. Seeing that hair now reminded Kate of the time when she'd seen him without the hindrance of clothing, and that put her in mind of something she'd been deliberately trying to forget, the night they'd spent together, the only time in life she'd ever felt fully alive. He'd made her feel things that night that she knew she would never feel again.

Which only made her cry harder.

"Kate," he said, from the duskiness of his corner. It had grown steadily darker outside as the rain grew heavier. Now it pounded down upon the roof of the chaise, which had slowed to a crawl, due to the mud on the road, and the fact that the driver surely couldn't see where he was going.

She didn't reply. She couldn't reply. She was crying silently, hoping it had grown too dark within the carriage for him to see her tears. But she couldn't speak without giving herself away. She didn't dare.

"What I don't understand," he said, ignoring her silence, "is why you felt compelled to run away. If you didn't want . . . if you didn't want to be my mistress, Kate, why didn't you just say so? It wasn't as if I would have tried to force you. You surely can't think me as base as *that*."

She bit her lower lip. His voice, coming out from the darkness like that, was gentler than she'd ever heard it, soft as velvet.

"I can understand," he went on, when she did not reply, "your being angry with me. I'm only asking that you try to understand. I didn't know what I was saying that night. I'm not just saying it now because I know you're a gentleman's daughter. I should have said it to you that night—I *would* have said it to you the next morning, I swear it, if you'd stayed. I realized as soon as you left that I was in love with you—"

He continued speaking, of course. That was not all he said. He spoke for some time, and with a good deal of energy. But Kate did not hear him. Because he had said that he loved her. He had said that he was in love with her.

Oh, God. Of all the things he could have said, why had he said *that*? The one thing, the one thing guaranteed to make her melt! How had he known? *How had he known?* And how was she supposed to harden herself to him *now*? It wasn't true. It couldn't be true. He was only saying it because he knew— he *knew*, dammit—what it did to a girl, hearing the man she loved say something like that. He was using weapons against her for which she had no defense, no defense at all. *Oh, God*, she told herself.

"I should have realized it before, I know that," Burke was saying, when she was able once again to focus on his words. "But it had been so long since I felt anything, anything at all but rage, I didn't recognize it for what it was, and . . . Well, after all, Kate, you know how my first marriage ended. I haven't exactly been anxious to try *that* experiment again. But you, Kate. Since you left, I've been doing everything I could think of to hasten the end of this empty, blockheaded life of mine. . . ."

Remember, she said to herself, trying to summon up the sort of indignation she knew she ought to feel. For he was, after all, the enemy. One of them. A member of the tribe that had, in the end, betrayed her family, and let their killer go unpunished. He could not be trusted.

She said aloud, her voice constricted, "A *black* phaeton. With *yellow* trim."

"Kate!" He launched himself across the chaise, and this time, it wasn't her hand he snatched up, but all of her, taking her in his arms as if she were no weightier than a doll.

"What," he demanded, giving her a shake, his livid face just inches from hers, "am I going to have to do to make you forget I ever said any of those things? What am I going to have to do? This?"

And then he was kissing her.

As simple as that, he was kissing her, and she . . .

Well, she thawed.

He was an excellent kisser, Burke Traherne. Not that she hadn't known that before. She remembered, only too well. But as if he wanted to be sure—perfectly sure—she hadn't for-gotten, he reminded her, his mouth moving over hers in a slightly inquisitive manner—not tentatively, by any means, but as if he were asking a question for which only she, Kate, had the answer.

It wasn't until Kate felt the intrusion of his tongue inside her mouth that she realized she'd answered that question, somehow—though she hardly knew how, much less what that question had been . . . until suddenly there was nothing ques-tioning at all in his manner; he'd launched the first volley and realized that Kate's defenses were down. That, then, had been the question. Now he attacked, showing no mercy.

It was then that it struck Kate, as forcibly as a blow, that this kiss was something out of the ordinary, and that perhaps she was not in as much control of the situation as she would have liked. Though she struggled against the sudden, dizzying assault on her senses, she could no sooner free herself from the hypnotic spell of his lips than the iron grip in which he held her. She went completely limp in his arms, except for her hands, which, as if of their own volition, slipped around his neck, tangling in the surprisingly soft hair at the nape of his neck. What was it, she wondered dimly, about the introduction of this man's tongue into her mouth that seemed to have a direct correlation to a very sudden and very noticeable tightening sensation between her thighs?

Even in her heightened state of arousal, Kate was not unaware of the fact that Burke seemed to be suffering a similar discomfort. She could feel it, pressing urgently through the rings of her crinoline. He had let out a low moan, smothered against her mouth, when she'd slid her hands around his neck, and now, as his need for her chafed against the front of his trousers, his strong arms tightened possessively around her. Callused fingers caressed her through the thin material of her dress, and she realized they were moving inexorably close to her breasts. If she let him touch her *there*, she'd be lost, she knew.

And she *had* to stop him, because she was no Sara Woodhart, who was loose enough to enjoy without compunction the attentions of men she had no intention of marrying. She was Kate Mayhew, who had a reputation to uphold. Granted, that reputation was not exactly a flawless one, but it *was* all she had, after all. . . .

And then those strong, yet incredibly gentle, fingers closed over one of her breasts, the nipple of which had already gone hard against the heat of his palm.

Tearing her mouth away from his and placing a restraining hand against his wide chest, Kate brought accusing eyes up to his face, and was startled by what she saw there, a mouth slack with desire and green eyes filled with . . . with what? Kate could not put a name to what she saw within those orbs, but it frightened as much as it thrilled her.

She had to put a stop to this madness, before things went too far again.

"Burke," she said, through lips that felt numb from the bruising pressure of his kiss. "Let go of me."

Burke lifted his head, his expression as dazed as a man who'd just been roused from sleep. Blinking down at her, he gave every indication of having heard her, and yet his hand, still anchored upon her breast, tightened, as if he had no intention of releasing her. When he spoke, it was with a hoarse voice, his intonations slurred.

"I don't think so," he said. "The last time I let go of you, you went away, and it was three months before I saw you again."

So what if in response, she seized his face in both her hands and dragged it down until his lips were on hers again? Who could blame her? It wasn't as if she could help it. It wasn't as if it made her happy, the ease with which he was able, with the merest touch, to render her so helpless in his hands. Especially when those hands were *doing* things to her, as they were just then. For though he kept one hand clamped firmly around the back of her neck, beneath the fall of her hair, obviously to keep her from pulling away—as if she'd ever be foolish enough to want to do that—the other was still singeing her breast straight through the material of her dress, and threatening to dip even lower. . . .

But not before the carriage driver was rapping on the door, telling them that the roads were too flooded to travel, and would his lordship mind waiting out the storm at this inn to which he'd just now pulled up?

Chapter Twenty-six

$\mathcal{I}$t was the thunder that woke her. It rattled the glass in the window beside her bed.

Kate sat up in the darkness, and stretched out to move the small curtain aside. Outside was only darkness, covered in a blanket of streaming water. She knew it had to be very late, because she could not see the lights in the windows of the hostelry across the road. The small village at which they'd been forced to make their unscheduled stop was asleep. Everyone in England, she imagined, was asleep.

Except for her.

It was a mercy, she supposed, that the thunder had wakened her when it did. She had been caught in the net of another one of those dreams—those horrible, wonderful dreams she'd been having ever since that fateful day she'd happened to spy the marquis at his bath; dreams she'd continued to have long after she'd left his company, dreams that left her, every time she waked from one of them, hot and breathless, with a hand between her legs. It was shocking. It wasn't any way for a lady to behave.

And yet she could no more stop herself from dreaming of him, it seemed, than she could stop herself from breathing.

And so, in the end, she'd been forced to give up trying. She now never even bothered putting on a nightdress, because she knew perfectly well it would only end up over her head and tangled in her bedclothes by morning. And when she woke with her hand clenched between her legs, she simply kept it there.

It had seemed the best way, overall, to handle the situation. Certainly better than doing what she'd longed to, which was to return to Park Lane, knock on Lord Wingate's door, and beg him to take her back.

But now he wasn't miles away in London. He was in the room next door, sleeping soundly, like any good British citizen should have been, at such an hour. He had been politely attentive to her all through dinner, and had not renewed his wild proposal from the chaise . . . nor the more physical proposal he'd made a little later. Possibly that was because now that he'd had time to reflect, he realized marrying the daughter of the notorious Peter Mayhew was not, perhaps, the wisest course of action.

Not, Kate supposed, that she could blame him.

Lightning filled her bedroom. Ten seconds later, thunder rumbled again, not as loudly as before. The storm, which had followed them from Lynn Regis, was moving away at last. With any luck, by morning it would be gone, and they'd have clear roads to Scotland.

Which was why, Kate told herself, she was a fool to lie here, blinking in the darkness. She ought to get some sleep. She had a long, arduous day of travel ahead of her.

She had just closed her eyes when she heard something that wasn't thunder or the rain. Opening her eyes again, she sat up and looked about the night-shrouded room. Roadhouses were notoriously rat infested, although this one had appeared to her to be cleaner than most, and she'd seen more than a few cats slinking about the place. Still, even Lady Babbie had been known to let a big one get away. Sweeping a hand to the floor, Kate snatched up one of her boots, and hurled it in the direction from which she'd heard the noises.

Kate, whose aim had always been good, knew she had scored a hit when she heard someone say, "Oof!"

But rats didn't say "Oof."

Then, after a clatter which was undoubtedly the boot falling to the floor, Lord Wingate's voice cut through the darkness. "Dammit, Kate," he hissed. "It's only me."

It was Lord Wingate—opening the small adjoining door between their two rooms, a door Kate had not, of course, thought to lock before she'd retired. Well, she certainly hadn't thought he might be bold enough to try for a nocturnal assault. She had requested, a bit nervously, that they take separate rooms, and Lord Wingate had not argued.

Now she saw why. They had separate rooms, all right. Separated by a door.

She heard the strike of a match, and then light flooded the little room. He had brought a candle with him, and now he raised it, and looked at her by the light of its flame. Too late, she remembered she hadn't a stitch of clothing on, and she snatched the sheets close to her chest.

"What do you want?" She averted her eyes from what the candlelight revealed, which was that he wore only a dressing gown, the front of which had fallen open above the sash when he'd raised the candle, revealing a long vee of exposed chest.

"I thought I heard you call me," he said.

"Well," she said. "I didn't."

Although even as she said it, she was not at all certain it was true. She had certainly been dreaming of him just minutes before, and she very well might have cried out his name during one of the dream's more erotic moments.

"Kate," he said, placing the candle on the small table beside her bed. "I heard you distinctly. I was reading, and—"

She pulled the sheets higher, the closer he came to the bed. "I may have called you," she admitted grudgingly. "But only in my sleep. I'm sorry if I disturbed you."

Only unfortunately, instead of being insulted and going away, Lord Wingate actually lowered himself onto the mattress beside her, and put his elbows on his knees, and his face in his hands.

"It's all right. I couldn't sleep anyway," he said to the floorboards. "There's no possible way we'll get there in time, you know, Kate. Not with all this rain."

Isabel. That was all he wanted. To speak of Isabel.

"Oh, no," she said, with a certainty she was far from feeling. "We'll find her. Of course we will."

"No." His back was to her, his face hidden from view, but everything about him conveyed the enormous pain and guilt he was feeling. "We won't. We'll be too late. And then she'll *have* to marry him."

Kate, struck by the pathos in his deep, masculine voice, reached out in spite of herself, and laid a hand sympathetically upon his broad, strong back. For the situation was far graver than Burke had imagined. Daniel Craven would never marry Isabel. Kate knew that.

But she couldn't, of course, tell the girl's father that.

"Not necessarily," she said, with an optimism she was far from feeling. "I mean, Isabel is headstrong, yes, but she isn't stupid, Lord Wingate."

"For God's sake," he said, and it sounded to Kate as if he were speaking through gritted teeth, although she couldn't tell for sure, since he still didn't turn to face her. "Call me by name, Kate. When you say 'Lord Wingate,' it sounds so cold, I can't bear it."

She hesitated. "All right," she said finally. "All right. Burke, then. Certainly you've spoken to your daughter about . . . well, about what goes on between a man and a woman. Haven't you?"

He still didn't turn around. "Of course not," he said bitterly. "I thought you did."

"Me?" Kate raised her eyebrows. "Certainly not! Whatever would have made you think—"

"Well, you taught her everything else. You taught her how to dress, and do her hair. I just assumed—"

"But Lord—I mean, Burke. Really, it's up to the *parent* to speak to his child about such things. . . ."

"Well, I never did, all right?"

He swung around then, and faced her. Kate instantly wished he hadn't. The candlelight brought into high relief the planes of his face, which, though not at all handsome, had a strength and undeniable masculinity that Kate had always found perfectly irresistible. And now, creased as it was with concern for his daughter, Lord Wingate's face was, to her, more attractive than ever.

"It never occurred to me," he said. "I raised her from a baby, Kate. I'm the one who saw that she bathed, and dressed, and ate. I couldn't do everything. You know how she is. It was all I could do just to make sure she wore clothes every day. And it wasn't exactly a subject upon which she ever expressed the slightest curiosity. Not that, if she had, I'd have known what to say. There are some things—very few, but some—that fathers simply can't explain to their daughters."

Kate dropped her gaze. She had to, or risk transferring the hand that had been on his back to his cheek, which, though rough with a day's growth of bristles, looked eminently strokable. *Remember,* she told herself.

"Well," she said. "Then perhaps, if he should try something, Isabel will be so shocked, she'll leave him."

She could feel his gaze on her, though she hadn't the strength to look him in the eye. "It was Craven," he said abruptly.

Kate blinked at him. "I beg your pardon?"

"It was Craven," he said again. "Isabel told me it was Daniel Craven that night in the garden, and not Lord Palmer. And yet you let me think it was. Why?"

Kate, startled by this sudden change of subject, swallowed, but still she did not lift her gaze from the quilt she'd kicked in her sleep to the bottom of her bed. "It doesn't matter," she said. "Not anymore."

"It does matter," he said urgently. "It matters a good deal, indeed. Why didn't you tell me?"

She licked her lips. Her mouth had suddenly gone very dry. "Well," she said. "I suppose . . . I suppose because I didn't want you to kill him. I thought. . . . I thought that would just cause another scandal, and it seemed to me there'd been enough of those to go round. . . ."

"You were *protecting* me?" he asked incredulously. "You allowed me to believe something terrible about you, in order to protect *me*?"

She made the mistake of looking up, then. "And Isabel,"

she said, not wanting him to think she'd done it for him. Because then, of course, he might think she cared. Which she did not. She most definitely did not.

And yet it seemed doubtful, when he looked into her eyes, that he was going to continue to believe that for long. Because she was certain that penetrating gaze of his had seen right through the charade of uncaring she'd been trying so carefully to construct. Just as, it seemed, he could see right through the sheet she'd held hiked up to her chin, as if its meager shelter could protect her from what she knew—with mingled feelings of excitement and nervousness—was about to happen.

"Then," he said, in that same deceptively gentle voice he'd used in the carriage, "you must have liked me a little, Kate. If you wanted to protect me from scandal, I mean."

She wanted to look away. She wanted more than anything to look away. So why couldn't she? All she seemed able to do was sit there and stare into his eyes, noticing, now that he was sitting so close, that they weren't completely green, after all. There were tiny gold specks in them, like tiny goldfish, swimming in a green pond.

"I suppose I did," Kate said. "Then."

"But you don't," he said, reaching for the sheet she was holding on to, "anymore?"

"Correct," she said, tightening her grip on the thin linen.

"Then why," he asked, giving the sheet the gentlest of tugs, "are you here?"

"I told you," she said. "I came for Isabel—"

But that was all she managed to get out before he leaned down and covered her mouth with his own.

As far as kisses went, she supposed this one was fairly devastating. It wasn't like the hard, possessive kisses he had given her that night in his library. Nor was it like the sweet, exploratory kisses they'd shared afterward, in his bedroom, before he'd started talking so wildly of bookshops and phaetons. It was more like the one in the carriage. . . .

Although not exactly like that one, either. Because this one was filled with something Kate couldn't recognize, not having encountered it before. And yet, as Lord Wingate—*Burke*.

When was she going to remember to call him Burke?—kissed her, she began to realize what that something was.

And what it was, was longing.

She was quite certain of it. Because of course, she was feeling it, too. Had been feeling it, for all the time they'd been apart. It was as if, though her mind knew differently, all her body knew was that here was another body that had once given hers great pleasure.

And now all it wanted was to experience that pleasure again.

Which would explain why Kate didn't protest when Burke gave the sheet she held a final, emphatic tug, and pulled it from her grasp entirely. She reached out, blindly—because of course he was still kissing her, his tongue easily breaking past the token resistance she put up with her lips—to stop him, but all she succeeded in doing was touching his chest where the dressing gown fell open. Her hand met with that hard wall of muscle and crisp dark hair—and his hand, the one that had tugged away the sheet, closed over one of her warm, bare breasts . . . and that was all.

She was lost.

It was so easy. It was so easy to give in to him, to his kissing, which was soon no longer filled with longing, but with hunger, a demanding hunger. It was so much easier to give in to him than to fight him. Because what did fighting get her? Nothing, except maybe some slim sort of intellectual satisfaction. But what was that, when his fingers were giving her so much physical satisfaction, first spinning tiny circles around her straining nipples, then eliciting gasps of shock from her as he skimmed them across the smooth flat surface of her stomach? It was an assault, she knew that. A skillful assault on all her senses, meant to make her forget everything that had happened between them, except how his body had once made hers feel.

And her body had not forgotten. How could it, when everything about him, from the intoxicating smell of him, that musky odor which he alone possessed—and the merest whiff of which made her knees feel as if they were dissolving—to the caress of his callused fingers on her tender skin, reminded her?

Not only reminded her, but goaded her into launching an attack on her own. No sooner had her hand come into contact with the bare flesh of his chest than she was pushing away the folds of his robe, and fumbling, with embarrassing eagerness, at the knot in the sash which kept that robe closed. He, of course, had no such concerns, as she was so conveniently naked beneath the sheet he'd pulled away. He had already torn his mouth away from hers, and was dragging his lips—his day-old growth of whiskers were singeing her every place they touched—down her throat, and toward the breast he'd captured.

Still, she would not be put off. She tugged once more at the knot, but when it continued to evade her, she plunged her hand beneath it, and found satisfaction by curling her fingers around the stiffening rod the robe had kept hidden from view. Burke, who had by that time discovered and conquered one of her nipples with his mouth, and was busy branding it with his tongue, let out a violent hiss at this, and lifted his head. He pinned her with an inscrutable glance, at which Kate only widened her eyes, and tightened her grip on him, mostly just to see what would happen.

What happened was that Burke caught hold of her hand by the wrist, and a second later, he'd pinned it to the pillow beside her head.

"What," he whispered hoarsely, "are you trying to do? End this before it's even begun?"

With her free hand, Kate tugged on the sash to his robe. "Take this off," she said.

He needed no further urging. The robe came off.

And when it was flung away, he thrust a hard thigh between her legs, parting them enough to allow him the room he needed to lower himself between them, until he lay atop her, both hands raised to cover her breasts. Then he brought his mouth down to smother hers once again, this time in a kiss that revealed, all too clearly, how very close he was to bursting from need of her—as if that hadn't been made perfectly obvious by the size of his erection, which she could feel pressing urgently against her inner thighs.

And once again, Kate's body, quite independent of her mind, remembered what to do, reacting instinctively to the familiar smell of him, the welcome weight of him. A second later, she had raised her hips, pressing her pelvis against him.

And he, with an unintelligible murmur that was lost inside her mouth, suddenly plunged into her, burying himself as deeply as he was able, feeling her heat and moisture close around him far more tightly than her fingers ever could. Beneath him, Kate gasped as he entered her, just as she had the first time. Only this night, there were no tears, just a sudden sinking of her fingernails into his shoulders, which she clung to the way a capsized sailor might cling to a piece of driftwood.

And perhaps, in a way, that's how Kate thought of those shoulders of his—as the only stable things in a world suddenly awash in desire. Wave after wave of it rolled over her as she brought her hips up to meet his each time he thrust himself into her. He wasn't being gentle about it this time, either. How could he? The first night, he'd been careful, careful not to frighten her with the intensity of his need for her. This night, his need for her was too great, and had been left too long unsatiated, for him to control it. Each time he plunged into her, he drove her deeper into the featherbed beneath them.

And each time he plunged into her, mindless with the pleasure of it, it was if he were coming home.

She drowned first. She simply let go of his shoulders and let the waves take her, no longer caring whether or not she kept afloat above them, no longer capable of keeping her head above them. They caught her up in a violent eddy, and down she went. Deeper and deeper she spiraled, until suddenly, she crashed onto the beach as if she had been pushed there by a veritable wall of water.

And there she lay, spent and panting beneath him, hardly conscious of the fact that at some point, he'd slipped down into the vortex with her, and had now collapsed atop her, his heart hammering at breakneck speed against her breast.

Kate opened her eyes, and saw that the candle had gone out. They lay in utter darkness. Somewhere, off in the distance, thunder rumbled, but the rain no longer beat down upon the window beside her bed. The storm was over, both outside the bedroom, and within it, as well.

Burke seemed to realize it, too. Wordlessly, he slid from her. Kate almost cried out at the coolness of the air that rushed in where he'd lain.

But he wasn't parted from her for long. He only sat up to find the quilt she'd so carelessly tossed aside in her sleep. He pulled it up over both of them, tucking the ends carefully about her, then circled an arm around her waist, and cradled her against the curl of his larger body.

There were things that needed to be said. Kate thought of them sleepily, and even opened her lips to say them, to remind him that he was not to think, just because their bodies found pleasure in one another's, that there was any reason to think she had in any way changed her mind about—

But as if he'd sensed what she was about to say, he leaned down and whispered, "Shhh. . . ." then smoothed a lock of hair from her cheek, and kissed her good-night.

And really, she was far too tired to argue anymore.

Chapter Twenty-seven

*B*urke was dreaming. He knew he was dreaming, because there was a weight upon his chest, and when he opened his eyes to see what that weight was, he saw that it was Kate. She had flung her torso across his in her sleep, and now lay with her cheek pressed to his heart, her hair spilling, like burnished gold, all across his shoulders. A strand of it tickled him beneath the chin.

But then he realized he could not possibly be dreaming, because they were not in his enormous bedroom back on Park Lane, but in a low-ceilinged, cramped room in a roadhouse outside some obscure village, and below them, he could hear the sounds of the innkeeper's wife as she began preparing breakfast. Outside the small window beside the bed, he could see that dawn was streaking the sky—at least, he assumed it was. It was rather hard to tell, with the thick fog that had rolled in. The rain had stopped during the night, but it was still utterly grey outside, and looked cold, as well. Autumn was well and truly upon them. All the more reason, he thought, to stay abed.

And yet they couldn't stay abed. Because there was Isabel to think of. Isabel, who with every passing minute was slipping farther and farther out of his reach.

And yet . . .

And yet, Isabel wasn't very likely going anywhere this

early, on so foggy a morning, either. And here he was, with
Kate in his arms at last.

It wasn't likely he was going anywhere anytime soon, either.

It still filled him with wonder, her beauty. Oh, it wasn't the
traditional beauty of, say, a Sara Woodhart. With the exception
of those enormous grey eyes, Kate's features were too small
to be classically beautiful. And her hair was neither pale
enough to be truly blond, nor dark enough to be brunette, but
somewhere in the middle, a color impossible to classify. And
she was small, almost small enough to make her seem insignificant, fine-boned and lacking in breadth of both hip and
breast for the current definition of what the *haut monde* considered beautiful.

And yet.

And yet her skin was flawless, smooth as satin and the color
of the palest blossom. Her waist was narrow enough for him
to circle with his hands, and have his fingers meet in the middle. And below that waist, her legs were long and slender,
tapering down to ankles of bewitching slimness, and feet of
elegant proportions. And between those legs lay a patch of
silken hair that enticed him more than any other woman's, for
in it he had found he could bury his entire length, the whole
of himself, in a nest of such sweet warmth and closeness, he
never wanted to leave it.

But that wasn't all, of course. There were her hands, so
small his own could swallow them up. Hers were the graceful
hands of a ballerina, or a musician. Her fingers, dancing across
his body the night before, had very nearly been his undoing.
And of course there was that mouth. Even now, he traced its
shape with his finger, as she lay atop him, sleeping so peacefully. He liked the feel of the weight of her upon him, chest,
enjoyed the softness of her breasts against him.

Perhaps he enjoyed it a little *too* much, since he could feel
himself swelling beneath the sheet which only partially covered him. Soon, the sheet became tent-poled from his erection,
and it occurred to him that this time, as opposed to all the

other mornings he'd wakened with this particular need, there was something he could do about it.

And so he did it. Only instead of rolling Kate over and plunging into her, which was his initial inclination, he had a better idea, and with only a little trouble, he slid her over him until she was astride his body. This woke her, of course, and she lifted her head sleepily from where it lay on his shoulder, and blinked in the dim grey morning light.

"What?" she said blearily.

He answered by placing steadying hands on her hips, and sliding himself slowly inside of her. She was still slick from the night before, and so he knew he could not have hurt her. And yet her eyelids flew apart, and, as always when he entered her, she sucked in her breath.

"What," she gasped breathlessly, "are you *doing*?"

He showed her, by moving her hips forward and then back again, and keeping himself still. Again, she sucked in her breath . . . but this time for a different reason. She tried moving her hips on her own, the way he had shown her, and was rewarded by a groan from him that she could feel reverberating all through her thighs, locked as they were around his waist. The groan was not so much because of the exquisite feel of her, as she moved up and down his shaft, enveloping him with her heat, as it was because of the way she looked perched there above him, her hair thrown back until it resembled a glorious cape behind her, her nipples pointed so insouciantly toward the ceiling. He wanted to reach for those nipples, to graze them with his palms, but he was compelled to hold on to her hips, as suddenly he could no longer keep himself still beneath her, and instead found himself driving into her with a force that, he was quite certain, threatened to rend her in two.

But Kate was not nearly so fragile as she looked, and matched him thrust for thrust, throwing her head back and marveling at the apparently numberless ways her softness could accommodate his hardness, all the while making her *feel* things, incredible things, she had never felt before.

And then she was slipping from him, slipping again into

that vortex between pleasure and pain, and she reached out for him, blindly grasping for his hand, his shoulder, anything that would keep her teetering on the edge just a little longer . . . but it was too late. She was gone, her back arching, her head thrown back, her hair spilling down until it brushed his knees.

And beneath her, he saw it all, watched as her climax took her, reveled in the way her lips parted to let out a soft, helpless cry . . . and then followed her with a mind-numbing orgasm of his own, one that caused him to shudder violently from his scalp to the arches of his feet, until he was convinced he was going to drown her in his own seed.

When Kate came back, it was to find that she had thrown herself across his chest. She raised her head, and realized, when she looked down at his smiling face, just a few inches from her own, that her hair had fallen around them, enclosing them in a soft, silken tent. She moved to push it away, but Burke caught her hand and said, "Don't. I like it."

And then she had to kiss him, of course. What else could she do?

And yet, when he reappeared a half hour later, after having left her to consult with his driver about the condition of the roads, even Kate was not quite prepared for her sudden change in mood. The root of it, of course, was the fact that she had just been violently ill—or as violently ill as someone with nothing in her stomach could be, after retching repeatedly and unproductively. Burke, finding her in the exact spot he'd left her, only asked, as anyone would, "Kate? Aren't you getting up?"

"*Get out,*" was all she could bring herself to say.

He continued to stand there, however, looking infuriatingly healthy and well rested, while she could hardly move without incurring waves of nausea.

"Kate," he said, obviously annoyed, but trying not to show it. "We do have to be going soon, you know . . ."

"*Get out!*" This time the request—which was a polite way of putting what, in actuality, it was—was accompanied by the mate to the boot she had hurled at him the night before. Burke made haste to do as she asked, and went downstairs to partake of breakfast, wondering how much her lolly-gagging was going to delay them. The road to Scotland was bad, according to his driver, but not impassable. If they traveled hard, they might be able to make it most, if not all, of the way by nightfall. But not if their start was a late one, as it appeared, thanks to Kate, it was going to be.

And yet no sooner was he finishing his coffee that she appeared in the dining room. She offered no explanation for her strange behavior. She eschewed the eggs and bacon he pressed upon her, but accepted toast and a cup of tea. And when she was finished with them, she declared herself ready to leave—but declared it in a voice that lacked real conviction.

But that was merely, he supposed, due to embarrassment, or extreme self-consciousness. She had, after all, spent the wee hours engaged in activities that might make a wife of long standing blush. And here she was, forced to face the other guests who'd slept beneath the very same roof that had been witness to her disreputable behavior.

He made haste to pay the innkeeper and rush Kate into the carriage, so as not to prolong her embarrassment.

But if he'd expected Kate to notice this gallant behavior, he was sadly disappointed. No sooner had he lowered himself onto the seat beside hers, and curled his arm around her shoulders, than she stiffened, and pointed at the padded bench across the way.

"No," she said. "I think you ought to sit over there."

He looked down at her incredulously. "Kate," he said. "You aren't going to start that again, are you? I thought we'd settled all that."

"Settled all what?" Kate demanded. "I don't believe we've settled anything. I agreed to come with you to help you find your daughter. Nothing more."

"If that's true," Burke challenged, "then why did you call to me last night?"

"I told you," she said, turning to stare out the window. "I was dreaming."

"Well, then maybe you should pay attention to your dreams, Kate," he said seriously. "Maybe they're trying to tell you something. Maybe they're trying to say what you apparently cannot, which is that you love me, and want to marry me—"

Still not looking in his direction, Kate gave a quick, negative shake of her head.

"Are you telling me," he said, speaking very carefully, "that even after last night—not to mention this morning—you still haven't any intention of marrying me?"

"That is correct," she said to the window.

He had never felt as much like throwing something as he did just then. His fingers curled into fists, but he kept them carefully hidden from view. He hadn't, he told himself, any intention of using them.

"You little hypocrite," he growled.

That brought her head whipping round at last. Her grey eyes wide with effrontery, she echoed, *"Hypocrite?"*

"Well," he said, with a calmness that impressed even himself. "That's the polite word for it."

The grey eyes, already so enormous, widened even further. "Polite word for *what?*"

"For a woman who behaves as you have, Kate. You claim to want nothing to do with me, and yet you made love to me last night and this morning like a woman who seemed to be thoroughly enjoying herself. Since I am not paying you for those particular services, I can only assume that you did it because you like me, at least a little, which makes your behavior now seem, if you'll excuse me, hypocritical."

She had not had much color in her face before. Now, what little of it there had been left her face in a rush. She stared at him, her lips slightly parted, as if she were quite incapable of speech. Then, as he watched, all the color which had previously washed away returned, in a sudden flood. Her lips and cheeks flushed red, she said, "I—That was because you—If you hadn't—"

Furious that she could do nothing but stammer, she looked away from him, and, with burning cheeks, said to the chaise floor, "It's all your fault. If you had only got out when I told you to. . . . I don't understand how I can be expected to resist you when you're so . . . ." Her voice trailed off, until it wasn't any more than a whisper, barely audible above the rumble of the wheels beneath them. "Irresistible."

"Kate," he said. His fists had started to unclench—not just the ones at the end of his arms, but the one that had been growing again in his stomach. It wasn't so much because of what she'd said, either . . . though what she had said had been enough, more than enough, to assuage his rage. It was more because of the way she'd said it, the throb in her voice, the blush, the fact that she couldn't meet his gaze. Suddenly, the reason behind her animosity toward him became clear. At least, he thought so.

"Kate," he said again, longing to reach for her hand, but restraining himself, since he felt he'd already scored victory enough simply by getting her to admit as much as she had. "Listen to yourself. Did you hear what you just said? If what you just said is true, how can you even think of not marrying me?"

To his utter astonishment, Kate—even-tempered, rational Kate—let out a sob. She turned her face away, so he could not see it past the wide brim of her bonnet . . . but he saw her slender shoulders shake, and quite definitely heard the sob.

But when he instinctively reached out toward her, those shoulders stiffened at once. The next thing he knew, she had crushed herself against the side of the chaise farthest from him, and cried, still without looking at him, "For God's sake, can't you sit over there and leave me *alone*?"

Burke did as she asked, but only because he could see she was in no mood to be appealed to rationally. Slumping against the back of the seat, he eyed her, wondering if it was possible that sometime during the night—or rather, the early hours of the morning, perhaps after he'd left to talk to the driver— someone had come along and taken the sweet, reasonable Kate he'd known, and replaced her with this irrational, upsetting Kate. He had long thought her the least changeable woman he had ever met, not at all prone to the sort of temperamental sulks and fits he'd grown accustomed to from other women of his acquaintance, most notably his own daughter.

And yet now he was discovering that any woman, no matter how rationally she carried herself the majority of the time, could be struck by these sudden and completely unexplainable mood swings.

Unless, of course, there was some reason Kate was behaving this way. Some reason, aside from the obvious one, that she was still angry with him for trying to make her his mistress. But he had already apologized for that, as well as tried to make it up to her by proposing. So why was she still so upset? He did not believe she was the type of woman to hold a grudge. If she were, she never would have agreed to help him search for Isabel.

Well, she'd get over it, he supposed. When all this was over—when, God willing, they found Isabel, and Kate, as he knew she would, reasoned her out of this mad plan to marry that bastard Craven—then he would make it all up to her.

See if he didn't.

Chapter Twenty-eight

*I*t was past midnight by the time they arrived in Gretna Green. Kate had long since sunk into an uneasy and not very comfortable sleep, and when the chaise finally stopped moving, she didn't wake up. Instead, she settled herself more deeply into the seat, appreciative that the jolting she'd endured for so many hours was halted at long last.

But she wasn't allowed to sleep for long. Soon she was being rocked again, not by the motion of the moving carriage, but by a hand upon her shoulder.

"Kate, wake up." The marquis's breath was warm upon her ear. "We're here."

She rolled over irritably until her back was to him—not an easy feat, since the seat was narrow, and her crinoline very wide, indeed. Still, she was comfortable—well, more comfortable than she'd been all day, anyway—and couldn't bear the thought of moving.

"I don't care," she said, keeping her eyes tightly closed, as if doing so would make him disappear. "Just let me sleep."

"You can't sleep in the chaise, Kate."

Burke's voice was filled with something undefinable. In her sleepy haze, Kate took it for tolerant amusement, and she wanted to say, *I am* not *a child*, even though she knew she was acting like one. Only she was so *tired*. Why couldn't he just go away and let her sleep?

Then, the next thing she knew, he'd slipped one arm behind her back, and another beneath her knees, and was lifting her bodily out of the chaise.

Kate was awake at once, fully awake and extremely unhappy. She expressed this unhappiness by sending a fist in the direction of the marquis's breastbone.

"Put me down," she said. "I'm not an invalid. I can walk."

The marquis looked down at the ground. "But Kate—"

"Put me *down,* I said."

Burke sighed, and did as she asked. She immediately sank up to her ankles in an enormous puddle of muddy rainwater.

"Oh. . . ." Dismayed, Kate lifted her hem and looked down at her thoroughly soaked feet. Burke, beside her, looked down at them, as well, as she turned her ankle this way and that, squinting at the damage in the light that spilled from the windows of the inn.

"I tried to tell you," he said. He didn't sound tolerant anymore, but he definitely sounded amused. "But you just hit me—"

"I know," she said.

"You're the one who insisted on being put down."

"I know," she said.

"If you hadn't found my proximity so repugnant," he said, "I would happily have carried you all the way up to the room."

"I *know,*" she said, this time through gritted teeth. The water was really quite cold.

Beside her, the marquis sighed. Then, bending down, he lifted her again.

This time, Kate did not protest. In fact, she threw her arms around his neck, and held on for all she was worth as he carried her across the stable yard, up the stairs to the inn door, through the door and into the firelit front room . . .

Where Kate saw so many people glance up at them from the tavern tables at which they sat, that she instantly buried her face in his shoulder, so that she did not have to meet their gazes. Burke noticed, of course, and found *that* amusing, too. She heard him chuckle, deep in his throat.

Well, wasn't that nice? Wasn't it just so nice that she was

able to provide him with so much amusement?

"It's not funny," she said, her voice muffled against his coat.

"It isn't," he agreed with her, as he began mounting the stairs to the second floor. "But you are."

"I'm not," she said, her voice still muffled. "I'm embarrassed. And tired and hungry and wet and miserable, that's all. I don't need people gawking at me."

"You needn't worry," he informed her conversationally. "They think we're married."

That made her raise her head. "They do?" she asked. "Why?"

"Well, I had to tell them so, when I found out they only had the one room left." He stopped walking, suddenly. "And here it is."

He flung open the door without even jostling her, then placed her gently on a deeply cushioned settle before a huge, roaring fire. Its heat instantly pervaded her damp boots and stockings, making her realize what she hadn't before, which was that not only was she tired and hungry and wet and miserable, but she'd been quite cold, too.

But the heat, comforting as it was, wasn't enough to keep her from reflecting that Burke Traherne had an infuriating tendency to get his own way, where she was concerned.

"Supper's on its way," Burke said, straightening, and stripping off his gloves and coat. "I can't vouch for its being edible, this late in the night, but the innkeeper assures me his wife has a meat pie or two tucked away somewhere. So long as it isn't haggis, I suppose it will be all right."

Kate felt the heat from the fire warming her face and hands, as well as her near frozen feet. It was a delicious feeling, to have gone so suddenly from such discomfort to such total luxury. Well, not total. She still had to get her boots off, of course, which was going to take some doing, considering that the laces were surely wet through, which would not make them at all easy to manipulate.

"Ah," she heard Burke say, when there was a tap upon the door. "That must be the food."

Then he disappeared for a while, and Kate was left by herself in the settle, which wasn't at all bad, considering the leth-
argy that was stealing over her, the delightful sleepiness she
could feel returning. Really, there was no need to fuss over
the fact that he'd managed to make it so that they would once
again be sharing a bed. She could sleep right here, right on
the settle, and not feel the worse for it. That was what she'd
do. She'd sleep right here, without even bothering about her
boots. So her toes were wet? They'd dry during the night. And
then tomorrow morning, when she was bound to feel horrible
again, she would have that many fewer things to worry
about. . . .

"Here." The marquis shoved something under her nose that
steamed. "Drink this."

The steam, she had to admit, smelled delicious. She asked,
"What is it?", even as she was wrapping her fingers around
the handle of the tankard, and tilting it toward her lips.

"Hot buttered rum," he said.

She made a face, and silently handed the tankard back to
him. But he pushed it toward her. He said, "It might help."

"I feel fine," Kate said. "But I definitely won't tomorrow,
if I drink *that*."

He took the tankard and, with a disapproving frown, removed it from her sight. But just as she was starting to relax
a little again, he was back, this time kneeling down beside the
settle. He seized her left ankle.

"What," Kate demanded, bolting upright, "do you think
you're doing?"

"You can't sit here, Kate, in these wet shoes." He had lifted
her left foot, and placed it on his upright thigh. Now he
plucked at the laces of her boot, not meeting her gaze, apparently completely absorbed in his work. "You'll catch cold."

She knew he was right, and that what he was doing was
hardly as shocking as some of the other activities in which the
two of them had engaged the night before. And yet somehow,
her modesty—the shreds of it she had left—was outraged.

"You can't just," she sputtered, and then realizing she was
speaking loudly enough to be heard down the hall, perhaps

even all the way belowstairs, lowered her voice. "You can't just start—start taking off my *boots* like that."

"Certainly I can," he said, sounding infuriatingly reasonable.

"No you can't," she insisted. "And you can't just tell people that we're married when you know perfectly well we're not."

He asked, quite calmly, "What would you have wanted me to do instead, Kate?"

"Well, is this the only inn in Gretna Green? Couldn't we have found one with *two* rooms available?"

"After midnight? In this weather? At this time of year, with the hunting so good?" He regarded her humorously above her knee. "Besides, what would have been the point? You know we'd only have ended up together again, in the end."

She sucked in her breath to hiss, "Burke, last night was a—"

"Mistake," he said, turning back to her soaked laces. "Yes, yes, I know. This morning, too. You've made your feelings on that matter perfectly clear. Turn your foot a little this way, would you, sweetheart?"

"And that's another thing," she said. "You can't call me sweetheart. I am not your sweetheart." He had pried off her left boot. Now his fingers started to slide up her leg, beneath her skirt. She immediately snatched her foot away.

"What do you think you're doing?" she asked with a gasp.

He snatched her foot right back again. "Removing your stocking," he said, keeping a firm grip on her ankle. "It's drenched."

He was right, her stocking was drenched. And bending over to remove it herself, with her corset stays pinching, and her crinoline bunching up, was not something she relished. She was so tired. And his fingers were so warm. . . .

What was it she'd been saying? Oh, yes. She'd been reminding him—and herself—of how futile it was, this dream that they might, one day, find happiness together.

"I am *not* your sweetheart," she repeated, as he went to work on her stocking, which was buttoned to the cuffs of her pantaloons. "I am your daughter's former chaperone, whom you debauched and—"

"I didn't debauch you," Burke interrupted, concentrating very hard on the buttons, which happened to be well under her skirt and crinoline, just above her knee. "You debauched me."

Kate could feel his breath, as well as the heat from the fire, on her thighs. It was a singularly unusual sensation, despite the fact that she still had the linen of her pantaloons to act as a shield between her bare skin and the heat of both his breath and the fire.

Despite these distractions, she went on, a bit grandly for a woman whose lover's head was between her knees. "In case you've forgotten, I was a *virgin*. Virgins are incapable of debauching anyone."

"What kind of virgin," he wanted to know, having successfully navigated the buttons, and now gently peeling the stocking down her calf, his fingertips just skimming the smooth white skin of her leg, "goes running about the house in the middle of the night dressed the way you happened to be dressed that evening?"

"Are you saying that I *wasn't* a virgin?"

"No," he said, having brought the stocking down past her heel, and up over her toes, then flinging it aside. "I'm just saying that anyone who was guarding her innocence as closely as you seem to think you were would have selected nightwear that was a little less . . . arousing."

He tucked her left foot, now bare, back onto the cushion of the settle, then seized hold of her right foot.

"That," Kate said, "is the most ridiculous thing I've heard in my life."

"The person who lures the other," Burke said, unlacing her right boot a good deal faster than he had her other, now that he'd got the hang of unlacing ladies' boots, "into sin through the use of her sensuality, is, by definition, the debaucher. Which makes you, Miss Mayhew, the guilty party. And you are not only guilty of debauching me, by the way, but of cruelly deserting me the following day, as well."

"Only," she declared, "because you were trying to make me your mistress."

"And then," he went on, as if she hadn't spoken, "when I proposed, I was again coldly rebuffed."

"You only asked me to marry you because you found out I come from a family that once had some money and property."

"Not to be offensive, Kate," he said, as he slowly lifted her skirt again and went to work on her right stocking, having made short work of her right boot. "But though I'm certain you loved your father very much, and he certainly might once have been a gentleman, he died under very different circumstances—"

"It isn't true," Kate declared truculently. "What everyone says about him. It isn't true."

"—and yet, knowing those circumstances full well, I still want to marry you. So how do you explain that?"

"Lunacy?" she suggested.

But it was becoming difficult to speak, because his fingers were on her again. She felt his knuckles graze the inside of her leg. This sensation, much more so than the feel of the heat of the fire, was what was making it very hard to remember what they were arguing about or even that they were arguing at all.

"I've retained enough of my wits to have gotten us to Scotland in record time, haven't I?" Burke pointed out.

"Only," Kate said, "out of fear that your daughter might meet the same fate as I did."

"Not so," he said, gently peeling the stocking down the curve of her calf. "If I thought Daniel Craven loved Isabel half so much as I love you, I would not have been opposed to the match."

She suddenly found it extremely difficult to speak. She cleared her throat. "That," she said, and had to clear it again. "That—"

"It's true," he said. He ran his hand along the skin from which he'd just peeled the sodden stocking. "You know it's true."

"I don't," she said, having even more trouble speaking now. "I can't—"

And then speech became completely impossible, because he had lowered his lips to the place where his hand had been. Kate nearly catapulted off the bench when she felt the prickly bite of his whiskers against the silken skin of her thigh, followed immediately afterward by the infinitely gentle caress of his lips—and then the feather-light but white-hot stroke of his tongue.

Kate's hand flew out. She didn't know what she was trying to do, stop him, or urge him on. But when her fingers met his thick, dark hair, they seemed to curl instinctively, until she was grasping him closer to her, and not pushing him away. No, not pushing him away at all.

"Burke," she said, but the name came out sounding funny, more like a gasp than an actual word.

And it didn't have the effect she'd wanted at all. Instead of stopping, instead of lifting his head, the marquis only became more persistent. He had tugged up the lace-trimmed cuffs of her pantaloons until they were bunched around the middle of her thighs. Now his mouth moved steadily up her leg, seeming to incinerate every inch of skin it encountered along the way—in a manner not unlike the way the fire, blazing before them, was rapidly turning the wood at its center to ash. Kate felt as if the marquis's tongue was turning *her* to ash. . . .

And it wasn't an unpleasant sensation, this being consumed in flame.

Oh, no. Not at all.

And then his fingers, sly and knowing, were slipping through the slit in the gusset of her pantaloons. Kate inhaled sharply as she felt them brush against her warm, moist core—not once, which might have been accidental, nor even twice, but three times, each contact sending jolts of pleasure through her.

And then they stayed there, those strong, competent fingers, purposefully pressing against that part of her which for so long had craved his touch. Kate's own fingers gripped his hair very tightly now, tightly enough to have hurt, if he'd been in a state of mind to notice anything except her breathless excitement, and the eager pounding of his own heart.

But when, a few seconds later, he replaced the fingers with his mouth, Kate experienced a rush of sensations unlike any other she had ever known. The wet warmth of his mouth on that tenderest of all places, the infinite gentleness of his lips, contrasting with the purposeful thrust of his tongue and the roughness of the razor stubble on his chin and jaw grazing the softness of her thighs . . . it was too much. It was wicked. It was wrong. It had to be wrong, because nothing that felt this good could possibly be right.

Kate wanted to tell him as much. She wanted to tell him to stop. After all, she still had her *bonnet* on, for God's sake. It couldn't be right to have a man's head between's one thighs when one was still wearing one's bonnet.

And yet it was extremely difficult to think about things like right and wrong when his lips and tongue were doing things to her, making her feel things she'd never imagined in her life were possible to feel. A part of her wanted to break away, push him back, clamp her legs shut and shove her skirts back into place, and stare down at him in outraged modesty. How else was she going to preserve her sanity? And yet another part of her—the stronger part—thought that sanity was over-rated, and what was the point of pushing him away, when with every flick of his tongue, every movement of his lips, he was bringing her closer to heaven?

Besides, even if she'd wanted to, she couldn't push him away. He had his arms wrapped around her hips, his broad shoulders wedged between her knees. His face was buried deeply between her thighs. She wasn't touching him—not purposely—anywhere now. She'd flung both her arms up over her head, and was gripping the back of the settle, as if somehow, that contact with the world beyond the one he was creating with his lips and tongue would keep her grounded.

It was then, almost senseless with pleasure, Kate said his name—a gasp, really, just a breathless movement of her lips. But he heard. He heard. And his name on her lips was, as always, his undoing. Before she was even fully aware of what was happening, Kate felt his head rise—his whiskers raking the sensitive skin between her thighs in the most delightfully painful way—and his arms tighten around her hips.

Then, next thing she knew, he was lifting her, right off the settle, her skirts bunched up around her waist, her heart hammering like a rabbit's, the gusset of her pantaloons drenched with her own desire. Lifted her straight up into the air, leaving her frantically pushing aside the rings of her crinoline, searching for his shoulders to seize and steady herself. Only by the time she found them, through all those yards of wool and lace, he was already setting her down again. She felt a mattress yield beneath her back, and then he was between her legs again, only this time, it was a knee nudging hers apart, as, above her, Burke struggled to undo his breeches. She watched him in a sort of daze, noticing, with a dizzy sort of sense of satisfaction, that his hands were trembling, and that, when he finally managed to unloose himself, he was huge with his need for her. *Ha*, she thought. I *did that.* I *did that to him.*

But then she didn't have a chance to think anything more, because, without so much as another caress, he was burying himself into her.

Not that Kate minded. Oh, it was startling, of course—startling enough to cause her to gasp in astonishment, though certainly, this was not something they hadn't done before. Still, it was startling to have this thick, solid mass suddenly invading her, where just seconds before, there'd been only the tenderest of kisses. Startling to have the full of his weight on top of her. Startling to reach out and feel the starched folds of his cravat, since they were both still fully dressed.

But perhaps most startling of all was how very little any of that bothered her, how very much she'd been craving this, how empty she had been feeling before, and now, how full—more than full, brimming . . . brimming with *him*. It seemed he only had to enter her, and she was already teetering on the edge of climax. Only because, she told herself, he'd brought her so close before, with his lips and tongue. That was the only reason. It wasn't that she wanted him. It wasn't that she needed him.

His lips were on her neck, just below her right earlobe. He'd pinned her wrists to the mattress when she'd tried to touch him, as if her touch were somehow dangerous. He was plunging into her, driving her deeper and deeper back into the mattress. And she was lifting her hips to meet him with every lunge.

All right. All right. She wanted him. She needed him.

And then she was slipping over the edge again. She didn't want to go there, didn't want to leave so soon. But he was pushing her there, with the raw emotion of his kisses, with the urgency of his thrusts. She wanted to cling to him, to keep from losing herself in the mindless pleasure toward which he was urging her. But his fingers were still wrapped around her wrists, as if she were a captive he was determined to keep from escaping, a prisoner upon whom he was intent on practicing the sweetest of tortures. . . .

She surrendered.

Waves of erotic pleasure rolled over her. Caught up in their inexorable grip, she could only writhe beneath him, her back arching, her hips raised against him. She let out a sound—a cry of helplessness—and then he released her wrists at last, and cradled her face with his hands as his body, too, was rocked with climactic release.

Kate, feeling much better than she had all day, was nevertheless a little bit ashamed. She found her voice after a few moments, and said sheepishly, "I never even had a chance to take my bonnet off," sounding as if somehow, the fact that she'd been wearing her bonnet the whole time was infinitely more shocking than anything else that had happened.

Burke raised his face from her throat, where he'd buried it after the last of the spasms that had racked his body had left him. He looked down at her bruised lips and storm-cloud grey eyes. A long strand of her dark blond hair had escaped from beneath the bonnet, and lay across her neck. He rose up to his elbows, shifting some of his weight from her much smaller frame, and lifted that strand.

"Most improper," he said, bringing the silken threads to his lips. "In the future, I shall remember always to remove your bonnet first."

"I should hope so," she said sleepily, quite forgetting that a future with him was the last thing she wanted.

Or was it the *only* thing she wanted?

Chapter Twenty-nine

$\mathcal{W}$hen Kate woke the next morning, she hadn't the slightest idea where she was, or how she had gotten there.

All she knew was that it had to be early, because she didn't yet feel sick. And she always felt sick, like clockwork, by eight.

It wasn't until she reached out, expecting to feel Lady Babbie's silken fur, and felt something a good deal more coarse, that she realized she was not still at White Cottage. When she opened one eye to investigate, she saw her hand resting in a nest of ink-black chest hair. Chest hair, she realized, when she bent forward to examine it more closely, that belonged to the Marquis of Wingate, who was lying—quite naked—in her bed.

Or was it that she was lying naked in *his* bed? She wasn't certain.

Then the events of the night before came back to her, and she sank back against the pillows with a quiet "Ohhh . . ." of comprehension.

Of course. They were in Gretna Green. They were there to find Isabel, who'd run off with Daniel Craven. Daniel Craven, who had once taken from Kate everything she held dear, and was now attempting, for reasons she could not begin to fathom, to do the same to Burke Traherne.

They were in an inn. The proprietors of which believed them to be married.

Well, they had certainly carried on as if they were. If married people even did things like that, which Kate highly doubted. She did not believe for an instant that her father had ever . . . Or that her mother had ever . . .

Her cheeks hot, Kate decided it was probably better not to think things like that. What had gone in her parents' bed had absolutely no relation to what went on in her own. None whatsoever. Particularly when what went on in her bed included Burke.

Burke. She turned her gaze toward him. He was still sleeping, his furred chest rising and falling in heavy slumber. That was how she thought of him now. As Burke. Not as Lord Wingate. As his name, Burke. It was a strange name, more of a last name than a Christian name, and much too small a name for the complex man who held it. Burke.

She leaned up on an elbow so that she could look at him more closely.

He had, she saw, with some surprise, a few grey hairs intermingled with the black, both on his head as well as on his chest. Well, and why not? He was in his late thirties, after all. He had a full-grown daughter. Well, practically full-grown, anyway. He had been how old when Kate was born? Thirteen.

Well, thirteen years' difference wasn't that much. And he certainly didn't look it. No one, seeing him now, would think him as old as thirty-six. Thirty, maybe. Maybe thirty-one or two. But not thirty-six. Oh, no. He was much too vital, too robust, for so advanced an age. Not that thirty-six was old. Just old for a man who was capable of doing . . . well, what they'd done, as many times as they had the past few days.

But they were going to have to stop doing *that,* she thought to herself, drawing her hand away from his chest. Really. Because how, after they found Isabel, and Kate kept Burke from killing Daniel Craven, could they continue? It wouldn't work. It couldn't work. She couldn't marry him, much as she wanted to.

She had reached out again, to touch him. He seemed to

draw her in that way. She constantly felt like touching him. Which was why, of course, she'd made him sit on the opposite seat all during those long hours in the chaise. She couldn't have him near her, within arm's reach, or she'd start touching him. She couldn't help herself. He drew her. It was shocking how he made her feel.

Shocking. Pathetic, was more like it.

Well, she wasn't going to let it happen again. In fact, she could nip it in the bud right now if she could only be up and dressed before he was . . . and before the nausea hit. It never lasted long, and if she could only dress without waking him.

Too late. She had merely pushed the blanket back and set one bare foot on the icy cold floor. But that small action had roused him. Suddenly, the furred chest she'd been admiring was on top of her, his weight pinning her to the bed. Both her wrists, engulfed in just one of his hands, were secured to the pillow above her head while he regarded her, his face just a few inches away from hers.

"Going somewhere?" he inquired quite casually, as if they were back in the town house on Park Lane, and they were passing one another in the hallway.

She said, her tongue feeling as if it had turned to lead in her mouth, "Um. No."

"I'm pleased to hear that," he said. "Because it occurs to me that this is quite a pleasant way to wake up. Don't you think so?"

Kate could hardly say no. Not with his heavy warmth pressing against her . . . especially between her legs, which he'd easily pried apart with his knee.

"In fact," Burke said, his voice a lazy drawl. "I think this is the way I want to wake up every morning." With the thumb of his free hand, he was tracing the outline of her lips, the rest of his fingers curled around her neck. "With you beneath me, I mean."

"That," Kate said, her own voice a husky shell of itself, "might be. . . ." He moved a little, and she was surprised to feel that he was already hard. Surprised and, to be strictly truthful, pleased.

"Uncomfortable," she finished.

"Uncomfortable?" Now he was kissing her where his thumb had been, the corners of her mouth, the place where her upper lips dipped in the middle, to form the shape of a hunter's bow. "What's uncomfortable about it?"

"Well," she said. "You do weigh a lot."

"Ah," he said. Now he was kissing her on the eyelids. "I can take care of that for you, actually."

A second later, he was beneath her, with Kate straddling his hips, and not having a very clear idea how she'd gotten there. When she pushed her hair out of her eyes, however, she could see that he was looking enormously pleased with himself.

"How about," he said, with a crooked grin, "we wake like *this* every morning? With *me* beneath *you*?"

She could feel his erection beneath her, prodding urgently at the soft furrow between her legs. And, much to her shame, her body reacted to his touch, sending a rush of warmth to her loins, and making it easy—oh, so very easy—for him simply to slide inside her, without her having to move an inch.

She sucked in her breath, and looked down at him with wide, reproachful eyes. But it was hard to be indignant when what he was doing felt so very right.

"Or better yet," he said, grinning up at her, "waking up *inside* you. Now that's"—on the word "that," he raised his hips, burying himself even more deeply within her—"more like it."

It was on the tip of Kate's tongue to remind him that this wasn't what they were here for. No, they were here to find Isabel. Weren't they?

But it was extremely difficult for Kate to think of anything else but Burke when he was inside her—about as difficult as it was for Burke to think of anything but Kate when she was anywhere near.

She certainly couldn't think of anything but him when his hands, as they were just then, were on her breasts, cupping them, caressing them. And she certainly couldn't think of anything but him when he was moving—with a slowness that was causing her toes to curl—in and then out of her. And when he slipped one of his hands beneath the fall of her hair, and around the back of her neck, and brought her face down until it was level with his, how was she supposed to remember anything but the way his lips felt on her mouth?

Then he was kissing her, his tongue forcing her mouth to open to him, just as he'd forced her legs to open to him. The tips of her breasts were skimming the thick forest of his chest hair. Suddenly, and in spite of her best intentions, she was moving a little on top of him. Not much, and certainly not consciously. But enough so that his hands slipped around eagerly to cup her buttocks, and bring her down harder against him.

This was *not* how she'd intended to start the day. She would have thought, after last night . . . Was the man insatiable?

Apparently so.

And apparently she was, too, since she was clinging to him in a disgraceful manner, not just with her lips and hands, but gripping him with her thighs, as well, as if he were a horse she'd mounted.

But this wasn't like riding. Well, not your average horse, anyway. Maybe . . . maybe a winged horse. Because she certainly felt as if she were flying—or rather, being flown, higher and higher. Not toward the burning sun, which would have been thoroughly unpleasant. And not toward the moon, either, ice-cold and distant. But instead toward the stars, sparkling in a sky of velvet black. She could reach out, it seemed, and if she stretched far enough, touch those stars. . . .

And then it was if she'd flown a little too high, and bumped her head into that velvet sky, because suddenly, all the stars were tumbling down around her, as if it were raining stars. She was trapped in a shower of diamonds. But she didn't mind. She held out her arms, trying to catch as many as she could, laughing, delighted. . . .

And then she opened her eyes, and realized she had collapsed against Burke's chest, and he was laughing at her. Well, not really laughing. He was having too much trouble catching his own breath for that. Plus his heart was thundering with unnatural speed against her breasts. But he definitely looked smug.

"Are you all right?" he asked, between pants.

She moved a little against him. Had he—oh, yes, he most assuredly had. She pushed her hair back from her eyes and looked at him, trying to assume a blank expression.

"Of course I'm all right," she said. "Why wouldn't I be all right?"

He looked so self-satisfied, she thought it was a wonder his head didn't burst. "Well, with all that screaming, I'm afraid we're probably going to have people banging on the door, thinking I've murdered you."

Indignant, Kate slid from him.

"Careful," he warned. "You'll endanger our chances at a family."

"I don't think," she said, dryly, pulling the sheets back up to her chin, "that's going to be something we need to worry about."

But he still didn't understand. He obviously thought she was referring to their future together—or lack thereof—and reacted accordingly, leaning over to grip her by the shoulders.

"You can't mean," he said, glaring down at her, "that you *still* don't intend to marry me? After *that*? And last night?"

It had to be getting close to eight. Kate could feel the first warning signs of impending nausea.

"Don't you think," she said, swallowing hard, "that you ought to be concerning yourself with finding your daughter, and not whether or not I want to marry you?"

He opened his mouth, but seemed unable to find an adequate retort. Instead, he let go of her, and rolled away, his disgust evident.

Still, even disgusted, the Marquis of Wingate, sans apparel, was something to look at. And Kate did look, despite how ill she was beginning to feel. He stormed about the room, throwing on his trousers, and then his shirt. He wouldn't look at her.

Which was fine. She didn't want him to look at her. The more he ignored her, the easier it would be, in the end. . . .

It was a half hour later—it had to be, because Kate was well into her nausea—when Burke came back into the room he'd left in such a huff. He carried with him an enormous tray, from which the odors of bacon and coffee drifted. Pleasant enough odors under normal circumstances. But in the present one, deadly.

"Here, Kate," Burke said, closing the door with his foot. "I took this off the maid in the hallway. I didn't figure you'd be up yet. Funny, I never pegged you for a laze-about. Well, get up now, and come eat some breakfast."

Kate could only pull the sheet up over her head.

Burke was not amused. "Come along, Kate," he said. "We haven't all day, you know. I'm going to have a devil of a time finding Craven. Do you know how many places they could be hiding? This isn't a big town, it's true, but—"

It was too much for her. The smell, the sight of that bacon . . . Suddenly, she threw the sheet back, sat up, and leaned over the side of the bed.

She hadn't anything inside of her to vomit up, of course. She hadn't eaten any supper the night before. Nevertheless, she retched and retched. As she retched, she cried. She couldn't help it. She was completely humiliated, the more so because he'd rushed toward her, and laid a cool hand upon her forehead, twisting her hair out of her face with his other hand. Now he was holding her, whispering tender endearments to her as she retched.

"Shhh," he said, when she tried, unsuccessfully, to make her feelings for him, which were not very friendly just then, known. "It's all right. I'm sorry, Kate. I didn't know."

He tugged strands of hair from her damp forehead, picking it up off her neck, letting air, sweet, cold air, cool her. After a while—a long while, it seemed, but probably no longer than five or ten minutes—she began to feel better. She made a movement, and he let go of her. She sank back against the pillows, and looked everywhere but at him.

But manlike, he didn't notice. He sat beside her, his green eyes soft with concern. "Why, Kate?" he asked, reaching out to push more hair from her sweaty face. "Why didn't you tell me?"

She could only shake her head.

"You can't be feeling missish, can you," he persisted, "because I didn't guess? I admit I ought to have known when you had so much trouble getting up yesterday, but I'm afraid I wasn't quite quick enough. But now. . . . Well, of course, now I know." He looked down at her. There wasn't much compassion in his expression anymore. "Which leads me back to the original question. Why didn't you tell me, Kate?"

She rolled over, but he was sitting on the sheet. She tugged at it wearily. When he moved, with a sigh, she wrapped the cloth around her, and turned her back on him. It was the only way, she was convinced, she was going to survive this conversation, which she'd been dreading since he had appeared beside the washline back at White Cottage.

"I didn't want to tell you," she said to the wall.

"Why, Kate?" His deep voice was filled with perplexity.

She groaned. She couldn't help it. She'd known this was going to happen. She'd known it. If only she hadn't slept with him, this wouldn't be happening now. Furious with herself, she reached up and swiped at the corners of her eyes with her wrists. "You don't understand."

"No," he said. His voice was filled with the tenderest of concern, but coupled with incomprehension. He didn't make another move to touch her, however, for which she was grateful. "No, I don't understand. You're pregnant with my child, and you weren't even going to tell me. Were you ever going to tell me, Kate?"

She couldn't speak. Not if she didn't want to start sobbing.

"Were you?"

She inhaled. "I wanted to. Only I couldn't. Because, you see, I can't . . ."

Burke knit his eyebrows. "You can't what?"

"I can't marry you." She said it in a rush, to get it over with. "I just can't do it, Burke."

Now his expression was not so much one of concern as one of total exasperation. "Why the devil not?"

"I can't," she said between gritted teeth, "go back."

"Go back?" Burke shook his head. Her words were oddly familiar, and yet he couldn't, for the life of him, remember where he'd heard them before. "Go back where?"

"To your world, the one . . . the one I used to live in."

"My world? What are you talking about, my world?"

"London," Kate explained. "You don't know—you *can't* know—what it was like, after my father was accused of having swindled all of those people." Kate shook her head, her gaze far away. "They were our friends—at least, they'd professed to be. But every one of them—every last one—turned on us. No one believed in my father's innocence. No one believed it was Daniel, and not my father, who—"

She broke off, choking back a sob. Burke, staring down at her in stunned silence, realized why her words had sounded familiar. Nanny Hinkle. Nanny Hinkle had tried to warn him. *She won't go back*, the old woman had said. This, then, was what she'd meant.

He opened his mouth to say something, but she went on, in a ragged whisper. "And then when he died . . . when he died, even though the fire was ruled officially as accidental, everyone—*everyone*—believed the rumor that my father had set it on purpose, that he had deliberately tried to kill himself and my mother. They believed they'd driven him to it, you see. That he couldn't bear the shame."

She swung the gaze she'd fastened unseeingly onto the bedpost toward him. "But he didn't do it," she said fiercely. "He didn't steal that money, and he didn't set that fire. They hadn't any right to say what they did. No right at all! Do you understand now, Burke? I can't go back. I could hardly bring myself to do it before. You had to offer me three hundred pounds to do it. But now . . . now I've got the baby to think of. I won't go back to that world. And I know I can't ask you to leave it."

He stared down at her. "Can't you?"

"Don't you see?" Kate shook her head wildly. "I'd rather raise this child on my own, in disgrace, than amongst the people who let Daniel Craven . . ."

"Let Daniel Craven what, Kate?" Burke asked carefully, when she did not go on.

This time, when she looked at him, there was nothing distant at all about her gaze. She was there, right there with him, and now there was an emotion other than angry sorrow in her eyes. If Burke wasn't mistaken, there was fear there now, as well.

"Nothing," Kate said quickly. Too quickly.

"Kate." He reached out and laid a heavy hand across the fingers with which she was twisting the edge of the sheet that covered her. "Tell me. The people who let Daniel Craven what?"

Her voice, though it was no louder than a whisper, seemed to slice through the silence between them like a scream. "Get away," she murmured, unable to meet his gaze, "with murder."

Chapter Thirty

*H*ere it is," Kate said, looking down at the slip of paper she held in her gloved hand. They were strolling, on foot, down a narrow street. To an observer, they might have looked like any happy couple, paying a call on friends or family. A closer inspection, however, would have revealed that the gentleman's jaw was very firmly set, and that the lady seemed to fear for the fingers she'd slipped into the crook of his arm, as the gentleman kept tensing his muscles.

"Number twenty-nine," Kate said, looking at the brass numbers by the unlit gaslight above the door. "This must be it."

It was not a particularly bad street—middle class, Burke supposed. But it was not the sort of street on which he'd ever hoped to find his daughter hiding with her lover.

Then again, there wasn't any sort of street on which he hoped to find his daughter hiding with her lover.

A lover who may—or may not—have killed.

One thing was certain: it had been far too easy to track him. The man had made himself conspicuous—much too much so, for someone who ought to have been doing everything in his power to avoid detection. Kate's tearful confession—that it had been Daniel Craven who'd set the fire that had killed her parents—had been interrupted by a tap at the door. When Burke went to answer it, he discovered a man there to whom he had, while ordering their breakfast, put a few questions concerning newcomers to the neighborhood.

Sure enough, the man had found someone who, for a small reward, had been quite ready to admit that someone fitting Craven's description—and Isabel's, as well—had taken a nearby house.

"They've just rented it," Burke had informed Kate, as she'd hurried to dress. "And they were most definitely there this morning. The fellow I spoke to said a milk delivery had been made there just an hour ago."

"Well, then," Kate had replied, with a bravery she had been far from feeling. "We'd best go then, hadn't we?"

But now, standing outside the door, Kate looked a good deal less brave, and Burke himself felt nothing but a violent desire to punch something.

"Supposing," he said, as they stood there, staring at the door. "She won't come with us."

"She will," Kate said, though she did not sound very certain.

"And if we're too late?"

She looked up at him. It was another grey day. Not raining, thank God. But unseasonably cold and dank. In spite of her fear, bright spots of color stood out on her cheeks, and the tip of her nose was pink.

"Burke," she said, in a warning tone. "If we are, you mustn't kill him. Do you understand? I don't care if this is Scotland. They still have laws. You mustn't commit murder. For Isabel's sake, Burke."

The sound of his name on her lips was almost enough to make him forget himself, and snatch her up, and rain kisses down upon that impossibly small mouth.

Almost.

The reminder of what she had *almost* gotten away with kept him from doing anything so sentimental, so foolish. She could only have known for certain that she was carrying his child for about eight weeks, or so. Two months. That wasn't so terribly long to have kept it from him. But if Isabel hadn't run off, and he hadn't come looking for her—

She reached out and turned the crank doorbell.

Burke heard it ring, deep inside the house. After a minute or two, a step was heard behind the door, and then it swung open. A maid, no more than a child in a frilled apron and oversized cap, looked out at them expectantly.

"Yes, sir?" she said. "Mum?"

Burke wanted to speak. He wanted to do this part, at least, on his own, without Kate's help. But he was perfectly incapable of forming the necessary words. All he could think of was taking Daniel Craven's face and grinding it, as hard as he could, into some dirt.

"Hello," Kate said sweetly to the girl. "Is Mr. Craven at home?"

"Oh, no, mum," the maid said. "Mr. Craven is gone back to London."

Burke had not been aware of how tense he'd become until Kate let out a little cry of pain, and drew her fingers away from the crook of his elbow, where they'd been resting. Apparently, he had inadvertently crushed them between his bicep and forearm.

Recovering herself, Kate said to the maid, "Back to London?"

"Yes, mum. You've only just missed him. He left not half an hour ago."

Kate had not even realized how much she'd been dreading a confrontation with Daniel until she felt the relief that flooded through her at hearing he was gone. This was not, however, a feeling apparently shared by Burke, who looked staggered by the information.

"And . . . Mrs. Craven?" Kate asked, since it appeared that Burke's disappointment in having to delay his pummeling of Daniel Craven had temporarily rendered him incapable of speech. "Did she escort Mr. Craven back to London?"

"Mrs. Craven?" The girl looked perplexed.

"There was a young lady with him," Kate questioned quickly, not daring to look in Burke's direction. "Was there not?"

"Oh," the maid said, relief—and, if Kate wasn't mistaken,

a bit of scorn—in her rosy-cheeked face. "You mean the Lady Isabel?"

"Yes," Kate said. "The Lady Isabel. Did she go back to London with Mr. Craven?"

An expression that could only be called indignant crossed the girl's face. "Indeed *not*," the maid declared, as if such an idea were preposterous—almost as preposterous as the idea of a Mrs. Craven.

"Then," Kate asked, fighting for patience. The parlormaid had clearly not been hired because of her pretty manners, or sharp intellect. "Could you tell us where we might find her ladyship?"

The maid's quick, darting glance over her shoulder, up the narrow staircase behind her, was all Burke needed. He thrust out a hand, giving the door a violent shove. The maid let out a startled shriek, and jumped hastily out of the way. It was a good thing she did, too, since Burke strode past her without so much as a beg-your-pardon.

"Where is she?" he growled, striding down a narrow, unattractively decorated hallway.

"See here," the girl squealed. "You can't come bustin' in here like this. Who d'you think you are? The master isn't goin' to like this, not one bit—"

But Burke was already climbing the stairs, taking them two at a time. Kate hurried after him, steadying herself with one hand on the banister.

"Burke," she called urgently. "Please—"

The first room he tried was empty. The second, however, revealed a figure slumped in a deep chair by a miserable fire. In the dismal light thrown by the embers, it was impossible to tell the identity of the person within the chair.

But the heart-wrenching sobs that wracked the figure's shoulders could belong to only one person: Isabel.

And yet, to Kate's astonishment, Burke did not fly to his daughter's side. Instead, he hung back from the doorway, peering uncertainly into the room. At Kate's questioning look, he murmured, "I can't."

"Burke," Kate said softly, but he only shook his head.

"No," he said. "She doesn't want me. You go."

It was Kate's turn to shake her head. "But—"

"She won't want to see me," Burke assured her.

"Burke, that's—"

"You don't know." His tone was flat. "You don't know how it was when . . . when last I saw her. She won't want to see me. You go."

Kate, recognizing the perilous look in his eyes, said, "All right."

And she went. Moved from the hallway into the darkened room, tugging on her gloves as she did so, so that when she knelt down beside the chair in which Isabel lay curled, she was able to place her fingers on the girl's hand.

Isabel broke off from her noisy sobbing and peered at Kate through tear-swollen eyelids.

"Oh!" she cried, upon recognizing who knelt beside her. "Oh, Miss Mayhew!"

And in a flurry of lace and petticoats, Isabel threw herself from the chair, and wrapped her arms so tightly about Kate's neck that she very nearly choked. "Oh, Miss Mayhew," she cried again. The sobbing began again, with a renewed note of anguish.

Kate, stroking the girl's tangled hair, attempted to comfort her as best she could. Bit by bit, Isabel spilled her pathetic story, beginning with an impassioned, "Oh, Miss Mayhew, if only I had listened to you! You never did like him, and I ought to have known you had good reason not to. Only he was so much more attentive than Geoffrey ever was, and he said he loved me, and you can't imagine how wretched I was, after you left," and ending with, "And then not an hour ago, he strode in and told me he was going back to London—going back to London without me. He wouldn't let me come with him! And he wasn't coming back. He said he'd had enough— enough of my being so spoiled and demanding. Only I wasn't, Miss Mayhew! I swear I wasn't! But he didn't care. He abandoned me—in *Scotland*. I didn't know what I was going to do. I couldn't imagine Papa would ever let me come home, not after . . . Oh, Miss Mayhew, I never imagined anyone could be so cruel! Why did he do it? *Why?*"

Kate, holding on to the girl's quivering shoulders, tried to maintain a calm, rational demeanor. But inwardly, she was a good deal unsettled. Why *had* Daniel done it? What could he have been thinking? Because, if Isabel was telling the truth— and Kate could not believe the girl capable of prevarication, not in her impassioned state—they had not only not married, but Daniel had not laid so much as a finger upon her. The two had kept separate bedrooms throughout their journey together, a fact Isabel seemed to view as perfectly natural—an example of Daniel's innate sense of "chivalry."

But what Isabel called chivalry, Kate called suspicious. Daniel Craven was no gentleman. She knew that better than anyone. And as he was in no need of Isabel's money, she had assumed—although it had been with some degree of disbe- lief—that the reason he'd embarked upon this wild scheme was that he had actually found himself attracted to the girl, and had been unable to think of any other way to get her.

But now it appeared that that had not been the case, either. So why on earth had he bothered? Why had he gone to all the time and trouble, if only to end up abandoning the poor child in the end?

But these were questions to which Kate was going to have to wait for an answer.

"What do you mean, you couldn't imagine your father would ever let you come home?" She gave the girl a gentle shake. "Why, he's been out of his mind with worry, these past few days."

Isabel applied the handkerchief Kate had given her to the corners of her eyes.

"Oh," she said shakily. "I knew what I was doing was wicked. Only I couldn't stand it, being home with him. You never saw such a beast as he was after you left, Miss May- hew."

Kate smoothed some of Isabel's tumbled hair back from her face. "Whom do you mean?" she asked, only half listening.

"Why, Papa, of course," Isabel said matter-of-factly. "I

want you to know that I don't blame you a bit for leaving us like that, Miss Mayhew. I *know* how horrid he was that night . . . the night he caught you in the garden with—with Daniel. He was even more horrid to *me,* after you left. I suppose he wired you to come and get me, since he doesn't want to see me anymore."

Kate, conscious that Burke was standing in the hallway, undoubtedly overhearing every word, hurried to interrupt the girl before she said something that would cause irreparable damage.

"What utter nonsense," she said briskly. "Your father's right outside this door. He thought *you* wouldn't want to see *him*—"

And then there was a great flurry of lace and crinoline as Isabel hurried to her feet, having finally spied her father lurking in the doorway. A second later, he stepped into the room, and she flung herself into his arms, with a delighted cry of "Papa!"

It was a joyous reunion. So joyous, in fact, that Kate felt it only proper to withdraw, and leave the two of them alone to enjoy it. Discreetly, she made her way down the hallway to the staircase, at the bottom of which she noticed the little maid, pacing back and forth across the foyer, looking furious.

Determined to discover the truth about Daniel's whereabouts—or at the very least, his motives—Kate made her way down the stairs, trying to appear as unconcerned as possible.

"Oy," the maid said, when she noticed Kate. "Listen here. You've got no cause to come bustin' in here like you did. Dan—I mean, Mr. Craven's not done anything wrong."

"Of course he hasn't," Kate said soothingly, when she reached the bottom of the staircase. "No one is suggesting any such thing."

"I don't know what *she's* been telling you"—the maid lifted a reproachful gaze toward the ceiling—"but it ain't true. Mr. Craven's a right gentleman, he is. He didn't lay a finger on her."

"So I've heard," Kate said, pausing in front of an ormoluframed mirror to tuck a few loose strands of hair back beneath her bonnet.

The maid's face, which Kate could see plainly reflected in the mirror, lost some of its pinched look.

"She told you that, then?" The girl nodded. "Well, it's the truth. He's got no interest in *her*. Not *that* way."

It was quite evident from the maid's tone where she believed Daniel Craven's interests lay instead.

"Indeed?" Kate turned, and looked down at the young woman. "I don't believe I've introduced myself. Kate Mayhew." She extended her hand.

The girl blinked at the gloved hand for a second or two before taking it loosely in hers, and giving it a squeeze. "Martha," she said quickly. Only because she seemed to have trouble pronouncing the *th*, it came out sounding like "Marfa."

"How do you do, Martha?" Kate asked. She busied herself with rifling through her reticule, as if she were looking for something.

"I do all right," Martha said sullenly.

"It's strange, don't you think, Martha," Kate went on mildly, "that Mr. Craven should have left you so suddenly."

The girl threw back her shoulders. "He only went," she said importantly, "to settle a few business matters in town. He'll be back by week's end. He told me so."

This was an entirely different version of events leading up to Daniel's departure than the one told by Isabel.

"And the Lady Isabel?" Kate asked casually. "Was she to wait for his return?"

Martha's expression turned scornful again. "Not her. He said she'd be well gone by the time he got back. He said her family would come. . . ." Martha's blue eyes widened, and her mouth clamped shut. Apparently, it occurred to her that she had said too much.

But what little she had said was all that Kate needed to hear. She was still uncertain as to the reasons behind Daniel's scheme, but that it went beyond a mere elopement she had now ascertained beyond a doubt.

"Go upstairs," Kate said, closing her reticule and looking

down at the maid, not without compassion, "and pack up her ladyship's things. We'll leave as soon as you're finished."

The girl shifted her weight uncertainly from one foot to another. "You . . . you're her family, then?" Martha asked.

"Yes," Kate said decidedly. "We're her family."

Chapter Thirty-one

$\mathcal{S}$moke.

It was what had wakened Kate that night, so many years ago. The smell of smoke. It was a smell which had stayed with her for months afterward, and not just because it had clung to everything she owned—everything that was not lost to the fire or to the debt collectors after her parents' deaths. It was an odor to which she'd grown so sensitive, so alert, that the slightest burning of a tea scone sent her scurrying down to the kitchens, even from several floors above.

But it seemed unlikely, when she opened her eyes that night, that anyone was burning scones at three o'clock in the morning.

That was what the face of the watch she'd placed by her bedside read, and Kate had no reason to disbelieve it. Her sleep had not exactly been restful, but rather fitful, and not just because she was sharing her bed with another. Another who, even as she lay there, blinking in the semidarkness, was snoring fitfully.

Not the Marquis of Wingate. No, the marquis never snored. But his daughter, the Lady Isabel, did, and quite noisily, too.

Kate turned her head on her pillow, wondering whether she ought to wake the sleeping girl. Isabel had dozed off in the midst of one of the many tearful fits she'd suffered since they'd found her. Isabel had her own room, of course, but she seemed to prefer Kate's. Now she slept, fully clothed, in the room to which Kate had been shown by the innkeeper's garrulous wife, leaving Kate to wonder whether or not she was really smelling smoke, or had only dreamed she did. . . .

And to continue pondering the topic that had kept her awake long after Isabel had dozed off, a topic she had not dared bring up with the girl. . . .

What was she going to do?

Not about Daniel Craven. That subject, as far as Kate was concerned, was closed. Burke had made it more than clear that he intended to find the man and dispatch him at his earliest convenience. Kate's attempts to convince him that, though Daniel had treated Isabel very shabbily, indeed, he had not actually caused any irreparable damage, had fallen upon deaf ears. The Marquis of Wingate intended to find Daniel Craven and kill him, just as soon as he'd safely delivered his daughter back to London.

And Kate found that she couldn't blame him. Daniel had outdone himself this time. Though she tried, Kate could not, for the life of her, imagine what he'd hoped to accomplish in his mad dash with Isabel. . . .

Well, that wasn't quite true. She had one theory about why he might have done it. But it was so perfectly ridiculous— and so thoroughly frightening—that she pushed it immediately from her mind.

No. Daniel, being Daniel, had seen in Isabel an invitation to a fortune, and he'd accepted that invitation, only to find that in the end, for some reason known only to him, he could not quite bring himself to go through with it.

But what was the point of wondering at the motives of such a man, when there was another so much more complicated— and so much more appealing—man to consider? For the real reason Kate could not sleep was that she could not stop thinking about Burke.

And not just about Burke, but about what she was going to do tomorrow, when he ordered the carriage round.

For she realized now that what she'd said to the maid Martha that morning was true: they were a family.

And there wasn't a blessed thing she could do about it. Not when she was as hopelessly in love with Burke as she knew she was. Not when she knew she would never be happy without him.

How could Kate turn her back on such love, when all that was keeping her from embracing it was her dislike of the social circle in which he traveled? She felt now that she could endure it—endure it all, the sneers, the cuts, the stares—as long as she had Burke at her side. Even toward Isabel, she knew now, she felt as protective and affectionate a love as if the girl were her own child. With such love to support her, no social slight could hurt her. Not anymore.

The problem, of course, was that now that she'd finally realized her love for Burke was stronger than her hatred for his social set, she had no idea how to go about letting him know it.

They had not had a private moment together since discovering Isabel. And Burke's attitude toward her during the course of the day had been decidedly unloverlike. Oh, he'd been unfailingly polite. But he had certainly never made anything like another proposal.

And as firmly as she'd put his last proposal down, he wasn't likely to make another.

Nor could she blame him. He had been appalled, Kate knew, by what she'd revealed to him that morning—first about the baby, and the fact that she would not marry him, and then, later, the truth about Daniel Craven. Appalled and, she knew, disbelieving. And why should he have believed her—about Daniel, anyway—when no one else ever had?

In any case, he'd made no reference to it afterward. All through the rest of the day, the marquis had not said a word to her, except when obligated to do so out of politeness. His attentions had, rightfully, been focused on Isabel. It was in deference to Isabel's still fragile state that the marquis decided they would stay another night in Gretna Green to allow her to rest, before starting back for London the next morning. It had been for Isabel's sake that Burke had sought out the finest hotel in the town, and bribed the innkeeper to turn over three of his best rooms to the marquis, in spite of the fact he'd not reserved them beforehand.

And now it was three o'clock in the morning, and though Kate was in what was surely the most comfortable bed, in the prettiest hotel room, in all of Scotland, she couldn't sleep.

She had been, she knew, a fool. And like any fool, now she would be forced to suffer for her folly. She would have to go back to Lynn Regis, and to Nanny Hinkle. The marquis would, of course, offer support for their unborn child, and Kate supposed she would have to take it, since she truly had no other source of income. And he would doubtless insist on seeing the child from time to time, which would necessitate her being in his company, making it all the more difficult for her to forget him.

Miserable, Kate rolled over . . .

. . . and smelled it again.

This time it was unmistakable. Smoke. Wafting through her bedroom.

But not, she realized, smoke from a fire. No, this was the smell of burning, all right, but burning tobacco. Someone was smoking. Someone was smoking, and quite close by.

Bemused, Kate sat up and reached for her peignoir. The rooms to which the party belonging to the Marquis of Wingate had been assigned were on the third floor, where each chamber contained a pair of French doors that opened out onto a small terrace, upon which, the innkeeper's wife had explained, when she'd shown it to Kate, guests liked to breakfast, weather permitting. Getting out of bed, Kate could see that the woman had left the doors to this terrace open a crack, allowing not only the autumn chill to seep in, but the smoke she kept smelling.

Could it be—Kate's heart leapt a little—that Burke was out there, on the terrace belonging to his own room? Had he gone outside to smoke in solitude? She had known the marquis to partake of a cigar now and then. Perhaps he, like herself, was finding it difficult to sleep, and had stepped outside to enjoy some fresh air. . . .

She didn't hesitate another second.

She swung open the French door, and stepped outside.

The rain of the past few days had passed, though the sky was still not completely cloudless. It was dark, but a bit of moonlight shone . . . enough so that she could plainly see such things as the small wrought-iron table at the center of her narrow terrace, and the fountain—shut off, this time of year—in the hotel's courtyard below.

She did not need the moonlight, however, to trace the source of the pungent aroma of burning tobacco. She saw that quite clearly when the person smoking it inhaled, and sent the tip of the cigar glowing bright red. He was not sitting, however, on the adjacent terrace, or even on the one after that. Instead, he was leaning against the railing of Kate's, and it was clear, from the light which spilled from the open doors to the terrace belonging to the room next door to hers, how he'd gotten there.

If he was surprised to see Kate join him so suddenly, he didn't show it. Instead, he only said softly, "Well, isn't this fortuitous. I was just sitting here thinking, How in hell am I to wake her without alerting the bloody child?, when out you step. Good show, Kate."

Kate, shaken to the core, reached up and gripped the collar of her peignoir, as if clutching the flimsy material together would keep out not only the chilly air, but his unwelcome presence, as well.

"Daniel," she said, through lips that had gone bloodless. "What . . . what are you doing here?"

But the truth was, she knew. She had known all along.

And it hadn't anything at all to do with Isabel.

"The marquis is right next door," Kate said quickly, before he had a chance to reply. She pointed at the balcony to her right, though truthfully, she hadn't the slightest idea if that was Burke's room, or the room Isabel had eschewed for hers. No light came through the tightly sealed French doors. "He's furious with you. He'll kill you, if he finds out you're here."

"I know it," Daniel said, calmly exhaling another long plume of blue smoke. "I took care, however, not to make my way upstairs until I'd received word he'd retired for the night."

His expression grew thoughtful. "It's amazing what a man can discover when he ventures into the kitchens of an establishment."

"Oh, you have quite a way with the help," Kate said bitterly. "I'm certain it will be months before Martha recovers from your venturing into *her* establishment."

He cocked up an inquisitive eyebrow. "Martha?" he asked. And then, brightening, he continued, "Oh, Martha. Yes, yes. Charming girl. Not quite as charming, perhaps, as the wife of the proprietor of this fine old place, but quite equally . . . malleable."

Kate set her jaw. "So you secured from that charmingly *malleable* woman a key to the room next to mine," she said coolly.

"Indeed." Daniel stretched out his long legs, and crossed them at the ankles. "You are an extremely difficult person to locate, Kate. You know I tried for some time to contact you after that fascinating conversation we had—what was it, now? Three months ago?—at Lady Tetmiller's ball, that night many weeks ago. I attempted to continue this conversation in Lord Wingate's garden, but . . . well, you remember. Lord Wingate had a serious objection to our tête-à-tête, you'll recall. I suppose I ought to apologize for leaving you so suddenly—but then, I'm opposed to bullets entering my person, and I was quite certain he'd never shoot *you*."

Kate stared at him. It was just as she'd thought, of course. She really shouldn't have been surprised. And yet. . . .

And yet she was, a little.

It's all my fault, she thought. *Everything—every bit of it—was my fault. Poor Isabel. Poor, sweet, stupid Isabel.*

She felt cold, but knew that her chill had nothing to do with the temperature outside.

"I had, of course, a devil of a time figuring out what happened to you when you disappeared from London so suddenly," Daniel went on. "I didn't want to flatter myself, but I couldn't help wondering if your disappearance and our little conversation had something to do with one another. You were never one to run from a fight, but then, a good deal of time had gone by since I'd last seen you, and so . . ." Daniel shrugged. "I thought it might behoove me to establish a friendship with Lady Isabel, in order to better ascertain your whereabouts."

"Friendship?" Kate echoed bitterly. "Is that what you call it? You seduced her, you vile—"

"Good Lord." Daniel actually heaved a shudder of distaste. "Bite your tongue. I never laid a finger on the child. Well, all right, a finger, but 'seduction' is entirely too strong a word for it. Especially when it became all too clear that the silly chit was not only ignorant of your location, but suspicious of your motives for abandoning her, which led me to believe you had, indeed, fled London because of me."

Kate said nothing. She wasn't about to admit the truth, which was that until Burke had come to her with the astonishing news of Isabel's elopement, Kate had not given her conversation with Daniel that fateful night a second thought. She'd had far more pressing concerns.

But now she remembered it. She remembered it all too clearly.

"I devised, as I'm sure you are now more than aware," Daniel continued, "a plan by which, since the mountain wouldn't come to Mohammed, Mohammed must come to the mountain. I knew how fond you were of that insipid offspring of Traherne's. If you thought her in danger, you'd most definitely come out of hiding—even at the risk of encountering me. And you see, of course, that I was right. Here you are. And here"—he smiled, and she noticed, not for the first time, what a reptilian smile he had—"am I."

Kate realized she was shaking, shaking all over, and not with cold. No, she was shaking with something she couldn't explain. . . .

Or maybe she could, but didn't want to.

"You can't possibly think," she said, in a voice that trembled every bit as much as her fingers, "that after what you've just told me, I'm going to stand out here and speak with you as if nothing has happened. Quite frankly, I think you're mad. And I don't care to converse with madmen. Good night, sir."

She turned to go back inside, intending to slam and lock the French doors behind her. But before she'd gone two steps, he had leapt up from the terrace railing, and seized her by the wrist.

"Not so fast, Katie," he said, the words coming out a bit garbled, thanks to the cigar he still kept clenched between his teeth.

Kate twisted in his iron grip. "Let go of me!"

"Little cat." The moonlight showed that Daniel's expression, while calm, was eerily so, the way the wind, just before a storm, often calmed to a deathlike hush. "Where do you think you're going? We haven't finished our chat."

"Please let go of me, Daniel," Kate said, realizing that struggling against his grip was proving not only painful, but useless, as well. She decided to try pleading instead. "If you let me go, I swear I won't tell anyone you were here. You can trust me. No one believed me when I told the last time, did they?"

He gazed down at her, his face no longer calm at all, but tight with stark emotion.

"The last time?" He dragged her forward and bent down so that his face was just inches from hers. His breath, when he spoke, was hot on her face, and stank of cigar smoke. "My God, there was no last time, do you understand? *I had nothing to do with that fire.*" He thrust her suddenly away, though he still kept a firm hold on her wrist. *"Nothing."*

Tears had begun to slide down Kate's cheeks, but she paid not the slightest heed to them. They were not from the pain of his grip—though it was hurtful. They weren't from fear, either. They were the result of something else. Something that Kate, up until that moment, had never dared to allow herself to feel, not in seven years.

"You're lying," she whispered, staring up at him, oblivious to everything—the pain in her arm, the cold, the stench of his cigar—all of it. None of it mattered. None of it mattered at all. All that mattered now was the truth. And the truth, at last, was going to come out.

"You know perfectly well you were there," Kate hissed. "I

saw you. You stood there and watched them burn."

Her gaze had become unfocused. Suddenly, she was no longer standing on a hotel terrace, but instead in the smoke-filled hallway of her childhood home, having just flung open her bedroom door and found, to her horror, that flames were leaping from her parents' open bedroom door.

"You were standing there," she repeated, not struggling at all now to free herself from him. "Just to one side of the stairway. And you were holding something. A canister of some kind. And there was a smell—a horrible smell, worse than the smoke. Kerosene. I thought Father had accidentally knocked over his bedside lamp. But even that wouldn't have caused flames to reach that high, that fast. Everything, everything was in flame. You must have soaked the bed curtains, the carpet, everything, with kerosene. And then I was trying to go to them, and you . . . you reached out. And stopped me."

As if he wanted to wake her from whatever trance it was she'd slipped into, Daniel released her wrist, threw the cigar away, and grasped her by both shoulders and shook her.

"It wasn't supposed to have happened like that," he said, and now there was something she had never seen before in his face. Desperation. "You and your mother—you weren't even supposed to have been there. You were supposed to have left London. Your father wanted you both in the country for the duration of the trial, to protect you, to shield you."

"Of course," Kate whispered. "But Mother refused to go. She said it would look cowardly, like we were running away."

"And so she died," Daniel said fiercely. "She wasn't supposed to have been there, and neither were you. I had to stop your father from testifying. He found proof, you see. Proof that I'd known all along the mine was dry. I couldn't allow that, now, could I? But I never meant to hurt your mother, and I never wanted to hurt you. *You weren't supposed to have been there.*"

He accompanied each syllable with a shake. Kate, limp from spent emotion, could only stand there, numb. That was all she seemed capable of feeling. Just a numbness. Here was her parents' murderer, standing in front of her, confessing . . .

confessing at last. She wasn't mad. She hadn't imagined it. She had seen him—seen Daniel Craven—in her house, the night of the fire that had killed her parents.

"I thought you were unconscious," he went on, in tones of what sounded—curiously—like despair. "I thought you'd fainted. But just to be safe, I went away. *Seven years* I was gone. *Seven years*, Kate, in that miserable hot country. I had to come back. I couldn't stand it anymore. I thought surely, after seven years. . . . But no. Oh, no. You remembered. Like a bloody elephant, you remembered. And you blamed me."

What was it he was trying to say? That it had all been an accident? Yes, he'd meant to do it, but not to both of them. Only her father. He'd only meant to kill her father. He hadn't meant to burn both of her parents alive in their bed.

That was when the numbness wore off. When she looked up again, her eyes were blazing more hotly than any fire.

"Did you honestly expect me," she asked in an icy voice, "to *forgive* you for what you did? For taking their lives, and destroying mine?"

Now the fingers on her shoulders tightened, and he said with a laugh, "Good God, no. Do you think I'd have gone to all this trouble—dragging that chattering little chit of Traherne's halfway across the country—if all I wanted was your *forgiveness*? Certainly not."

Kate blinked at him. "Well, then, what—"

"Oh, I intend to kill you, too, of course," he said lightly.

Chapter Thirty-two

I should," he informed her, as she stared up at him in horror, "have let you die that night along with your parents. But I was foolishly sentimental back then. I saved your life, instead of taking it. But then I return to London seven years later, thinking I had nothing to worry about, that the fire would have long ago been forgotten, only to find that you not only haven't forgotten it, but are still quite openly blaming me for it—"

"As well I should," Kate declared vehemently. "You started it! You started it, and then you went off, and let it look as though my father killed himself, and took Mother with him. Do you have any idea what it was like, Daniel? Any idea what it was like to live through that? Through the funeral, the investigation? My God, I almost wish you had let me die. It would have been easier. But no, you ran off. You ran off, like the money-grasping coward you are—"

"Now, you see," Daniel said, "it's that kind of attitude right there that I simply don't have patience for."

More quickly than she would have thought possible, he'd pulled her against him, his arm wrapped tightly about her neck. She threw up both hands in an attempt to pry the rock-hewn limb from around her throat, but quickly realized such an attempt was futile. She struggled, instead, with her feet, kicking back at him with her heeled slippers, and elbowing him as hard as she could in the stomach. The result was that he only squeezed harder with his casual grip.

"You know, Katie, I'm actually doing you a favor," he remarked, as she felt the breath being pressed from her throat. "You oughtn't to think so ill of me."

Kate's vision began to swim. Her frantic efforts to break free quickly grew more sluggish.

"What kind of life have you had lately?" Daniel asked. "Slaving away as chaperone to insufferable society misses like Isabel Traherne. That's hardly what I'd call a life. You should be thanking me for putting you out of your misery. Well, little Isabel will undoubtedly be sorry she gave you so much trouble, when tomorrow you're found with your neck broken at the bottom of this courtyard—"

She regretted that she hadn't told Daniel she was pregnant. It probably wouldn't have made a difference, but he'd spoken so regretfully over having killed her mother, maybe, just maybe, he'd have spared her. . . .

"They'll probably think," Daniel was saying, "you were sleepwalking. That's what I thought you were doing, Kate, that night you stepped out into the hallway, into all that smoke. You looked so white, like a ghost. Then you started screaming, and I knew—"

Stars. Kate saw stars, and not overhead, either. Bright pinpricks of light danced before her eyes as she choked for breath. But it was impossible. She was dying. She knew she was dying. . . .

And it was all her own fault. She had seen the trap—oh, yes. From the very first moment the name Daniel Craven had fallen from the marquis's lips that day in Lynn Regis, she had seen it. And yet she had walked right into it, knowing full well that there was no way—no earthly way—Daniel Craven would ever actually elope with Isabel Traherne. She had known full well why he'd done it.

And yet she'd gone with Burke. She'd gone with him because he'd asked her to.

Stars, floating before her eyes. She was dying. It wasn't so terrible, dying. Like falling, really.

And then, suddenly, miraculously, she was free.

Free and falling forward, the world suddenly turned upside down as air, sharp and cold, poured into her lungs. Something hard bit into her knees and palms, scraping them, and then she was lying on cold, wet stone, gasping, gasping for breath.

Behind her, she heard a loud scuffle. What were those noises? If only she could see. The stars had disappeared into inky blackness, which was only just now starting to fade. Was someone dancing? It sounded like someone was dancing. Only there was no music.

And then Kate smelled it. It burned her lungs, the same lungs into which she'd been so gratefully gulping the sweet autumn air. Smoke. Again.

And not tobacco smoke. No, not this time. This was the acrid scent of something burning that was never meant to burn.

And then she saw it, just a ruddy glow before her swimming eyes, but coming more and more swiftly into focus. The curtains. The curtains to the French doors of her hotel room were on fire. When Daniel had thrown his cigar away, he must have tossed it toward the doors, rather than away from them. And now the curtains were on fire.

And Isabel. Isabel was inside.

Kate turned her head. She could see now. She was lying on the balcony floor, her hands and knees scraped raw from the stones, her throat aching terribly. And not five feet from her was Daniel. . . .

Only not just Daniel. No, he wasn't alone. He was being held in a grip very similar to the one in which he'd been holding her, only he was being held there by Burke. Burke was on her balcony. How, Kate wondered hazily, had Burke gotten there?

Then she smelled the smoke again, and remembered Isabel, sleeping so peacefully inside. Isabel. She had to save Isabel from the fire.

Staggering to her feet, using the balcony railing to pull herself up, Kate stumbled toward the French doors. The curtains weren't the only things on fire. The carpet was smolder-ing, as well. Reaching up, Kate gave the flimsy cloth a tug. The curtain came away from the rod that had supported it, and fell to sizzle on the wet terrace floor. She did the same with the other curtain, then hurried to stomp on the smoldering carpet. When it continued to smoke, she seized the water basin from the stand in one corner of her room, and poured it over both the carpet and the curtains, outside.

Dense grey smoke filled the night air. Through it, she was only dimly able to see that there was only one figure—besides herself—left on the terrace. He was silhouetted in the moon-light, and she could not see his features, but she realized, in one panicked moment, her head finally clear, that something might have happened to Burke, that it might be Daniel ap-proaching her. . . .

And she smashed the china water basin against the side of the doorframe, and held one jagged piece of it in the air threat-eningly.

"Stop," she said to the man coming at her through the smoke. Or at least that's what she tried to say. Only what came out of her mouth was a croak. Her throat hurt too badly to say another word. Certainly not what she wanted to say, which was, "I'll kill you, Daniel, I swear I will, if you come any closer."

But it turned out she didn't need to say a word, because a voice she recognized, a voice she dearly loved was saying, "Kate, it's me. Are you all right?"

And then she found herself snatched up into the warmest, most comforting embrace she could imagine.

"Burke," she said. Or tried to say. What came out sounded nothing like his name.

"Are you all right?" He took his arms away from her, but only so that he could thrust her away from him and examine her. "My God, Kate, I thought he'd killed you."

She found that she wanted to laugh and cry at the same time. She plucked at the lapels of the dressing gown he wore, trying to get his attention as he flipped over first one of her palms, and then the other, peering down at the scrapes on them.

"This isn't too bad," he said. "Not even bleeding. How about your throat? How does it feel? My God, your fingers are like ice. We should get inside."

"Burke," she croaked urgently, tugging on a lapel. "Isabel."

"Oh," he said, looking down at the smoldering curtains as if noticing them for the first time. "Isabel's not here. When she woke and heard a man talking on the balcony, she ran to fetch me. She didn't"—Kate felt a shudder run through him—"realize it was Craven."

Relief coursed through Kate's veins, warming them as no fire ever could. Poor Isabel! When the truth came out, how horrible it was going to be for her!

And then Kate looked around the terrace questioningly.

Burke read her unasked thought.

"He's gone, Kate," he said in a voice that was surprisingly hard, seeing as how it was accompanied by a tender gesture, as he pushed some of her tumbled hair from her eyes. "He won't be bothering you ever again."

But that wasn't enough of an answer for Kate, and so, reluctantly, he showed her. Daniel's body lay where hers would have, if he'd had his way, crumpled at the bottom of the courtyard. His head was tilted at an odd angle, revealing all too clearly the cause of his death.

Kate quickly looked away, regretting that she'd asked. But Burke, holding her, said, in the same hard voice, "He killed your parents, Kate. And he'd have killed you, too, not to mention our child. I wasn't wrong to have done it, Kate. I won't say I'm sorry for it, either."

"No," she said, against his chest. "No." She found that she could say no more. Her throat was much too tender.

Without another word, he swept her up into his arms, and carried her from the smoke-filled bedroom, and out into the hallway, where his daughter and the inn's proprietor stood, with any number of servants, holding candles and looking concerned.

"It's all right," Burke said, in his usual brusque tones. "Miss Mayhew is all right."

"Oh, Papa!" Isabel, still dressed in the rumpled gown in which she'd fallen asleep. "I was so worried! Are you sure—"

"Everyone can go back to bed now," Burke said firmly. "Except you." He gazed meaningfully at the hotel's owner. "There's a mess in the courtyard you'll want to have someone clean up. And you'd best send someone for the magistrate in the morning."

The innkeeper seemed to take this in stride, but his wife, who evidently was not aware of the nature of the mess in the courtyard, peered worriedly at Kate.

"Perhaps we ought to send for the surgeon right now, though, for the young lady—"

At Kate's adamant head shake, Burke said, "Miss Mayhew doesn't need a surgeon. If you could see to the Lady Isabel, however—"

This the woman appeared only too eager to do, though Isabel seemed markedly unimpressed by her kind attentions, and reluctant to leave Kate. She was finally compelled to go back to bed—in her own room, this time—when Kate assured her, in a hoarse whisper, that she was perfectly all right. The corridor emptied even further when Burke snapped, with typical authoritativeness, "Everyone go back to bed. *Now.*"

Burke Traherne was not master of this house, and yet his orders were obeyed with an alacrity that would have made a general jealous. The hallway cleared, and Burke conveyed Kate into his room, a chamber furnished in rich masculine tones. The light from the fire in the hearth revealed a large four-poster, the bedclothes thrown back, as if in haste.

It was onto his own bed that he lowered her, and in its comforter that he wrapped her, until she felt quite stifled by the heat of both the bedclothes and the fire, upon which he heaped multiple logs in an attempt to warm her.

She tried to protest, but he would hear none of it. He had said he would see to her himself, and he had meant it. Her scrapes and bruises were bathed by his own hands, her throat eased by tea he offered her himself. He was as attentive as any lover, as caring as any husband, and yet. . . .

He had to know. He had to have figured it out. That it was all—*all of it*—her fault: Daniel's seducing Isabel—well, more or less—and leading them on this mad, cross-country chase. It had all been her fault. If he had not hated her before—and God only knew, he had reason to, the way she'd treated him— he must surely hate her now.

She certainly deserved that hatred. And yet she couldn't let him go away thinking she wasn't sorry for what she'd done.

All she had to do, she realized, was say it. Just come out and say it.

She took a deep breath, and opened her mouth.

Chapter Thirty-three

I," Kate began. This, she realized, was not going to be easy. It was extremely difficult to think rationally with that penetrating gaze on her.

"I," she said again. "Am."

Good. That was a good beginning. Her voice was stronger now, thanks to the tea.

Now, what came after that?

"Sorry."

There. Perfect.

Except that Burke only sat there, looking at her expectantly. Perhaps it hadn't been so perfect. Kate took another deep breath.

"I'm sorry," she said, "about Daniel, Burke. What happened between him and Isabel was all my fault, you see."

He cocked his head, as if he weren't sure he'd heard her properly. "Your fault," he repeated.

She nodded. "Yes," she said. "Daniel realized that I'd seen him—really seen him—the night of the fire, and I suppose he thought I'd tell someone, and so he decided he couldn't let me live. Only he didn't know where I was, of course, so he figured that if he eloped with Isabel, I'd—"

Burke interrupted. "But you did tell someone. You told a lot of people."

"I—Well, of course I did. Seven years ago. Only no one believed me."

"But Craven didn't know that."

Kate, considering this, knit her brow. "No, I suppose not. But the truth is . . . well, I wasn't quite sure I believed it, either. I mean, I knew my father hadn't started the fire. And I knew I'd seen Daniel there. But in a part of my mind, I suppose I always thought there was a chance Freddy was right—that I had only imagined seeing Daniel that night, because . . . well, that would have been better than admitting the truth. At least what everyone else thought was the truth."

He studied her. The confusion was gone from his face. Now he wore no expression whatsoever.

"So you are vindicated," he said softly.

"Vindicated?" She raised the eyebrows that had been knit together a split second before. "Me?"

"Certainly. All those people," he said, "who turned against you when it first happened. You've proved them wrong. It *was* Daniel Craven, and not your father, who absconded with their money and started the fire, as you maintained all along."

Kate, surprised, sat up slowly. "Yes. I suppose you're right." Then she shook her head. "Only I haven't any proof of it, of course."

Burke, seated on the edge of the bed beside her, said with a shrug, "*I* heard him admit it."

"Did you?" Kate turned her stunned gaze toward him. "Did you really?"

"Of course I did. I'll tell the magistrate so, in my statement in the morning. Won't *that* make for some interesting reading in the London papers? By week's end, your father's name should be every bit as untarnished as the Queen's."

Kate shook her head, hardly daring to breathe in the face of such a reversal of fortune—not, of course, that she was any less penniless than she'd been before. No, she was still poor as a churchmouse. But having her father's reputation—his good name—restored meant more to her than any fortune in African diamonds.

"Not, of course," Burke went on, "that it will make any difference to you."

Kate threw him a startled glance. "What? What won't make any difference?"

Burke shrugged his broad shoulders again. "Well, what people say, of course."

"Are you mad?" Kate asked. "Of *course* it makes a difference. It makes all the difference in the world!"

"But I thought you didn't want anything to do with my set." Burke's tone was even, his face still expressionless. "At least, that's what you said this morning, is it not? I believe your exact words were that you couldn't go back. That you'd prefer to raise our child on your own, in disgrace, than amongst the people who believed your father guilty before he ever stood trial, and then allowed his killer to go free."

Kate felt her face heat up, and realized, with a start, that she was blushing. It seemed incredible to her that she could still blush after all she'd been through with this man, but apparently, there were still a few things which could make her feel shy.

It was, she supposed, no more than she deserved.

"Burke," Kate said uneasily. "I know that's what I said this morning. But I realized—even before Daniel came around— that it doesn't matter. All that matters is that—"

But he interrupted again.

"It must be gratifying," he said, "to have proved so many people wrong. It's something that at one time in my life, I should have liked to have done."

She blinked up at him, what she'd been intending to say forgotten. "You?"

"Certainly." He looked down at his hands, resting on his thighs. "You can't have been so busy refuting what they were saying about your father that you never heard what they say about *me,* Kate."

Kate immediately dropped her gaze. "I've heard some things," she said, keeping her gaze on the counterpane. "But I don't believe in gossip. Which is why I want you to know that—"

"But it can be quite useful, you know," he said. "Gossip, I mean. In my case, especially."

She risked a glance at his face. He was looking down at her with an expression of mingled bitterness and compassion. She looked away again, confused.

"I don't know what you mean," she said quickly. "Burke, I—"

"Of course you do. I'm sure your friend Freddy told you all about me. The heartless Marquis of Wingate, who threw his wife's lover from a window, then did everything within his power to keep the woman from seeing her infant daughter again. Isn't that how it goes?"

Kate said faintly, "Well, I suppose I did hear something along those lines. . . ."

"Of course you did. I wanted you to, you see. Because sometimes, Kate, rumors are . . . well, kinder than the truth."

He must have noticed her bewildered expression, since he continued, with a sigh, "I never kept Isabel's mother from seeing her, Kate. I did throw her lover out the window. That much I'll admit. But as for the rest. . . . If Elisabeth had ever expressed the slightest interest in seeing her daughter, I would have arranged it for her, even if it meant my bringing Isabel all the way to Italy. But she didn't. Elisabeth didn't care about Isabel at all. During the court proceedings—the divorce—the only thing she worried about was money. How much was I going to settle on her. That was all. Not a word, not a breath, about Isabel.

"That's why, after a while, I welcomed the rumors. I wanted Isabel to hear them, believe them," Burke went on. "That's why I never disputed them. The rumors were better than the truth. I'd rather people whispered that I was an ogre, keeping a mother from her child, than have them saying the truth, which was that Isabel's own mother didn't love her enough to make even the slightest attempt to see her."

"Oh," Kate said. Her throat felt as if it had closed up again. But this time, it wasn't because someone had been trying to choke the life from her. "I . . . I see."

He looked down at her, but there was something dispassionate about his gaze. It was almost as if he weren't quite seeing her.

"So there you have it," he said. "My whole bitter little history. Well, what's suitable for your ears, anyway. It's interesting, isn't it? The difference between us two, I mean. You abhor London society for its rumor-mongering hypocrisy, while I quite selfishly embraced it for my own purposes."

Suddenly, he stood up. The mattress, relieved of his weight, lurched before settling again.

"Well, not that any of this makes a difference now," he said. "You've made your decision. Still, it's a pity we couldn't come to any sort of understanding, you and I. For I think that together, we might have managed to pitch the whole self-deluded lot of them on their ears. But, as you said, it's better this way. And now I think we've had enough high emotion for one night. I had better let you sleep."

And he actually began striding toward the door.

Kate threw off the bedclothes that covered her, and scrambled from the bed.

"Wait," she called.

He had nearly reached the door. He turned, and looked back at her, his expression inscrutable. "Kate," he said. "You've had a shock. You need rest. Get back in bed."

Kate stayed where she was, twisting her fingers together anxiously. "No," she said. "I've got to talk to you." She nodded toward the bed. "Won't you sit down, just for a minute more?"

He looked as if he wanted to say something—probably another protestation—but gave up. He retraced his steps, moving past her to lower himself onto the bed she'd just vacated.

"So," he said. Seated on the bed, his face was only slightly lower than hers while she was standing. "What is it?"

Kate found it exceptionally difficult to meet his gaze. In the first place, it was a bit disturbing, standing this close to him. While they weren't touching anywhere at all, she nevertheless felt enveloped by him. Her senses were being assaulted on all sides. There was the heat she felt coming off his thighs, and from the vee his robe formed, over his naked chest. And there was the clean scent of him. And certainly, there was the way he looked, so tantalizingly masculine, so strong . . . and yet, at the same time, so vulnerable.

"I," Kate said, unable to meet his gaze. There was something so knowing, so expectant, in his eyes that she couldn't look at them, and instead tried to keep her own trained on the floor. Only she kept being distracted by the place where his dressing gown came open again, just beyond the knot in its sash. She could see nothing there but the dark shadow that existed beneath the satin, but she felt the heat—oh, yes, she felt the warmth emanating from there—on her thighs, right through the flimsy material of her negligee.

"I . . . I want to apologize," she managed to stammer out, at last.

"Didn't you do that already?"

She looked him in the eye, and for once didn't regret doing so. The knowingness was still there, true. But there was something else there, too. Something indefinable. Once, long ago, Kate's father had given her a ring for her birthday, a ring with an emerald in it that had been very much the same color as Burke's eyes. In the center of the emerald, she'd noticed, after hours of examination, was a flaw. A tiny crack. That's what she thought she saw in Burke's eyes just then. A tiny crack, through which, she was certain, if she just looked hard enough, she'd be able to see his soul.

"Not about Daniel," Kate said. She lifted a hand, and placed it on one of his broad shoulders. "I mean, I am more sorry than I can ever say about Daniel, about what he did to Isabel. But I'm also sorry about . . . about what I said this morning." Lord, had it only been that morning she'd sat there and said all of those horrid things to him?

"Well, I'm sorry about it, too," Burke said reasonably. "But being sorry doesn't change things, does it?"

"I suppose not," Kate murmured.

Crushed. He had crushed her, as easily as if she'd been an ant.

Still, she went on.

"But I might have been a bit . . . hasty," she said.

"Hasty," he repeated, his green eyes fixed very steadily upon her.

"Yes. About my refusing to . . ."

One of his ink-dark eyebrows slanted upward. "To what?"

He was going to be difficult about it. He knew perfectly well what she was talking about, but he seemed to want to torture her a little before admitting it.

Well. She deserved a little torture, she supposed.

"Burke." Kate moved her hand, lightly running her fingertips along the silky material of his dressing gown's lapels. "I want to go back to London with you and Isabel tomorrow."

Up went the other eyebrow. "Do you? This is an interesting turn of events. Though I suppose it's only natural for you to want to enjoy the apologies of all those people who were once so abominably rude to you."

"That's not why. You can't think I actually *care* what they say."

"Don't you? That's not the impression you gave me earlier. You seemed to care a good deal what they said. . . . Still, I suppose if you wish to return to London, we could arrange it. But if resuming your duties as Isabel's chaperone is part of your scheme, I'm afraid you'll have to rethink it."

She cocked her head. What game was he playing? "Why?"

"Well, she's obviously never going to be invited anywhere again, not after the scandalous way she ran off with Mr. Craven. She's quite thoroughly ruined her reputation. So she'll hardly have need of a chaperone, I think."

"No," Kate agreed, her gaze downcast. "But she's going to need a mother."

"Is she?" Burke's tone was dry. "And have you a suitable candidate for the job in mind?"

Kate raised her gaze. "Burke," she said firmly, "I'm sorry I didn't tell you sooner about my . . . *our* baby. I'm sorry I said I wouldn't marry you. And I'm sorry I acted like such a . . . hypocrite."

One corner of his mouth—just one—turned upward. "I rather liked the hypocrite part," he admitted.

Then, as if he couldn't help himself, he reached out and wrapped strong fingers around her wrist. Like a fisherman reeling in a line, he pulled her inexorably toward him, until she was standing between his legs, over which were draped the folds of his dressing gown. He looked up at her, his fingers looser now around her wrist, but still possessively encircling it.

She dropped her gaze. She couldn't help it. It wasn't that she didn't want to look into his soul. It was more that her hand, which she'd been running along his body, had reached the knot in his dressing gown's sash, and was now hovering just over the material covering another part of him in which Kate felt a deep and sincere interest.

"Me, too," Kate said, though she hadn't the slightest idea what she was admitting to. She was busy wondering what Burke would think if she gave that knot in the sash to his dressing gown a tug. He would probably think her more of a hypocrite than ever.

She must have struck something sensitive with her fingers—although her touch had been very light, indeed—since Burke suddenly stiffened, the hand around her wrist tightening its hold on her convulsively. But when she lifted her gaze to meet his, she noticed that the undefinable something she'd seen—dropped like a veil across his eyes—was still there.

"Kate," he began.

But she didn't let him finish. Instead, she took hold of one of the ends of his dressing gown's sash, and gave it a tug. The material bunched together, and then slowly parted, revealing the fact that underneath the robe, the marquis was as naked as he'd been that day she'd seen him stepping out of his bath. What was more, that part of him in which she'd felt such an all-consuming interest had reacted to her earlier, feather-light touch, and had grown to a proportion that surprised even Kate, who'd seen it in a good many states.

"Kate," Burke said, in a very different voice.

But she wasn't listening. Like someone in a trance, she

reached out and wrapped the fingers of her free hand around the thick shaft before her.

For once, it was Burke who sucked in his breath. A second later, he'd released her wrist, and had placed both hands on her hips, drawing her toward him with an unintelligible exclamation. Kate flattened one hand against his bare chest, but she kept the other where it was, even when his mouth captured hers, his tongue thrusting through the token barrier of her lips.

And then they were falling backward across the bed, in a tangle of satin and lace, Kate's long blond hair falling to form a tent around both their faces. Burke tried to roll over on top of her, but the hand she'd placed against his chest stopped him, though Kate applied only the slightest of pressure to it.

"Not yet," she whispered, when he reared back to look at her questioningly.

But the questioning look vanished the instant she replaced the hand she'd held against his sternum with her lips. She kissed his chest, giggling as the thick forest of hair there tickled her nose. Then she lowered her head to rain kisses on each of the ridges formed by his iron-hard stomach muscles. And then she dipped her head even lower.

That was when Burke felt obligated to stop her.

He didn't want to stop her. More than anything, he wanted to let her keep going, to allow her to do what he'd been secretly dreaming of her doing these many weeks. More than anything, he wanted to feel those sweet lips on him.

But not yet. Not when he was so swollen with need for her—having come so close to losing her—that he could hardly think.

But Kate wouldn't be put off. She looked up the length of his body, her hair spilling like a puddle of silk across his thighs, and said, quite tartly, "What's good for the goose is good for the gander, I imagine."

To which Burke could make no reply, because she'd already placed that mouth—that mouth which had both irritated and bewitched him for so many months—where he'd so longed to have it.

But not for long. Because he couldn't stand it for very long.

A few seconds only, and he reached out, cupping her face in his hands, his fingers embedded deeply in her smooth straight hair. He brought her mouth up to his—that impossibly small, impossibly soft mouth—plundering it with his lips and tongue, while pushing her back, back against the bed. It had been a day—just a day—since he'd last had her, and yet it felt as if years had gone by. He had to bury himself within her, or burst right then.

Maybe that was why he did what he did next, which was to release her face and reach down to fling up the hem of her nightdress. Then, his mouth still on hers, he ran a hand along the length of each of her legs, beginning with the insides of her thighs and ending with the arches of her feet. Then, abruptly wrenching his mouth from hers, and placing it instead against one of her breasts, his hot breath and tongue branding her nipple through the thin material of her nightdress, he reached down to circle each of her ankles with one of his large brown hands. Then, before she knew what he was about, he was spreading her legs, bending them at the knee, opening her to him, as wide and as far as she could go. He lifted his face from her breast as he did this, and looked into her eyes.

And that was when Kate finally saw through the crack in the emeralds of his eyes. And what she saw there—the naked longing; the possessive need; the desperate anguish; and most of all, the fierce protective love—made her wonder how she'd ever left this man, how she'd ever even entertained the idea of spending her life without him.

And then his mouth was on hers again, not so much kissing her as consuming her, devouring her, even as his hands left her ankles and went to cup her buttocks, raising them up, bringing her, softly damp, radiating a hypnotic, welcoming heat, against his straining erection. . . .

He dove into that heat with a groan, burying himself in that tight, wet sheath. As always, she gasped as he entered her, tensing as if afraid something inside of her was going to be ripped apart by his tremendous need. And then, when she realized it was all right, that she wasn't broken, she opened to him almost shyly, embracing him with her warmth, but only allowing him to sink into her by degrees, the way one sank into a hot, steaming bath.

Only that wasn't enough. That wasn't enough for him. He needed to sink in all at once. He needed to pour himself into her, to lose himself in her. Raising his head, breaking their kiss, he tightened his grip on her hips. Then he watched her face as he lifted her toward him, and then drove himself—all of himself, all at once—into her.

She arched against him, her head falling back, exposing the long white column of her throat. Her breasts—their hard buds of nipples seeming to singe him, as if they were made of fire, and not flesh—were crushed against him. She was, he saw, senseless in her need for him. And that was how he wanted her. Because that was how she made him. Senseless. No other woman he had ever known had been capable of rendering him so perfectly senseless with lust. No other woman had ever opened up to him—both physically and emotionally—the way Kate had. No other woman had ever let herself become so mindless with passion as the one writhing beneath him just then.

That mindlessness—the fact that Kate was as caught up in her desire for him as he was in his desire for her—was what finally sent him over the edge. One minute he was plunging deeper and deeper into her—knowing this was not how he'd wanted it; he'd wanted it sweet and gentle, not rough and forceful, but with Kate, it seemed, he had no self control, none at all—and the next, he was teetering on the edge of sanity. What pushed him over that edge was the sudden tightening of all of Kate's muscles, including the ones gripping him between her legs. Suddenly, she was climaxing, her orgasm ripping through her the way lightning ripped through a summer sky. And then he too was lost in a thunderclap of a release, his entire body shuddering as he finally did pour himself into her, bathing her with liquid fire.

Even after he'd emptied himself within her, he stayed where he was, buried deep inside. She didn't protest. In fact, he wasn't sure she could if she wanted to. She seemed completely spent, as well, her limbs tangled in the heavy folds of his dressing gown, which he had neglected to remove. He could feel her heart beating beneath his, however—proof she was still amongst the living—sporadically at first, getting gradually slower, and more even.

After a while, he lifted his head, and looked down at her.

Her face was flushed, her lips and cheeks a deep pink. There was an unnatural brightness to her eyes, which looked at him with shrewd knowingness.

"Burke," she said. He could feel her voice, sweetly hoarse, reverberate through both of their bodies. "There's something I've been wanting to ask you."

"Indeed?" He brushed those rosy lips lightly with his mouth. "And what is that?"

"Will you marry me?"

"Hmmm," he said. "I think, if we don't, people will talk. Don't you agree?"

She showed him that she did, on no uncertain terms.

Chapter Thirty-four

⟨urke," Kate said with a laugh, as she walked alongside him, one hand on the grip of a perambulator, and the other in the crook of his arm. "It's nothing but an old wives' tale."

"Nevertheless," Burke said somberly. "We shouldn't take any chances. We're talking about my heir, you know."

"But it's perfectly ridiculous." Kate looked up at him from the beneath the brim of her new spring bonnet, which had been delivered, all the way from London, only the day before. "Have you actually *seen* Lady Babbie anywhere near the baby's cradle?"

"Every morning," he asserted. "When I go in. There she is, sitting by it."

"Well, certainly. Because she adores him. But you'll note you said sitting *by* the cradle. Not *in* it."

"Nevertheless—"

"Nevertheless, it simply isn't true. Ask Nanny. Cats do not sit on babies' chests and smother them while they sleep, Burke. I can't believe you've been listening to servants' gossip." She nodded her head toward Isabel, who was strolling several yards ahead of them, her fingers through the arm of a tall, fair-haired young man. "You're worse than Isabel."

At the mention of his daughter's name, Burke glanced in her direction. "And that's another thing," he said. "How long are we going to let this go on?"

"Let what go on, Burke?"

"This." He lifted a hand and gestured toward Isabel, who was twirling a lace parasol above her head and laughing rather coquettishly at something her companion had said. "This . . . *flirtation*, I suppose you'd have to call it, between Isabel and Freddy Bishop."

Kate, pausing to reach inside the perambulator and adjust the baby's cap, said, without looking up, "Really, Burke. It's a very good match. You ought to be overjoyed. I was perfectly convinced, when the truth came about Daniel, that she'd never look at another man. You remember how she cried for days? But now she's like a different person. And she could do *much* worse."

"Worse?" Burke rolled his eyes. "What could possibly be worse than having one of *your* old beaux as my son-in-law?"

"Geoffrey Saunders," Kate said, straightening up again, and slipping her fingers back through his arm. This time, Burke took hold of the baby carriage's handle, and pushed it as they strolled along the grounds of Wingate Abbey.

"At least Geoffrey Saunders," Burke said, "was sufficiently young enough for her. Bishop's old enough to be her father."

"Nonsense. He's only ten years older than she is, Burke. You're *thirteen* years older than I am. And acting it, I must say."

He glared down at her. "What's that supposed to mean?"

Kate smiled teasingly. "Only that I think you need to prepare yourself for the inevitability of Duncan beginning to lay out flannel waistcoats for you. I wouldn't be surprised to see you turning rheumatic, what with the fact that you're starting to believe old wives' tales, and are so thoroughly jealous of your daughter's suitors. What's next, Burke? Warm milk before bed?"

He said, with wounded dignity, "I will have you know, Lady Wingate, that I have never needed a flannel waistcoat in my life, and that I am about as close to being a rheumatic as you are to needing a cane. And furthermore, it's not my daughter's suitors I'm jealous of. It's the fact that this particular one used to be an admirer of yours."

"Oh," Kate said, with a dismissive wave of her hand. "That's all water under the bridge. I'm a distant memory, as far as Freddy is concerned, same as that soprano of his. He's vowed to me that Isabel is the only true interest in his life, for now and forever after."

Burke made a sound that very closely resembled a harrumph. Kate restrained herself from pointing out that this was a hopelessly middle-aged thing to say. Burke was, after all, still hearty at thirty-seven. Hadn't he proved it just that morning, by making good on his long-ago threat—or perhaps it had been a promise—of waking every day with her beneath him?

"Besides," Kate said, with a laugh. "If you think you don't like the idea of Isabel and Freddy, think how Lady Palmer must feel, having *me* as her son's future mother-in-law. Well, stepmother-in-law, anyway. Even now that the truth's come out about Papa, I think she still blames him for sending her husband to an early grave. Now she's going to have to put up with the ignominy of being related to me, at least through marriage. And I'm not even going to mention what you did to her drawing room."

"Morning room," Burke corrected her. "And it served her right for blaming you, even indirectly, for anything. Well," he added, with a sigh, "I suppose you're right. Bishop's not as bad as all that. He did, after all, finally tell me how to find you." Burke grinned at her, then rocked the perambulator, and smiled as his son eyed him sleepily. "Chaperones," he said to the baby. "Troublesome things. At least I won't ever have to worry about finding one for you, now, will I?"

"Not for him," Kate agreed dryly. "But he might have a sister or two coming along someday."

Burke stopped rocking the perambulator. "Oh, God," he said. He raised his gaze toward Isabel, who'd reached out to give the Earl of Palmer a playful slap. "*No,*" he said with horror.

Kate only laughed, and hugged his arm. "Oh, God, *yes,*" she said.